THE
BROKEN
KINGDOMS

I am, you see, a woman plagued by gods.

It was worse once. Sometimes it felt as if they were everywhere: underfoot, overhead, peering around corners, and lurking under bushes. They left glowing footprints on the sidewalks. (I could see that they had their own favorite paths for sightseeing.) They urinated on the white walls. They didn't have to do that, urinate I mean; they just found it amusing to imitate us. I found their names written in splattery light, usually in sacred places. I learned to read in this way.

Sometimes they followed me home and made me breakfast. Sometimes they tried to kill me. Occasionally they bought my trinkets and statues, though for what purpose I can't fathom. And, yes, sometimes I loved them.

I even found one in a muckbin once. Sounds mad, doesn't it? But it's true. If I had known this would become my life when I left home for this beautiful, ridiculous city, I would have thought twice. Though I would still have done it.

THE
BROKEN
KINGDOMS

Book Two of the Inheritance Trilogy

N. K. JEMISIN

orbitbooks.net

ORBIT

First published in Great Britain in 2010 by Orbit

1 3 5 7 9 10 8 6 4 2

A CIP catalogue record for this book
is available from the British Library.

ISBN 978-1-84149-818-8

Printed and bound in Great Britain by
Clays Ltd, Elcograf S.p.A.

Papers used by Orbit are from well-managed forests
and other responsible sources.

Orbit
An imprint of
Little, Brown Book Group
Carmelite House
50 Victoria Embankment
London EC4Y 0DZ

An Hachette UK Company
www.hachette.co.uk

www.orbitbooks.net

I REMEMBER THAT IT WAS MIDMORNING.

Gardening was my favorite task of the day. I'd had to fight for it, because my mother's terraces were famous throughout the territory, and she didn't quite trust me with them. I couldn't really blame her; my father still laughed over whatever I'd done to the laundry that one time I tried.

"Oree," she would say whenever I sought to prove my independence, "it's all right to need help. All of us have things we can't do alone."

Gardening, however, was not one of those things. It was the weeding that my mother feared, because many of the weeds that grew in Nimaro were similar in form to her most prized herbs. Fakefern had a fan-shaped frond just like sweet ire; running may was spiky and stung the fingers, same as ocherine. But the weeds and the herbs didn't *smell* anything alike, so I never understood why she had such trouble with them. On the rare occasions that both scent and feel stumped me, all I had to do was touch a leaf edge to my lips or brush my hand through the leaves to hear the way they settled into place, and I would know. Eventually, Mama had to admit that I hadn't tossed out a single good plant all season. I was planning to ask for my own terrace the following year.

I usually lost myself in the gardens for hours, but one morning something was different. I noticed it almost the moment I left the house: a strange, tinny flatness to the air. A pent-breath tension. By the time the storms began, I had forgotten the weeds and sat up, instinctively orienting on the sky.

And *I could see.*

What I saw, in what I would later learn to call *the distance*, were vast, shapeless blotches of darkness limned in power. As I gaped, great spearing shapes—so bright they hurt my eyes, something that had never happened before—jutted forth to shatter the blotches. But the remnants of the dark blotches became something else, darting liquid tendrils that wrapped about the spears and swallowed them. The light changed, too, becoming spinning disks, razor-sharp, that cut the tendrils. And so on, back and forth, dark against light, neither winning for more than an instant. Through it all, I heard sounds like thunder, though there was no scent of rain.

Others saw it, too. I heard them coming out of their houses and shops to murmur and exclaim. No one was really afraid, though. The strangeness was all up in the sky, too far above our very earthly lives to matter.

So no one else noticed what I did as I knelt there with my fingers still sunk in the dirt. A tremor in the earth. No, not quite a tremor; it was that tension I'd felt before, that *pent* feeling. It hadn't been in the sky at all.

I sprang to my feet and grabbed my walking stick, hurrying for the house. My father was out at the market, but my mother was home, and if some sort of earthquake was in the offing, I needed to warn her. I ran up the porch steps and yanked open the rickety old door, shouting for her to come out, and hurry.

Then I heard it coming, no longer confined to the earth, rolling across the land from the northwest—the direction of Sky, the Arameri city. *Someone's singing*, I thought at first. Not one someone but many—a thousand voices, a million, all vibrating and echoing together. The song itself was barely intelligible, its lyrics a single word—yet so powerful was that word that the whole world shook with its imminent force.

The word that it sang was *grow.*

You must understand. I have always been able to see magic, but Nimaro had been mostly dark to me until then. It was a placid land of sleepy little towns and villages, of which mine was no exception. Magic was a thing of the cities. I got to see it only every once in a while, and then always in secret.

But now there was light and color. It burst across the ground and the street, traced up every leaf and blade of grass and paving stone and wooden slat around the front yard. So much! I had never realized there was so much to the world, right there around me. The magic washed the walls with texture and lines so that for the first time in my life, I could see the house where I'd been born. It outlined the trees around me and the old horse cart around the side of the house—I couldn't figure out what that was at first—and the people who stood in the street with mouths hanging open. *I saw it all*—truly saw, as others did. Maybe more than they did, I don't know. It is a moment I will hold in my heart forever: the return of something glorious. The reforging of something long broken. The rebirth of life itself.

That evening, I learned my father was dead.

One month after that, I set out for the city of Sky to start my own new life.

And ten years passed.

1

"Discarded Treasure"
(encaustic on canvas)

PLEASE HELP ME," said the woman. I recognized her voice immediately. She, her husband, and two children had looked over—but not bought—a wall hanging at my table perhaps an hour before. She had been annoyed then. The hanging was expensive, and her children were pushy. Now she was afraid, her voice calm on the surface but tremolo with fear underneath.

"What is it?" I asked.

"My family. I can't find them."

I put on my best "friendly local" smile. "Maybe they wandered off. It's easy to get lost this close to the trunk. Where did you last see them?"

"There." I heard her move. Pointing, probably. She seemed to realize her error after a moment, with the usual sudden awkwardness. "Ah...sorry, I'll ask someone else—"

"Up to you," I said lightly, "but if you're talking about a nice clean alley over near the White Hall, then I think I know what happened."

Her gasp told me I'd guessed right. "How did you..."

I heard a soft snort from Ohn, the nearest of the other art sellers along this side of the park. This made me smile, which I hoped the woman would interpret as friendliness and not amusement at her expense.

"Did they go *in* the alley?" I asked.

"Oh...well..." The woman fidgeted; I heard her hands rub together. I knew the problem already, but I let her muddle through. No one likes to have their errors pointed out. "It's just that...my son needed a toilet. None of the businesses around here would let him use theirs unless we bought something. We don't have a lot of money...."

She'd given that same excuse to avoid buying my wall hanging. That didn't bother me—I'd have been the first to say no one *needed* anything I sold—but I was annoyed to hear that she'd taken it so far. Too cheap to buy a wall hanging was one thing, but too cheap to buy a snack or a trinket? That was all we businesspeople asked in exchange for letting out-of-towners gawk at us, crowd out regular customers, and then complain about how unfriendly city dwellers were.

I decided not to point out that her family could have used the facilities at the White Hall for free.

"That particular alley has a unique property," I explained instead. "Anyone who enters the alley and disrobes, even partially, gets transported to the middle of the Sun Market." The market dwellers had built a stage on the arrival spot, actually— the better to point and laugh at hapless people who appeared there bare-assed. "If you go to the Market, you should find your family."

"Oh, thank the Lady," the woman said. (That phrase has always sounded strange to my ears.) "Thank you. I'd heard things about this city. I didn't want to come, but my husband— he's a High Norther, wanted to see the Lady's Tree..." She let out a deep breath. "How do I get to this market?"

Finally. "Well, it's in West Shadow; this is East Shadow. Wesha, Easha."

"What?"

"Those are the names people use, if you stop to ask directions."

"Oh. But...*Shadow*? I've heard people use that word, but the city's name is—"

I shook my head. "Like I said, that's not what it's called by the people who live here." I gestured overhead, where I could dimly perceive the ghostly green ripples of the World Tree's ever-rustling leaf canopy. The roots and trunk were dark to me, the Tree's living magic hidden behind foot-thick outer bark, but its tender leaves danced and glimmered at the very limit of my sight. Sometimes I watched them for hours.

"We don't get a lot of sky here," I said. "You see?"

"Oh. I...I see."

I nodded. "You'll need to take a coach to the rootwall at Sixth Street, then either ride the ferry or walk the elevated path through the tunnel. This time of day, they'll have the lanterns at full wick for out-of-towners, so that's good. Nothing worse than walking the root in the dark—not that it makes much difference to *me*." I grinned to put her at ease. "But you wouldn't believe how many people go crazy over a little darkness. Anyway, once you get to the other side, you'll be in Wesha. There are always palanquins around, so you can either catch one or walk to the Sun Market. It's not far, just keep the Tree on your right, and—"

There was a familiar horror in her voice when she interrupted me. "This city...how am I supposed to...I'll get lost. Oh, demons, and my husband's even worse. He gets lost all the time. He'll try to find his way back here, and I have the purse, and—"

"It's all right," I said with practiced compassion. I leaned across my table, careful not to dislodge the carved-wood sculptures, and pointed toward the far end of Art Row. "If you want, I can recommend a good guide. He'll get you there fast."

She would be too cheap for that, I suspected. Her family could've been assaulted in that alley, robbed, transformed into rocks. Was the risk really worth whatever money they'd saved? Pilgrims never made sense to me.

"How much?" she asked, already sounding dubious.

"You'll have to ask the guide. Want me to call him over?"

"I..." She shifted from foot to foot, practically reeking of reluctance.

"Or you could buy this," I suggested, turning smoothly in my chair to pick up a small scroll. "It's a map. Includes all the god spots—places magicked-up by godlings, I mean, like that alley."

"Magicked— You mean, some godling did this?"

"Probably. I can't see scriveners bothering, can you?"

She sighed. "Will this map help me reach this market?"

"Oh, of course." I unrolled it to give her a look. She took a long time staring at it, probably hoping to memorize the route to the Market without buying it. I didn't mind her trying. If she could learn Shadow's convoluted streets that easily, interrupted on the map by Tree roots and occasional notes about this or that god spot, then she deserved a free peek.

"How much?" she asked at last, and reached for her purse.

After the woman left, her anxious footsteps fading into the general mill of the Promenade, Ohn ambled over. "You're so nice, Oree," he said.

I grinned. "Aren't I? I could have told her to just go into the alley and lift her skirts a bit, which would've sent her to her family in a heartbeat. But I had to look out for her dignity, didn't I?"

Ohn shrugged. "If they don't think of it on their own, that's their fault, not yours." He sighed after the woman. "Shame to come all the way here on a pilgrimage and spend half of it wandering around lost, though."

"Someday she'll savor the memory." I got up, stretching. I'd been sitting all morning and my back was sore. "Keep an eye on my table for me, will you? I'm going for a walk."

"Liar."

I grinned at the coarse, growly voice of Vuroy, another of the Row's sellers, as he ambled over. He stood close to Ohn; I imagined Vuroy hooking an affectionate arm around Ohn. They and Ru, another of the Row's sellers, were a triple, and Vuroy was possessive. "You just want to look in that alley, see if her dumb-as-demons man and brat dropped anything before the magic got 'em."

"Why would I do that?" I asked as sweetly as I could, though I couldn't help laughing. Ohn was barely holding in a snicker himself.

"If you find something, be sure to share," he said.

I blew a kiss in his direction. "Finders keepers. Unless you want to share Vuroy in return?"

"Finders keepers," he retorted, and I heard Vuroy laugh and pull him into an embrace. I walked away, concentrating on the *tap-tap* of my stick so that I wouldn't hear them kiss. I'd been joking about the sharing, of course, but there were still some things a single girl didn't enjoy being around when she couldn't have a little of it herself.

The alley, across the wide Promenade from Art Row, was easy to find, because its walls and floor shimmered pale against the ambient green glow of the World Tree. Nothing too bright; by godling standards, this was minor magic, something even a mortal could've done with a few chiseled sigils and a fortune in activating ink. Ordinarily, I would've seen little more than a scrim of light along the mortar between the bricks, but this god spot had been activated recently and would take time to fade back to its usual quiescence.

I stopped at the mouth of the alley, listening carefully. The Promenade was a wide circle at the city's relative heart, where foot traffic met the carriageways and came together to encircle a broad plaza of flower beds, shade trees, and walkways. Pilgrims liked to gather there, because the plaza offered the city's best view of the World Tree—which was the same reason we artists liked it. The pilgrims were always in a good mood to buy our wares after they'd had a chance to pray to their strange new god. Still, we were always mindful of the White Hall perched nearby, its shining walls and statue of Bright Itempas seeming to loom disapprovingly over the plaza's heretical goings-on. The Order-Keepers weren't as strict these days as they had once been; there were too many gods now who might take exception to their followers being persecuted. Too much wild magic altogether in the city for them to police it all. That still didn't make it smart to do certain things right under their noses.

So I entered the alley only after I'd made sure there were no priests in the immediate vicinity. (It was still a gamble—the street was so noisy that I couldn't hear everything. I was prepared to say I was lost, just in case.)

As I moved into the relative silence of the alley, tapping my stick back and forth in case I happened across a wallet or other valuables, I noticed the smell of blood at once. I dismissed it just as quickly, because it didn't make sense; the alley had been magicked to keep itself clean of detritus. Any inanimate object dropped in it disappeared after half an hour or so—the better to lure in unwary pilgrims. (The godling who'd set this particular trap had a wicked mind for detail, I had decided.) Yet the deeper I moved into the alley, the more clearly the scent came to me—and the more uneasy I grew, because I recognized it. Metal and salt, cloying in that way blood becomes after it has grown cold and clotted. But this was not the heavy, iron scent of mortal blood; there was a lighter, sharper tang to it. Metals that had no name in any mortal tongue, salts of entirely different seas.

Godsblood. Had someone dropped a vial of the stuff here? An expensive mistake, if so. Yet the godsblood smelled...flat somehow. Wrong. And there was far, far too much of it.

Then my stick hit something heavy and soft, and I stopped, dread drying my mouth.

I crouched to examine my find. Cloth, very soft and fine. Flesh beneath the cloth—a leg. Cooler than it should have

11

been, but not cold. I felt upward, my hand trembling, and found a curved hip, a woman's slightly poochy belly—and then my fingers stilled as the cloth suddenly became sodden and tacky.

I snatched my hand back and asked, "A-are you...all right?" That was a foolish question, because obviously she wasn't.

I could see her now, a very faint person-shaped blur occluding the alley floor's shimmer, but that was all. She should have glowed bright with magic of her own; I should have spotted her the moment I entered the alley. She should not have been motionless, since godlings had no need for sleep.

I knew what this meant. All my instincts cried it. But I did not want to believe.

Then I felt a familiar presence appear nearby. No footsteps to forewarn me, but that was all right. I was glad he'd come this time.

"I don't understand," Madding whispered. That was when I had to believe, because the surprise and horror in Madding's voice were undeniable.

I had found a godling. A *dead* one.

I stood, too fast, and stumbled a little as I backed away. "I don't, either," I said. I gripped my stick tightly with both hands. "She was like this when I found her. But—" I shook my head, at a loss for words.

There was the faint sound of chimes. No one else ever seemed to hear them, I had noticed long ago. Then Madding manifested from the shimmer of the alley: a stocky, well-built man of vaguely Senmite ethnicity, swarthy and weathered of face, with tangled dark hair caught in a tail at the nape of his neck. He did not glow, precisely—not in this form—but I could see him, contrasting solidly against the walls' shimmer. And I had never seen the stricken look that was on his face as he stared down at the body.

"Role," he said. Two syllables, the faintest of emphasis on the first. "Oh, Sister. Who did this to you?"

And how? I almost asked, but Madding's obvious grief kept me silent.

He went to her, this impossibly dead godling, and reached out to touch some part of her body. I could not see what; his fingers seemed to fade as they pressed against her skin. "It doesn't make sense," he said, very softly. That was more proof of how troubled he was; usually he tried to act like the tough, rough-mannered mortal he appeared to be. Before this, I had seen him show softness only in private, with me.

"What could kill a godling?" I asked. I did not stammer this time.

"Nothing. Another godling, I mean, but that takes more raw magic than you can imagine. All of us would have sensed that and come to see. But Role had no enemies. Why would anyone hurt her? Unless..." He frowned. As his concentration slipped, so did his image; his human frame blurred into something that was a shining, liquid green, like the smell of fresh Tree leaves. "No, why would either of them have done it? It doesn't make sense."

I went to him and put a hand on his glimmering shoulder. After a moment, he touched my hand in silent thanks, but I could tell the gesture had given him no comfort.

"I'm sorry, Mad. I'm so sorry."

He nodded slowly, becoming human again as he got a hold of himself. "I have to go. Our parents...They'll need to be told. If they don't know already." He sighed and shook his head as he got to his feet.

"Is there anything you need?"

He hesitated, which was gratifying. There are some reactions a girl always likes to see from a lover, even a former one. This former one brushed my cheek with a finger, making my skin tingle. "No. But thank you."

While we'd spoken, I hadn't paid attention, but a crowd had begun to gather at the mouth of the alley. Someone had seen us and the body; in the way of cities, that first gawker had drawn others. When Madding picked up the body, there were gasps from the watching mortals and one horrified outcry as someone recognized his burden. Role was known, then—possibly even one of the godlings who'd gathered a small following of worshippers. That meant word would be all over the city by nightfall.

Madding nodded to me, then vanished. Two shadows within the alley drew near, lingering by the place Role had been, but I did not look at them. Unless they worked hard not to be noticed, I could always see godlings, and not all of them liked that. These were probably Madding's people; he had several siblings who worked for him as guards and helpers. There would be others, though, coming to pay their respects. Word spread quickly among their kind, too.

With a sigh, I left the alley and pushed through the crowd—giving no answers to their questions other than a terse, "Yes, that was Role," and "Yes, she's dead"—eventually returning to my table. Vuroy and Ohn had been joined by Ru, who took my hand and sat me down and asked if I wanted a glass of water—or a good, stiff drink. She started wiping my hand with a piece of cloth, and belatedly I realized there must've been godsblood on my fingers.

"I'm all right," I said, though I wasn't entirely sure of that.

"Could use some help packing up, though. I'm heading home early." I could hear other artists along the Row doing the same. If a godling was dead, then the World Tree had just become the second-most-interesting attraction in the city, and I could look forward to poor sales for the rest of the week.

So I went home.

*   *   *

I am, you see, a woman plagued by gods.

It was worse once. Sometimes it felt as if they were everywhere: underfoot, overhead, peering around corners and lurking under bushes. They left glowing footprints on the sidewalks. (I could see that they had their own favorite paths for sightseeing.) They urinated on the white walls. They didn't have to do that, urinate I mean, they just found it amusing to imitate us. I found their names written in splattery light, usually in sacred places. I learned to read in this way.

Sometimes they followed me home and made me breakfast. Sometimes they tried to kill me. Occasionally they bought my trinkets and statues, though for what purpose I can't fathom. And, yes, sometimes I loved them.

I even found one in a muckbin once. Sounds mad, doesn't it? But it's true. If I had known this would become my life when I left home for this beautiful, ridiculous city, I would have thought twice. Though I would still have done it.

The one in the muckbin, then. I should tell you more about him.

*   *   *

I'd been up late one night—or morning—working on a painting, and I had gone out behind my building to toss the leftover paint before it dried and ruined my pots. The muckrakers usually came with their reeking wagons at dawn, carting off the bin contents to sift for night soil and anything else of value, and I didn't want to miss them. I didn't even notice a man there, because he smelled like the rest of the muck. Like something dead—which, now that I think about it, he probably was.

I tossed the paint and would have gone back inside had I not noticed an odd glimmer from the corner of one eye. I was tired enough that I should have ignored that, too. After ten years in Shadow, I had grown inured to godling leavings. Most likely one of them had thrown up there after a night of drinking or had spent himself in a tryst amid the fumes. The new ones liked to do that, spend a week or so playing mortal before settling into whatever life they'd decided to lead among us. The initiation was generally messy.

So I don't know why I stopped, that chilly winter morning. Some instinct told me to turn my head, and I don't know why I listened to it. But I did, and that was when I saw glory awaken in a pile of muck.

At first I saw only delicate lines of gold limn the shape of a man. Dewdrops of glimmering silver beaded along his flesh and then ran down it in rivulets, illuminating the texture of skin in smooth relief. I saw some of those rivulets move impossibly upward, igniting the filaments of his hair, the stern-carved lines of his face.

And as I stood there, my hands damp with paint and my door standing open behind me, forgotten, I saw this glowing man draw a deep breath—which made him shimmer even more beautifully—and open eyes whose color I would never be able to fully describe, even if I someday learn the words. The best I can do is compare it to things I do know: the heavy thickness of red gold, the smell of brass on a hot day, desire and pride.

Yet, as I stood there, transfixed by those eyes, I saw something else: pain. So much sorrow and grief and anger and guilt, and other emotions I could not name because when all was said and done, my life up to then had been relatively happy. There are some things one can understand only by experience, and there are some experiences no one wants to share.

*   *   *

Hmm. Perhaps I should tell you something about me before I go on.

I'm something of an artist, as I've mentioned. I make, or made, my living selling trinkets and souvenirs to out-of-towners. I also paint, though my paintings are not meant for the eyes of others. Aside from this, I'm no one special. I see magic and gods, but so does everyone; I told you, they're everywhere. I probably just notice them more because I can't see anything else.

My parents named me Oree. Like the cry of the southeastern weeper-bird. Have you heard it? It seems to sob as it calls, *oree*, gasp, *oree*, gasp. Most Maroneh girls are named for such sorrowful things. It could be worse; the boys are named for vengeance. Depressing, isn't it? That sort of thing is why I left.

Then again, I have never forgotten my mother's words: *it's all right to need help. All of us have things we can't do alone.*

So the man in the muck? I took him in, cleaned him up, fed him a good meal. And because I had space, I let him stay. It was the right thing to do. The human thing. I suppose I was also lonely, after the whole Madding business. Anyhow, I told myself, it did no harm.

But I was wrong about that part.

* * *

He was dead again when I got home that day. His corpse was in the kitchen, near the counter, where it appeared he'd been chopping vegetables when the urge to stab himself through the wrist had struck. I slipped on the blood coming in, which annoyed me because that meant it was all over the kitchen floor. The smell was so thick and cloying that I could not localize it—this wall or that one? The whole floor or just near the table? I was certain he dripped on the carpet, too, while I dragged him to the bathroom. He was a big man, so that took a while. I wrestled him into the tub as best I could and then filled it with water from the cold cistern, partly so that the blood on his clothes wouldn't set and partly to let him know how angry I was.

I'd calmed down somewhat—cleaning the kitchen helped me vent—by the time I heard a sudden, violent slosh of water from the bathroom. He was often disoriented when he first returned to life, so I waited in the doorway until the sounds of sloshing stilled and his attention fixed on me. He had a strong personality. I could always feel the pressure of his gaze.

"It's not fair," I said, "for you to make my life harder. Do you understand?"

Silence. But he heard me.

"I've cleaned up the worst of the kitchen, but I think there might be some blood on the living-room rugs. The smell's so thick that I can't find the small patches. You'll have to do those. I'll leave a bucket and brush in the kitchen."

More silence. A scintillating conversationalist, he was.

I sighed. My back hurt from scrubbing the floor. "Thanks for making dinner." I didn't mention that I hadn't eaten any. No way to tell—without tasting—if he'd gotten blood on the food, too. "I'm going to bed; it's been a long day."

A faint taste of shame wafted on the air. I felt his gaze move away and was satisfied. In the three months he'd been living with me, I'd come to know him as a man of almost compulsive fairness, as predictable as the tolling of a White Hall bell. He did not like it when the scales between us were unbalanced.

I crossed the bathroom, bent over the tub, and felt for his face. I got the crown of his head at first and marveled, as always, at the feel of hair like my own—soft-curled, dense but yielding, thick enough to lose my fingers in. The first time I'd touched him, I'd thought he was one of my people, because only Maroneh had such hair. Since then I'd realized he was something else entirely, something not human, but that early surge of fellow-feeling had never quite faded. So I leaned down and kissed his brow, savoring the feel of soft smooth heat beneath my lips. He was always hot to the touch. Assuming we could come to some agreement on the sleeping arrangements, next winter I could save a fortune on firewood.

"Good night," I murmured. He said nothing in return as I headed off to bed.

*   *   *

Here's what you need to understand. My houseguest was not suicidal, not precisely. He never went out of his way to kill himself. He simply never bothered to avoid danger—including the danger of his own impulses. An ordinary person took care while walking along the roof to do repairs; my houseguest did not. He didn't look both ways before crossing the street, either. Where most people might fleetingly imagine tossing a lighted candle onto their own beds and just as fleetingly discard that idea as mad, my houseguest simply did it. (Though, to his credit, he had never done anything that might endanger me, too. Yet.)

On the few occasions I had observed this disturbing tendency of his—the last time, he had casually swallowed something poisonous—I'd found him amazingly dispassionate about the whole thing. I imagined him making dinner this time, chopping vegetables, contemplating the knife in his hand. He had finished dinner first, setting that aside for me. Then he had calmly stabbed the knife between the bones of his wrist, first holding the injury over a mixing bowl to catch the blood. He did like to be neat. I had found the bowl on the floor, still a quarter full; the rest was splashed all over one wall of the kitchen. I gathered he'd lost his strength rather faster than expected and had struck the bowl as he fell, flipping it into the air. Then he'd bled out on the floor.

I imagined him observing this process, still contemplative, until he died. Then, later, cleaning up his own blood with equal apathy.

I was almost certain he was a godling. The "almost" lay in the fact that he had the strangest magic I'd ever heard of. Rising from the dead? Glowing at sunrise? What did that make him, the god of cheerful mornings and macabre surprises? He never spoke the gods' language—or any language, for that matter. I suspected he was mute. And I could not see him, save in the mornings and in those moments when he came back to life, which meant he was magical only at those times. Any other time, he was just an ordinary man.

Except he wasn't.

The next morning was typical.

*   *   *

I woke before dawn, as was my longtime habit. Ordinarily, I would just lie there awhile, listening to the sounds of morning: the rising chorus of birds, the heavy erratic *bap-plink* of dew dripping from the Tree onto rooftops and street stones. This time, however, the urge for a different sort of morning overtook me, so I rose and went in search of my houseguest.

He was in the den rather than the small storage pantry where he slept. I felt him there the instant I stepped out of my room. He was like that, filling the house with his presence, becoming its center of gravity. It was easy—natural, really—to let myself drift to wherever he was.

I found him at the den window. My house had many windows—a fact I often lamented since they did me no good and made the house drafty. (I couldn't afford to rent better.) The den was the only room that faced east, however. That did me no good, either, and not just because I was blind; like most of the city's denizens, I lived in a neighborhood tucked between two of the World Tree's stories-high main roots. We got sunlight for a few minutes at midmorning, while the sun was high enough to overtop the roots but not yet hidden by the Tree's canopy, and a few more moments at midafternoon. Only the nobles could afford more constant light.

Yet my houseguest stood here every morning, as regular as clockwork, if he wasn't busy or dead. The first time I'd found him doing this, I thought it was his way of welcoming the day. Perhaps he made his prayers in the morning, like others who still honored Bright Itempas. Now I knew him better, if one could ever be said to know an indestructible man who never spoke. When I touched him on these occasions, I got a better sense of him than usual, and what I detected was not reverence or piety. What I felt, in the stillness of his flesh and the uprightness of his posture and the aura of peace that he exuded at no other time, was *power*. Pride. Whatever was left of the man he'd once been.

Because it was clearer to me with every day that passed that there was something broken, *shattered*, about him. I did not know what, or why, but I could tell: he had not always been like this.

He did not react as I came into the room and sat down in one of the chairs, wrapping myself in the blanket I'd brought against the house's early-morning chill. He was doubtless used to me making a show of his morning displays, since I did it frequently.

And sure enough, a few moments after I got comfortable, he began, again, to glow.

The process was different every time. This time his eyes took the light first, and I saw him turn to glance at me as if to make sure I was watching. (I had detected these little hints of phenomenal arrogance in him at other times.) That done, he turned his gaze outward again, his hair and shoulders beginning to shimmer. Next I saw his arms, as muscled as any soldier's, folded across his chest. His long legs, braced slightly apart; his posture was relaxed, yet proud. Dignified. I had noticed from the first that he carried himself like a king. Like a man long used to power, who had only lately fallen low.

As the light filled his frame, it grew steadily brighter. I squinted—I loved doing that—and raised a hand to shield my eyes. I could still see him, a man-shaped blaze now framed by the jointed lattice of my shadowy hand bones. But in the end, as always, I had to look away. I never did this until I absolutely had to. What was I going to do, go blind?

It didn't last long. Somewhere beyond the eastern rootwall, the sun moved above the horizon. The glow faded quickly after that. After a few moments, I was able to look at him again, and in twenty minutes, he was as invisible to me as every other mortal.

When it was over, my houseguest turned to leave. He did chores around the house during the day and had lately begun hiring himself out to the neighbors, giving me whatever pittance he earned. I stretched, relaxed and comfortable. I always felt warmer when he was around.

"Wait," I said, and he stopped.

I tried to gauge his mood by the feel of his silence. "Are you ever going to tell me your name?"

More silence. Was he irritated, or did he care at all? I sighed.

"All right," I said. "The neighbors are starting to ask questions, so I need something to call you. Do you mind if I make something up?"

He sighed. Definitely irritated. But at least it wasn't a no.

I grinned. "All right, then. Shiny. I'll call you Shiny. What about that?"

It was a joke. I said it just to tease him. But I will admit that I'd expected some reaction from him, if only disgust. Instead, he simply walked out.

Which annoyed me. He didn't have to talk, but was a smile too much to ask for? Even just a grunt or a sigh?

"Shiny it is, then," I said briskly, and got up to start my day.

2

"Dead Goddesses"
(watercolor)

APPARENTLY I AM PRETTY. Magic is all I see, and magic tends to be beautiful, so I have no way of properly judging the mundane myself. I have to take others' word for it. Men praise parts of me endlessly—always the parts, mind you, never the whole. They love my long legs, my graceful neck, my storm of hair, my breasts (especially my breasts). Most of the men in Shadow were Amn, so they also commented on my smooth, near-black Maro skin, even though I told them there were half a million other women in the world with the same feature. Half a million is not so many measured against the whole world, though, so that always got included in their qualified, fragmentary admiration.

"Lovely," they would say, and sometimes they wanted to take me home and admire me in private. Before I got involved with godlings, I would let them, if I felt lonely enough. "You're beautiful, Oree," they would whisper as they positioned and posed and polished me. "If only—"

I never asked them to complete this sentence. I knew what they almost said: *if only you didn't have those eyes.*

My eyes are more than blind; they are deformed. Disturbing. I would probably attract more men if I hid them, but why would I want more men? The ones I already attract never really want me. Except Madding, and even he wished I were something else.

My houseguest did not want me at all. I did worry at first. I wasn't stupid; I knew the danger of bringing a strange man into my home. But he had no interest in anything so mundane as mortal flesh—not even his own. His gaze felt of many things when it touched me, but covetousness was not one of them. Neither was pity.

I probably kept him around for that reason alone.

* * *

"I paint a picture," I whispered, and began.

Each morning before leaving for Art Row, I practiced my *true* art. The things I made for the Row were junk—statues of godlings that were inaccurate and badly proportioned; watercolors depicting banal, inoffensive images of the city; pressed and dried Tree flowers; jewelry. The sorts of trinkets potential buyers expected to see from a blind woman with no formal training who sold nothing over twenty meri.

My paintings were different. I spent a good portion of my income on canvas and pigment, and beeswax for the base. I spent hours—when I really lost myself—imagining the colors of air and trying to capture scent with lines.

And, unlike my table trinkets, I could see my paintings. Didn't know why. Just could.

When I finished and turned, wiping my hands on a cloth, I was not surprised to find that Shiny had come in. I tended to notice little else around me when I was painting. As if to rebuke me for this tendency, the scent of food hit my nose, and my stomach immediately set up a growl so loud that it practically filled the basement. Sheepishly I grinned. "Thanks for making breakfast."

There was a creak on the wooden stairs and the faint stir of displaced air as he approached. A hand took hold of mine and guided it to the smooth, rounded edge of a plate, heavy and slightly warm underneath. Warmed cheese and fruit, my usual, and—I sniffed and grinned in delight. "Smoked fish? Where on earth did you get that?"

I didn't expect an answer and I didn't get one. He guided me over to a spot at my small worktable, where he'd arranged a simple place setting. (He was always proper about things like that.) I found the fork and began to eat, my delight growing as I realized the fish was velly from the Braided Ocean, near Nimaro. It wasn't expensive, but it was hard to find in Shadow—too oily for the Amn palate. Only a few Sun Market merchants sold it, as far as I knew. Had he gone all the way to Wesha for me? When the man wanted to apologize, he did it right.

"Thank you, Shiny," I said as he poured me a cup of tea. He paused for just a moment, then resumed pouring with the faintest of sighs at his new nickname. I stifled the urge to giggle at his annoyance, because that would've just been mean.

He sat down across from me, though he had to push a pile of beeswax sticks out of the way to do it, and watched me eat. That sobered me, because it meant I'd been painting long enough that he'd gone ahead and eaten. And that meant I was late for work.

Nothing to be done for it. I sighed and sipped tea, pleased to find that it was a new blend, slightly bitter and perfect for the salty fish.

"I'm debating whether I should even go to the Row today," I said. He never seemed to mind my small talk, and I never minded that it was one-sided. "It will probably be a madhouse. Oh, that's right—did you hear? Yesterday, near the Easha White Hall, one of the godlings was found dead. Role. I was the one who found her; she was actually, really dead." I shuddered at the memory. "Unfortunately, that means her worshippers will come to pay respects, and the Keepers will be all over the place, and the gawkers will be as thick as ants at a picnic." I sighed. "I hope they don't decide to block off the whole Promenade; my savings are down to fumes as it is."

I kept eating and did not at first realize Shiny's silence had changed. Then I registered the shock in it. What had caught his attention—my worrying about money? He'd been homeless before; perhaps he feared I would turn him out. Somehow, though, that didn't feel right.

I reached out, found his hand, and groped upward until I found his face. He was a hard man to read at the best of times, but now his face was absolute stone, jaw tight and brows drawn and skin taut near the ears. Concern, anger, or fear? I couldn't tell.

I opened my mouth to say that I had no intention of evicting him, but before I could, he pushed his chair back and walked away, leaving my hand hovering in the air where his face had been.

I wasn't sure what to think of this, so I finished eating, carried my plate upstairs to wash, and then got ready to head to the Row. Shiny met me at the door, putting my stick into my hands. He was going with me.

*   *   *

As I had expected, there was a small crowd filling the nearby street: weeping worshippers, curious onlookers, and very snappish Order-Keepers. I could also hear a small group off at the far end of the Promenade, singing. Their song was wordless, just the same melody over and over, soothing and vaguely eerie. These were the New Lights, one of the newer religions that had appeared in the city. They had probably come looking for recruits among the dead goddess' bereft followers. Along with the Lights, I could smell the heavy, soporific incense of the Darkwalkers—worshippers of the Shadow Lord. There weren't many of them, though; they tended not to be morning people.

In addition to these were the pilgrims, who worshipped the Gray Lady; the Daughters of the New Fire, who favored some godling I'd never heard of; the Tenth-Hellers; the Clockwork League; and half a dozen other groups. Amid this rabble I could hear street-children, probably picking pockets and playing pranks. Even they had a patron god these days, or so I'd heard.

Small wonder the Order-Keepers were snappish, with so many heretics crowding their own hall. Still, they had managed to cordon off the alley and were allowing mourners to approach it in small groups, letting them linger long enough for a prayer or two.

With Shiny beside me, I crouched to brush my hand over the piles of flowers and candles and offertory trinkets that had been placed at the mouth of the alley. I was surprised to find the flowers half wilted, which meant they had been there awhile. The godling who'd marked the alley must have suspended the self-cleaning magic for the time being, perhaps out of respect for Role.

"A shame," I said to Shiny. "I never met this one, but I hear she was nice. Goddess of compassion or something like that. She worked as a bonebender down in South Root. Anyone who could pay had to give her an offering, but she never turned away those who couldn't." I sighed.

Shiny was a silent, brooding presence beside me, unmoving, barely breathing. Thinking this was grief, I stood and fumbled for his hand and was surprised to find it clenched tight at his side. I'd completely mistaken his mood; he was angry, not sad. Puzzled by this, I slid my hand up to his cheek. "Did you know her?"

He nodded, once.

"Was she ... *your* goddess? Did you pray to her?"

He shook his head, cheek flexing beneath my fingers. What had that been, a smile? A bitter one.

"You cared for her, though."

"Yes," he said.

I froze.

He had never spoken to me. Not once in three months. I hadn't even realized he *could* talk. For a moment I wondered whether I should say something to acknowledge this momentous event—and then I inadvertently brushed against him and felt the hard, tension-taut muscle of his arm. Foolish of me to fixate on a single word when something far more momentous had occurred: he had shown concern for something in the world besides himself.

I coaxed his fist open and laced my fingers with his, offering the same comfort of contact that I had given Madding the day before. For an instant, Shiny's hand quivered in mine, and I dared to hope that he might return the gesture. Then his hand went slack. He did not pull away, but he might as well have.

I sighed and stayed by him for a little while, then finally pulled away myself.

"I'm sorry," I said, "but I have to go." He said nothing, so I left him to his mourning and headed over to Art Row.

Yel, the proprietor of the Promenade's biggest food stand, allowed us artists to store things in her locked stand overnight, which made my life much easier. It didn't take long to set up my tables and merchandise, though once I sat down, it was exactly as I'd feared. For two whole hours, not a single person came to peruse my goods. I heard the others grumbling about it as well, though Benkhan was lucky; he sold a charcoal drawing of the Promenade that happened to include the alley. I had no doubt he would have ten more drawings like it by the next morning.

I hadn't gotten enough sleep the night before, since I'd been up late cleaning Shiny's mess. I was beginning to nod off when I heard a soft voice say, "Miss? Excuse me?"

Starting awake, I immediately plastered on a smile to cover my grogginess. "Why, hello, sir. See something that interests you?"

I heard his amusement, which confused me. "Yes, actually. Do you sell here every day?"

"Yes, indeed. I'm happy to hold an item if you like—"

"That won't be necessary." Abruptly I realized he hadn't come to buy anything. He didn't sound like a pilgrim; there wasn't the faintest hint of uncertainty or curiosity in his voice. Though his Senmite was cultured and precise, I could hear the slower curves of a Wesha accent underneath. This was a man who had lived in Shadow all his life, though he seemed to be trying to conceal that.

I took a guess. "Then what would an Itempan priest want with someone like me?"

He laughed. Unsurprised. "So it's true what they say about

the blind. You can't see, but your other senses grow finer. Or perhaps you have some other way of perceiving things, beyond the abilities of ordinary folk?" There was the faint sound of something from my table being picked up. Something heavy. I guessed it was one of the miniature Tree replicas that I grew from linvin saplings and trimmed to resemble the Tree. My biggest-selling item, and the one that cost the most in time and effort to produce.

I licked my lips, which were abruptly and inexplicably dry. "Other than my eyes, everything about me is ordinary enough, sir."

"Is that so? The sound of my boots probably gives me away, then, or the incense clinging to my uniform. I suppose those would tell you a great deal."

Around me I could hear more of those characteristic boots, and more cultured voices, which were answered in uneasy tones by my fellow Row denizens. Had a whole troop of priests come out to question us? Usually we had to deal with only the Order-Keepers, who were acolytes in training to become priests. They were young and sometimes overzealous, but generally all right unless antagonized. Most of them hated street duty, so they did a lazy job of it, which left the people of the city to find their own ways of resolving problems—exactly as most of us preferred it. However, something told me this man was no lowly Order-Keeper.

He hadn't asked a question, so I didn't speak, which he seemed to take as an answer in itself. I felt my front table shift alarmingly; he was sitting on it. The tables weren't the sturdiest things in the world, since they had to be light enough for me to carry home if necessary. My stomach clenched.

"You look nervous," he said.

"I'm not," I lied. I'd heard Order-Keepers used such techniques to throw their targets off-balance. This one worked. "But it might help if I knew your name."

"Rimarn," he said. A common name among lower-class Amn. "Previt Rimarn Dih. And you are?"

A previt. They were full-fledged priests, high-ranking ones, and they didn't leave the White Halls often, being more involved in business and politics. The Order must've decided that the death of a godling was of great importance.

"Oree Shoth," I said. My voice cracked on my family name; I had to repeat it. I thought that he smiled.

"We're investigating the death of the Lady Role and were hoping you and your friends could assist. Especially given that we've been kind enough to overlook your presence here at the Promenade." He picked up something else. I couldn't tell what.

"Happy to help," I said, trying to ignore the veiled threat. The Order of Itempas controlled permits and licenses in the city, among many other things, and they charged dearly for them. Yel's stand had a permit to sell on the Promenade; none of us artists could afford one. "It's so sad. I didn't think gods could die."

"Godlings can, yes," he said. His voice had grown noticeably colder, and I chided myself for forgetting how prickly devout Itempans could be about gods other than their own. I had been too long away from Nimaro, damn it—

"Their parents, the Three, can kill them," Rimarn continued. "And their siblings can kill them, if they're strong enough."

"Well, I haven't seen any godlings with bloody hands, if that's what you're wondering. Not that I see much of anything." I smiled. It was weak.

"Mmm. You found the body."

"Yes. There was no one around, though, that I could tell. Then Madding—Lord Madding, another godling who lives in town—came and took the body. He said he was going to show it to their parents. To the Three."

"I see." The sound of something being put back on my table. Not the miniature Tree, though. "Your eyes are very interesting."

I don't know why this made me more uneasy. "So people tell me."

"Are those...cataracts?" He leaned close to peer at me. I smelled mint tea on his breath. "I've never seen cataracts like those."

I've been told my eyes are unpleasant to look at. The "cataracts" that Rimarn had noticed were actually many narrow, delicate fingers of grayish tissue, layered tight over one another like the petals of a daisy yet to bloom. I have no pupils, no irises in the ordinary sense. From a distance, it looks as though I have matte, steely cataracts, but up close the deformity is clear.

"The bonebenders call them malformed corneas, actually. With some other complications that I can't pronounce." I tried to smile again and failed miserably.

"I see. Is this...malformation...common among Maroneh?"

There was a crash from two tables over. Ru's table. I heard her cry out in protest. Vuroy and Ohn started to join in. "Shut up," snapped the priest who was questioning her, and they all fell silent. Someone from the onlooking crowd—probably a Darkwalker—shouted for the priests to leave us alone, but no one else took up his cry, and he was not brave or stupid enough to repeat it.

I have never been very patient, and fear shortened my temper even more. "What is it you want, Previt Rimarn?"

"An answer to my question would be welcome, Miss Shoth."

"No, of course my eyes aren't common among Maroneh. *Blindness* isn't common among Maroneh. Why would it be?"

I felt the table shift slightly; perhaps he shrugged. "Some aftereffect of what the Nightlord did, perhaps. Legend says the forces he unleashed on the Maroland were...unnatural."

Implying that the survivors of the disaster were unnatural as well. Smug Amn bastard. We Maroneh had honored Itempas for just as long as they had. I bit back the retort that first came to mind and said instead, "The Nightlord didn't do anything to us, Previt."

"Destroying your homeland is nothing?"

"Nothing beyond that, I mean. Demons and darkness, he didn't *care* enough to do anything to us. He destroyed the Maroland only because he happened to be there at the time the Arameri let his leash slip."

There was a moment's pause. It lasted just long enough that my anger withered, leaving only horror. One did not criticize the Arameri—certainly not to an Itempan priest's face. Then I jumped as a loud crash sounded right in front of me. The miniature Tree. He'd dropped it, shattering the ceramic pot and probably doing fatal damage to the plant itself.

"Oh, dear," Rimarn said, his voice ice cold. "Sorry. I'll pay for that."

I closed my eyes and drew in a deep breath. I was still trembling from the crash, but I wasn't stupid. "Don't worry about it."

Another shift, and suddenly fingers took hold of my chin. "A shame about your eyes," he said. "You're a beautiful woman otherwise. If you wore glasses—"

"I prefer for people to see me as I am, Previt Rimarn."

"Ah. Should they see you as a blind human woman, then, or as a godling only pretending to be helpless and mortal?"

What the— I stiffened all over, and then did another thing I probably shouldn't have done. I burst out laughing. He was already angry. I knew better. But when I got angry, my nerves sought an outlet, and my mouth didn't always guard the gates.

"You think—" I had to work my hand around his to wipe a tear. "A *godling*? *Me*? Dearest Skyfather, is *that* what you're thinking?"

Rimarn's fingers tightened suddenly, enough to hurt the sides of my jaw, and I stopped laughing when he forced my face up higher and leaned close. "What I'm thinking is that you reek of magic," he said in a tight whisper. "More than I've ever smelled on any mortal."

And suddenly I could see him.

It was not like Shiny. Rimarn's glow was there all at once, and it didn't come from inside him. Rather, I could see lines and curlicues all over his skin like fine, shining tattoos, winding around his arms and marching over his torso. The rest of him remained invisible to me, but I could see the outline of his body by those dancing, fiery lines.

A scrivener. He was a scrivener. A good one, too, judging by the number of godwords etched into his flesh. They weren't really there, of course; this was just the way my eyes interpreted his skill and experience, or so I'd come to understand over the years. Usually that helped me spot his kind long before they got close enough to spot me.

I swallowed, no longer laughing now, and terrified.

But before he could begin the real questioning, I felt a sudden shift of the air, signaling movement nearby. That was my only warning before something yanked the previt's hand off my face. Rimarn started to protest, but before he could, another body blurred my view of him. A larger frame, dark and empty of magic, familiar in shape. Shiny.

I could not see precisely what he did to Rimarn. But I didn't have to; I heard the gasps of the other Row artists and onlookers, Shiny's grunt of effort, and Rimarn's sharp cry as he was bodily lifted and flung away. The godwords on Rimarn's flesh blurred into streaks as he flew a good ten feet through the air. He stopped glowing only when he landed in a bone-jarring heap.

No. Oh, no. I scrambled to my feet, knocking over my chair, and fumbled desperately for my walking stick. Before I could find it, I froze, realizing that though Rimarn's glow had vanished, I could still see.

I could see *Shiny.* His glow was faint, barely noticeable, but growing by the second and pulsing like a heartbeat. As Shiny interposed himself between me and Rimarn, the glow brightened still more, racheting up from a gentle burn toward that eye-searing peak that I had never seen from him outside of the dawn hour.

But it was the middle of the day.

"What the hells are you doing?" demanded a harsh voice from farther away. One of the other priests. This was followed by other shouts and threats, and I snapped back to awareness.

No one could see Shiny's glow except me and maybe Rimarn, who was still groaning on the ground. They had simply seen a man—an unknown foreigner, dressed in the plain, cheap clothing that was all I'd been able to afford for him—attack a previt of the Itempan Order. In front of a full troop of Order-Keepers.

I reached out, caught one of Shiny's blazing shoulders, and instantly snatched my hand back. Not because he was hot to the touch—though he was, hotter than I'd ever felt—but because the flesh under my hand seemed to *vibrate* in that instant, like I'd touched a bolt of lightning.

But I pushed that observation aside. "Stop it!" I hissed at him. "What are you doing? You have to apologize, right now, before they—"

Shiny turned to look at me, and the words died in my mouth. I could see his face now completely, as I always could in that perfect instant before he blazed too bright and I had to look away. "Handsome" did not begin to describe that face, so much more than the collection of features that my fingers had explored and learned. Cheekbones did not have their own inner light. Lips did not curve like living things in their own right, sharing with me a slight, private smile that made me feel, for just an instant, like the only woman in the world. He had never, ever smiled at me before.

But it was vicious, that smile. Cold. Murderous. I drew back from it, stunned—and for the first time since I'd met him, afraid.

Then he glanced around, facing the Keepers who were almost surely converging upon us. He considered them and the crowd of onlookers with the same detatched, cold arrogance. He seemed to make some decision.

I kept gaping as three of the Order-Keepers grabbed him. I saw them, dark silhouettes limned by Shiny's light, throw him to the ground and kick him and haul his arms back to tie them. One of them put his knee on the back of Shiny's neck, bearing down, and I screamed before I could stop myself. The Order-Keeper, a malevolent shadow, turned and shouted for me to shut *up*, Maro bitch, or he would have some for me, too—

"*Enough!*"

At that fierce bellow, I started so badly that I lost my grip on my stick. In the silence that fell, it clattered on the Promenade's walkstones loudly, making me jump again.

Rimarn had been the one to shout. I could not see him; whatever he'd done to conceal his nature from me before, it was back in effect now. Even if I'd been able to see his godwords, I think Shiny would have drowned out his minor light.

Rimarn sounded hoarse and out of breath. He was on his feet, near the cluster of men, and spoke to Shiny. "Are you a fool? I've never seen a man do anything so stupid."

Shiny had not struggled as the priests bore him down. Rimarn waved away the Order-Keeper who'd put a knee on Shiny's neck—my own shoulder muscles unknotted in sympathetic relief—and then shoved the back of Shiny's head with a toe. "Answer me!" he snapped. "Are you a fool?"

I had to do something. "H-he's my cousin," I blurted. "Fresh from the territory, Previt. He doesn't know the city, didn't know who you were..." This was the worst lie I had ever told. Everyone, no matter their nation or race or tribe or class, knew Itempan priests on sight. They wore shining white uniforms and they ruled the world. "Please, Previt, I'll take responsibility—"

"No, you won't," Rimarn snapped. The Order-Keepers got up and hauled Shiny to his feet. He stood calmly between them, glowing so brightly that I could see half the Promenade by the light that poured off his flesh. He still had that terrible, deadly smile on his face.

Then they were dragging him away, and fear soured my mouth as I fumbled my way around my tables. Something else fell over with a crash as I groped toward Rimarn without a stick. "Previt, wait!"

"I'll be back for you later," he snapped at me. Then he, too, walked away, following the other Order-Keepers. I tried to run after them and cried out as I tripped over some unseen obstacle. Before I could fall, I was caught by rough hands that smelled of tobacco and sour alcohol and fear.

"Quit it, Oree," Vuroy breathed in my ear. "They're too pissed off to feel guilty about kicking the shit out of a blind girl."

"They'll kill him." I gripped his arm tight. "They'll beat him to death. Vuroy—"

"Nothing you can do about it," he said softly, and I went limp, because he was right.

*   *   *

Vuroy, Ru, and Ohn helped me get home. They carried my tables and goods, too, out of the unspoken understanding that I would not need to store my things with Yel, because I would not be going back to the Row anytime soon.

Ru and Vuroy stayed with me while Ohn went out again. I tried to keep calm and look passive, because I knew they would be suspicious. They had looked around the house, seen the pantry that served as Shiny's bedroom, found his small pile of clothes—neatly folded and stacked—in the corner. They thought I'd been hiding a lover from them. If they'd known the truth, they would've been much more afraid.

"I can understand why you didn't tell us about him," Ru was saying. She sat across the kitchen table from me, holding my hand. The night before, Shiny's blood had covered the place where our hands now rested. "After Madding...well. But I wish you had told us, sweetheart. We're your friends—we would've understood."

I stubbornly said nothing, trying not to show how frustrated I was. I had to look dejected, depressed, so they would decide that the best thing for me was privacy and sleep. Then I could pray for Madding. The Order-Keepers probably wouldn't kill Shiny immediately. He had defied them, disrespected them. They would make him suffer for a long time.

That was bad enough. But if they killed him, and he pulled his little resurrection trick in front of them, gods knew what they would do. Magic was power meant for those with other kinds of power: Arameri, nobles, scriveners, the Order, the wealthy. It was illegal for commonfolk, even though we all used a little magic now and again in secret. Every woman knew the sigil to prevent pregnancy, and every neighborhood had someone who could draw the scripts for minor healing or hiding valuables in plain sight. Things had been easier since the coming of the godlings, actually, because the priests—who could not always tell godlings and mortals apart—tended to leave us all alone.

Shiny wasn't a godling, though; he was something else. I

didn't know why he'd begun to shine back at the Promenade, but I knew this: it wouldn't last. It never did. When he became weak again, he would be just a man. Then the priests would tear him apart to learn the secret of his power.

And they would come after me again for harboring him.

I rubbed my face as if I was tired. "I need to lie down," I said.

"Demonshit," Vuroy said. "You're going to pretend to go to bed, then call your old boyfriend. Think we're stupid?"

I stiffened, and Ru chuckled. "Remember we know you, Oree."

Damn. "I have to help him," I said, abandoning the pretense. "Even if I can't find Madding, I have a little money. The priests take bribes—"

"Not when they're this angry," said Ru, very gently. "They'd just take your money and kill him, anyway."

I clenched my fists. "Madding, then. Help me find Mad. He'll help me. He owes me."

I heard chimes on the heels of those words, which made my cheeks heat as I realized just how badly I'd underestimated my friends.

Someone opened the front door. I saw Madding's familiar shimmer through the walls even before he stepped into the kitchen, with Ohn a taller shadow at his side. "I heard," Madding said quietly. "Are you calling in a debt, Oree?"

There was a curious shiver in the air, and a delicate tension like something unseen holding its breath. This was Madding's power beginning to flex.

I stood up from the table, more glad to see him than I'd been in months. Then I noticed the somberness of his expression and recalled myself. "I'm sorry, Mad," I said. "I forgot...your sister. If there was any other way, I would never ask for your help while you're in mourning."

He shook his head. "Nothing to be done for the dead. Ohn tells me you've got a friend in trouble."

Ohn would've told him more than that, because Ohn was an inveterate gossipper. But..."Yes. I think the Order-Keepers might have taken him somewhere other than their White Hall, though." Itempas Skyfather—*Dayfather*, I kept forgetting—abhorred disorder, and killing a man was rarely neat. They would not profane the White Hall with something like that.

"South Root," Madding said. "Some of my people saw them headed that way with your friend, after the incident at the Promenade."

I had an instant to digest that he'd had his people watching me. I decided that it didn't matter, reached for my stick, and went over to him. "How long ago?"

"An hour." He took my hand with his own smooth, warm, uncallused one. "I won't owe you after this, Oree," he said. "You understand?"

I smiled thinly, because I did. Madding never reneged on an agreement; if he owed you, he would do anything, go through anyone, to repay. If he had to go through the Itempan Order, however, that would make business in Shadow difficult for him for quite some time. There were things he could not do—kill them, for example, or leave the city except to return to the gods' realm. Even gods had their rules to follow.

I stepped closer and leaned against the comforting strength of his arm. Hard not to feel that arm without remembering other nights and other comforts and other times I'd relied on him to make all my troubles go away.

"I'd say that's worth the price of breaking my heart," I said. I spoke lightly, but I meant every syllable. And he sighed, because he knew I was right.

"Hang on, then," he said, and the whole world went bright as his magic carried us to wherever Shiny was dying.

3

"Gods and Corpses"
(oil on canvas)

THE INSTANT MADDING and I appeared in South Root, a blast of power staggered us both.

I perceived it as a wave of brightness so intense that I cried out as it washed past, dropping my stick to clap both hands over my eyes. Mad gasped as well, as if something had stricken him a blow. He recovered faster than me and took my hands, trying to pull them away from my face. "Oree? Let me see."

I let him push my hands aside. "I'm fine," I said. "Fine. Just... too bright. Gods. I didn't know these things could hurt like that." I kept blinking and tearing up, which made him peer closely into each eye.

"They're not 'things'; they're eyes. Is the pain fading?"

"Yes, yes, I'm fine, I told you. What in the infinite hells was that?" Already the brightness had vanished, subsumed into the dark that was all I usually saw. The pain was fading more slowly, but it *was* fading.

"I don't know." Madding cupped my face in his hands, thumbs grazing my underlids to brush away the tears. I allowed this at first, but abruptly his touch was too intimate, triggering memories more painful than the light had been. I pulled away, probably more quickly than I should have. He sighed a little but let me go.

There was a faint stir on either side of me, and I heard a light patter, as of feet touching the ground. Madding's tone shifted to something more authoritative, as it always did when he spoke to his underlings. "Tell me that wasn't who I thought it was."

"It was," said one voice, which I thought of as pale and androgynous even though I had seen its owner once, and she was the exact opposite, brown and voluptuous. She was also one of the godlings who didn't like it when I saw her, so I had never glimpsed her since.

"Demons and darkness," Mad said, sounding annoyed. "I thought the Arameri were keeping him."

"Not anymore, apparently," said the other voice. This one was definitively male. I had seen him, too, and he was a strange creature with long, wild hair that smelled like copper. His skin was Amn-white but with irregular darker patches here and there; I gathered the patches were his idea of decoration. I certainly found them pretty, whenever I managed to see him undisguised. This was business, though, so now he was just part of the darkness.

"Lil has come," said the woman, and Madding groaned. "There are bodies. The Order-Keepers."

"The—" Madding suddenly pulled back and looked hard at me. "Oree, please don't tell me *this* is your new boyfriend."

"I don't have a boyfriend, Mad, not that it's any of your business." I frowned, suddenly understanding. "Wait. Are you talking about Shiny?"

"Shiny? Who the—" Madding cursed, then stooped swiftly to collect my walking stick and press it into my hands. "Enough. Let's go."

His underlings vanished, and Madding began to pull me along toward wherever that white-hot power had come from.

South Root—Where Sows Root, went the local joke—was the worst neighborhood in Shadow. One of the Tree's main roots had forked off a side branch nearby, which meant the area was bracketed on three sides rather than the usual two. On rare days, South Root could be beautiful. It had been a respectable crafters' neighborhood before the Tree, so the white-painted walls were inlaid here and there with mica and smooth agate, and the streets were cobbled in patterns of large and small bricks, with gates of iron wrought in magnificent shapes. If not for the three roots, it would have gotten more sunlight than parts of Shadow closer to the Tree's trunk. I'd been told that it still did, on windy days in late autumn, for an hour or two a day. Any other time, South Root was perpetually dark.

No one lived there anymore but desperate, angry poor people. This made it one of the few places in the city where Order-Keepers might feel comfortable beating a man to death in the street.

Their consciences must've bothered them more than usual, however, because the space into which Madding finally dragged me did not feel open. I smelled garbage and mildew, and there was the bitter acridity of stale urine on my tongue. Another alley? One that had no magic to keep it clean.

And there were other smells here, stronger and even less pleasant. Smoke. Charcoal. Burned meat and hair. I could hear something still sizzling faintly.

Near this sound stood a tall, languid female figure, the only thing I could see aside from Madding. Her back was to me, so at first I noticed only her long, ragged hair, straight like a High Norther's but an odd mottled gold in color. This was not the gold of Amn hair; it was somehow not pretty at all. She was also thin—disturbingly, unhealthily so. She wore an incongruously elegant gown with a low back, and the shoulder blades that I could see on either side of her hair were sharp-angled, like knife edges.

Then the woman turned, and I clapped both hands over my mouth to keep from crying out. Above the nose, her face was normal. Below, her mouth became a distorted, impossible monstrosity, her lower jaw hanging all the way to her knees, the too-long expanse of her gums lined with several rows of tiny, needlelike teeth. *Moving* teeth, each row marching along her jaw like a restless trail of ants. I could hear them whirring faintly. She drooled.

And when she saw my reaction, she smiled. That was the most hideous sight I had ever seen.

Then she shimmered and became an ordinary-looking woman, nondescriptly Amn, with a nondescriptly human mouth. She was still smiling, though, and there was still something disturbingly *hungry* in her expression.

"My gods," Madding murmured. (Godlings said this sort of thing all the time.) "It *is* you."

His words confused me because of their direction; he was not speaking to the blonde woman. Then I jumped at the response, because it came from another unexpected direction—above.

"Oh, yes," said this new, soft voice. "It's him."

Madding suddenly went still in a way that I knew meant trouble. His two lieutenants suddenly flickered into view, equally tense. "I see," Madding said, speaking low and carefully. "It's been a while, Sieh. Have you come to gloat?"

"A little." The voice was that of a young, prepubescent boy. I looked up, trying to gauge where he was—a rooftop, maybe, or a window on the second or third floor. I could not see him. A mortal? Or another godling who was feeling shy?

There was a sudden feel of movement before me, and abruptly the boy spoke from the ground only a few feet away. Godling, then.

"You look worn out, old man," the boy said, and belatedly I realized he, too, was addressing someone other than me, Madding, or the blonde woman. Finally I noticed that off to the side of the alley, near the wall, there was someone low to the ground. Sitting or kneeling, maybe. Panting for some reason. Something about those weary breaths was familiar.

"Mortal flesh is bound by physical laws," the boy continued, speaking to the panting person. "If you don't use sigils to channel the power, you get more, it's true—but then the magic drains your strength. Use enough and it can even kill you—for a while, anyhow. Just one of a thousand new things you'll have to learn, I'm afraid. Sorry, old man."

The blonde woman uttered a laugh like pebbles grinding underfoot. "You're not sorry."

She was right. The voice of the boy—Sieh, Madding had

called him—was utterly devoid of compassion. He sounded pleased, in fact, in the way that most people would be pleased to see an enemy brought low. I cocked my head, listening close and trying to understand.

Sieh chuckled. "Of course I'm sorry, Lil. Do I look like the kind of person who would hold a grudge? That would be petty of me."

"Petty," agreed the blonde woman, "and childish and cruel. Does his suffering please you?"

"Oh, yes, Lil. It pleases me very much."

Not even the pretense of friendliness this time. There was nothing in that boyish voice but sadistic relish. I shivered, even more afraid for Shiny. I had never seen a godling child before, but I had an inkling they were not all that different from human children. Human children could be merciless, especially when they had power.

I stepped away from Madding, intending to go to the panting man. Madding pulled me sharply back, his hand like a vise on my arm. I stumbled, protesting, "But—"

"Not now, Oree," Madding said. He didn't use that tone with me often, but I had learned long ago that it meant danger when he did.

If this had been any other situation, I would have happily stepped behind him and tried to make myself as unnoticeable as possible. I was in a dark alley in the back end of beyond, surrounded by dead men and gods whose tempers were up. For all I knew, there wasn't another mortal anywhere in shouting distance. Even if there had been, what in the infinite hells could they have done to help?

"What's happened to the Keepers?" I whispered to Madding.

It was an unnecessary question; they had finally stopped sizzling. "How did Shiny kill them?"

"Shiny?"

To my great dismay, it was Sieh's voice. I hadn't wanted to draw his attention or that of the blonde woman. Yet Sieh seemed honestly delighted. "*Shiny?* Is that what you call him? Really?"

I swallowed, tried to speak, then tried again when the first try failed. "He won't give me his name, so... I had to call him something."

"Did you, now?" The boy, sounding amused, came closer. I was a good deal taller than him, I guessed by the direction of his voice, but that was not as comforting as it should have been. I could still see nothing of him, not even an outline or a shadow, which meant that he was better than most godlings at concealing himself. I couldn't even smell him. I could *feel* him, though; his presence filled the whole alley in a way that none of the other godlings' did.

"Shiny," the boy said again, contemplative. "And he answers to that name?"

"Not exactly." I licked my lips and decided to take a chance. "Is he all right?"

The boy abruptly turned away. "Oh, he'll be fine. He has no *choice* but to be fine, doesn't he?" He was angrier now, I realized, my heart sinking into my stomach. I had made things worse. "No matter what happens to his mortal body, no matter how many times he abuses it—and, yes, oh yes, I know about that, did you think I didn't?" He was speaking to Shiny again, and his voice practically trembled with fury. "Did you think I wouldn't laugh at you, so proud, so *arrogant*, dying over and over because you can't be bothered to take the most basic care?"

There was a sudden jostling sound and a grunt from Shiny. And another sound, unmistakable: a blow. The boy had hit or kicked him. Madding's hand tightened on my arm, inadvertently I think. A reaction to whatever he was seeing. Sieh was barely coherent, snarling out his words. "Did you think"— another kick, this one harder; godlings were far stronger than they seemed—"I wouldn't"—Kick—"love to help you along?" *Kick*.

And an echo: the wet snap of bone. Shiny cried out, and at this I could not help myself; I opened my mouth to protest.

But before I could, another voice spoke, so softly that I almost missed it. "Sieh."

Stillness.

All at once, Sieh became visible. He was a boy, small and spindly looking, almost Maroneh-colored, though with an unkempt flop of straight hair. Not at all threatening to look at. As he appeared, he stood frozen, his eyes wide with surprise, but all at once he turned.

In the space that he faced, another godling appeared. This one was also a tiny thing, a full head shorter than me and barely larger than Sieh, yet there was something about her that hinted at strength. Possibly her attire, which was strange: a long, gray sleeveless vest that bared her slim, tight brown arms, and leggings that stopped at midcalf. Below them she was barefoot. She looked, I thought at first, the way I'd heard High Northers described, but her hair was wrong—curled and wild instead of straight, and chopped boyishly short. And her eyes were wrong, too, though I could not quite fathom how. What color was that? Green? Gray? Something else entirely?

At the corner of my vision, I saw Madding stiffen, his eyes going wide and round. One of his lieutenants uttered a swift, soft curse.

"Sieh," the quiet woman said again, her tone disapproving.

Sieh scowled, in that moment looking like nothing more than a sulky little boy caught doing something wrong. "What? It's not like he's really mortal."

Off to the side, the blonde goddess, Lil, looked at Shiny with interest. "He smells mortal enough. Sweat and pain and blood and fear, so nice."

The new goddess glanced at her, which didn't seem to bother Lil at all, then focused on Sieh again. "This wasn't what we had in mind."

"Why shouldn't I kick him to death now and again? He's not even trying to fulfill the terms you set. He might as well entertain me."

The goddess shook her head, sighing, and went to him. To my surprise, Sieh did not resist as she pulled him into an embrace, cupping one hand at the back of his head. He held stiff against her, not reciprocating, but even I could see that he did not mind being held.

"This serves no purpose," she said in his ear, and so tender was her tone that I could not help thinking of my own mother, miles away in Nimaro Territory. "It doesn't help. It doesn't even hurt him, not in any way that matters. Why do you bother?"

Sieh turned his face away, his hands clenching at his sides. "You know why!"

"Yes, I know. Do you?"

When Sieh spoke again, I could hear the strain in his voice. "No! I hate him! I want to kill him forever!"

But then the dam broke, and he sagged against her, dissolving into tears. The quiet goddess sighed and pulled him closer, seemingly content to comfort him for however long it took.

I marveled at this for a moment, torn between awe and pity, then remembered Shiny on the ground nearby, his breathing labored now.

Surreptitiously I edged away from Madding, who was watching the tableau with the oddest look on his face, something I could not interpret. Sorrow, maybe. Chagrin. It didn't matter. While he and the others were preoccupied, I went over to Shiny. It was definitely him; I recognized his peculiar spice-and-metal scent. When I crouched to examine him, I found his back as hot as a fever and completely drenched in what I hoped was only sweat. He had bent in on himself in a huddle, his fists clenched tight, in obvious agony.

His condition enraged me. I lifted my eyes to glare at Sieh and the quiet goddess—and with a deep chill, I found her watching me over Sieh's bony shoulder. Hadn't her eyes been gray-green before? They were yellowish green now, and not at all warm.

"Interesting," she said. Beside her, Sieh turned to peer at me, too, rubbing one eye with the back of his hand. She kept a hand on his shoulder with absent affection and said to me, "Are you his lover?"

"She's not," said Madding.

The woman threw him the mildest of looks, and Madding's jaw flexed. It was as close to fear as I had ever seen him come.

"I'm not," I blurted. I didn't know what was going on, why Madding seemed so wary of this woman and the child-god, but I knew I didn't want Madding getting in trouble for my folly. "Shiny lives with me. We...he's..." What should I say? *Never lie to a godling*, Mad had warned me long ago. Some of them had spent millennia studying humankind. They could not read minds, but the language of our bodies was an open book. "I'm his friend," I said at last.

The boy exchanged a look with the goddess, and then both of them turned unnerving, enigmatic gazes on me. I noticed only then that Sieh's pupils were slitted, like those of a snake or cat.

"His friend," said Sieh. His face was expressionless now, his eyes dry, his voice without inflection. I didn't know if that was good or bad.

It sounded so weak. "Yes," I said. "It's...how I...think of myself, anyway." Another silence fell, and in it, I grew ashamed. I didn't even know Shiny's real name. "Please just stop hurting him." It was a whisper this time.

Sieh sighed, and so did the woman. The feeling that I was walking a narrow bridge over a very deep chasm began to fade.

"You call yourself his friend," the woman said. There was compassion in her voice, to my surprise. And her eyes were darker green now, shading toward hazel. "Does *he* call *you* the same?"

So they had noticed. "I don't know," I said, hating her for asking that question. I did not look at Shiny, who was still beside me. "He doesn't talk to me."

"Ask yourself why," drawled the boy.

I licked my lips. "There are many reasons why a man would hesitate to speak about his past."

"Few of those reasons are good. *His* certainly aren't." With a last contemptuous look, Sieh turned and walked away.

He paused, however, a look of surprise crossing his face, when the quiet woman suddenly moved forward, coming over to Shiny and me. When she crouched, balancing easily on her bare toes, I caught a fleeting sense of the real her, the goddess underneath her unimposing shell, and it staggered me. Where Sieh had filled the alley, she filled…what? It was too vast to grasp, too detailed. The ground beneath my knees. Every brick and speck of mortar, every struggling weed and smear of mildew. The air. The muckbins at the back of the alley. *Everything.*

And then it was gone, just as fast, and she was just a small High Norther woman with eyes that made me think of a dark, wet forest.

"You're very lucky," she said. I was confused at first; then I realized she was speaking to Shiny. "Friends are precious, powerful things—hard to earn, harder still to keep. You should thank this one for taking a chance on you."

Shiny twitched beside me. I could not see what he did, but the woman's expression changed to one of annoyance. She shook her head and got to her feet.

"Be careful of him," she said. To me this time. "Be his friend if you like—if he lets you. He needs you more than he realizes. But for your own sake, don't love him. He's not ready for that."

I could only stare at her, mute with awe. She turned away, then paused as she walked past Madding.

"Role," she said.

He nodded, as if he'd been expecting her attention. "We're doing everything we can." He threw me a quick, uneasy glance. "Even the mortals are looking into it. Everyone wants to know how this happened."

She nodded, slowly and solemnly. For an instant too long she was silent. Gods did that sometimes, contemplating the unfathomable, though they usually tried not to do it when mortals were around. Perhaps this one wasn't used to mortals yet.

"You have thirty days," she said suddenly.

Madding went stiff. "To find Role's killer? But you promised—"

"I said we wouldn't interfere in *mortal* affairs," she said sharply. Madding fell silent at once. "This is family."

After a moment, Madding nodded, though he still looked uncomfortable. "Yes. Yes, of course. And, ah—"

"He is angry," said the woman, and for the first time she looked troubled herself. "Role didn't take sides in the war. But even if she had...you're still his children. He still loves you." She paused and glanced at Madding, but Madding looked away. I guessed that she spoke of Bright Itempas, who was said to be the father of all the godlings. Naturally, He would take exception to the death of His child.

The woman continued. "So, thirty days. I've convinced him to stay out of it for that long. After that"—she paused, then shrugged—"you know his temper better than I do."

Madding went very pale.

With that, the woman turned to join the boy, both of them clearly intending to leave. From the corner of my eye, I saw one of Madding's lieutenants exhale in relief. I should have been relieved, too. I should have stayed quiet. But as I watched the woman and boy walk away, I could think of only one thing: *they knew Shiny.* Hated him, perhaps, but knew him.

I groped for my walking stick. "Wait!"

Madding looked at me like I had lost my mind, but I ignored him. The woman stopped, not turning back, but the child did, looking at me in surprise. "Who is he?" I asked, pointing at Shiny. "Will you tell me his name?"

"Oree, gods damn it." Madding stepped forward, but the woman held up a graceful hand and he went still.

Sieh only shook his head. "The rules are that he live among mortals *as* a mortal," he said, glancing beyond me at Shiny. "None of you comes into this world with a name, so neither does he. He gets nothing unless he earns it himself. Since he's not trying very hard, that means he'll never have much. Except a friend, apparently." He eyed me briefly and looked sour. "Well ... like Mother said, even he gets lucky sometimes."

Mother, I noted, with the part of my mind that remained fascinated by such things even after years of living in Shadow. Godlings did mate among themselves sometimes. Was Shiny Sieh's father, then?

"Mortals don't come into the world with nothing," I said carefully. "We have history. A home. Family."

Sieh's lip curled. "Only the fortunate ones among you. He doesn't deserve to be *that* lucky."

I shuddered and inadvertently thought of how I'd found Shiny, light and beauty discarded like trash. All this time I had assumed misfortune on his part; I had speculated that he suffered from some godly disease, or an accident that had stripped all but a vestige of his power. Now I knew his condition had been deliberately imposed. Someone—these very gods, perhaps—had *done this to him*, as a punishment.

"What in the infinite hells did he *do*?" I murmured without thinking.

I didn't understand the boy's reaction at first. I would never be as good at perceiving things with my eyes as I was with my other senses, and the look on Sieh's face alone was not enough for me to interpret. But when he spoke, I knew: whatever Shiny had done, it had been truly terrible, because Sieh's hate had once been love. Love betrayed has an entirely different sound from hatred outright.

"Maybe he'll tell you himself one day," he said. "I hope so. He doesn't deserve a friend, either."

Then he and the woman vanished, leaving me alone among gods and corpses.

4

"Frustration"
(watercolor)

By now you're probably confused. That's all right; so was I. The problem wasn't just my misunderstanding—though that was part of it—but also history. Politics. The Arameri, and maybe the more powerful nobles and priests, probably know all this. I'm just an ordinary woman with no connections or status, and no power beyond a walking stick that makes an excellent club in a pinch. I had to figure everything out the hard way.

My education didn't help. Like most people, I was taught that there were three gods once, and then there was a war between them, which left two. One of them wasn't actually a god anymore—though he was still very powerful—so really that left just one. (And a great many godlings, but we never saw them.) For most of my life, I was raised to believe that this state of affairs was ideal, because who wants a bunch of gods to pray to when one will do? Then the godlings returned.

Not just them, though. Suddenly the priests began to say odd prayers and write new teaching poems into the public scrolls. Children learned new songs in the White Hall schools. Where once the world's people had been required to offer their praises only to Bright Itempas, now we were urged to honor two additional gods: a Lord of Deep Shadows and someone called the Gray Lady. When people questioned this, the priests simply said, *The world has changed. We must change with it.*

You can imagine how well that went over.

It wasn't as chaotic as it might have been, though. Bright Itempas abhors disorder, after all, and the people who were most upset were the ones who had taken His tenets to heart. So quietly, peacefully, and in an orderly fashion, those people just stopped attending services at the White Halls. They kept their children at home for schooling, teaching them as best they could on their own. They stopped paying tithes, even though this had once meant prison or worse. They committed themselves to preserving the Bright, even as the whole world seemed determined to turn a little darker.

Everyone else held their breath, waiting for the slaughter to begin. The Order answers to the Arameri family, and the Arameri do not tolerate disobedience. Yet no one was imprisoned. There were no disappearances, of individuals or towns. Local priests visited parents, exhorting them to bring their children back to school for the children's sake, but when the parents refused, their children were not taken away. The Order-Keepers issued an edict that everyone was to pay a basal tithe to cover public services; those who didn't do this *were* punished. But for people who chose not to tithe *to the Order*—nothing.

No one knew what to make of that. So there were other quiet rebellions, these more challenging to the Bright. Everywhere, heretics started worshipping their gods openly. Some nation up in High North—I can't recall which one—declared that it would teach children its own language first, then Senmite, instead of the other way around. There were even people who chose to worship no god at all, despite new ones appearing in Shadow every day.

And the Arameri have done nothing.

For centuries, *millennia*, the world has danced to a single flute. In some ways, this has been our most sacred and inviolable law: *thou shalt do whatever the hells the Arameri say*. For this to change... well, that's more frightening to most of us than any shenanigans the gods might pull. It means the end of the Bright. And none of us knows what will come after.

So perhaps my confusion on a few points of metaphysical cosmology is understandable.

I figured things out pretty quickly after that, thank goodness. When I turned back to the alley—

* * *

—the blonde godling was licking something on the ground.

I thought at first it was Shiny. As I came closer, though, I realized the positioning was wrong. Shiny was on *that* side of the alley. The only things on the side where she crouched were—

My gorge rose. The dead Order-Keepers.

She looked up at me. Her eyes were the same as her hair: gold mottled with irregular spots of darker color. I stared at her and suffered a pang of epiphany. When people looked at my eyes, was this what they saw? Ugliness that should have been beauty?

"Flesh freely given," the godling said, and flashed me a hungry smile.

I skirted wide around her and moved back to Shiny's side.

"You try me, Oree," Madding said, shaking his head as I passed him. "You really do."

"All I did was ask a question," I snapped, and crouched to examine Shiny. Gods knew what the Order-Keepers had done to him, even before Sieh's attack. I didn't let myself think about the bodies behind me, and who had done that.

"He was trying to keep you alive," replied Madding's lieutenant, the female one.

I ignored her, though she was probably right. I just didn't feel like admitting it. When I explored Shiny's face with my fingers, I discovered his mouth was cut, and someone had blacked his eye; it was swollen almost shut. Those wounds did not concern me. I felt my way to his ribs, trying to find the break—

Something planted itself on my chest and shoved. Hard. Startled, I cried out, flying backward with such force that my back struck the far alley wall, knocking the sense out of me.

"Oree! *Oree!*"

Hands pulled at me. I blinked away stars and saw Madding crouched before me. I didn't realize at first what had happened. Then I saw Madding swing around, his face contorting with fury—at Shiny.

"I'm all right," I said vaguely, though I was not at all sure of this. Shiny had not been gentle. My head rang dully where the back of my skull had impacted stone. I let Madding help me to my feet, grateful for his support when the shining forms of him and the blonde woman blurred unpleasantly. "I'm all right!"

Madding snarled something in the gods' singsong, guttural language. I saw the words spill from his mouth as glittering arrows that darted away to strike Shiny. Most of the words were harmless, I gathered by the way they shattered into nothing, but a few of them seemed to land and sink in.

The blonde godling's rusty laugh interrupted this tirade. "Such disrespect, little brother," she said, licking charcoal and grease from her lips. No blood; she hadn't nibbled. Yet.

"Respect is earned, Lil." Madding spat off to the side. "Did he ever try to earn ours, instead of demanding it?"

Lil shrugged, bowing her head until ragged hair obscured her face. "What does it matter? We did what we had to do. The world changes. As long as there is life to be lived and food to be savored, I am content."

With that, she abandoned her human guise. Her mouth opened wide, wider, stretching impossibly as she bent over the Order-Keepers' huddled forms.

I covered my mouth, and Madding looked disgusted. "Flesh freely given, Lil. I thought that was your creed?"

She paused. "This was given." Her mouth did not move as she spoke. It could not possibly have formed words in the human fashion, as it was.

"By whom? I doubt those men volunteered to be roasted for your pleasure."

She lifted an arm, pointing one skeletal finger at the place where Shiny huddled. "His kill. His flesh to give."

I shuddered as she confirmed my fears. Madding noticed this and leaned close to examine me, touching my shoulders and head gingerly. The soreness where he touched warned me there would be bruises come morning.

"I'm all right," I said again. My head was clearing, so I let Madding help me to my feet. "I'm fine. Let me see him."

Madding scowled. "He really tried to hurt you, Oree."

"I know." I stepped around Madding. Beyond him, I heard the unmistakable, hideous sounds of flesh being torn and bone crunching. I made certain not to move far from Madding, whose broad body blocked my view.

Instead I focused on Shiny, or where I guessed he was. Whatever magic he'd used to kill the Order-Keepers was long gone. He was weak now, wounded, lashing out in his pain like a beast—

No. I had spent my life knowing the hearts of others through the press of skin to skin. I had felt the petulant anger in that shove. Perhaps it was only to be expected: the quiet goddess had told him to be grateful for having me as a friend. I might never know Shiny well, but I could tell he was too proud to take that as anything but an insult.

He was panting again. Shoving me had spent what little strength he'd regained. But I felt it when he managed to lift his head and glare at me.

"My home is still open to you, Shiny," I said, speaking very softly. "I've always helped people who needed me, and I don't intend to stop now. You *do* need me, whether you like it or not." Then I turned away, extending my hand. Madding put my stick into it. I took a deep breath, tapping the ground twice to hear the comforting clack of wood on stone.

"Find your own way back," I told Shiny, and left him there.

*　　*　　*

Madding did not delegate the task of caring for me to someone else. That was what I'd expected, since things had been awkward between us since the breakup. Yet he stayed, bathing me as I knelt shivering in the cold water. (Madding could have heated the water for me—gods were handy that way—but the cold was better for my back.) When that was done, he bundled me into a soft, fluffy robe that he had conjured, tucked me into bed on my belly, and settled in beside me.

I didn't protest, though I gave him an amused look. "I suppose this is just to keep me warm?"

"Well, not *just*," he said, snuggling closer and resting a hand on the small of my back. That part was unbruised. "How's your head?"

"Better. I think the cold helped." It felt nice, having him there against me. Like old times. I told myself not to get used to it, but that was like telling a child not to want candy. "There isn't even a lump."

"Mmm." He brushed aside a few coils of hair and sat up to kiss the nape of my neck. "Might be one come morning. You should rest."

I sighed. "It's hard to rest if you keep doing things like that."

Madding paused, then sighed, his breath tickling my skin. "Sorry." He lingered there for a moment with his face pressed against my neck, breathing my scent, and finally he sat up, shifting to put a few inches between us. I missed him immediately and turned my face away so that he would not see.

"I'll have someone bring...Shiny...back, if he hasn't made it on his own by morning," he said finally, after a long, uncomfortable silence. "That was what you asked me to do."

"Mmm." There was no point in thanking him. He was the god of obligation; he kept his promises.

"Be careful of him, Oree," he said quietly. "Yeine was right. He doesn't think much of mortals, and you saw what his temper's like. I have no idea why you took him in—I have no idea why you do half the things you do—but just be careful. That's all I ask."

"I'm not sure I should let you ask anything of me, Mad."

I knew I'd pissed him off when the room lit up in bright, rippling blue-green. "It doesn't all go one way between us, Oree," he snapped. His voice was softer in this form, cool and echoing. "You know that."

I sighed, started to turn over, and thought better of it when my bruises throbbed. Instead I turned just my face to him. Madding had become a shimmering, humanoid shape that was only vaguely male, but the look that boiled in his face was wholly that of an injured lover. He thought I was being unfair. He might even have been right.

"You say you still love me," I said. "But you don't want to be with me anymore. You won't share anything. You drop these vague warnings about Shiny rather than telling me anything *useful*. How do you expect me to feel?"

"I *can't* tell you anything more about him." The liquid of his form abruptly became hard crystal, delicately faceted aquamarine and peridot. I loved it when he went solid, though it usually meant stubbornness on his part. "You heard Sieh. He must wander this world, nameless and unknown—"

"Tell me about Sieh, then, and that woman. Yeine, you called her? You were afraid of them."

Madding groaned, setting all his facets ashiver. "You're like a magpie, dropping one subject to jump after a prettier one."

I shrugged. "I'm mortal. I don't have all the time in the world. Tell me." I wasn't angry anymore. Neither was he, really. I knew he still loved me, and he knew that I knew. We were just taking a hard day out on each other. It was easy to fall into old habits.

Madding sighed and leaned back against the bed's headboard, resuming his human form. "It wasn't fear."

"Looked like fear to me. All of you were afraid, except that one with the mouth. Lil."

He made a face. "Lil isn't capable of fear. And it wasn't fear. It was just..." He shrugged, frowning. "It's hard to explain."

"Everything is with you."

He rolled his eyes. "Yeine is... Well, she's very young, as our kind goes. I don't know what to think of her yet. And Sieh, despite how he looks, is the oldest of us."

"Ah," I said, though I didn't really understand. That child had been older than Madding? And why had Sieh called the woman his mother if she was younger? "The respect due a big brother—"

"No, no, that doesn't matter to us."

I frowned in confusion. "What, then? Is he stronger than you?"

"Yes." Madding grimaced in consternation. I had a momentary impression of aquamarine shading to sapphire, though he did not change; just my imagination.

"Because he's older?"

"Partly, yes. But also..." He trailed off.

I groaned in frustration. "I want to sleep tonight, Mad."

"I'm trying to say it." Madding sighed. "Mortal languages don't have words for this. He... *lives true*. He is what he is. You've heard that saying, haven't you? It's more than just words for us."

I had no idea what he was talking about. He saw that in my

face and tried again. "Imagine you're older than this planet, yet you have to act like a child. Could you do it?"

Impossible to even imagine. "I . . . don't know. I don't think so."

Madding nodded. "Sieh does it. He does it *every day*, all day; he never stops. That makes him strong."

I was beginning to understand, a little. "Is that why you're a usurer?"

Madding chuckled. "I prefer the term *investor*. And my rates are perfectly fair, thank you."

"Drug dealer, then."

"I prefer the term *independent apothecary*—"

"Hush." I reached out, wistful, to touch the back of his hand where it rested on the sheets. "It must have been hard for you during the Interdiction." That was what he and the other godlings called the time before their coming—the time when they hadn't been permitted to visit our world or interact with mortals. Why they'd been forbidden to come, or who had forbidden them, they would not say. "I can't see gods having many obligations."

"Not true," he said. He watched me for a moment, then turned his hand over to grasp mine. "The most powerful obligations aren't material, Oree."

I looked at his hand clasped around the nothingness of my own, understanding and wishing that I didn't. I wished he had just fallen out of love with me. It would have made things easier.

His grip loosened; I had let him see more in my expression than I'd meant to. He sighed and lifted my hand, kissing the back of it. "I should go," he said. "If you need anything—"

On impulse, I sat up, though it made my back ache something awful. "Stay," I said.

He looked away, uneasy. "I shouldn't."

"No obligation, Mad. Just friendship. Stay."

He reached up to brush my hair back from my cheek. His expression, in that one unguarded moment, was the softest I ever saw it outside of his liquid form.

"I wish you were a goddess," he said. "Sometimes it feels as if you *are* one. But then something like this happens..." He brushed my robe back and grazed a bruise with his fingertip. "And I remember how fragile you are. I remember that I'll lose you one day." His jaw flexed. "I can't bear it, Oree."

"Goddesses can die, too." I realized my error belatedly. I'd been thinking of the Gods' War, millennia before. I had forgotten Madding's sister.

But Madding smiled sadly. "That's different. We *can* die. You mortals, though...Nothing can stop you from dying. All we can do is stand by and watch."

And die a little with you. That was what he'd said before, on the night he'd left me. I understood his reasoning, even agreed with it. That didn't mean I'd ever like it.

I put my hand on his face and leaned in to kiss him. He did it readily, but I felt how he held himself back. I tasted nothing of him in that kiss, even though I pressed close, practically begging for more. When we parted, I sighed and he looked away.

"I should go," he said again.

This time I let him. He rose from the bed and went to the door, pausing in the frame for a moment.

"You can't go back to Art Row," he said. "You know that, don't you? You shouldn't even stay in town. Leave, at least for a few weeks."

"And go where?" I lay back down, turning my face away from him.

"Maybe visit your hometown."

I shook my head. I hated Nimaro.

"Travel, then. There must be somewhere else you want to visit."

"I need to eat," I said. "Rent would be nice, too, unless you intend for me to carry all my household possessions when I go."

He sighed in faint exasperation. "Then at least set up your table at one of the other promenades. The Easha Order-Keepers don't bother with those parts of the city as much. You'll still get a few customers there."

Not enough. But he was right; it would be better than nothing. I sighed and nodded.

"I can have one of my people—"

"I don't want to owe you anything."

"A gift," he said softly. There was a faint, unpleasant shiver of the air, like chimes gone sour. Generosity was not easy for him. On another day, under other circumstances, I would've been honored that he made the effort, but I was not feeling particularly generous in that moment.

"I don't want *anything* from you, Mad."

Another silence, this one reverberating with hurt. That was like old times, too.

"Good night, Oree," he said, and left.

Eventually, after a good cry, I slept.

*   *   *

Let me tell you how Madding and I met.

I came to Shadow—though I still thought of it as Sky then— when I was seventeen. Very quickly I fell in with others like me—newcomers, dreamers, young people drawn to the city in spite of its dangers because sometimes, for some of us, tedium and familiarity feel worse than risking your life. With their help, I learned to make a living off my knack for crafts and to protect myself from those who would have exploited me. I slept in a tenement with six others at first, then got an apartment of my own. After a year's time, I sent a letter to my mother letting her know I was alive, and received in return a ten-page missive demanding that I come home. I was doing well.

I remember it was the end of a day, and wintertime. Snow is rare and light in the city—the Tree protects us from the worst of it—but there had been some, and it was cold enough for the cobbled paths to become icy death traps. Two days before, Vuroy had fractured his arm falling, much to the dismay of Ru and Ohn, who had to put up with his incessant complaining at home. I had no one at home to take care of me if I fell, and I couldn't afford a bonebender, so I went even more slowly than usual on the sidewalks. (Ice sounds much like stone when tapped with a walking stick, but there is a subtle difference to the air above a patch; it is not only colder but also palpably heavier.)

I was safe enough. Just slow. But because I was so intent on not breaking a limb, I paid less attention to my route than I should have, and given that I was still relatively new to the city, I got lost.

Shadow is not a good city to get lost in. The city had grown haphazardly over the centuries, springing up at the foot of Sky-the-palace, and its layout made little sense despite the constant efforts of the nobles to impose order on the mess. Long-time denizens tell me it's even worse since the growth of the Tree, which bifurcated the city into Wesha and Easha and caused other, more magical changes. The Lady had been kind enough to keep the Tree from destroying anything when it grew, but entire neighborhoods had been shifted out of place, old streets erased and new ones created, landmarks moved. Get lost and one could wander in circles for hours.

That was not the real danger, however. I noticed it quickly that chilly afternoon: someone was following me.

The steps trailed twenty feet or so behind, keeping pace. I turned a corner and hoped, to no avail; the feet moved with me. I turned again. The same.

Thieves, probably. Rapists and killers didn't much care for the cold. I had little money on me, and I did not look wealthy by any stretch, but most likely it was enough that I looked alone and lost and blind. That made me easy pickings on a day when the pickings would be slim.

I did not walk faster, though of course I was afraid. Some thieves didn't like leaving witnesses. But to hurry would let this thief know that he had been spotted, and worse, I might still break my neck. Better to let him come, give him what he wanted, and hope that would be enough.

Except…he wasn't coming. I walked a block, two blocks, three. I heard few other people on the street, and those few were moving quickly, some of them muttering about the cold and paying no attention to anything but their misery. For long stretches, there was only me and my pursuer. *Now he will come*, I thought several times. But there was no attack.

As I turned my head for a better listen, something glinted at the corner of my vision. Startled—in those days I was not quite used to magic—I forgot wisdom, stopped, and turned to see.

My pursuer was a young woman. She was plump, short, with curly pale green hair and skin of a nearly similar shade. That alone would have alerted me as to her nature, though it was obvious in the fact that I could see her.

She stopped when I did. I noticed that her expression was very sad. She said nothing, so I ventured, "Hello."

Her eyebrows rose. "You can see me?"

I frowned a bit. "Yes. You're standing right there."

"How interesting." She resumed walking, though she stopped when I took a step back.

"If you don't mind me saying so," I said cautiously, "I've never been mugged by a godling."

If anything, her expression grew even more mournful. "I mean you no harm."

"You've been following me since that street back there. The one with the clogged sewer."

"Yes."

"Why?"

"Because you might die," she said.

I stumbled back, but only one step, because my heel slipped on a bit of ice alarmingly. "*What?*"

"You will very likely die in the next few moments. It may be difficult... painful. I've come to be with you." She sighed gently. "My nature is mercy. Do you understand?"

I had not met many godlings at that point, but anyone who dwelled for long in Shadow learned this much: they drew their strength from a particular thing—a concept, a state of being, an emotion. The priests and scriveners called it *affinity*, though I had never heard any godling use the term. When they encountered their affinity, it drew them like a beacon, and some of them could not quite help responding to it.

I swallowed and nodded. "You ... You're here to watch me die. Or"—I shivered as I realized—"or to *kill* me, if something only does the job halfway. Is that right?"

She nodded. "I'm sorry." And she really did seem sorry, her eyes heavy-lidded, her brow furrowed with the beginnings of grief. She wore only a thin, shapeless shift—more proof of her nature, since any mortal would have frozen to death in that. It made her look younger than me, vulnerable. Like someone you'd want to stop and help.

I shuddered and said, "Well, ah, maybe you could tell me what's going to kill me, and I can, ah, walk *away* from it, and then you won't have to waste time on me. Would that be all right?"

"There are many pathways to any future. But when I am drawn to a mortal, it means most paths have exhausted themselves."

My heart, already beating fast, gave an unpleasant little lurch. "You're saying it's inevitable?"

"Not inevitable. But likely."

I needed to sit down. The buildings on either side of me were not residential; I thought they might be storehouses. Nowhere to sit but the cold, hard ground. And for all I knew, doing that might kill me.

That was when I became aware of how utterly quiet it was.

There had been three other people on the street two blocks back. Only the green woman's steps had stood out to me, for obvious reasons, but now there were no other footfalls at all. The street was completely empty.

Yet I could hear... something. No—it was not a sound so much as a feeling. A pressure to the air. A lingering whiff of scent, teasingly unidentifiable. And it was...

Behind me. I turned, stumbling again, my heart leaping into my throat as I saw *another* godling standing across the street from me.

This one was paying no attention to me, however. She looked middle-aged, islander or Amn, black-haired, ordinary enough except that I could see her, too. She stood with legs apart and hands fisted at her sides, body taut, an expression of pure fury on her face. When I followed her gaze to see who this fury was directed at, I spied a third person, equally tense and still but on my side of the street, closer by. A man. Madding, though I didn't know this at the time.

The air between these two godlings was a cloud the color of blood and rage. It curled and shivered, flexing larger and flinching compact with whatever forces they were using against each other. Because that was, indeed, what I had walked into, for all that it was silent and still: a battle. One did not need magic-seeing eyes to know that.

I licked my lips and glanced back at the green-skinned woman. She nodded: this was how I might die, caught in the cross fire of a duel between gods.

Very quickly, as quietly as I could, I began to back up, toward the green woman. I didn't think she would protect me—she'd made her interest clear—but there was no other safe direction.

I'd forgotten the ice patch behind me. Of course I slipped and fell, jarring a grunt of pain from my throat and my stick from my hand. It landed on the cobblestones with a loud, echoing clatter.

The woman across the street jerked in surprise and looked at me. I had an instant to register that her face was not as ordinary as I'd thought, the skin too shiny, hard-smooth, like porcelain. Then the stones under me began to shake, and the wall behind me buckled, and my skin prickled all over.

Suddenly the man was in front of me, opening his mouth to utter a roar like surf crashing in an ocean cave. The porcelain-skinned woman screamed, flinging up her arms as something (I could not see what, exactly) shattered around her. That same force flung her backward. I heard mortar crack and crumble as her body struck a wall, then crumpled to the ground.

"What the hells are you doing?" the man shouted at her. Dazed, I stared up at him. A vein in his temple was visible, pounding with his anger. It fascinated me because I hadn't realized godlings had veins. But of course they did; I had not been in the city long, but already I had heard of godsblood.

The woman pushed herself up slowly, though the blow she had taken would have crushed half her bones if she'd been mortal. It did seem to have weakened her, as she stayed on one knee while glaring at the man.

"You can't stay here," he said, calmer now, though still visibly furious. "You're not careful enough. By threatening this mortal's life, you've already broken the most important rule."

The woman's lip curled in a sneer. "*Your* rule."

"The rule agreed upon by all of us who chose to dwell here! None of us wants another Interdiction. You were warned." He held up a hand.

And suddenly the street was *full* of godlings. Everywhere I looked, I could see them. Most looked human, but a few had either shed their mortal guises or had never bothered in the first place. I caught glimpses of skin like metal, hair like wood, legs with animal joints, tentacle fingers. There must have been two, maybe three dozen of them standing in the street or sitting on the curbs. One even flitted overhead on gossamer insect wings.

The porcelain-faced woman got to her feet, though she still looked shaky. She looked around at the assemblage of godlings, and there was no mistaking the unease on her face. But she straightened and scowled, pushing her shoulders back. "So this is how you fight your duels?" This was directed at the man.

"The duel is over," the man said. He stepped back, closer to me, and then to my surprise bent to help me up. I blinked at him in confusion, then frowned as he moved in front of me, blocking my view of the woman. I tried to lean around him to keep an eye on her, since I had a notion she'd almost killed me a moment before, but the man moved with me.

"No," he said. "You don't need to see this."

"What?" I asked. "I—"

There was a sound like the tolling of a great bell behind him, followed by a sudden swift concussion of air. Then all the godlings around us vanished. When I craned my head around the man this time, I saw only an empty street.

"You killed her," I whispered, shocked.

"No, of course not. We opened a door, that's all—sent her back to our realm. *That's* what I didn't want you to see." To my surprise, the man smiled, and I was momentarily caught by how human this made him look. "We try not to kill each other. That tends to upset our parents."

Before I could stop myself, I laughed, then realized I was laughing with a god and fell silent. Which confused me more, so I just stared up at his strangely comforting smile.

"Everything all right, Eo?" The man didn't turn from me as he raised his voice to speak. I suddenly remembered the green woman.

When I looked at her, I started again. The green woman—Eo, apparently—was smiling at me as fondly as a new mother. Her coloring had changed, too, from green to a soft pale pink. Even her hair was pink. As I stared at her, she inclined her head to me and again to the man, then turned and walked away.

I gaped after her for a moment, then shook my head.

"I suppose I owe you my life," I said, turning back to the man.

"Since it was in danger partly because of me, let's just call it even," he said, and there was a faint ringing in the air, as of wind chimes, though there was no wind. I looked around, confused. "But I wouldn't mind buying you a drink, if you're feeling the need to celebrate life."

That startled me into another laugh as I finally realized what he was up to. "Do you try to pick up all the mortal girls you almost kill?"

"Just the ones who don't scream and run," he said. And then he startled me further by touching my face, just under one eye. I tensed just a little, as I always did when someone noticed my eyes. Bracing myself for the *if only*.

But there was no revulsion in his gaze and nothing but fascination in his touch. "And the ones with pretty eyes," he added.

You can imagine the rest, can't you? That smile, the strength of his presence, his calm acceptance of my strangeness, the fact that he was stranger still. I barely stood a chance. Two days after we met, I kissed him. He took the opportunity to pour a taste of himself into my mouth, the wretch, trying to lure me into bed. It didn't work then—I had some principles—but a few days later, I went home with him. Naked before Madding, I felt for the first time that someone saw the whole of me, not just my parts. He found my eyes fascinating, but he also waxed eloquent about my elbows. He liked it all.

I miss him. Gods, how I miss him.

* * *

I slept late the next day and woke up in agony. My back hurt all over, and because I was not used to sleeping on my belly, my neck was stiff. Between that, my sore and puffy eyes, and the headache that had returned with a vengeance, I could perhaps be forgiven for not realizing at first that there was someone new in the house.

I stumbled blearily into the kitchen, drawn by the smells and sounds of cooking breakfast. "Good morning," I mumbled.

"Good morning," said a cheery woman's voice, and I nearly fell. I caught myself against a counter, spun, and grabbed for the block of kitchen knives.

Hands caught mine and I cried out, immediately struggling. But the hands were warm, big, familiar.

Shiny, thank the gods. I stopped trying to reach for a weapon, though my heart was still racing. Shiny, and a woman. Who?

Then I recalled her greeting. That raspy, too-sweet voice. *Lil* was in my home, making me breakfast, after eating some Order-Keepers that Shiny had murdered.

"What in the Maelstrom are you doing here?" I demanded. "And show yourself, damn it. Don't hide from me in my own home."

She sounded amused. "I didn't think you liked my looks."

"I don't, but I'd rather *know* you're not standing there slavering at me."

"You won't know that even if you see me." But she appeared, facing me in her deceptively normal form. Or maybe the other shape—the mouth—was normal for her, and this was only a courtesy that she offered me. Either way, I was grateful. "As for why I'm here, I brought him home." She nodded beyond me, where I heard Shiny breathing.

"Oh." I was beginning to feel calm again. "Er. Thank you, then. But, um, Lady Lil—"

"Just Lil." She beamed and turned back to the stove. "Ham."

"What?"

"*Ham.*" She turned and looked past me, at Shiny. "I would like some ham."

"There's no ham in the house," he said.

"Oh," she said, sounding heartbroken. Her face fell, too, almost comically tragic. I hardly noticed, stunned by Shiny's response.

He moved behind me to the cupboard and took something out, setting it on the counter. "Smoked velly."

Lil brightened immediately. "Ah! Better than ham. Now we'll have a proper breakfast." She turned back to her preparations, beginning to hum some toneless song.

I was beginning to feel light-headed. I went to the table and sat down, not sure what to think. Shiny sat down across from me, watching me with his heavy gaze.

"I must apologize," he said softly.

I jumped. "You're talking *more?*"

He didn't bother to respond to that question, since the answer was obvious. "I didn't expect Lil to impose on your hospitality. That was not my intention."

For a moment I did not respond, distracted. He'd spoken at the site of Role's murder, but this was the first time I'd heard him say several sentences in a row.

And dear *gods*, his voice was beautiful. Tenor. I'd expected him to be baritone. And it was rich, every precisely enunciated word reverberating through my ears all the way down to my toes. I could listen to a voice like that all day.

Or all night...Sternly, I turned my thoughts away from that path. I had enough gods in my love life.

Then I realized I'd been staring blankly at him. "Oh, ah, I don't mind that so much," I said at last. "Though I wish you'd asked first."

"She insisted."

That threw me. "Why?"

"I have a warning to pass on," Lil interjected, coming over to the table. She put a plate in front of me, then another in front of Shiny. My kitchen had only two chairs, so she hoisted herself up on a counter, then picked up a plate she'd apparently set aside for herself. Her eyes gleamed as she gazed at her food, and I looked away, afraid she would open her mouth wide again.

"A warning?" In spite of everything, the food smelled good. I poked it a bit and realized she'd incorporated the velly into the eggs, along with peppers and herbs I'd forgotten I had. I tried it—delicious.

"Someone is looking for you," Lil said.

It took a moment to figure out she meant me, not Shiny. Then I sobered, realizing who might be looking for me.

"Everyone saw Previt Rimarn talking to me yesterday. Now that he's, um, gone, I imagine his fellow previts will come around."

"Oh, he's not dead," said Lil, surprised. "The three I ate last night were just Order-Keepers. Young, healthy, quite juicy beneath the crust." She uttered a lascivious sigh. I put down my fork, appetite gone. "There was no magic on them to spoil the taste, except that used to kill them. I imagine they were just there to do the beating."

In spite of myself, I groaned inwardly. That had been the one benefit I could see in the priests' deaths; Rimarn was the only one who knew of my magic and suspected me of being Role's killer. Now, with his men dead, he would definitely be looking for me.

Madding's words came back to me: *leave town*. Yet the problem of money haunted me. And I did not want to leave. Shadow was my home.

"He's not the one I meant, in any case," Lil said, interrupting my thoughts. Surprised, I focused on her. Her plate, faintly visible to me in the reflected glow of her body, was empty—clean, as if she'd polished it. She was licking her fork now, with long, slow strokes of her tongue that seemed obscene.

"What?"

She turned and looked at me, and abruptly I was pinned by her mottled gaze. The dark spots in her eyes *moved*, spinning about her pupils in a slow, restless dance. I found myself wondering if the spots in her hair moved, too.

"So much hunger," she said in a soft, raspy purr. "It wraps about you like a layered cloak. A previt's anger. Madding's desire." My cheeks grew warm. "And one other, more hungry than the others. Powerful. Dangerous." She shivered, and I shivered with her. "He could reshape the world with such hunger, especially if he gets what he wants. And what he wants is *you*."

I stared at her, confused and alarmed. "Who is this person? What does he want me for?"

"I don't know." She licked her lips, then regarded me thoughtfully. "Perhaps if I stay near you, I can meet him."

I frowned, too unnerved to comment on this. Why would anyone powerful want me? I was nothing, nobody. Even Rimarn would be disappointed if he knew the truth of the magic he'd sensed in me. All I could do was *see*.

And... I frowned. There were also my paintings. I kept those out of sight; only Madding and Shiny knew about them. There was something magical to those. I didn't know what, but my father had taught me long ago that it was important to keep such things hidden, and so I did.

Was it those, then, that this mysterious person wanted?

No, no, I was jumping to conclusions. I didn't even know if this person existed. All I had to go on was the word of a goddess who saw nothing wrong with eating human beings. She might see nothing wrong with lying to them, too.

Shiny was still there, though I had not heard him eat. I licked my lips, wondering if he would answer. "Do you know what she's talking about?" I asked him.

"No."

So far, so good. "Your injuries," I began.

"He's fine," Lil said. She was eyeing my unfinished plate. "I killed him, and he came back whole."

I blinked in surprise. "You healed him... by *killing* him?"

She shrugged. "Should I have left him as he was, taking weeks to heal on his own? He isn't like the rest of us. He is mortal."

"Except at sunrise."

"Even then." Lil hopped down from the counter, leaving her empty plate behind. "He has been diminished to only a fraction of his true self—enough for a pretty light show now and then, but no more. And enough to protect you." She drew close, her eyes fixed on my plate.

I was so busy pondering her words that I did not notice her approach until her expression turned... Gods, I have no words for the horror of her. It was as if her other face, the long-mouthed predator, had appeared underneath the benign one. I could not see that face, as she had warned me, but I could feel its presence and its raw, bottomles hunger. I realized it only when she lunged, not at my plate but at *me*.

I didn't even have time to cry out. Her bony, sharp-nailed hand shot at my throat and might have torn it out by the time I registered the danger. But an instant later, her hand stilled and quivered, an inch away. I stared at it, then at the dark blotch around her wrist. Just like the day before, at my table. And just as then, Shiny suddenly became visible to me, his glow rising from within, his face hard and eyes irritated as he glared at Lil.

Lil smiled at him, then at me. "You see?"

I dragged my mind back from silent screaming fits and took a deep breath to calm down. I did see. But it made no sense. I said to Shiny, "Your power comes back to you when... when you protect me?"

I could still see him, which made it easy to see the contemptuous look he threw at me. I nearly flinched in surprise. What had I done to merit that look? Then I remembered what Madding had said. *He doesn't think much of mortals.*

Lil grinned, reading my face. "Any mortal," she said, and eyed Shiny. "'*You will wander among mortals as one of them.*'" I blinked in surprise and saw Shiny stiffen. The words were not hers, I could tell. They did not sound like Lil at all; I heard darker echoes. "'*Unknown, commanding only what wealth and respect you can earn with your deeds and words. You may call upon your power only in great need, and only to aid these mortals for whom you hold such contempt.*'"

Shiny released her wrist and turned away from her, sitting down with a bleak expression—what little of it I could see, because his glow was fading already. Ah, he had dealt with the threat, so he no longer needed his power.

I took a deep breath and faced Lil. "I appreciate the information. But if you don't mind, in the future, just *explain* things to me. No more demonstrations."

She laughed, which set the little hairs arise on my skin. She did not sound entirely sane. "I'm glad you can see me, mortal girl. It makes things so much more interesting." Her eyes shifted to the table. "Are you going to eat that?"

My plate—or did she mean my hand, which rested near it? Very carefully I moved my hand to my lap. "Be my guest."

Lil laughed again, delighted, and bent over the plate. There was a movement too fast for me to follow. I had the impression of whirring needles, and a quick, fetid breeze wafted past my nose. When she lifted her head half a breath later, the plate was clean. She took my napkin, too, to dab at the corners of her mouth.

I swallowed hard and pushed myself to my feet, edging around her. Shiny was a barely visible shadow across from me, eating. Lil had begun to throw glances at his plate, too. There were things I wanted to say to him, though not in front of Lil. He had been humiliated enough the night before. But we would have to reach an understanding, he and I, and soon.

I washed the dishes slowly, and Shiny ate slowly. Lil sat in my chair, glancing from one to the other of us and laughing to herself now and again.

* * *

The sun was high by the time I left the house—later than I'd hoped to set out. I had farther to go this time and tables to carry. Though I'd hoped that Shiny would join me again and perhaps help me carry things, he remained where he was after breakfast was done. He was brooding, in a darker mood than usual; I almost missed his old apathy.

Lil left when I did, to my great relief. One problematic godling houseguest was enough for me. She bid me a fond farewell before she left, however, and thanked me so profusely for the breakfast that I actually felt better about her. Madding had always hinted to me that some godlings were better than others at interacting with mortals. Some of them were too alien in their thought processes, or too monstrous in our eyes, to fit in easily despite their best efforts. I had an idea that Lil was among these.

I carried my tables and the best-selling of my merchandise to the southern promenade of Gateway Park. The northwestern promenade was where Art Row stood, the better to take advantage of the crowds that came for the best view of the Tree and other noteworthy sights of the city. The south promenade, where the view was passable but not ideal and where the attractions were less impressive, was a mediocre spot. Still, it was the only option I had left; the northeastern entrance of the park had been occluded years ago by a root of the Tree, and the east gate had a lovely view of Sky's freight gate.

As I entered the south promenade, I heard a few other sellers at work, calling out to passersby to hawk their wares. Not a good sign, that—it meant potential cutomers were sparse enough that the sellers had to compete over them. There would be none of the companionable looking out for one another that I was used to at the Row; this would be every seller for herself. I could hear three—no, four—other sellers in the vicinity: one with decorative headscarves, another selling "Tree pies" (whatever those were; they did smell nice), and two people apparently selling books and souvenirs. I felt the glares of the latter two as I began setting up, and I worried that I might have to deal with unpleasantness. As often happened once they got a good look at me, however, no one bothered me. There are times—rare, I'll admit—when blindness comes in handy.

So I set up and waited. And waited. I didn't know the area and hadn't had a chance to fully explore. Although I could hear foot traffic passing relatively nearby (pilgrims remarking over how dark the city had become and how beautiful the Tree-entangled palace Sky still was), it was possible I'd managed to set myself up in a bad area. I had no doubt the other sellers had already laid claim to the best spots, so I resolved to do the best I could with what I had.

By midafternoon, however, I knew I was in trouble. My wares had lured over a few pilgrims—working folk mostly, Amn from less-prosperous towns and lands near Shadow. That was part of the problem, I realized; High Northers and island folk had always been my best customers. The faith of Itempas had always been precarious in those lands, so they bought my miniature Trees and statues of godlings eagerly. But Senmites were mostly Amn, and Amn were mostly Itempan. They were less easily impressed by the Tree and Shadow's other heretical wonders.

Which was fine. I never begrudged people their beliefs, but I needed to eat. My stomach had begun to rumble in a vocal reminder of this fact—my own fault for letting Lil's presence deter me from breakfast.

Then an idea came to me. I rummaged among my bags and was relieved to find I'd brought the sidewalk chalk. I moved around to the front of my tables, crouched, and considered what to sketch.

The idea that came to me was so fiercely powerful that I rocked back on my toes for a moment, startled. Usually my creative urges came in the morning, when I painted in my basement. I'd meant to sketch only a few silly doodles to draw eyes toward my trinkets and goods. But the image in my head...I licked my lips and considered whether it was safe.

It was dangerous, I decided. No doubt about it. I was *blind*, for the gods' sake; I shouldn't have been able to visualize anything, much less depict it recognizably. Most people in the city wouldn't notice the paradox, or care, but to Order-Keepers and others whose job it was to watch for unauthorized magic, it would be suspect. I had survived all these years by being careful.

But...I picked up a piece of chalk, rubbing its smooth, fat length between my fingers. Colors meant little to me except as a detail of substance, but I had picked up the habit of naming my paints and chalks nevertheless. There is more to color than what can be seen, after all. The chalk smelled faintly bitter—not the bitterness of food, but the bitterness of air too rarefied to breathe, like when one climbed a high hill. I decided it was white, and perfect for the image in my head.

"I paint a picture," I whispered, and began.

I sketched the bowl of a sky. Not Sky, or any part of it—not even the sky that existed somewhere above the Tree, which I had never seen. This would be a thin, nearly empty firmament, wheeling above in layers of rising color. I laid down a thick base of white chalk, using both of my available sticks until there was just a sliver remaining. Lucky. Then I grazed in blue—not much of it, though. It felt wrong for the sky in my head—too vibrant, thick, almost greasy between my fingers. I used my hands to thin out the blue, then added another color that made a good yellow. Yes, that was right. I thickened the yellow, rolling it on, feeling its growing intensity and warmth and following it until at last it coalesced into light at the center of my composition. *Two* suns, one great and one smaller, spinning about each other in an eternal dance. Perhaps I could—

"Hey."

"Just a minute," I murmured. The clouds in this sky would be powerful things, thick and dark with impending rain. I reached for something that smelled silver and drew one, wishing I had more blue, or black.

Now birds. Of course there would be birds flying in this bright, empty sky. But they would not have feathers—

"Hey!" Something touched me and I started, dropping the chalk and blinking out of my daze.

"Wh-what?" Almost at once, my back protested, bruises and

muscles twinging. How long had I been drawing? I groaned, reaching back to knead the small of my back.

"Thanks," said the voice. Male, older. No one I knew, though he reminded me vaguely of Vuroy. Then I recalled hearing his voice—one of my fellow souvenir sellers, the loudest of the three who'd been hawking his wares. "That's a nice trick," he continued. "You pulled a good crowd. But the south promenade closes at sunset, so you might want to catch a few of 'em while you can, huh?"

Crowd?

I abruptly became aware of voices around me—dozens of them, clustered around my drawing. They were murmuring, exclaiming over something. I got to my feet and hissed at the agony in my knees.

As I straightened, the cluster of people around me burst into applause.

"What—" But I knew. They were clapping for *me*.

Before I could wrap my thoughts around this, my onlookers pushed forward—I heard them jostling each other in an effort to avoid stepping on the drawing—and began asking me the price of my wares, and whether I painted professionally, and how I managed to draw such beautiful things when I couldn't see, and whether I *really* couldn't see, and, and, and. I had enough wits left to get behind the table and answer the most uncomfortable questions with silly pleasantries ("No, I really can't see! I'm glad you like it!"), before I was inundated with eager customers buying everything I had. Most of them weren't even haggling. It was the best sales day I'd ever had, and it all happened in a span of minutes.

When they were done with me, most of the customers moved

on to the other tables—as they had been doing since I'd begun drawing, I realized belatedly. No wonder the hawker had come to thank me. But I could hear the distant tolling of the White Hall bells, marking sunset; the park would be closing soon.

"I thought it might be you," said a voice nearby, and I jumped, turning to smile at what I thought was yet another customer. But the man who'd spoken did not come to the table. When I oriented on him, I realized he was just beyond the chalk drawing.

"Pardon?" I asked.

"You were at the other promenade," he said, and I tensed in alarm, though he did not sound threatening at all. "The day after you found that godling's body. I saw you then, thought there was something... interesting... about you."

I began to pack up, less alarmed now; perhaps this was some sort of awkward attempt on the man's part to chat me up. "Were you in the crowd?" I asked. "One of the heretics?"

"Heretics?" The man chuckled. "Hmm. I suppose the Order would think so, though I honor the Bright Lord, too."

One of the New Lights, then; they were supposedly some other branch of Itempan. Or maybe a newer sect. I could never keep them straight. "Well... I'm a traditional Itempan myself." I said it to forestall any attempts on his part to convert me. "But if Role was your god, then I'm sorry for your loss."

I almost heard his eyebrows rise. "An Itempan who does not condemn the worshippers of another god or celebrate that god's death? Aren't you a bit heretical yourself?"

I shrugged, putting the last of the small boxes into my carry-sack. "Maybe so." I smiled. "Don't tell the Order-Keepers."

The man laughed and then, to my relief, turned away. "Of

course not. Until later, then." He walked off, humming to himself, and that confirmed it: he was singing the New Lights' wordless song.

I sat down for a moment to recoup before starting the trip back. My pockets were full of coins, and my purse, too. Madding would be pleased; I'd have to take a few days off to replenish my stock before I could sell again, and maybe I'd take a few days beyond that, as a vacation. I'd never had a vacation before, but I could afford it now.

Boots approached from the far end of the promenade. I was so tired and dazed that I thought nothing of it; there were many people milling around the south promenade now, though the other sellers were packing up as well. If I had listened more carefully, however, I would've recognized the boots. I did, too late, when their owner spoke.

"Very good, Oree Shoth," said a voice I'd dreaded hearing all day. Rimarn Dih. Oh, no.

"Very good of you, indeed, to draw such a lovely beacon," he said, coming to stop just beyond the chalk drawing. There were three other sets of footsteps approaching beyond him, all with those horribly familiar heavy boots. I rose to my feet, trembling.

"I'd expected you to be halfway to Nimaro by now," he continued. "Imagine my surprise when I caught the scent of familiar magic, not so very far away at all."

"I don't know anything," I stammered. I gripped my stick as if that would help me. "I have no idea who killed Lady Role, and I'm not a godling."

"My dear, I don't really care about that anymore," he said, and by the cold fury in his tone, I knew he'd found whatever Lil had left of his men. That meant I was lost, utterly lost. "I want your friend. That white-haired Maro bastard; where is he?"

For a moment I was confused. Shiny's hair was white? "He didn't do anything." Oh, gods, that was a lie and Rimarn was a scrivener; he would know. "I mean, there was a godling, a woman named Lil. She—"

"Enough of this," he snapped, and turned away. "Take her."

The boots came forward, closing in. I stumbled back, but there was nowhere to go. Would they beat me to death and avenge their comrades right here, or take me to the White Hall for questioning first? I began to gasp in panic; my heart was pounding. What could I do?

And then many things happened at once.

*   *   *

Why? I'd asked my father long ago. Why could I not show my paintings to others? They were just paint and pigment. Not everyone liked them—some of the images were too disturbing for that—but they did no harm.

They're magic, he told me. Over and over again he told me, but I didn't listen enough. I didn't believe. *There's no such thing as magic that does no harm.*

*   *   *

The Order-Keepers stepped onto my drawing.

"No," I whispered as they drew closer. "Please."

"Poor girl," I heard a woman, one of those who'd wanted to know if I painted professionally, murmuring amid the crowd from some ways off. They had loved me a moment before. Now they were going to just stand there, useless, while the Keepers took their revenge.

"Put that stick down, woman," said one of the Keepers, sounding annoyed. I clutched my walking stick tighter. I couldn't breathe. Why were they doing this? They knew I hadn't killed Role, that I wasn't a godling. I had magic, but they would laugh to know what phenomenal powers I was concealing. I was no threat.

"Please, please," I said. I almost sobbed it, like my name: *please*—gasp—*please*. They kept coming.

A hand grabbed my stick, and suddenly my eyes burned. Heat boiled behind them, pushing to get out. I shut them in reflex, the pain fueling my terror.

"Get away from me!" I screamed. I tried to fight, flailed with hands and stick. My hand found a chest—

Shiny's hand on my chest, lashing out at the witness to his shame. And I *pushed.*

* * *

This is difficult to describe, even now. Bear with me.

Somewhere, elsewhere, there is a sky. It is a hot, empty sky, overhead as skies should be, blazing with the light of twin suns. The sky I drew—do you understand? Somewhere it is real. I know this now.

When I screamed and pushed at the Order-Keepers, the heat behind my eyes flared into light. In my mind's eye, I saw legs fall into this sky, upside down. Legs and hips, appearing out of nowhere, kicking, twisting. Falling.

There was nothing else attached to them.

* * *

Something changed.

When I became aware of it, I blinked. Screaming all around

me. Running, pounding feet. Something jostled one of my tables, knocking it over; I stumbled back. I could smell blood and something fouler: excrement and bile and stark, stinking fear.

Abruptly I realized I could not see my entire drawing any-more. It was there—I could still see the edges of it. Its glow was oddly faded and growing fainter by the second, as if its magic had been spent. However, what remained of it was occluded by three large dark blotches, spreading and overlapping. Liquid, not magical.

Rimarn Dih's voice was distraught, almost unintelligible with horror. "What did you do, Maro bitch? *What in the Father's name have you done?*"

"Wh-what?" My eyes hurt. My head hurt. The smell was making me ill. I felt wrong, off balance, all my skin aprickle. My mouth tasted of guilt, and I did not know why.

Rimarn was shouting for someone to help him. He sounded like he was exerting himself, pulling at something heavy. There was a sound, something wet...I shuddered. I did not want to know what that sound was.

Two presences suddenly appeared on either side of me. They took me by the arms, gingerly.

"Time to go, little one," said a bright male voice. Madding's lieutenant. Where the hells had he come from? Then the world flared and we were somewhere else. Quiet settled around us, along with warm, scented humidity and a blue-green feeling of calm and balance. Madding's house.

It should have been a sanctuary for me, but I did not feel safe.

"What happened?" I asked the godling beside me. "Please tell me. Something...I did something, didn't I?"

"You don't know?" Madding's other lieutenant, the female one, on my other side. She sounded incredulous.

"No." I did not want to know. I licked my lips. "Please tell me."

"I don't know how you did it," she said, speaking slowly. There was something in her tone that was almost... awed. That made no sense; she was a god. "I've never seen a mortal do anything like that. But your drawing..." She trailed off.

"It became *enarmhukdatalwasl*, though not quite *shuwao*," said the male godling, his godwords briefly stinging my eyes. I shut them in reflex. Why did my eyes hurt? It felt like I'd been punched in the back of each. "It carved a path across half a billion stars and connected one world with another, just for a moment. Damnedest thing."

I rubbed at my eyes in frustration, though this did no good; the pain was inside me. "I don't understand, damn you! Speak mortal!" *I did not want to know.*

"You made a door," he said. "You sent the Order-Keepers through it. Not all the way, though. The magic wasn't stable. It burned out before they passed through completely. Do you understand?"

"I..." No. "It was just a chalk drawing," I whispered.

"You dropped them partway into another world," snapped the female godling. "And then you closed the door. *You cut them in half*. Do you understand now?"

I did.

I began to scream, and kept screaming until one of the godlings did something, and then I passed out.

5

"Family"
(charcoal study)

I HAVE A FAVORITE MEMORY of my father that I sometimes recall as a dream.

In the dream, I am small. I have only recently learned to climb the ladder. The rungs are very far apart and I cannot see them, so for a long time I was afraid I would miss a rung and fall. I had to learn not to be afraid, which is much harder than it sounds. I am very proud of having accomplished this.

"Papa," I say, running across the small attic room. This is, by my parents' mutual agreement, *his* room. My mother does not come here, not even to clean. It is neat anyhow—my father is a neat man—yet it is permeated all over with that indefinable feeling that is *him*. Some of it is scent, but there is something more to his presence, too. Something that I understand instinctively, even if I lack the vocabulary to describe it.

My father is not like most people in our village. He goes to White Hall services only often enough to keep the priest from sanctioning him. He makes no offerings at the household altar. He does not pray. I have asked him whether he believes in the gods, and he says that of course he does; are we not Maroneh? *But that is not the same thing as honoring them,* he sometimes adds. Then he cautions me not to mention this to anyone else. Not the priests, not my friends, not even Mama. One day, he says, I will understand.

Today he is in a rare mood—and for a rare once, I can see him: a smaller-than-average man with cool black eyes and large, elegant hands. His face is lineless, almost youthful, though his hair is salt-and-pepper and there is something in his gaze, something heavy and tired, that shows his long life more clearly than wrinkles ever could. He was old when he married Mama. He never wanted a child, yet he loves me with all his heart.

I grin and lean on his knees. He's sitting down, which puts his face in reach of my searching fingers. Eyes can be fooled, I have learned already, but touch is always sure.

"You've been singing," I say.

He smiled. "Can you see me again? I thought it would have worn off by now."

"Sing for me, Papa," I plead. I love the colors his voice weaves in the air.

"No, Ree-child. Your mother's home."

"She never hears it! Please?"

"I promised," he says softly, and I hang my head. He promised my mother, long before I was born, never to expose her or me to the danger that comes of his strangeness. I am too young to understand where the danger comes from, but the fear in his eyes is enough to keep me silent.

But he has broken his promise before. He did it to teach me, because otherwise I might have betrayed my own strangeness out of ignorance. And because, I later realize, it kills him a little to stifle that part of himself. He was meant to be glorious. With me, in these small private moments, he can be.

So when he sees my disappointment, he sighs and lifts me into his lap. Very softly, just for me, he sings.

* * *

I awoke slowly, to the sound and smell of water.

I was sitting in it. The water was nearly body temperature; I barely felt it on my skin. Under me, I could feel hard, sculpted stone, as warm as the water; nearby was the smell of flowers. Hiras: a vining plant that had once been native to the Maroland. Its blooms had a heavy, distinctive perfume that I liked. That told me where I was.

If I hadn't been to Madding's place before, I would've been disoriented. Madding owned a large house in one of the richer districts of Wesha, and he had brought me here often, complaining that my little bed would give him a bad back. He had filled the ground floor of the house with pools. There were at least a dozen of them, carved out of the bedrock that underlay this part of Shadow, sculpted into pretty shapes and screened by growing plants. It was the sort of design choice godlings were infamous for; they thought first of aesthetics and lastly of convenience or propriety. Madding's guests had to either stand or strip and get into a pool. He saw nothing wrong with this.

The pools were not magical. The water was warm because Mad had hired some mortal genius to concoct a mechanism that kept boiled water in the piping system at all times. Madding had never bothered to learn how it worked, so he couldn't explain it to me.

I sat up, listening, and promptly became aware that someone was with me, sitting nearby. I saw nothing, but the breathing pattern was familiar. "Mad?"

He resolved out of the darkness, sitting at the pool's edge with one knee drawn up. His hair was loose, clinging to his damp skin. It made him look strangely young. His eyes were somber.

"How do you feel?" he asked.

The question puzzled me for a moment, and then I remembered.

I sat back against the side of the pool, barely feeling the throb of my old bruises, and turned my face away from him. My eyes still ached, so I closed them, though that didn't help much. How did I feel? Like a murderess. How else?

Madding sighed. "I suppose it does no good to point this out, but what happened wasn't your fault."

Of course it did no good. And it wasn't true.

"Mortals are never good at controlling magic, Oree. You weren't built for it. And you didn't know what your magic could do. You didn't intend to kill those men."

"They're still dead," I said. "My *intentions* don't change that."

"True." He shifted, putting the other foot into the water. "They probably intended to kill *you*, though."

I laughed softly. It echoed off the shifting surface of the water and sounded demented. "Stop trying, Mad. Please."

He fell silent for a while, letting me wallow. When he decided I'd done enough of that, he slipped into the waist-high water and came over, lifting me against him. That was all it took, really. I buried my face in his chest and let myself turn to noodle in his arms. He rubbed my back and murmured soothing things in his language while I cried, and then he carried me out of the room of pools and up curving stairs and laid me down in the tumbled pile of cushions that served as his bed. I fell asleep there, not caring whether I ever woke up again.

* * *

Of course, I did wake up eventually, disturbed by voices talking softly nearby. When I opened my eyes and looked around, I was surprised to see a strange godling sitting beside the cushion pile. She was very pale, with short black hair molded like a cap around a pleasant, heart-shaped face. Two things struck me at once: first, that she looked ordinary enough to pass for human, which marked her as a godling who regularly did business with mortals. Second, for some reason, she sat in shadow, though there was nothing nearby that could have thrown a shadow on her, and I shouldn't have been able to see the shadow in any case.

She had been talking with Madding but paused as I sat up. "Hello," I said, nodding to her and rubbing my face. I knew all his people, and this one wasn't one of them.

She nodded back, smiling. "So you're Mad's killer."

I stiffened. Madding scowled. "Nemmer."

"I meant no insult," she said, shrugging, still smiling. "I like killers."

I glanced at Madding, wondering whether it was all right for me to tell this kinswoman of his to go to the infinite hells. He didn't seem tense, which told me she was no threat or enemy, but he wasn't happy, either. He noticed my look and sighed. "Nemmer came to warn me, Oree. She runs another organization here in town—"

"More like a guild of independent professionals," Nemmer put in.

Madding threw her a look that was pure brotherly annoyance, then focused on me again. "Oree...the Order of Itempas just contacted her, asking to commission her services. Hers specifically, not one of her people."

I picked up a big pillow and pulled it against me, not to hide my nudity but to cover my shiver of unease. Madding noticed and went to his closet to fetch something for me. To Nemmer I said, "Not that I know much about it, but I was under the impression that the Order could call upon the Arameri assassin corps whenever they had need."

"Yes," said Nemmer, "when the Arameri approve of, or care about, what they're doing. But there are a great many small matters that are beneath the Arameri's notice, and the Order prefers to take care of such matters itself." She shrugged.

I nodded slowly. "I take it you're a god of...death?"

"Oh, no, that's the Lady. I'm just stealth, secrets, a little infiltration. The sort of business that takes place under the Nightfather's cloak."

I could not help blinking at this title. She was referring to one of the new gods, the Lord of Shadows, but her term had sounded much like *Nightlord*. That could not be, of course; the Nightlord was in the keeping of the Arameri.

"I don't mind the odd elimination," Nemmer continued, "but only as a sideline." She shrugged, then glanced at Madding. "I might reconsider, though, given how much the Order is offering. Probably a big unexploited market in taking out godlings who piss off mortals."

I gasped and whirled toward Mad, who was coming back to the bed with a robe. He lifted an eyebrow, unworried. Nemmer laughed and reached over to poke my bare knee, which made me jump. "I could be here for *you*, you know."

"No," I said softly. Madding could take care of himself. There was no reason for me to worry. "No one would send a godling to kill me. Easier to pay some beggar twenty meri and make it look like a robbery gone wrong. Not that they need to hide it at all; they're *the Order*."

"Ah, but you forget," Nemmer said. "You used magic to kill those Keepers at the park. And the Order thinks you killed three others who'd been assigned to discipline a Maro man, reportedly your cousin, for assaulting a previt. They couldn't find the bodies, but word's going around about how your magic works." She shrugged.

Oh, gods. Madding knelt behind me, putting a robe of watered silk around my shoulders. I slumped back against him. "Rimarn," I said. "He thought I was a godling."

"And you don't hire a mortal to kill a godling. Even one who's apparently goddess of chalk drawings come to life." Nemmer winked at me. But then she sobered. "It's you they want, but you're not the one they think is behind Role's death, not ultimately. Little brother, you should've been more discreet." She nodded toward me. "All her neighbors know about her godling lover; half the *city* knows it. You might've been able to save her from this otherwise."

"I know," Mad said, and there was a millennium's worth of regret in his tone.

"Wait," I said, frowning. "The Order thinks Madding killed Role? I know a godling must have done it, but—"

"Madding is in the business of selling our blood," Nemmer said. Her tone was neutral as she said this, but I heard the disapproval in it, anyway, and heard Madding's sigh. "And I hear business is good. It's not a far stretch to think he might want to increase production, maybe by obtaining a large amount of godsblood at one time."

"Which would be a fair assumption," Madding snapped, "if Role's blood had been *gone*. There was plenty of it left in and around her body—"

"Which you took away, in front of witnesses."

"To Yeine! To see if there was any hope of bringing her back to life. But Role's soul had already gone elsewhere." He shook his head and sighed. "Why in the infinite hells would I kill her, dump her body in an alley, then *come back to fetch it*, if her blood was what I wanted?"

"Maybe that wasn't what you wanted," Nemmer said very softly. "Or at least, you didn't want *all* her blood. Some of the witnesses got close enough to see what was missing, Mad."

Madding's hands tightened on my shoulders. Puzzled, I covered one of them with my own. "Missing?"

"Her heart," said Nemmer, and silence fell.

I flinched, horrified. But then I remembered that day in the alley, when my fingers had come away from Role's body coated thickly with blood.

Madding cursed and got up; he began to pace, his steps quick and tight with anger. Nemmer watched him for a moment, then sighed and returned her attention to me.

"The Order thinks this was some sort of exotic commission," she said. "A wealthy customer wanting a more potent sort of godsblood. If the stuff from our veins is powerful enough to give mortals magic, how much stronger might heartblood be? Maybe even strong enough to give a blind Maroneh woman—known paramour of the very godling they suspect—the power to kill three Order-Keepers."

My mouth fell open. "That's insane! No godling would kill another for those reasons!"

Nemmer's eyebrows rose. "Yes, and anyone who knows us would understand that," she said, a note of approval in her voice. "Those of us who live in Shadow enjoy playing games with mortal wealth, but none of us *needs* it, nor would we bother to kill for it. The Order hasn't figured that out yet, or they wouldn't have tried to hire me, and they wouldn't suspect Madding—at least, not for this reason. But they follow the creed of the Bright: that which disturbs the order of society must be eliminated, regardless of whether it *caused* the disturbance." She rolled her eyes. "You'd think they'd get tired of parroting Itempas and start thinking for themselves after two thousand years."

I drew up my legs and wrapped my arms around them, resting my forehead on one knee. The nightmare kept growing, no matter what I did, getting worse by the day. "They suspect Madding because of me," I murmured. "That's what you're saying."

"No," Madding snapped. I could hear him still pacing; his voice was jagged with suppressed fury. "They suspect me because of your damned houseguest."

I realized he was right. Previt Rimarn might have noticed my magic, but that meant little in and of itself. Many mortals had magic; that was where scriveners like Rimarn came from. Only *using* that magic was illegal, and without seeing my paintings,

Rimarn would've had no proof that I'd done so. If he had questioned me that day, and if I'd kept my wits about me, he would've realized I couldn't possibly have killed Role. At worst, I might have ended up as an Order recruit.

But then Shiny had intervened. Even though Lil had eaten the bodies in South Root, Rimarn knew that four men had gone into that alley and only one had emerged, somehow unscathed. Gods knew how many witnesses there were in South Root who would talk for a coin or two. Worse, Rimarn had probably sensed the white-hot blast of power Shiny used to kill his men, even from across the city. Between that and what I'd done to the Order-Keepers with my chalk drawing, it did not seem so far-fetched a conclusion: one godling dead, another standing to profit from her death, and the mortals most intimately connected with him suddenly manifesting strange magic. None of it was proof—but they were Itempans. Disorder was crime enough.

"Well, I've said my piece." Nemmer got up, stretching. As she did so, I saw what her posture had hidden: she was all wiry muscle and acrobatic grace. She looked too ordinary to be a spy and an assassin, but it was there when she moved. "Take care of yourself, little brother." She paused and considered. "Little sister, too."

"Wait," I blurted, drawing a surprised look from both of them. "What are you going to tell the Order?"

"What I *already* told them," she said with firm emphasis, "was that they'd better never try to kill a godling again. They don't understand: it's not Itempas they have to deal with now. We don't know what this new Twilight will do. No one sane wants to find out. And Maelstrom help the entire mortal realm if they ever ignite the Darkness's wrath."

"I..." I fell silent in confusion, having no idea what she was talking about. *The Twilight* I knew; it was another name for the Lady. *The Darkness*—was that the Shadow Lord? And what had she meant by "it's not Itempas they have to deal with now"?

"They're wasting time on this stupidity," Madding snapped, "grasping at straws instead of actually trying to find our sister's killer! I could kill them for that myself."

"Now, now," said Nemmer, smiling. "You know the rules. Besides, in twenty-eight days, it will be a moot point." I wondered at this, too, then remembered the words of the quiet goddess, that day in South Root. *You have thirty days.*

What would happen when thirty days had passed?

Nemmer sobered. "Anyway...it's worse than you think, little brother. You'll hear about this soon enough, so I might as well tell you now: two of our other siblings have gone missing."

Madding started, as did I. Nemmer's sources of information were good indeed if she'd learned this before Mad's people or before the gossip vine of the streets could pass it on.

"Who?" he asked, stricken.

"Ina and Oboro."

I had heard of the latter. He was some sort of warrior-god, making a name for himself among the illegal fighting rings in the city. People liked him because he fought fair—had even lost a few times. Ina was new to me.

"Dead?" I asked.

"No bodies have been found, and none of us has felt the deaths occur. Though no one felt Role, either." She paused for a moment, growing still within her ever-present shadow, and abruptly I realized she was furious. It was hard to tell behind her jocularity, but she was just as angry as Madding. Of course; these were her brothers and sisters missing, possibly dying. I would have felt the same in her position.

Then, belatedly, it occurred to me: I *was* in her position. If someone was targeting godlings, killing them, then every godling in the city was in danger—including Madding. And Shiny, if he still counted.

I got to my feet and went over to him. He had stopped pacing; when I took his hands in a fierce grip, he looked surprised. I turned to Nemmer and could not help the tremor in my voice.

"Lady Nemmer," I said, "thank you for telling us all this. Would you mind if Madding and I spoke in private now?"

Nemmer looked taken aback; then she grinned wolfishly. "Oh, I like this one, Mad. Shame she's mortal. And, yes, Miss Shoth, I'd be happy to leave you two alone now—on the condition that you never call me 'Lady Nemmer' again." She shuddered in mock horror. "Makes me feel old."

"Yes, L—" I bit my tongue. "Yes."

She winked, saluted Madding, and then vanished.

As soon as she was gone, I turned to Madding. "I want you to leave Shadow."

He rocked back on his heels, staring at me. "You *what?*"

"Someone is killing godlings here. You'll be safe in the gods' realm."

He gaped at me, speechless for several seconds. "I don't know whether to laugh or kick you out of my house. That you would think so little of me...that you would honestly think I'd *run* rather than find the bastards who are doing this—"

"I don't care about your pride!" I squeezed his hands again, trying to make him listen. "I know you're not a coward; I know you want to find your sister's killer. But if someone is killing godlings, and if none of the gods know how to *stop* that person... Mad, what's wrong with running? You just urged me to do the same thing to get away from the Order, right? You spent aeons in the gods' realm, and only, what, ten years in this one? Why should you care what happens here?"

"Why should I—" He shook off my hands and took hold of my shoulders, glaring at me. "Have you gone mad? You're standing here in front of me, asking me why I don't leave you behind to face the Order-Keepers and gods know what else! If you think—"

"It's *you* they want! If you leave, I'll turn myself in. I'll tell them you went back to the gods' realm; they'll draw their own conclusions from that. Then—"

"Then they'll kill you," he said. That startled me silent. "Of course they will, Oree. Scapegoats restore order, don't they? People are upset about what happened to Role; mortals don't like to think that their gods can die. They also want to see her killer brought to justice. The Order will have to give them *someone*, if not the killer. With me gone, you'd have no protection at all."

It was true, every word of it; I knew it with instinctive certainty. And I was afraid. But...

"I couldn't bear it if you died," I said softly. I could not meet his eyes. It was a variation on the same thing he'd told me months before, and it hurt to say now as much as his words had hurt to hear then. "It's different, knowing I'll lose you when I die. That's...right, natural. The way things have to be.

But—" And I could not help it; I imagined *his* body in that alley, his bluegreen scent fading, his warmth cooling, his blood staining my fingers and nothing, nothing, where the sight of him should be.

No. I would rather die than allow that to happen.

"So be it," I said. "I've killed three men. It was an accident, but they're still dead. They had dreams, maybe families . . . You know all about debts owed, Mad. Isn't it right that I repay? As long as you're safe."

He said a word that rang of fury and fear and sour chimes, and it burst against my vision in a splash of cold aquamarine, silencing me. He let go of me then, moving away, and belatedly I realized that I had hurt him in my willingness to give my life. Obligation was his nature; altruism was its antithesis.

"You will not do this to me," he said, cold in his anger, though I heard the taut fear that lay under it. "You will not throw away your life because you were unlucky enough to be nearby when those fools started their blundering 'investigation.' Or because of that selfish bastard who lives with you." He clenched his fists. "And you will never, ever again offer to die for my sake."

I sighed. I didn't want to hurt him, but there was no reason for him to stay in the mortal realm and put up with petty mortal politics. Not even for me. I had to make him see that.

"You said it yourself," I said. "I'm going to die one day; nothing can prevent that. What does it matter whether that happens now or in fifty years? I—"

"*It matters*," he snarled, rounding on me. In two strides, he crossed the room and took me by the shoulders again. This caused a ripple in the surface of his mortal shape. For an instant, he flickered blue and then settled back, sweat sheening his face. His hands trembled. He was making himself sick to make a point. "Don't you dare say it doesn't matter!"

I knew what I should have said then, what I should have done. I had encountered this with him before—this fierce, dangerous, all-consuming need that drove him to love me no matter how much pain that caused. He was right; he needed a goddess for a lover, not some fragile mortal girl who would let herself get killed at the drop of a hat. Dumping me had been the smartest thing he'd ever done, even if letting him do it had been the hardest choice I'd ever made.

So I should have pushed him away. Said something terrible, designed to break his heart. That would've been the right thing to do, and I should've been strong enough to do it.

But I've never been as strong as I would like.

Madding kissed me. And gods, was it sweet. I felt him this time, all the coolness and fluid aquamarine of him, the edges and the ambition, everything he'd held back two nights before. I heard the chimes again as he flowed into me and through me, and when he pulled away, I clutched at him, pulling him close again. He rested his forehead on mine, trembling for a long, pent moment; he knew what he should do, too. Then he picked me up and carried me back to the pile of cushions.

We had made love before, many times. It was never perfect—it couldn't be, me being mortal—but it was always good. Best of all when Mad was needy the way he was now. He lost control at such times, forgot that I was mortal and that he needed to hold back. (By this I don't mean his strength, though that was part of it. I mean that sometimes he took me places, showed me visions. There are things mortals aren't meant to see. When he forgot himself, I saw some of them.)

I liked that he lost control, dangerous though it was. I liked knowing I could give him that much pleasure. He was one of the younger godlings, but he had still lived millennia to my decades, and sometimes I worried that I wasn't enough for him. On nights like this, though, as he wept and groaned and strained against me, and scintillated like diamond when the moment struck, I knew that was a silly fear. Of course I was enough, because he loved me. That was the whole point.

*   *   *

Afterward we lay, spent and lazy, in the cool humid silence of the late-night hours. I could hear others moving about in the house, on that floor and the one above: mortal servants, some of Madding's people, perhaps a valued customer who'd been given the rare privilege of buying goods direct from the source. There were no doors in Madding's home, because godlings regarded them as a nuisance, so the whole house had probably heard us. Neither of us cared.

"Did I hurt you?" His usual question.

"Of course not." My usual answer, though he always sighed in relief when I gave it. I lay on my belly, comfortable, not yet drowsy. "Did I hurt *you*?"

He usually laughed. That he stayed silent this time made me remember our earlier argument. That made me fall silent, too.

"You're going to need to leave Shadow," he said at last.

I said nothing, because there was nothing to say. He wasn't going to leave the mortal realm, because that would get me killed. Leaving Shadow might get me killed, too, but the chances were lower. Everything depended on how badly Previt Rimarn wanted me. Outside of the city, Madding had less power to protect me; no godling was permitted to leave Shadow by decree of the Lady, who feared the havoc they might cause worldwide. But the Order of Itempas had a White Hall in every sizable town, and thousands of priests and acolytes all over the world. I would be hard-pressed to hide from them if Rimarn was determined to have me.

Madding was betting Rimarn wouldn't care, however. I was easy prey, but not really the prey he wanted.

"I have a few contacts outside the city," Madding said. "I'll have them set things up for you. A house in a small town somewhere, a guard or two. You'll be comfortable. I'll make sure of that."

"What about my things here?"

His eyes unfocused briefly. "I've sent one of my siblings to take care of it tonight. We'll store your belongings here for now, then send them all to your new home by magic. Your neighbors will never even see you move out."

So neat and quick, the destruction of my life.

I rolled onto my belly and put my head down on my folded arms, trying not to think. After a moment, Mad sat up and leaned away from the pile of cushions, opening a small cabinet set into the floor and rummaging through it. I could not see what he picked up, but I saw him use it to prick his finger, at which I scowled.

"I'm not in the mood," I said.

"It'll make you feel better. Which will make *me* feel better."

"Doesn't it bother you, selling godsblood now that people think you're willing to kill over it?"

"No," he said, though his voice was sharper than usual, "because I'm *not* willing to kill over it, and I don't give a damn what others think." He held the finger out to me. A single dark drop of blood, like a garnet, sat there. "See? It's already shed. Shall I waste it?"

I sighed, but finally leaned forward and took his finger into my mouth. There was a fleeting taste of salt and metal, along with other, stranger flavors that I had never been able to name. The taste of other realms, maybe. Whatever it was, I felt the tingle of it in my throat as I swallowed, all the way down into my belly.

I licked his finger before I let go. As I had suspected, the wound was already closed; I just liked teasing him. He let out a soft sigh.

"This is why the Interdiction happened," he said, lying back down beside me. He rubbed little circles on the small of my back with one hand; this usually meant he was thinking about sex again. Greedy bastard.

"Hmm?" I closed my eyes and shivered, just a little, as the godsblood spread its power throughout my body. Once, when Madding had given me a taste of his blood, I had begun floating precisely six inches off the floor. Hadn't been able to get down for hours. Madding was no help; he'd been too busy laughing his ass off. Fortunately, all I *usually* felt was a pleasant relaxing sensation, like drunkenness but without the hangover. Sometimes I had visions, but they were never frightening. "What are you talking about?"

"You." He brushed his lips against my ear, sending a lovely shiver down my spine. He noticed it and traced the shiver with his fingertips, making me arch and sigh. "You mortals and your intoxicating insanity. So many of us have been seduced by your kind, Oree; even the Three, long ago. I used to think anyone who fell in love with a mortal was a fool."

"But now that you've tried it, you see the error of your ways?"

"Oh, no." He sat up, straddled my legs, and slid his hands under me to cup and knead my breasts. I sighed in languid pleasure, though I couldn't help giggling when he nibbled at the back of my neck. "I was right. It *is* a kind of insanity. You make us want things we shouldn't."

My smile faded. "Like eternity."

"Yes." His hands stilled for a moment. "And more than that."

"What else?"

"Children, for one."

I sat up. "Tell me you're joking." He had promised me long before that I didn't have to take the same precautions with him that I would with a mortal man.

"Hush," he said, pressing me back down. "Of course I'm joking. But I *could* give you a child, if I wanted. If you wanted me to. And if I was willing to break the only real law the Three have ever imposed on us."

"Oh." I settled back into the cushions, relaxing as he resumed his slow, coaxing caresses. "You're talking about demons. Children of mortals and immortals. Monsters."

"They weren't monsters. It was before the Gods' War, before even I was born, but I hear they were just like us—godlings, I mean. They could dance among the stars as we do; they had the same magic. Yet they grew old and died, no matter how powerful they were. It made them...very strange. But not monstrous."

115

He sighed. "It's forbidden to create more demons, but...ah, Oree. You'd make such beautiful children."

"Mmm." I was beginning to not pay attention to him. Madding loved to talk while his hands were doing lovely things that transcended words. He had slipped one hand between my legs during this last ramble. Lovely things. "So the Three were afraid you'd all...ah...fall in love with mortals and make more dangerous little demons."

"Not all the Three. In the end, it was only Itempas who ordered us to stay away from the mortal realm. But he does not brook disobedience, so we did as he commanded." He kissed my shoulder, then nuzzled my temple. "I never realized how cruel that order was, before I met you."

I smiled, feeling wicked, and reached back to catch hold of the warm, hard lump that lay against my backside. I gave him a practiced stroke and he shuddered against me, his breath quickening in my ear. "Oh, yes," I teased. "So cruel."

"Oree," he said, his voice suddenly low and tight. I sighed and lifted my hips a little, and he slipped back into me like he belonged nowhere else.

Somewhere in the delicious, floating pleasure that followed, I became aware that we were being watched. I didn't think anything of it at first. Madding's siblings seemed fascinated by our relationship, so if watching us helped them whenever they decided to try a mortal, I didn't mind. But there had been something different about this gaze, I realized afterward, when I lay pleasantly exhausted and drifting toward sleep. It did not have the usual air of curiosity or titillation; there was something heavier about this. Something disapproving. And familiar.

Of course. Madding had sent someone to collect all my belongings. Naturally that would include Shiny: my brooding, arrogant, selfish bastard of a pet. I had no idea why my being with Madding angered him, and I didn't care. I was tired of his moods, tired of everything. So I ignored him and went to sleep.

*   *   *

Madding was gone when I woke. I sat up, bleary, and listened for a moment, trying to get my bearings. From downstairs I could hear the ceaseless ripple of water and could smell hiras perfume. Upstairs, someone was walking, making the floorboards creak. Intuition told me it was very late, but most of Madding's people were godlings; they didn't sleep. From somewhere on the same floor, I heard a woman laughing and two men talking.

I yawned and put my head back down, but the voices impinged gently on my consciousness.

"—didn't tell you—"

"—your business, damn it! You have no—"

It sank in slowly: Shiny. And Madding. Talking? It didn't matter. I didn't care.

"You're not listening," Madding said. He spoke in a low voice but intently; that made the sound carry. "She gave you a real chance and you're throwing it away. Why would you do that when so many of us fought for you, died..." He faltered, silent for an instant. "You never consider others—only yourself! Do you have any idea what Oree has gone through because of you?"

My eyes opened.

Shiny's reply was a low murmur, unintelligible. Madding's was anything but, almost a shout: "You're destroying her! Isn't it enough that you destroyed your own family? Do you have to kill what *I* love, too?"

I got up. My stick was there on my side of the pillow pile, right where Mad had always put it. The robe was tangled in the pillows where I'd dropped it. I shook it out and put it on.

"—tell you this now—" Madding had regained some of his composure, though he was still plainly furious. He'd lowered his voice again. Shiny was silent, as he had been since Madding's outburst. Madding kept talking, but I couldn't tell what he was saying.

I stopped at the door. I didn't care, I told myself. My life was ruined and it was Shiny's fault. *He* didn't care. Why did it matter what he and Madding said to each other? Why did I still bother trying to understand him?

"—he could love you again," Madding said. "Pretend that means nothing to you, Father, if you like. But I know—"

Father. I blinked. *Father?*

"—in spite of everything," Madding said. "Believe that or not, as you will." The words had an air of finality. The argument was over, one-sided as it had been.

I stepped back against the bedroom wall and out of the doorway, though that would do me little good if Madding came back into the room. But although I heard Madding's footsteps leave whatever room they'd been in and stomp away, they headed downstairs, not back to his bedroom.

As I stood there against the wall, mulling over what I'd heard, Shiny left the room as well. He walked past Madding's room, and I braced myself for him to notice that I was out of bed and perhaps come in and find me. His footsteps didn't even slow. He headed upstairs.

Which one to follow? I wavered for a moment, then went after Madding. At least I knew he would talk to me.

I found him standing atop the largest of his pools, glowing bright enough to make the whole chamber visible as his magic reflected off walls and water. I stopped behind him, savoring the play of light across his facets, the shift and ripple of liquid aquamarine flesh as he moved, the patterned flicker of the walls. He had folded his hands together, head bowed as if to pray. Perhaps he *was* praying. Above the godlings were the gods, and above the gods was Maelstrom, the unknowable. Perhaps even it prayed to something. Didn't we all need someone to turn to sometimes?

So I sat down and waited, not interrupting, and presently Madding lowered his hands and turned to me.

"I should have kept my voice down," he said softly, amid the chime of crystal.

I smiled, drawing up my knees and wrapping my arms around them. "I find it hard not to yell at him, too."

He sighed. "If you could have seen him before the war, Oree. He was glorious then. We all loved him—competed for his love, basked in his attention. And he loved us back in his quiet, steady way. He's changed so much."

His body gave off one last liquid shimmer and then settled back into his stocky, plain-featured human shell, which I had come to love just as much over the years. He was still naked, his hair still loose, still standing on water. His eyes carried memories and sorrow far too ancient for any mortal man. He would never look truly ordinary, no matter how hard he tried.

"So he's your father." I spoke slowly. I did not want to voice aloud the suspicion I'd begun to develop. I hardly wanted to believe it. There were dozens, perhaps hundreds, of godlings, and there'd been even more before the Gods' War. Not all of them had been parented by the Three.

But most of them had been.

Madding smiled, reading my face. I'd never been able to hide anything from him. "There aren't many of us left who haven't disowned him."

I licked my lips. "I thought he was a godling. *Just* a godling, I mean, not..." I gestured vaguely above my head, meaning the sky.

"He's not just a godling."

Confirmation, unexpectedly anticlimactic. "I thought the Three would be...different."

"They are."

"But Shiny..."

"He's a special case. His current condition is temporary. Probably."

Nothing in my life had prepared me for this. I knew I was not especially knowledgeable about the affairs of gods, despite my personal association with some of them. I knew as well as anyone that the priests taught what they wanted us to know, not necessarily what was true. And sometimes even when they told the truth, they got it wrong.

Madding came over, sitting down beside me. He gazed out over the pools, his manner subdued.

I needed to understand. "What did he do?" It was the question I had asked Sieh.

"Something terrible." His smile had faded during my moment of stunned silence. His expression was closed, almost angry. "Something most of us will never forgive. He got away with it for a while, but now the debt has come due. He'll be repaying it for a long time."

Sometimes they got it *very* wrong. "I don't understand," I whispered.

He lifted a hand and drew a knuckle across my cheek, brushing a stray curl of hair aside.

"He really was lucky to find you," he said. "I have to confess, I've been a bit jealous. There's still a little of the old him left. I can see why you'd be drawn to him."

"It's not like that. He doesn't even like me."

"I know." He dropped his hand. "I'm not sure he's capable of caring for anyone now, not in any real way. He was never good at changing, bending. He broke instead. And he took all of us with him."

He fell silent, reverberating pain, and I understood then that, unlike Sieh, Madding still loved Shiny. Or whoever Shiny had once been.

My mind fought against the name that whispered in my heart.

I found his hand and laced our fingers together. Madding glanced down at them, then up at me, and smiled. There was such sorrow in his eyes that I leaned over and kissed him. He sighed through it, resting his forehead against mine when we parted.

"I don't want to talk about him anymore," he said.

"All right," I said. "What shall we talk about instead?" Though I thought I knew.

"Stay with me," he whispered.

"I wasn't the one who left." I tried for lightness and failed utterly.

He closed his eyes. "It was different before. Now I realize I'm going to lose you either way. You'll leave town, or you'll grow old and die. But if you stay, I'll have you longer." He fumbled for my other hand, not as good at doing things without his eyes as I was. "I need you, Oree."

I licked my lips. "I don't want to endanger you, Mad. And if I stay..." Every morsel of food I ate, every scrap of clothing I wore, would come from him. Could I bear that? I had traveled across the continent, left my mother and my people, scrabbled and struggled, to live as I pleased. If I stayed in Shadow, with the Order hunting me and murder dogging my steps, would I even be able to leave Madding's house? Freedom alone, or imprisonment with the man I loved. Two horrible choices.

And he knew it. I felt him tremble, and that was almost enough. "Please," he whispered.

Almost, I gave in.

"Let me think," I said. "I have to...I can't think, Mad."

His eyes opened. Because he was so near, touching me, I could feel the hope fade in him. When he drew back, letting go of my hand, I knew he had begun to draw back his heart as well, steeling it against my rejection.

"All right," he said. "Take as long as you like."

If he had gotten angry, it would have been so much easier.

I started to speak, but he had turned away. What was there to say, anyhow? Nothing that would heal the pain I'd just caused him. Only time could do that.

So I sighed and got up, and headed upstairs.

*   *   *

Madding's house was huge. The second floor, where his room was located, was also where he and his siblings worked, pricking themselves to produce tiny vials of their blood for sale to mortals. He had grown wealthy from this and from his other lines of business; there were many skills godlings possessed that mortals were willing to pay a premium for. But he was still a godling, and when his business had grown, he hadn't considered opening an office; he'd simply made his house bigger and invited all his underlings to come live with him.

Most of them had taken him up on the offer. The third floor held the rooms of those godlings who liked having a bed, a few scriveners who'd slipped the Order's leash, and a handful of mortals with other useful talents—record-keeping, glassblowing, sales. The next floor up was the roof, which was what I sought.

I found two godlings lounging at the bottom of the roof stairs when I came up from below: Madding's patch-skinned male lieutenant/guard and a coolly handsome creature who'd taken the form of a middle-aged Ken man. The latter, whose gaze held wisdom and disinterest in equal measure, did not acknowledge my presence. The former winked at me and shifted closer to his sibling to let me pass.

"Up for a breath of night air?" he asked.

I nodded. "I can feel the city best up there."

"Saying good-bye?" His eyes were too sharp, reading my face like a sigil. I mustered a weak smile in response, because I did not trust myself to keep my composure if I spoke. His expression softened with pity. "It'd be a shame to see you go."

"I've caused him enough trouble."

"He doesn't mind."

"I know. But at this rate, I'll end up owing him my soul, or worse."

"He doesn't keep an account for you, Oree." It was the first time he'd used my name. I shouldn't have been surprised; he'd been with Madding for longer than I had. Perhaps they'd even come to the mortal world together, two eternal bachelors seeking excitement amid the grit and glory of the city. The idea made me smile. He noticed and smiled himself. "You have no idea how much he cares for you."

I had seen Mad's eyes when he'd asked me to stay. "I do know," I whispered, and then had to take a deep breath. "I'll see you later, ah . . ." I paused. All this time, I had never asked his name. My cheeks grew warm with shame.

He looked amused. "Paitya. My partner—the woman?—is Kitr. But don't tell her I told you."

I nodded, resisting the urge to glance at the older-looking godling. Some godlings were like Paitya and Madding and Lil, not caring whether mortals accorded them any particular reverence. Others, I had learned, regarded us as very much inferior beings. Either way, the older one already looked annoyed that I'd interrupted their relaxation. Best to leave him be.

"You'll have company," Paitya said as I moved past him. I almost stopped there, realizing who he meant.

But that was fitting, I decided, considering the churn of misery inside myself. I had been raised as a devout Itempan, though

I'd lapsed in the years since, and my heart had never really been in it, anyhow. Yet I still prayed to Him when I felt the need. I was definitely feeling the need now, so I proceeded up the steps, wrestled the heavy metal lever open, and stepped out onto the roof.

As the metallic echoes of the door faded, I heard breathing to one side, low to the ground. He was sitting down somewhere, probably against one of the wide struts of the cistern that dominated the rooftop space. I could not feel his gaze, but he must have heard me come onto the roof. Silence fell.

Standing there, knowing who he was, I expected to feel different. I should have been reverent, nervous, awed maybe. Yet my mind could not reconcile the two concepts: the Bright Lord of Order and the man I'd found in a muckbin. Itempas and Shiny; Him and him; they did not feel at all the same, in my heart.

And I could think of only one question, out of the thousands that I should have asked.

"All that time you lived with me and never spoke," I said. "Why?"

At first I thought he wouldn't answer. But at last I heard a faint shift in the gravel that covered the rooftop and felt the solidity of his gaze settle on me.

"You were irrelevant," he said. "Just another mortal."

I was growing used to him, I realized bitterly. That had hurt far less than I'd expected.

Shaking my head, I went over to another of the cistern's struts, felt about to make sure there were no puddles or debris in the way, and sat down. There was no true silence up on the roof; the midnight air was thick with the sounds of the city. Yet

I found myself at peace, anyhow. Shiny's presence, my anger at him, at least kept me from thinking about Madding or dead Order-Keepers or the end of the life I'd built for myself in Shadow. So in his own obnoxious way, my god comforted me.

"What the hells are you doing up here, anyhow?" I asked. I could not muster the wherewithal to show him any greater respect. "Praying to yourself?"

"There's a new moon tonight."

"So?"

He did not reply, and I did not care. I turned my face toward the distant, barely there shimmers of the World Tree's canopy and pretended they were the stars I'd heard others talk about all my life. Sometimes, amid the ripples and eddies of the leafy sea, I would see a brighter flash now and again. Probably an early bloom; the Tree would be flowering soon. There were people in the city who made a year's living from the dangerous work of climbing the Tree's lower branches and snipping off its silvery, hand-wide blossoms for sale to the wealthy.

"All that happens in darkness, he sees and hears," Shiny said abruptly. I wished he would stop talking again. "On a moonless night, he will hear me, even if he chooses not to answer."

"Who?"

"Nahadoth."

I forgot my anger at Shiny, and my sorrow over Madding, and my guilt about the Order-Keepers. I forgot everything but that name.

Nahadoth.

*   *   *

We have never forgotten his name.

These days, our world has two great continents, but once

there were three: High North, Senm, and the Maroland. Maro was the smallest of the three but was also the most magnificent, with trees that stretched a thousand feet into the air, flowers and birds found nowhere else, and waterfalls so huge that it was said you could feel their spray on the other side of the world.

The hundred clans of my people—called just "Maro" then, not "Maroneh"—were plentiful and powerful. In the aftermath of the Gods' War, those who had honored Bright Itempas above other gods were shown favor. That included the Amn, a now-extinct people called the Ginij, and us. The Amn were ruled by the Arameri family. Their homeland was Senm, but they built their stronghold in our land, at our invitation. We were smarter than the Ginij. But we paid a price for our savvy politicking.

There was a rebellion of some sort. A great army marched across the Maroland, intent upon overthrowing the Arameri. Stupid, I know, but such things happened in those days. It would have been just another massacre, just another footnote in history, if one of the Arameri's weapons hadn't gotten loose.

He was the Nightlord, brother and eternal enemy of Bright Itempas. Hobbled, diminished, but still unimaginably powerful, he punched a hole in the earth, causing earthquakes and tsunamis that tore the Maroland apart. The whole continent sank into the sea, and nearly all its people died.

The few Maro who survived settled on a tiny peninsula of the Senm continent, granted to them by the Arameri in condolence for our loss. We began to call ourselves Maroneh, which meant "those who weep for Maro" in the common language we once spoke. We named our daughters for sorrow and our sons for rage; we debated whether there was any point in trying to rebuild our race. We thanked Itempas for saving even the handful of us who remained, and we hated the Arameri for making that prayer necessary.

And though the rest of the world all but forgot him outside of heretic cults and tales to frighten children, we remembered the name of our destroyer.

Nahadoth.

* * *

"I have been attempting," said Shiny, "to express my remorse to him."

That pulled me from one kind of shock into another. *"What?"*

Shiny got up. I heard him walk a few steps, perhaps over to the low wall that marked the edge of the rooftop. His voice, when he spoke, was diluted by wind and the late-night sounds of the city, but it came to me clearly enough. His diction was precise, unaccented, perfectly pitched. He spoke like a nobleman trained to give speeches.

"You wanted to know what I had done to be punished with mortality," he said. "You asked that of Sieh."

I pulled my thoughts from their endless litany of *Nahadoth, Nahadoth, Nahadoth.* "Well...yes."

"My sister," he said. "I killed her."

I frowned. Of course he had. Enefa, the goddess of earth and life, had conspired against Itempas with their brother, the Nightlord Nahadoth. Itempas had slain her for her treachery and had given Nahadoth to the Arameri as a slave. It was a famous story.

Unless...

I licked my lips. "Did she...do something to provoke you?"

The wind shifted for a moment. His voice drifted to me and away, then back again, singsong and soft. "She took him from me."

"She—" I stopped.

I did not want to understand. Obviously Itempas had been involved with Enefa at some point before their falling-out; the existence of the godlings was proof enough of that. But Nahadoth was the monster in the dark, the enemy of all that was good in the world. I didn't want to think of him as the Bright Lord's *brother*, much less—

But I had spent too much time among godlings. I had seen that they lusted and raged like mortals, hurt like mortals, misunderstood and nursed petty grudges and *killed each other over love like mortals.*

I got to my feet, trembling.

"You're saying *you* started the Gods' War," I said. "You're saying the Nightlord was your lover—that you love him *still*. You're saying *he's free now and he's the one who did this to you.*"

"Yes," said Shiny. Then, to my surprise, he let out a little laugh, so laden with bitterness that his voice wavered unsteadily for an instant. "That's precisely what I'm saying."

My hands tightened on my stick until it hurt my palms. I sank back to a crouch, planting the stick in the gravel to balance myself, pressing my forehead against the smooth old wood. "I don't believe you," I whispered. I *could not* believe him. I could not be that wrong about the world, the gods, everything. The entire human race could not be that wrong.

Could we?

I heard the gravel shift under Shiny's feet as he turned to me. "Do you love Madding?" he asked.

It was such an unexpected question, so nonsensical in the context of our discussion, that it took me several seconds to make my mouth work. "Yes. Dear gods, of course I do. Why are you asking me that now?"

More gravel, chuffing rhythmically as he came over to me. His warm hands took hold of mine where they gripped the stick. I was so surprised by this that I let him pry me loose and pull me up to stand. He did nothing then, for several moments. Just looked at me. I became aware, belatedly, that I wore nothing but a silk robe. The winter had been mild this year, and spring was coming early, but the night had begun to turn cold. Goose bumps prickled my skin, and my nipples tented the silk. I had worn as little in my own house—or less. Nudity meant nothing to me as titillation, and Shiny had never shown the slightest interest. Now, however, I was very aware of his gaze, and...it bothered me. I had never experienced this particular flavor of discomfort with him before.

He leaned closer, his hands sliding up to my arms. His hands were very warm, almost comforting. I didn't know what he meant to do until his lips brushed mine. Startled, I tried to pull away, and his hands tightened sharply—not enough to hurt, but it was a warning. I froze. He drew near again and kissed me.

I didn't know what to think. But as his mouth coaxed mine open with a skill I had never imagined he possessed, and his tongue flickered at my lips, I could not help relaxing against him. If he had forced the kiss, I would have hated it. I would have fought. Instead he was gentle—unnaturally, too-perfectly gentle. His mouth tasted of nothing, which was strange and somehow emphasized his inhumanity. It was not like kissing Madding. There was no flavor of Shiny's inner self. But when his tongue touched my own, I jumped a little, because it felt good. I had not expected that. His hands slid down to my waist, then my hips, pulling me closer. I breathed his peculiar, hot-spice smell. The heat and strength of his body—it was wholly different from Madding. Disturbing. Interesting. His teeth grazed my lower lip and I shivered, this time not wholly in fear.

He had not closed his eyes. I could feel them watching me, evaluating me, cold despite the heat of his mouth.

When he pulled back, he drew in a breath. Let it out slowly. Said, still in a terrible, soft voice, "You don't love Madding."

I stiffened.

"Even now, you want me." There was such contempt in his voice; each word dripped with venom. I had never before heard such emotion from him, and all of it hate. "His power intrigues you. The prestige of having a god for a lover. Perhaps you're even devoted to him in your small way—though I doubt that, since it seems any god will do." He let out a small sigh. "I know well the dangers of trusting your kind. I warned my children, kept them away while I could, but Madding is stubborn. I mourn the pain it will cause him when he finally realizes just how unworthy of his love you are."

I stood there, shocked to numbness. Believing him, for a long, horrifying moment. Shiny had been—still was, diminished or not—the god I had revered all my life. Of course he was right. Had I not hesitated at Madding's offer? My god had judged me and found me wanting, and it hurt.

Then sense reasserted itself, and with it came pure fury.

I was still backed against the cistern strut, which gave me perfect leverage as I planted my hands on Shiny's chest and shoved him back with all my strength. He stumbled back, making a sound of surprise. I followed, all my fear and confusion forgotten amid red-hot rage.

"*That's* your proof?" My hands found his chest and I shoved him again, throwing all my weight into it just for the satisfaction of hearing him grunt as I did so. "*That's* what makes you think I don't love Mad? You're a damned good kisser, Shiny, but do you honestly think you hold a candle to Madding in my heart?" I laughed, my own voice echoing harshly in my ears. "My gods, he was right! You really don't know anything about love."

I turned, muttering to myself, and began making my way back to the roof door.

"Wait," Shiny said.

I ignored him, sweeping my stick in a tight angry arc ahead of me. His hand caught my arm again, and this time I tried to shake him off, cursing.

"*Wait*," he said, not letting go. He turned away from me, barely noticing my rage. "Someone's here."

"What are you—" But I heard it, too, now, and froze. Footsteps, chuffing on the rooftop gravel, beside the door hatch.

"Oree Shoth?" The voice was male, cool and dark like the late-winter night. Familiar, though I could not place it.

"Y-yes," I said, wondering if this was some customer of Madding's, and what he was doing on the roof if that was the case. And how did he know my name? Maybe he'd overheard some of Madding's people gossiping. "Were you looking for me?"

"Yes. Though I had hoped you'd be alone."

Shiny shifted suddenly, moving in front of me, and I found myself trying to hear the man through his rather intimidating bulk. I opened my mouth to shout at him, too angry for politeness or respect—and then I stopped.

It was faint. I had to squint. But Shiny had begun to glow.

"Oree," he said. Calm, as always. "Go into the house."

Fear stopped anything else I might have said. "H-he's between me and the door."

"I will remove him."

"I wouldn't advise that," said the man, unruffled. "You aren't a godling."

Shiny sighed, and under other circumstances, I would have been amused by his annoyance. "No," he snapped, "I'm not."

And before I could speak again, he was gone, the space in front of me cold in his absence. There was a glimmer of magic—something occluded by the hazy shimmer of Shiny's body. Then a flurry of movement, cloth tearing, the struggle of flesh against flesh. A spray of wetness across my face, making me flinch.

And then silence.

I held still for a moment, my own breath loud and fast in my ears as I strained to hear the sound that I knew and feared would come: bodies, hitting the cobblestones of the street three stories below. But there was only that terrible silence.

My nerves snapped. I ran to the roof door, clawed it open, and flung myself into the house, screaming.

6

"A Window Opens"
(chalk on concrete)

THERE ARE THINGS he told me about himself. Not all of it, of course—some things I heard from other gods or remember from old stories of my childhood. But mostly he just told me. It was not his nature to lie.

In the time of the Three, things were very different. There were many temples but few holy texts, and no persecution of those with differing beliefs. Mortals loved whatever gods they wished—often several at once—and it was not called heresy. If there were disputes about a particular bit of lore or magic, it was simple enough to call on a local godling and ask about it. No point in getting possessive about one god or another when there were plenty to go around.

It was during this time that the first demons were born: offspring of mortal humans and immortal gods, neither one nor the other, possessing the greatest gifts of both. One of those gifts was mortality—a strange thing to call a gift, by my thinking, but people back then thought differently. Anyhow, all the demons possessed it.

But consider what this means: *all the demons died.* Doesn't make sense, does it? Children rarely take after just one of their parents. Shouldn't a few of the demons have inherited immortality? They certainly got the magic, in plenty—so much that they passed it on to us, when they mated with us. Scrivening and bonebending and prophecy and shadow-sending, all of this came to mortalkind through the demons. But even when the demons took godly lovers and had children with them, those children grew old and died, too.

For us, the divine inheritance was a blessing. For the gods, one drop of mortal blood doomed their offspring to death.

Apparently, no one realized what this meant for a very long time.

*   *   *

I scrambled downstairs much faster than I should have, given that I'd never gotten around to memorizing Madding's stairs. Behind me trailed Paitya; the middle-aged godling; Kitr, who had come out of nowhere at my shout and was visible for once; and Madding. As we reached the room of pools, two more people joined us: a tall mortal woman who shone with nearly as many godwords as Previt Rimarn, and a sleek racing dog who glowed white in my sight. As I reached the house's front door, I heard other calls upstairs; I'd woken the whole house.

I might have felt bad if my thoughts had not been filled with that awful silence.

"Oree!" Hands caught me before I got three steps out the door; I fought them. A blur of blue resolved into Madding. "You shouldn't leave the house, damn it."

"I have to—" I twisted to get around Madding. "He—"

"He who? Oree—" Madding abruptly went still. "Why is there blood on your face?"

That stopped my panic, though the hand that I lifted to my face shook badly. Wetness had splattered my face up on the roof; I'd forgotten.

"Boss?" Paitya had crouched to peer at something on the ground. I could not see what, but the grim expression on his face was unmistakable. "There's a lot more blood here."

Madding turned to look, and his eyes widened. He turned back to me, frowning. "What happened? Where were you, up on the roof?" Suddenly his frown deepened. "Did Father do something to you? So help me—"

Kitr, who had been scanning the street for danger, looked at us both sharply. "You *told* her?"

Madding ignored her, though I caught his wince of consternation. He turned me from one side to the other, checking for injuries. "I'm fine," I said, holding my stick to my chest as I grew calmer. "*I'm* fine. But, yes, I was on the roof, with...with Shiny. There was someone...a man. I couldn't see him; he must've been mortal. He knew my name, said he'd been looking for me—"

Paitya cursed and stood up, narrowing his eyes as he scanned the area. "Since when do Order-Keepers come by way of the damned roof? They usually have sense enough not to piss us off."

Madding muttered something in gods' language; it curled and spiked, a curse. "What happened?"

"Shiny," I said. "He fought with the man. There was magic…"
I clutched at Madding's arms, my fingers tightening on the cloth
of his shirt. "Mad, the man hit him with magic somehow, I
think that's what caused the blood, I think Shiny grabbed him
and pulled him off the roof, *but I didn't hear them hit the
ground…*"

Madding had already begun gesturing at his companions,
directing them to search around the house and nearby streets.
Kitr stayed nearby, as did Paitya. Madding had no real need of
bodyguards, but I did, and he had probably directed one of them
to spirit me away if it came down to any sort of fight.

"I'm going to raze that White Hall to the ground," he snarled,
his human shape flickering blue as he pushed me back toward
the front door. "If they've dared to attack my house, my people—"

"He wasn't after Shiny," I murmured, realizing it belatedly. I
stopped, clutching Madding's arm to get his attention. "Mad,
that man wasn't after Shiny at all! If he was an Order-Keeper,
he would've wanted Shiny, wouldn't he? They know he killed
the ones in South Root." The more I thought about it, the more
certain I became. "I don't think that man was an Order-Keeper
at all."

I didn't mistake the swift, startled look that crossed Madding's face. He exchanged a glance with Kitr, who looked equally
alarmed. Kitr then turned to look at one of the mortals, the
scrivener. She nodded and knelt, taking a pad of paper out of
her jacket and uncapping a thin ink-brush.

"I'll go see, too," said the middle-aged godling, vanishing.
Madding pulled me against him, holding me firm with one arm
and keeping the other free, in case of trouble. I tried to feel safe

there, in the arms of one god and protected by half a dozen others, but all my nerves were a-jangle, and the panic would not fade. I could not push aside the feeling that something was wrong, very wrong, that someone was watching, that something was going to happen. I felt it with every ounce of intuition that I possessed.

"There's no body," said Paitya, coming over to us. Beyond him, I could see other godlings winking in and out of sight about the street, on nearby windowsills, on the edge of a roof. "Enough blood that there *should* be, but nothing. Not even, er, parts."

"Is it—" I had to struggle to be heard, half muffled against Madding's shoulder.

"It's his." Paitya glanced back at the racing dog, who was sniffing at the spot now; the dog looked up and nodded in solemn confirmation. "No doubt about it. The blood's just splattered about; it fell from above. But he didn't *land* here."

Madding muttered something in his own tongue, then switched to Senmite so I would understand. "There must have been a weapon. Or magic, as you said." He looked down at me, scowling in irritation. "He's powerless now. He must have known he couldn't take a scrivener, if that's what the man was. On the roof of a house full of godlings—why didn't he just call for help? Stubborn bastard."

I closed my eyes and leaned against Madding, suddenly weary. I could have called for help, too, I realized belatedly, though I'd been too frightened to think of doing so. Shiny, however, hadn't been afraid at all. He hadn't *wanted* help. He'd done it again—charged into a dangerous situation, spent his life like currency, all so he could have a taste of his old power. It had been for my benefit this time, but did that really make it better? Godlings respected life, including their own. They were just as immortal, but they at least tried to defend themselves or evade blows when attacked. When they fought, they tried not to kill. While Shiny slaughtered even his own kin.

"The Nightlord should've just killed him," I said, filled with sudden bitterness. Madding raised his eyebrows in surprise, but I shook my head. "There's something wrong with him, Mad. I always suspected it, but tonight..."

I remembered the little break in Shiny's voice when he'd admitted his role in the Gods' War. Just an instant of instability, a crack in the bedrock of his stoicism. But it went deeper than that, didn't it? His carelessness with his flesh—how *had* he ended up dead in my muckbin, all those months ago? That vicious kiss he'd given me. His even more vicious words afterward, blaming me for all the duplicity of the human race.

He was—or had been—the god of order, the living embodiment of stability, peace, and rationality. The man he had become, here in the mortal realm, didn't make sense. Shiny did not feel like Itempas because Shiny *wasn't* Itempas, and no part of my proper Maro upbringing would let me accept him as such.

Madding sighed. "Nahadoth wanted to kill him, Oree. A lot of my siblings did, too, after what he'd done. But the Three created this universe; if any one of them dies, it all ends. So he was sent here, where he can do the least damage. And maybe..." He paused, and again I heard that hint of longing in his voice. Hope, not quite stifled. "Maybe, somehow, he can...get better. See the error of his ways. I don't know."

"He said he was trying to apologize. Up on the roof. To… to…" I shuddered. We did not forget his name, but we didn't say it, either, not if we could help it. "The Nightlord."

Madding blinked in surprise. "Did he? That's more than I ever thought he'd do." He sobered. "But I doubt that will do any good. He *killed my mother*, Oree. Murdered her with poison, mutilated her body. Then spent the next few millennia killing or imprisoning any of us who dared to protest. It takes a little more than an apology to atone for that."

I reached up to touch Madding's face, reading his expression with my fingers. This helped me catch what I had missed. "You're still angry about it."

His brow furrowed. "Of course I am. I loved her! But"—he sighed heavily, leaning down to press his forehead against mine—"I loved him, too, once."

I cupped his face in my hands, wishing I knew how to comfort him. This was family business, though, between father and son. It was Shiny's problem to solve, if we ever found him.

There was one thing I could do, though.

"I'll stay," I said.

He started, pulling back to stare at me. Of course he knew what I meant. After a long moment, he said, "Are you sure?"

I almost laughed. I was shaky inside, not just from leftover panic. "No. But I don't think I ever will be. I just…I know what's most important to me." I did laugh then, as I realized that Shiny had helped me decide, with that horrid kiss and the challenge in his words. I did, too, love Madding. And I wanted to be with him, even though it meant the end of the life I'd worked so hard to build and the end of my independence. Love meant compromise, after all—something I suspected Shiny did not understand.

Madding's face was solemn as he nodded, accepting my decision. I liked that he did not smile. I think he knew what the decision cost me.

Instead, after a moment, he sighed and glanced at Kitr, who had carefully paid more attention to the street than to us for the past few minutes.

"I'm calling everyone in," he said. "I don't like this. No mere scrivener should be able to hide from us." He glanced back, in the direction of the splashes of blood. "And I can't sense Father anywhere. I *especially* don't like that."

"Nor can I," said Kitr. "There are some of us with the power to hide him, but why would they? Unless..." She glanced at me, assessing and dismissing in a single sweep of her eyes. "You think this has something to do with Role? Your mortal there did find the body, but what's that got to do with anything?"

"I don't know, but—"

"Wait. There's something..." This came from the other side of the street. I followed the voice and saw the sigil-etched outline of Madding's scrivener. She stood looking up at the buildings nearby, holding a sheet of paper in her hands. A series of individual sigils had been drawn at the corners, with three rows of godwords in the middle. As I watched, one of the godwords and a sigil in the upper right corner began to glow more brightly. The scrivener, who apparently knew what this meant, gasped and took several steps back. I could not see her face, for she had no godwords written there, but terror filled her voice. "Oh, gods, I knew it! Look out! All of you, look—"

And suddenly hells filled the street.

No, not hells. *Holes.*

With a sound like tearing paper, they opened all around us, perfect circles of darkness. Some lay along the ground, some on the walls; some must've hung unsupported in midair. One of them opened right beneath the scrivener's feet, practically the instant the last word left her lips. She didn't have time to cry out before she fell into it and vanished. Another caught Kitr, who had turned to run to Madding's side. It opened before her between one step and another, and she was gone. The racing dog cursed in Mekatish and darted around the first hole that opened at his feet, but then another opened above him. I saw his short fur stand on end, pulled upward, and then with a yelp he was sucked in as well.

Before I could react, Madding suddenly shoved me away from him, into the doorway of the house. Stumbling over the doorway's raised step, I turned back, opening my mouth to speak—then saw the hole opening at his back. I felt the pull, its force powerful enough to jerk me forward a step even after I stopped.

No! I caught the door's elaborate handle in one hand to brace myself and used that leverage to raise my walking stick, hoping Madding would be able to grab it. Madding, his eyes wide and teeth bared, strained toward me. The sound of jangling chimes was barely audible, sucked away by the hole.

He mouthed something I couldn't hear. He ground his teeth, and I heard him in my head this time, in the manner of gods. *GET INSIDE!*

Then he flew backward, as if a great invisible hand had

grabbed him around the waist and yanked. The hole vanished. He was gone.

I fumbled with the door handle, my breath wild and loud in my ears, my palms so sweaty that the stick slipped loose to clatter on the ground. I could hear no one else on the street; I was alone. Except for the remaining holes, which hovered all around me, darker than the black of my sight.

Then I got the door open and ran into the house, away from the holes, toward the clean, empty darkness where I was blind but where at least I knew what dangers I faced.

I got three steps into the house before the air tore behind me, and I flew backward off my feet, and a sound like trembling metal filled the world as I tumbled away.

7

"Girl in Darkness"
(watercolor)

MY DREAMS HAVE BEEN more vivid lately. They told me that might happen, but still...I remembered something.

In the dream, I paint a picture. But as I lose myself in the colors of the sky and the mountains and the mushrooms that dwarf the mountains—this is a living world, full of strange flora and fungi; I can almost smell the fumes of its alien air—the door to my room opens and my mother comes in.

"What are you doing?" she asks.

And though I am still half lost in mountains and mushrooms, I have no choice but to pull myself back into this world, where I am just a sheltered blind girl whose mother wants what's best for me, even if she and I do not agree on what that is.

"Painting," I say, though this is obvious. My belly has clenched in defensive tension; I fear a lecture is coming.

She only sighs and comes closer, putting her hand on mine to let me know where she is. She is silent for a long while. Is she looking at the painting? I nibble my bottom lip, not quite daring to hope that she is, perhaps, trying to understand why I do what I do. She has never told me to stop, but I can taste her disapproval, as sour and heavy on my tongue as old, molding grapes. She has hinted at it verbally as well, in the past. *Paint something useful, something pretty.* Something that does not entrance viewers for hours on end. Something that would not attract the sharp, gleaming interest of the priests if they saw it. Something safe.

She says nothing this time, only stroking my braided hair, and at last I realize she is not thinking about me or my paintings at all. "What is it, Mama?" I ask.

"Nothing," she says, very softly, and I realize that for the first time in my life, she has just lied to me.

My heart fills with dread. I don't know why. Perhaps it is the whiff of fear that wafts from her, or the sorrow that underlies it, or simply the fact that my garrulous, cheerful mother is suddenly so quiet, so still.

So I lean against her and put my arms around her waist. She is trembling, unable to give me the comfort that I crave. I take what I can, and perhaps give a little of my own in return.

My father died a few weeks later.

*   *   *

I floated in numbing emptiness, screaming, unable to hear myself. When I clasped my hands together, I felt nothing, even when I dug in my nails. Opening my mouth, I sucked in another breath to scream again but felt no sensation of air moving over my tongue or filling my lungs. I *knew* that I did it. I willed my muscles to move and believed that they responded. But I could feel nothing.

Nothing but the terrible cold. It was bitter enough to be painful, or would have been if I could feel pain. If I had been able to stand, I might have fallen to the ground, too cold to do anything but shiver. If only there had been ground.

The mortal mind is not built for such things. I did not miss sight, but touch? Sound? Smell? I was used to those. I *needed* those. Was this how other people felt about blindness? No wonder they feared it so.

I contemplated going mad.

*   *   *

"Ree-child," says my father, taking my hands. "Don't rely on your magic. I know the temptation will be there. It's good to see, isn't it?"

I nod. He smiles.

"But the power comes from inside you," he goes on. He opens one of my small hands and traces the whorling print of one fingertip. It tickles and I laugh. "If you use a lot of it, you'll get tired. If you use it all ... Ree-child, you could die."

I frown in puzzlement. "It's just magic." Magic is light, color. Magic is a beautiful song—wonderful, but not a necessity of life. Not like food or water, or sleep, or blood.

"Yes. But it's also part of you. An important part." He smiles, and for the first time, I see how deeply the sadness has permeated him today. He seems lonely. "You have to understand. We're not like other people."

*   *   *

I cried out with my voice and my thoughts. Gods can hear the latter if a mortal concentrates hard enough—it's how they hear prayers. There was no reply from Madding, or anyone else. Though I groped around, my hands encountered nothing. Even if he'd been there, right beside me, would I have known? I had no idea. I was so afraid.

*   *   *

"Feel," says my father, guiding my hand. I hold a fat horsehair brush tipped with paint that stinks like vinegar. "Taste the scent on the air. Listen to the scrape of the brush. Then believe.*"*

"Believe . . . what?"

"What you expect to happen. What you want to exist. If you don't control it, it will control you, Ree-child. Never forget that."

*   *   *

I should have stayed in the house I should have left the city I should have seen the previt coming I should have left Shiny in the muck where I found him I should have stayed in Nimaro and never left.

*   *   *

"The paint is a door," my father says.

*   *   *

I put out my hands and imagined that they shook.

*   *   *

"A door?" I ask.

"Yes. The power is in you, hidden, but the paint opens the way to that power, allowing you to bring some of it out onto the canvas. Or anywhere else you want to put it. As you grow older, you'll find new ways to open the door. Painting is just the first method you've found."

"Oh." I consider this. "Does that mean I could sing my magic, like you?"

"Maybe. Do you like singing?"

"Not like I like painting. And my voice doesn't sound good like yours."

He chuckles. "I like your voice."

"You like everything I do, Papa." But my thoughts are turning, fascinated with the idea. "Does that mean I can do something besides make paintings? Like . . ." My child's imagination cannot fathom the possibilities of magic. There are no godlings in the world yet to show us what it can do. "Like turn a bunny into a bee? Or make flowers bloom?"

He is silent for a moment, and I sense his reluctance. He has never lied to me, not even when I ask questions he would rather not answer.

"I don't know," he says at last. "Sometimes when I sing, if I believe something will happen, it happens. And sometimes"—he hesitates, abruptly looks uneasy—"sometimes when I don't sing, it happens, too. The song is the door, but belief is the key that unlocks it."

I touch his face, trying to understand his discomfort. "What is it, Papa?"

He catches my hand and kisses it and smiles, but I have already felt it. He is, just a little, afraid. "Well, just think. What if you took a man and believed he was a rock? Something alive that you believed was something dead?"

I try to think about this, but I am too young. It sounds fun to me. He sighs and smiles and pats my hands.

*   *   *

I put out my hands, closed my eyes, and *believed* a world into being.

My hands ached to feel, and so I imagined thick, loamy soil. My feet ached to stand, so I put that soil under them, solid, hollow sounding when I stomped because of the air and life teeming within it. My lungs ached to breathe, and I inhaled air that was slightly cool, moist with dew. I breathed out and the warmth of my breath made vapor in the air. I could not see that, but I *believed* it was there. Just as I knew there would be light around me, as my mother had once described—misty morning light, from a pale, early-spring sun.

The darkness lingered, resistant.

Sun. *Sun.* SUN.

Warmth danced along my skin, driving away the aching cold. I sat back on my knees, drawing deep breaths and smelling fresh-turned dirt and feeling the glaze of light against my closed eyelids. I needed to hear something, so I decided there would be wind. A light morning breeze, gradually dispelling the fog. When the breeze came, stirring my hair to tickle my neck, I did not let myself feel amazement. That would lead to doubt. I could feel the fragility of the place around me, its inclination to be *something else.* Cold, endless dark—

"No," I said quickly, and was pleased to hear my own voice. There was air now to carry it. "Warm *spring* air. A garden ready to be planted. Stay here."

The world stayed. So I opened my eyes.

I could see.

And strangely, the scene around me was familiar. I sat in the terrace garden of my home village, where I had almost always been completely blind. Not much magic in Nimaro. The only time I had ever seen the village had been—

—the day my father died. The day of the Gray Lady's birth. I had seen everything then.

I had re-created that day now, falling back on the memory of that single, magic-infused glimpse. Silvery midmorning mists shivered in the air. I remembered that the big, boxy shape on the other side of the garden was a *house*, though I could not tell if it was mine or the neighbors' without smelling it or counting my steps. Prickly things near my feet danced in the breeze: *grass*. I had rebuilt everything.

Except people. I got to my feet, listening. In all my years in the village, I had never heard it so silent at this time of day. There were always small noises—birds, backyard goats, some-body's newborn fussing. Here there was nothing.

Like ripples in water, I felt the space around me tremble.

"It's home," I whispered. "It's home. Just early; nobody else is up yet. It's real."

The ripples ceased.

Real, yet terribly fragile. I was still in the dark place. All I'd done was create a sphere of sanity around myself, like a bubble. I would have to continue affirming its reality, believing in it, to keep it intact.

Trembling, I dropped to my knees again, pushing my fingers into the moist soil. Yes, that was better. Concentrate on the small things, the mundanities. I lifted a handful of earth to my nose, inhaled. My eyes could not be trusted, but the rest—yes. That I could do.

But I was tired suddenly, more tired than I should have been. As I squeezed the clod of dirt, I found my head nodding, my eyelids heavy. I hadn't slept much, but that did not account for this. I was in a strange place, scared out of my mind. Fear alone should have had me too tense to sleep.

Before I could fathom this new mystery, there was another of those curious rippling shivers—and then agony sizzled behind my eyes. I cried out, arching backward and clapping dirty hands to my face, my concentration broken. Even as I screamed, I felt the false Nimaro bubble shatter around me, spinning away into nothingness as the sickening, empty dark rushed in.

And then—

I landed on my side on a solid surface, hard enough that the breath was jarred from my body.

"Well, here you are," said a cool, male voice. Familiar, but I could not think. Hands touched me, turning me over and pushing my hair from my face. I tried to jerk away, but that jarred the racheting agony in my eyes, my head. I was too tired to scream.

"Is she all right?" That was a woman's voice, somewhere beyond the man.

"I'm not certain."

The words felt like godwords, slapping my ears. I clapped my hands over my ears and moaned, wishing they would all just be silent.

"This isn't the usual disorientation."

"Mmm, no. I think it's some effect of her own magic. She used it to protect herself from my power. Fascinating." He turned away from me, and I felt his smugness like a scrim of filth along my skin. "Your proof."

"Indeed." She sounded pleased as well.

At that point I passed out.

8

"Light Reveals"
(encaustic on canvas)

I AWOKE SLOWLY, and in some pain.

I was lying down. Heavy blankets covered me, soft linen and scratchy wool. I listened for a while, breathing, assessing. I was in a smallish room; my breath sounded close, though not claustrophobically so. It smelled of spent candlewax, dust, me, and the World Tree.

The lattermost scent was *very* strong, stronger than I'd ever known the Tree to smell. The air was laden with its distinctive wood resins and the bright sharp greenscent of its foliage. The Tree did not lose its leaves in autumn—a fact for which we in the city below were deeply grateful—but it did shed damaged leaves whenever they occurred, and it replaced those just before the spring flowering. It tended to smell more strongly during that time, but for the scent to be *this* strong, I had to be closer than usual.

That was not the only unusual thing. I sat up slowly, wincing as I discovered that my whole left arm was sore. I examined it and found fresh bruises there, and also on my hip and ankle. My throat was so scratchy that it hurt when I tried to clear it. And my head ached dully in a single area, from the middle of my scalp right down into my head and forward to press against my eyes—

Then I remembered. The empty place. My false Nimaro. Shattering, falling, voices. *Madding*.

Where the hells was I?

The room was cool, though I could feel watery sunlight coming from my left. I shivered a little as I got out of the warm blankets, though I was wearing clothing—a simple sleeveless shift, loose drawstring pants. Comfortable, if not the best fit. There were slippers beside the cot, which I avoided for the moment. Easier to feel the floor if I left my feet bare.

I explored the room and discovered that I had been imprisoned.

As prisons went, it was nice. The cot had been soft and comfortable, the small table and chairs were well made, and there were thick rugs covering much of the wooden floor. A tiny room off the main one contained a toilet and a sink. Yet the door I found was solidly locked, and there was no keyhole on my side. The windows were unbarred but sealed shut. The glass was thick and heavy; I would not be able to break through it easily, and certainly not without making a great deal of noise.

And the air felt strange. Not as humid as I was used to. Thinner, somehow. Sounds did not carry as well. I clapped experimentally, but the echoes came back all wrong.

I jumped when the door's lock turned, right on the heels of my thought. I was by the windows, so their solidity was suddenly comforting to me as I backed against them.

"Ah, you're awake at last," said a male voice I had never heard before. "Conveniently when I come to check on you myself, rather than sending an initiate. Hello."

Senmite, but no city accent I was familiar with. In fact, he sounded like someone rich, his every enunciation precise, his language formal. I couldn't tell more than that, since I didn't talk to many rich people.

"Hello," I said, or tried to say. My abused throat—from screaming in the empty place, I remembered now—let out a rusty squeak, and it hurt badly enough that I grimaced.

"Perhaps you shouldn't talk." The door closed behind him. Someone outside locked it. I jumped again at the sound of the latch. "Please, Eru Shoth, I mean you no harm. I imagine I can guess most of your questions, so if you'll sit down, I'll explain things."

Eru Shoth? It had been so long since I'd heard the honorific that for a moment I didn't recognize it. A Maro term of respect for a young woman. I was a bit old for it—generally it was used for girls under twenty—but that was all right; maybe he meant to flatter me. He didn't sound Maro, however.

He waited where he was, patiently, until I finally moved to sit down on one of the chairs.

"That's better," he said, moving past me. Measured steps, solid but graceful. A large man, though not as large as Shiny. Old enough to know his body. He smelled of paper and fine cloth, and a bit of leather.

"Now. My name is Hado. I'm responsible for all new arrivals here, which for the moment consists solely of you and your friends. 'Here,' if you're wondering, is the House of the Risen Sun. Have you heard of it?"

I frowned. The newly risen sun was one of the symbols of the Bright Father but was little used these days, since it was easily confused with the dawning sun of the Gray Lady. I had not heard anyone refer to the risen sun since my childhood, back in Nimaro.

"White Hall?" I rasped.

"No, not exactly, though our purpose is also votive. And we, too, honor the Bright Lord—though not in the same manner as the Order of Itempas. Perhaps you've heard the term used for our members instead: we are known as the New Lights."

That one I did know. But that made even less sense; what did a heretic cult want with me?

Hado had said he could guess my questions, but if he guessed that one, he chose not to address it. "You and your friends are to be our guests, Eru Shoth. May I call you Oree?"

Guest, hells. I set my jaw, waiting for him to get to the point.

He seemed amused by my silence, shifting to lean against the table. "Indeed, we have decided to welcome you among us as one of our initiates—our term for a new member. You'll be introduced to our doctrines, our customs, our whole way of life. Nothing will be hidden from you. Indeed, it is our hope that you will find enlightenment with us, and rise within our ranks as a true believer."

This time I turned my face toward him. I had learned that doing this drove the point home for seeing people. "No."

He let out a gentle, untroubled sigh. "It may take you some time to get used to the idea, of course."

"*No.*" I clenched my fists in my lap and forced the words out, despite the agony of speaking. "Where are my friends?"

There was a pause.

"The mortals who were brought here with you are also being inducted into our organization. Not the godlings, of course."

I swallowed, both to wet my throat and to push down a sudden queasy fear in my belly. There was no way they had managed to bring Madding and his siblings here against their will. No way. "What about the godlings?"

Another of those telling, damning pauses. "Their fate is for our leaders to decide."

I tried to figure out whether he was lying. These were godlings I was worrying about, not mortals. I had never heard of mortal magic that could hold a godling prisoner.

But Madding had not come for me, and that meant he could not, for some reason. I *had* heard of godlings using mortals as a cover for their own machinations. Perhaps that was what was happening here—some rival of Madding's, moving to take over the godsblood trade. Or perhaps another godling had taken the commission that Lady Nemmer had declined.

If either were true, though, wouldn't only Madding have been targeted, and not his whole crew?

Just then, there was a strange movement beneath my feet, like a shiver of the floor. It rippled through the walls, not so much audible as palpable. It was as if the whole room had taken a momentary chill. One of the thick windows even rattled faintly in its frame before going still.

"Where are we?" I rasped.

"The House is attached to the trunk of the World Tree. The Tree sways slightly now and again. Nothing to be concerned about."

Dearest gods.

I'd heard rumors that some of the wealthiest folk in the city—heads of merchant cartels, nobility, and the like—had begun to build homes onto the Tree's trunk. It cost a fortune, in part because the Arameri had laid down strict requirements for aesthetics, safety, and the health of the Tree, and in part because no one with the gall to build onto the Tree would bother building a *small* house.

That a group of heretics could command such resources was incredible. That they had the power to capture and hold half a dozen godlings against their will was impossible.

These aren't ordinary people, I realized with a chill. *This is more than money; it's power too. Magical, political—everything.*

The only people in the world with that kind of power were Arameri.

"Now, I see that you're still not feeling well—not well enough to carry on a conversation, anyhow." Hado straightened, coming over to me. I flinched when I felt his fingers touch my left temple, where I was surprised to realize I had another bruise. "Better," he said, "but I think I'll recommend that you be given another day to rest. I'll have someone bring you dinner here, then take you to the baths. When you've healed more, the Nypri would like to examine you."

Yes, I remembered now. After my false Nimaro had shattered, I had been brought out of the empty place somehow. I had fallen to the floor, hard. The ache in my eyes, though—that was more familiar. I had felt the same at Madding's after I'd used magic to kill the Order-Keepers at the park.

Then I registered what Hado had said. "Nypri?" It sounded like some sort of title. "Your leader?"

"One of our leaders, yes. His role is more specific, however; he's an expert scrivener. And he's very interested in your unique magical abilities. Most likely he'll request a demonstration."

The blood drained out of my face. They knew about my magic. How? It did not matter; they knew.

"Don't want to," I said. My voice was very small, not just because of the soreness.

Hado's hand was still on my temple. He moved it down and patted my cheek, twice, in a patronizing sort of way. Both slaps were just a little too hard to be comforting, and then his hand lingered on me, an implicit warning.

"Don't be foolish," he said very softly. "You're a good Maroneh girl, aren't you? We are all true Itempans here, Oree. Why wouldn't you want to join us?"

The Arameri had ruled the world for thousands of years. In that time, they had imposed the Bright on every continent, every kingdom, every race. Those who'd worshipped other gods were given a simple command: convert. Those who disobeyed were annihilated, their names and works forgotten. True Itempans believed in one way—their way.

How like Shiny, a small, bitter voice whispered in me before I forced it silent.

Hado chuckled again, but this time he stroked my cheek approvingly at my silence. It still stung.

"You'll do well here, I see," he said.

With that, he went to the door and knocked. Someone let him out and locked the door again behind him. I sat where I was for a long while after, with my hand on my cheek.

* * *

Wordless people entered my room twice the next day, bringing me a light Amn-style breakfast and soup for lunch. I spoke to the second one—my voice was better—asking where Madding and the others were. The person did not answer. No one else appeared in the interim, so I listened at the door awhile, trying to determine whether there were guards outside and whether there was any pattern to the movement I could hear in the halls beyond. My chances of escaping—alone, from a house full of fanatics, without even a stick to help me find my way—were slim, but that was no reason not to try.

I was fiddling with the thick-glassed window when the door opened behind me and someone small came in. I straightened without guilt. They weren't stupid. They expected me to try and escape, at least for the first few days or so. True Itempans were nothing if not rational.

"My name is Jont," said a young woman, surprising me by speaking. She sounded younger than me, maybe in her teens. There was something about her voice that suggested innocence, or maybe enthusiasm. "You're Oree."

"Yes," I said. She had not given a family name, I noticed. Neither had Hado, the night before. So neither did I—a small, safe battle. "I'm pleased to meet you." My throat felt better, thank the gods.

She seemed pleased by my attempt at politeness. "The Master of Initiates—Master Hado, whom you met—says I'm to give you anything you need," she said. "I can take you to the baths now, and I've brought some fresh clothing." There was the faint *pluff* of a pile of cloth being deposited. "Nothing fancy, I'm afraid. We live simply here."

"I see," I said. "You're an . . . initiate, too?"

"Yes." She came closer, and I guessed that she was staring at my eyes. "Was that a guess, or did you sense it somehow? I've heard that blind people can pick up on things normal people can't."

I tried not to sigh. "It was a guess."

"Oh." She sounded disappointed but recovered quickly. "You're feeling better today, I see. You slept for two whole days after they brought you out of the Empty."

"Two days?" But something else caught my attention. "The Empty?"

"The place our Nypri sends the worst blasphemers against the Bright," Jont said. She had dropped her voice, her tone full of dread. "Is it as terrible as they say?"

"You mean that place beyond the holes." I remembered being unable to breathe, unable to scream. "It was terrible," I said softly.

"Then it's fortunate the Nypri was merciful. What did you do?"

"Do?"

"To cause him to put you there."

At this, fury lanced down my spine. "I did nothing. I was with my friends when this Nypri of yours attacked us. I was *kidnapped* and brought here against my will. And my friends . . ." I almost choked as I realized. "For all I know, they're still in that awful place."

To my surprise, Jont made a compassionate sound and patted my hand. "It's all right. If they aren't blasphemers, he'll bring them out before too much harm is done. Now. Shall we go to the baths?"

Jont took my arm to lead me while I shuffled along, moving

slowly since I had no walking stick to help me gauge floor obstacles. Meanwhile, I mulled over the tidbits of information Jont had tossed at my feet. They might call their new members initiates instead of Order-Keepers, and they might use strange magic, but in every other way, these New Lights seemed much like the Order of Itempas—right down to the same high-handed ways.

Which made me wonder why the Order hadn't yet broken them up. It was one thing to permit the worship of godlings; there was a certain pragmatism in that. But another faith dedicated to Bright Itempas? That was messy. Confusing to the layfolk. What if the Lights began to build their own White Halls, collect their own offerings, deploy their own Order-Keepers? That would violate every tenet of the Bright. The Lights' very existence invited chaos.

What made even less sense was that the Arameri allowed it. Their clan's founder, Shahar Arameri, had once been His most favored priestess; the Order was their mouthpiece. I could not see how it benefitted them to allow a rival voice to exist.

Then a thought: *maybe the Arameri don't know.*

I was distracted from this when we entered an open room filled with warm humidity and the sound of water. The bath chamber.

"Do you wash first?" Jont asked. She guided me to a washing area; I could smell the soap. "I don't know anything about Maro customs."

"Not very different from Amn," I said, wondering why she cared. I explored and found a shelf bearing soap, fresh sponges, and a wide bowl of steaming water. Hot—a treat. I pulled off my clothes and draped them over the rack I found along the shelf's edge, then sat down to scrub myself. "We're Senmite, too, after all."

"Since the Nightlord destroyed the Maroland," she said, and then gasped. "Oh, darkness—I'm sorry."

"Why?" I shrugged, putting down the sponge. "Mentioning it won't make it happen again." I found a flask beside it, which I opened and sniffed. Shampoo. Astringent, not ideal for Maroneh hair, but it would have to do.

"Well, yes, but...to remind you of such a horror..."

"It happened to my ancestors, not to me. I don't forget—we never forget—but there's more to the Maroneh than some long-ago tragedy." I rinsed myself with the bowl and sighed, turning to her. "Which way is the soak?"

She took my hand again and led me to a huge wooden tub. The bottom was metal, heated by a fire underneath. I had to use steps built into the side to climb in. The water was cooler than I liked, and unscented, though at least it smelled clean. Madding's pools had always been just right—

Enough of that, I told myself sharply as my eyes stung with the warning of tears. *You can't do him any good if you don't figure out how to get out of here.*

Jont came with me, leaning against the side of the tub. I wished she would go away, but I supposed part of her role was to act as my guard as well as my guide.

"The Maroneh have always honored Itempas first among the Three, just like we Amn," she said. "You don't worship any of the lesser gods. Isn't that right?"

Her phrasing warned me immediately. I had met her type before. Not all mortals were happy that the godlings had come. I had never understood their thinking, because—until recently—I had assumed Bright Itempas had changed His mind about the Interdiction; I thought He'd *wanted* His children in the mortal realm. Of course, more devout Itempans would realize it before I, lapsed as I was. The Bright Lord did not change His mind.

"Worship the godlings?" I refused to use her phrasing. "No. I've met a number of them, though, and some of them I even call friend." Madding. Paitya. Nemmer, maybe. Kitr—well, no, she didn't like me. Definitely not Lil.

Shiny? Yes, I had once called him friend, though the quiet goddess had been right; he would not say the same of me.

I could almost hear Jont's face screwing up in consternation. "But...they're not human." She said it the way one would describe an insect, or an animal.

"What does that matter?"

"They're not like us. They can't understand us. They're dangerous."

I leaned against the tub's edge and began to plait my wet hair. "Have you ever talked to one of them?"

"Of course not!" She sounded horrified by the idea.

I started to say more, then stopped. If she couldn't see gods as people—she barely saw *me* as a person—then nothing I could say would make a difference. That made me realize something, however. "Does your Nypri feel the way you do about godlings? Is that why he dragged my friends into that Empty place?"

Jont caught her breath. "Your friends are *godlings?*" At once her voice hardened. "Then, yes, that's why. And the Nypri won't be letting *them* out anytime soon."

I fell silent, too revolted to think of anything to say. After a moment, Jont sighed. "I didn't mean to upset you. Please, are you finished? We have a lot to do."

"I don't think I want to do anything you have in mind," I said as coldly as I could.

She touched my shoulder and said something that would keep me from ever seeing her as innocent again: "You will."

I got out of the tub and dried myself, shivering from more than the cold air.

When I was dry and wrapped in a thick robe, she led me back to my room, where I dressed in the garments she'd brought: a simple pullover shirt and an ankle-length skirt that swirled nicely about my ankles. The undergarments were generic and loose, not a complete fit but close enough. Shoes too—soft slippers meant for indoor wear. A subtle reminder that my captors had no intention of letting me go outside.

"That's better," said Jont when I was done, sounding pleased. "You look like one of us now."

I touched the hem of the shirt. "I take it these are white."

"Beige. We don't wear white. White is the color of false purity, misleading to those who would otherwise seek the Light." There was a singsong intonation to the way Jont said this that made me think she was reciting something. It was no teaching poem I'd ever heard, in White Hall or elsewhere.

On the heels of this, a heavy bell sounded somewhere in the House. Its resonant tone was beautiful; I closed my eyes in inadvertent pleasure.

"The dinner hour," Jont said. "I got you ready just in time. Our leaders have asked you to dine with them this evening."

Trepidation filled me. "I don't suppose I could pass? I'm still a bit tired."

Jont took my hand again. "I'm sorry. It's not far."

So I followed her through what felt like an endless maze of hallways. We passed other members of the New Lights (Jont greeted most of them but did not pause to introduce me), but I paid little attention to them beyond realizing that the organiza-tion was much, much larger than I'd initially assumed. I noted a dozen people just in the corridor beyond my room. But instead of listening to them, I counted my paces as we walked so that I could find my way faster if I ever managed to escape the room. We moved from a corridor that smelled like varsmusk incense to another that sounded as though it had open windows along its length, letting in the late-evening air. Down two flights of stairs (twenty-four steps), around a corner (right), and across an open space (straight ahead, thirty-degree angle from the cor-ner), we came to a much larger enclosed space.

Here there were many people all around us, but most of the voices seemed to be below head level. Seated, maybe. I had been smelling food for some time, mingled with the scents of lanterns and people and the omnipresent green of the Tree. I guessed it was a huge dining hall.

"Jont." An older woman's contralto, soft and compelling. And there was a scent, like hiras blossoms, that also caught my atten-tion because it reminded me of Madding's house. We stopped. "I'll escort her from here. Eru Shoth? Will you come with me?"

"Lady Serymn!" Jont sounded flustered and alarmed and excited all at once. "O-of course." She let go of me, and another hand took mine.

"We've been expecting you," the woman said. "There's a private dining room this way. I'll warn you if there are steps."

"All right," I said, grateful. Jont had not done this, and I'd stubbed my toe twice already. As we walked, I pondered this new enigma.

Lady Serymn, Jont had called her. Not a godling, certainly, not among these godling haters. A noblewoman, then. Yet her name was Amn, one of those tongue-tangling combinations of consonants they so favored; the Amn had no nobility, except— But, no, that was impossible.

We passed through a wide doorway into a smaller, quieter space, and suddenly I had new things to distract me, namely the scent of food. Roasted fowl, shellfish of some kind, greens and garlic, wine sauce, other scents that I could not identify. Rich people's food. When Serymn guided me to the table where this feast lay, I belatedly realized there were others already seated around it. I'd been so fascinated with the food that I'd barely noticed them.

I sat among these strangers, before their luxurious feast, and tried not to show my nervousness.

A servant came near and began preparing my plate. "Would you like duck, Lady Oree?"

"Yes," I said politely, and then registered the title. "But it's just Oree. Not 'Lady' anything."

"You undervalue yourself," said Serymn. She sat to my right, perpendicular to me. There were at least seven others around the table; I could hear them murmuring to each other. The table was either rectangular or oval-shaped, and Serymn sat at its head. Someone else sat at the other end, across from her.

"It is appropriate for us to call you Lady," Serymn said. "Please allow us to show you that courtesy."

"But I'm *not*," I said, confused. "There isn't a drop of noble blood in me. Nimaro doesn't have a noble family; they were wiped out with the Maroland."

"I suppose that's as good an opening as any to explain why we've brought you here," Serymn said. "Since I'm certain you've wondered."

"You might say so," I said, annoyed. "Hado..." I hesitated. "*Master* Hado told me a little, but not enough."

There were a few chuckles from my companions, including two low, male voices from the far end of the table. I recognized one of them and flushed: Hado.

Serymn sounded amused as well. "What we honor is not your wealth or status, Lady Oree, but your lineage."

"My lineage is like the rest of me—common," I snapped. "My father was a carpenter; my mother grew and sold medicinal herbs. *Their* parents were farmers. There's nobody fancier than a smuggler in my entire family tree."

"Allow me to explain." She paused to take a sip of wine, leaning forward, and as she did, I caught a glimmer from her direction. I turned to quickly peer at it, but whatever it was had been obscured somehow.

"How curious," said another of my table companions. "Most of the time she seems like an ordinary blind woman, not orienting her face toward anything in particular, but just now she seemed to *see* you, Serymn."

I kicked myself. It probably would've done no good to conceal my ability, but I still hated giving them information inadvertently.

"Yes," said Serymn. "Dateh did mention that she seems to have some perception where magic is concerned." She did something, and suddenly I got a clear look at what I'd glimpsed. It was a small, solid circle of golden, glowing magic. No—the circle was not solid at all. In spite of myself, I leaned closer, narrowing my eyes. The circle consisted of dozens upon dozens of tiny, closely written sigils of the gods' spiky language. Godwords. *Sentences* of them, a whole treatise's worth, spiraling and overlapping each other so densely that from a distance the circle looked solid.

Then I understood, and drew back in shock.

Serymn moved again, letting her hair fall back into place, I realized by the way the sigil-circle vanished. Yes, it would be on her forehead.

That can't be. It doesn't make sense. I don't believe it. But I had seen it with my own two magic eyes.

I licked my suddenly dry lips, folded my shaking hands in my lap, and mustered all my courage to speak. "What is an Arameri fullblood doing with some little heretic cult, Lady Serymn?"

The laughter that broke out around the table was not the reaction I'd been expecting. When it died down—I sat through it, uneasily silent—Serymn said in a voice that still rippled with amusement, "Please, Lady Oree, do eat. There's no reason we can't have a good conversation *and* enjoy a fine meal, is there?"

So I ate a few bites. Then I wiped my mouth using my best manners and sat up, making a point of waiting politely for an answer to my question.

Serymn uttered a soft sigh and wiped her own mouth. "Very well. I'm with this 'little heretic cult,' as you put it, because I have a goal to accomplish, and being here aids that purpose.

But I should point out that the New Lights are neither little, nor heretical, nor a cult."

"I was given to understand," I said slowly, "that any form of worship other than that sanctioned by the Order was heretical."

"Untrue, Lady Oree. By the law of the Bright—the law as set down by my family—only the worship of *gods other than Itempas* is heretical. The form in which we choose to worship is irrelevant. It's true that the Order would prefer that the two concepts—obedience to the Bright Lord, obedience to the Order—be synonymous." There was another soft roll of chuckles from our table companions. "But to put it bluntly, the Order is a mortal authority, not a godly one. We of the Lights merely recognize the distinction."

"So you think the form of worship you've chosen is better than that of the Order?"

"We do. Our organization's beliefs are fundamentally similar to those of the Order of Itempas—indeed, many of our members are former Order priests. But there are some significant differences."

"Such as?"

"Do you really want to get into a doctrinal discussion right now, Lady Oree?" Serymn asked. "You'll be introduced to our philosophy over the next few days, like any new initiate. I thought your questions would be more basic."

They were. Still, I felt instinctively that the key to understanding the whole heaping pile of fanatics lay in understanding this woman. This *Arameri*. The fullbloods were the highest members of a family so devoted to order that they ranked and sorted themselves by how closely they could trace their lineage back to First Priestess Shahar. They were the power brokers, the decision makers—and sometimes, through the might of their god-slaves, the annihilators of nations.

Yet that had been before ten years ago, that strange and terrible day when the World Tree had grown and the godlings returned. There had always been rumors, but I knew the truth now, from Shiny's own lips. The Arameri's slaves had broken free; the Nightlord and the Gray Lady had overthrown Bright Itempas. The Arameri, though far from powerless, had lost their greatest weapons and their patron in one stunning blow.

What happened when people who'd once possessed absolute power suddenly lost it?

"All right," I said carefully. "Basic questions. Why are you here, and why am *I*?"

"How much do you know of what happened ten years ago, Lady Oree?"

I hesitated, unsure. Was it safer to play the ignorant commoner, or reveal how much I knew? Would this Arameri woman have me killed if I told her family's secret? Or was it a test to see if I would lie?

I tore off a piece of bread, more out of nervousness than hunger. "I...I know there are three gods again," I said slowly. "I know Bright Itempas no longer rules alone."

"Try 'at all,' Lady Oree," Serymn said. "But you've guessed that, haven't you? All true followers of Itempas know He would never permit the changes that have occurred in the past few years."

I nodded, inadvertently thinking of Madding's bed, and our

lovemaking, and Shiny's glowering disapproval. "That's true," I said, suppressing a bitter smile.

"Then we must consider His siblings, these new gods..."

One of Serymn's companions let out a bark of laughter. "New? Come, now, Lady Serymn; we are not the gullible masses." She glanced at me, and I was not fooled by the sweetness in her tone. "Most of us, anyhow."

I set my jaw, refusing to be baited. Serymn took this with remarkable equanimity, I thought; I wouldn't have expected an Arameri to brook much in the way of ridicule, even if most of it had been at someone else's expense.

"Granted, 'the Lord of Shadows' was a feeble attempt at diversion," she replied, then returned her attention to me. "But my family has had its hands full trying to prevent a panic, Lady Oree. After all, we spent centuries filling mortal hearts with terror at the prospect of the Nightlord's release. Better that we should keep him leashed than he break loose and wreak his vengeance upon the world; that was how it went. Now only a few feeble lies keep the populace from realizing we could *all* go the way of the Maro."

She referred to the destruction of my people—her family's fault—with neither rancor nor shame, and it made me seethe. But that was how Arameri were: they shrugged off their errors, when they could even be persuaded to admit them.

"He's angry," I said. Softly, because so was I. "The Nightlord. You know that, don't you? He has given a deadline for the Arameri and the godlings to find his children's killers."

"Yes," said Serymn. "That message was delivered to the Lord

Arameri several days ago, I'm told. One month, from Role's death. That leaves us approximately three weeks."

She spoke like it was nothing, a god's wrath. My hands fisted in my lap. "The Nightlord was *bored* when he destroyed the Maroland. He didn't even have his full power at the time. Can you even imagine what he'll do now?"

"Better than you can, Lady Oree." Serymn spoke very softly. "I grew up with him, remember."

The table fell silent. A clock somewhere in the room ticked loudly. All of us could hear the untold tales in her inflectionless tone—and then there was the biggest tale, lurking beneath the surface of the conversation like some leviathan: *why had a woman so powerful, so apparently fearless, fled from Sky in the first place?* And now, imagining horrors in the ticking stillness, I could not help wondering, *What the hells did the Nightlord do to her?*

"Fortunately," said Serymn at last, and I exhaled in relief when the silence broke, "his anger fits well into our plans."

I must have frowned, because she laughed. It sounded forced, though only a little.

"Consider, Lady Oree, that we have been saved once already by the third member of the Three. Consider what that means— what her presence means. Have you never wondered? Enefa of the Twilight, sister of Bright Itempas, has been dead for two thousand years. Who, then, is this Gray Lady? You're acquainted with many of the city's godlings. Did they explain this mystery to you?"

I blinked in surprise as I realized Madding had not. He had spoken of his mother's death, grief still thick in his voice. But he had also spoken of his parents, plural and present. It was just one of those contradictions that one had to accept when dealing with gods; it hadn't bothered me because I hadn't thought it was important. But then, until recently, I thought I'd understood the hierarchy of the gods.

"No," I said. "He—they never told me."

"Hmm. Then I will tell you a great secret, Lady Oree. Ten years ago, a mortal woman betrayed her god and her humanity by conspiring to set the Nightlord—her lover—free. She succeeded, and for her efforts was rewarded with the lost power of Enefa. She became, in effect, a *new* Enefa, a goddess in her own right."

I caught my breath in inadvertent surprise. I had never realized it was possible for a mortal to become a god. But that explained a great deal. The restrictions on the godlings, confining them within the city of Shadow; why the godlings so carefully policed each other to prevent mass destruction. A goddess who had once been mortal herself might take exception to the callous disregard for mortal life.

"The Gray Lady is irrelevant to us," Serymn said, "beyond the fact that we have her to thank for the current peace." She leaned forward, resting her elbows on the table. "We're counting on her intervention, in fact. Enefa—of whom this new goddess is essentially a copy—has always fought for the preservation of life. That is her nature; where her brothers are more extreme—quick to judge and quicker to wreak havoc—she *maintains*. She adapts to change and seeks stability within it. The Gods' War was not the first time Itempas and Nahadoth had fought, after all. It was simply the first time they'd done it, since the creation of life, without Enefa around to keep the world in balance."

I was shaking my head. "You mean you're counting on this new Enefa to keep us safe? Are you kidding? Even if she used to be human, she's not anymore. Now she thinks like any other god." I thought of Lil. "And some of them are crazy."

"If she'd wanted all humanity dead, she could have done it herself, many times over, during the past ten years." The table shifted slightly as Serymn made some gesture. "She is the goddess of death as well as life. And, please remember, when she was mortal, she was Arameri. We have always been predictable." I heard her smile. "I believe she will seek to channel the Nightlord's rage in the most expedient manner. He need not destroy the whole world, after all, to avenge his children. Just a part of it will do. A single city, perhaps."

I put my hands in my lap, my appetite gone.

Maroneh parents do not tell comforting bedtime tales. Just as we name our children for sorrow and rage, we also tell them stories that will make them cry and awaken in the night, shivering with nightmares. We *want* our children to be afraid and to never forget, because that way they will be prepared if the Nightlord should ever come again.

As he would soon come to Shadow.

"Why has the Order of Itempas..." I faltered, unsure of how to say it without offending a room full of former Order members. "The Nightlord. Why honor him just because he's free? He already hates us. Do they actually think an angry god would be deterred by that kind of hypocrisy?"

"The gods aren't who they're trying to deter, Lady Oree." This came from the man at the table's far end. I stiffened. "It's *us* they hope to appease."

I knew that voice. I had heard it before—three times, now. At the south promenade, just before I'd killed the Order-Keepers. On Madding's rooftop before all chaos had broken loose. And later, as I'd lain shivering and sick after my release from the Empty.

He sat at the far end of the table, opposite Serymn, radiating the same easy confidence as she. Of course he did; he was their Nypri.

As I sat there, trembling with fear and fury, Serymn chuckled. "Blunt as ever, Dateh."

"It's only the truth." He sounded amused.

"Hmm. What my husband means to say, Lady Oree, is that the Order, and through it the Arameri family, desperately hopes to convince the rest of mortalkind that the world is as it should be. That despite the presence of all our new gods, nothing *else* should change—politically speaking. That we should feel happy...safe...complacent."

Husband. An Arameri fullblood married to a heretic cultist?

"You're not making any sense," I said. I focused on the fork in my fingers, on the crackle of the dining room's fireplace in the background. Those helped me stay calm. "You're talking about the Arameri as if you're not one of them."

"Indeed. Let's just say that my activities aren't sanctioned by the rest of my family."

The Nypri sounded amused. "Oh, they might approve—if they knew."

Serymn laughed at this, as did others around the table. "Do you really think so? You're far more of an optimist than I, my love."

They bantered while I sat there, trying to make sense of nobility and conspiracy and a thousand other things that had never been a part of my life. I was just a street artist. Just an ordinary Maroneh, frightened and far from home.

"I don't understand," I said finally, interrupting them. "You've kidnapped me, brought me here. You're trying to force me to join you. What does all this—the Nightlord, the Order, the Arameri—have to do with *me*?"

"More than you realize," said the Nypri. "The world is in great danger at the moment—not just from the Nightlord's wrath. Consider: for the first time in centuries, the Arameri are vulnerable. Oh, they still have immense political and financial strength, and they're building an army that will make any rebel nation think twice. But *they can be defeated now*. Do you know what that means?"

"That someday we might have a different group of tyrants in charge?" Despite my efforts to be polite, I was growing annoyed. They kept talking in circles, never answering my questions.

Serymn seemed unoffended. "Perhaps—but which group? *Every* noble clan and ruling council and elected minister will want the chance to rule the Hundred Thousand Kingdoms. And if they all strive for it at once, what do you think will happen?"

"More scandals and intrigues and assassinations and whatever else you people do with your time," I said. Lady Nemmer would be pleased, at least.

"Yes. And coups, as weak nobles are replaced by stronger or more ambitious ones. And rebellions within those lands, as minority factions jostle for a share. And new alliances as smaller kingdoms band together for strength. And betrayals, because every alliance has a few." Serymn let out a long, weary sigh. "War, Lady Oree. There will be war."

Like the good Itempan girl I had never quite been, I nevertheless flinched. War was anathema to Bright Itempas. I had heard tales of the time before the Bright, before the Arameri had made laws to strictly regulate violence and conflict. In the old days, thousands had died in every battle. Cities had been razed to the ground, their inhabitants slaughtered as armies of warriors descended upon helpless civilians to rape and kill.

"Wh-where?" I asked.

"Everywhere."

I could not imagine it. Not on such a scale. It was madness. Chaos.

Then I remembered. Nahadoth, the Lord of Night, was also the god of chaos. What more fitting vengeance could he wreak upon humanity?

"If the Arameri fall and the Bright ends, war returns," Serymn said. "The Order of Itempas fears this more than any threat the gods pose, because it is the greater danger—not just to a city, but to our entire civilization. Already there are rumors of unrest in High North and on the islands—those lands that were forcibly converted to the worship of Itempas after the Gods' War. They have never forgotten, or forgiven, what we did to them."

"High Northers," said someone else at the table, in a tone of scorn. "Darkling barbarians! Two thousand years and they're still angry."

"Barbarians, yes, and angry," said Hado, whom I had forgotten was there. "But did we not feel the same anger when we were told to start worshipping the Nightlord?" There were grumbles of assent from around the table.

"Yes," said the Nypri. "So the Order permits heresy and looks the other way when Itempas's former faithful scorn their duties. They hope the exploration of new faiths will occupy the people and grant the Arameri time to prepare for the conflagration to come."

"But it's pointless," said Serymn, a note of anger in her voice. "T'vril, the Lord Arameri, hopes to put down the war swiftly when it comes. But to prepare for earthly war, he's taken his eyes off the threat in the heavens."

I sighed, weary in more ways than one. "That's a fine thing to concern yourself with, but the Nightlord is"—I spread my hands helplessly—"a force of nature. Maybe we should all start praying to this Gray Lady, since you say she's the one keeping him in line. Or maybe we should just start picking out our personal heavens in the afterlife now."

Serymn's tone chided me gently. "We prefer to be more proactive, Lady Oree. Perhaps it's the Arameri in me, but I'm not fond of allowing a known threat to fester unchecked. Better to strike first."

"Strike?" I chuckled, certain I was misunderstanding. "What, a god? That isn't possible."

"Yes, Lady Oree, it is. It's been done before, after all."

I froze, the smile falling from my face. "The godling Role. *You* killed her."

Serymn laughed noncommittally. "I was referring to the Gods' War, actually. Itempas Skyfather killed Enefa; if one of the Three can die, they all can."

I fell silent in confusion, but I wasn't laughing, not any longer. Serymn wasn't a fool. I did not believe an Arameri would hint at something like a goddess's murder unless she had the power to do it.

"Which, to come to the point at last, is why we kidnapped you." Serymn lifted her glass to me, the faint crystalline sound as loud as a bell in the room's silence. Our dining companions had fallen silent, hanging on her every word. When she saluted them, they lifted their glasses in return.

"To the return of the Bright," said the Nypri.

"And the White Lord," said the woman who had commented on my sight.

"'Til darkness ends," said Hado.

And other affirmations, from each person at the table. It had the feel of a solemn ritual—as they all committed themselves to a course of stunning, absolute insanity.

When they had all said their piece and fallen silent, I spoke, my voice hollow with realization and disbelief.

"You want to kill the Nightlord," I said.

"Yes," she said. She paused as another servant came over. I heard the cover being lifted from some sort of tray. "And we want you to help us do it. Dessert?"

9

"Seduction"
(charcoal)

THERE WAS NO FURTHER TALK of gods or insane plots after dinner. I was too stunned to think of further questions, and even if I had asked, Serymn made it clear she would answer no more. "I think we've spoken enough for tonight," she said, and then she'd laughed a rich, perfectly measured laugh. "You're looking a bit pale, my dear."

So they'd brought me back to my room, where Jont had left me nightclothes and spiced wine to drink before my evening prayers, in the Maroneh custom. Perhaps she'd looked it up in a book. Suspecting observation, I drank a glass and then prayed for the first time in several years—but not to Bright Itempas.

Instead I tried to fix my thoughts on Madding. He had told me that gods could hear the prayers of their devotees regardless of distance or circumstance, if they only prayed hard enough. I was not precisely a devotee of Madding's, but I hoped desperation would make up for it.

I know where you are, I whispered in my mind, since there might be listeners in the room. *I don't know how to get you out yet, but I'm working on it. Can you hear me?*

But though I repeated my plea, and waited on my knees for nearly an hour, there was no answer.

I knew Madding was in that dark, sensationless place—the Empty—but I wasn't sure where *that* was. For all I knew, only the Lights could open and close the way to it. Or perhaps only their scrivener-trained Nypri could. Figuring that out would be my next task.

The next morning I awoke at dawn, having slept fitfully on my cot. Already there was activity in the house. I could hear it through the door: people walking, brooms sweeping, casual chatter. I should have guessed that an organization of Itempans would start their day well before sunrise. More distantly, echoing through the corridors, I heard singing—the Lights' wordless hymn, which was far more soothing and uplifting than the Lights themselves had turned out to be. Perhaps there was some sort of morning ceremony taking place. If that was the case, then it would be only a matter of time before they came for me. Trying to quell unease, I dressed in the clothes they'd given me, and waited.

Not long afterward, the lock on my room's door opened and someone came in. "Jont?" I asked.

"No, it's Hado again," he said. My belly tightened, but I think I managed not to show my unease. There was something about this man that made me very uncomfortable. It was more than his participation in my kidnapping and forced assimilation into a cult; more than his veiled threat the night before. Sometimes I even thought I could see him, like a darker shadow etched against my vision. Mostly it was just the constant feeling, impossible to prove, that the face he showed me was just a veil, and behind it he was laughing at me.

"Sorry to disappoint you." He had caught my unease, and predictably it seemed to amuse him. "Jont has cleaning duty in the mornings. Something you'll become familiar with, too, eventually."

"Eventually?"

"It's traditional for a new initiate to be put on a work crew, but we're still trying to figure out a placement that can accommodate your unique needs."

I could not help bristling. "You mean that I'm blind? I can clean just fine, especially if you give me a walking stick." Mine, to my lament, had been left behind on the street outside Madding's house. I missed it like an old friend.

"No, Eru Shoth, I mean the fact that you'll escape first chance you get." I flinched, and he chuckled softly. "We don't usually put guards on the work crews, but until we're certain of your commitment to our way . . . Well, it would be foolish to leave you unsupervised."

I drew in a deep breath, let it out. "I'm surprised you have no procedures for handling recruits like me, if kidnapping and coercion are your usual practice."

"Believe it or not, most of our initiates are volunteers." He moved past me, inspecting the room. I heard him pick up a candle holder from one of the wall sconces, perhaps noting that I'd blown out the candle early. I didn't exactly need the light, and I'd never liked the idea of dying in my sleep from a fire. He continued. "We've done quite well at recruiting among certain groups—in particular, devout Itempan laity who are disaffected with the Order's recent changes. I imagine we'll do well in Nimaro when we start setting up a branch there."

"Even in Nimaro, Master Hado, there are those who feel no need to worship Itempas in the same way as everyone else. No one forces them to do what they don't want to."

"Untrue," he replied, which made me frown. "Before ten years ago, every mortal in the Hundred Thousand Kingdoms worshipped Itempas in the same way. Weekly offerings and services at a White Hall, monthly hours of service, lessons for children from three years to fifteen. Every holy day, all over the world, the same rituals were enacted and the same prayers chanted. Those who dissented..." He paused and turned to me, still radiating that cool amusement that I so hated about him. "Well. You tell me what happened to them, Lady. If there were so many dissenters in your land."

I said nothing, in consternation, because it was a pointed dig at me: a Maroneh who had fled Nimaro first chance. Worse, he was right. My own father had loathed the White Halls and the rituals and the rigid adherence to tradition. Long ago, he'd told me, the Maroneh had had their own customs for worshipping Bright Itempas—special poetic forms and a holy book and priests who had been warrior-historians, not overseers. We'd even had our own language back then. All that changed when the Arameri came to power.

"You see," said Hado. He could read my face like a book, and I hated him for it. "Itempas values order, not choice. That said"—he came over and took my hand, coaxing me up and letting me take his arm to be guided—"obviously it would be impractical to recruit many like you. We wouldn't have done it if you weren't so important to our cause."

That didn't sound good. "What exactly does that mean?"

"That instead of following the usual process of initiation, you will spend today with Lady Serymn and tomorrow with the Nypri. They'll decide how best to proceed from there." He patted my hand again, reminding me of his ungentle pats from the night before. Yes, this, too, was a warning. If I did not somehow please the Lights' leaders, what would happen? Without even knowing why they wanted me, I could not guess. I ground my teeth, angry—but in truth, I was more afraid than angry. These people were powerful and mad, and that was never a good combination.

Hado walked me out of my room and began guiding me through the corridors, moving at an unhurried pace. I counted my steps for as long as I could, but there were too many twists and turns in the House of the Risen Sun; I kept losing count. The corridors here were all slightly curved, perhaps some function of building a house partially wrapped around a tree trunk. And because the House's builders had been unable to extend the structure far from the trunk—I was no architect, but even I could see the folly in that—the House had been built narrow and high, with multiple levels and stair-connected sections, giving the whole place an oddly disjointed feel. Hardly a monument to the Bright Lord's love of order.

Then again, perhaps this, too, was a disguise, like the New Lights' carefully cultivated appearance of harmlessness. The Order of Itempas saw them as just another heretic cult. Would they feel the same if they knew this heretic cult had power enough to challenge the gods?

Hado said nothing while we walked, and neither did I in my preoccupation. I gauged his silence, trying to decide how much

I dared ask. Finally I braved it. "Do you know what those…
holes…are?"

"Holes?"

"The magic that was used to bring me here." I shivered. "The
Empty."

"Ah, that. I don't know, not exactly, but the Nypri was ranked
Scrivener Honor Class within the Order of Itempas. That's their
highest designation." He shrugged, jostling my hand on his arm.
"I'm told he was even a candidate to become First Scrivener to
the Arameri, though, of course, that ended when he defected
from the Order."

I let out a laugh in spite of myself. "So he married an Arameri
fullblood and started his own religion to remind himself of what
he almost had?"

Hado chuckled, too. "Not exactly, but I understand that
mutual dissatisfaction is a factor in their collaboration. I imagine it isn't a far step from mutual goals to mutual respect, and
from there to love."

Interesting—or it would have been, if the happy couple
hadn't kidnapped, tortured, and imprisoned me and my friends.
"That's lovely," I said as blandly as I could, "but I know something about scriveners, and I've never seen a scrivener do anything like that. Overpower one godling, much less several? I
didn't think that was even possible."

"Gods aren't invincible, Lady Oree. And your friends—well,
nearly all of the ones who live here in the city—are the younger,
weaker godlings." He shrugged, oblivious to my surprise; he had
just told me something I'd never realized. "The Nypri simply
found a way to exploit these facts."

I fell silent again, mulling over what he'd told me. Eventually we passed through a doorway into a smaller enclosed space, this one thickly carpeted. There were more food smells here, breakfast items—and a familiar hiras-scented perfume.

"Thank you for coming," said Serymn, coming over to us. Hado let go of my hand, and Serymn took it in a sisterly fashion, stepping close to kiss me on the cheek. I managed not to pull back at that, though it was a near thing. Serymn noticed, of course.

"Forgive me, Lady. I suppose street folk don't greet each other that way."

"I wouldn't know," I said, unable to keep a scowl off my face. "I'm not 'street folk,' whatever those are."

"And here I've offended you." She sighed. "My apologies. I have little experience with commoners. Thank you, Brightbrother Hado." Hado left, and Serymn guided me over to a large plush chair.

"Prepare a plate," she ordered, and someone off to the side of the room began doing so. Sitting down across from me, Serymn examined me in silence for a moment. She was like Shiny in that; I could feel her gaze, like the brush of moth wings.

"Did you rest well last night?"

"Yes," I said. "I appreciate your hospitality, up to a point."

"That point being your fate and the fates of your godling friends, yes. Understandable." Serymn paused as the servant came over, placing a plate in my hands. No formal service this time. I relaxed.

"And your own fate," I said. "When Madding and the others get free, I doubt they'll be very forgiving of their treatment. They're immortal; you can't hold them *forever*." Though if she could somehow kill them, that rendered my argument moot....

"True," she said. "And how convenient you mentioned this fact, as it's the cause of the mess we find ourselves in now."

I blinked, realizing she was no longer talking about Madding and the others, but another set of captive gods. "You mean the Arameri's gods. The Nightlord." Their ridiculous target.

"Not just the Nightlord, but also Sieh the Trickster." It took all my self-control not to start at this. "Kurue the Wise, and Zhakkarn of the Blood. It was inevitable they would find their way to freedom eventually. Perhaps the millennia they spent imprisoned didn't even seem like a long time to them. They are endlessly patient, our gods, but they never forget a wrong, and they never let that wrong go unpunished."

"Do you blame them? If I had power and someone harmed me, I'd get back at them, too."

"So would I. So *have* I, on more than one occasion." I heard her cross her legs. "But any person on whom I sought vengeance would be equally within her rights to try and defend herself. That's all we're doing here, Lady Oree. Defending ourselves."

"Against *one of the Three*." I shook my head and decided to try honesty. "I'm sorry, but if you're trying to convert me by appealing to...street logic, or whatever you think motivates us lowly, common folk, then there's a flaw in your reasoning. Where I come from, if someone that powerful is angry with you, you *don't* fight back. You make amends as best you can, or you go into hiding and never come out, and meanwhile you pray that no one you care about gets hurt."

"Arameri do not hide, Lady Oree. We do not make amends, not when we believe our actions to have been correct. Those are the ways of Bright Itempas, after all."

And look where that got him, I almost said, but I held my tongue. I had no idea whether Shiny was all right, or where he was. If he had managed to escape, I had little hope he would bother to help us, but on the off chance that he might, I didn't intend to tell the New Lights about him.

"I think I should warn you," I said, "that I don't consider myself much of an Itempan."

Serymn was silent for a moment. "I'd wondered about that. You left home at the age of sixteen—the year your father died, wasn't it? Only a few weeks after the Gray Lady's ascension."

I stiffened. "How in the gods' names did you know that?"

"We investigated you when you first came to our attention. It wasn't difficult. There aren't many towns on the Nimaro reservation, after all, and your blindness makes you memorable. Your White Hall priest reported that you enjoyed arguing with him during lessons, as a child." She chuckled. "Somehow that doesn't surprise me."

My stomach twisted, threatening to return my meal. They had gone to my village? Spoken with my priest? Would they threaten my mother now?

"Please, Lady Oree. I'm sorry. I didn't mean to alarm you. We mean you no harm, nor anyone in your family." There was the clink of a teapot and the sound of liquid pouring.

"You'll understand if I find that hard to believe." I found a table beside my chair and set my plate on it.

"Nevertheless, it's true." She leaned forward and put something in my hands—a small cup of tea. I held it tightly to conceal my shaking fingers. "Your priest thinks you left Nimaro because you lost your faith. Is that true?"

"That priest was *my mother's* priest, Lady, far more than he ever was mine, and neither of them knew me very damned well." My voice was just a hair too loud for polite conversation; anger had frayed my self-control. I took a deep breath and tried again to mimic her calm, cultured manner of speaking. "You can't lose faith you never had to begin with."

"Ah. So you never believed in the Bright at all?"

"Of course I believed. Even now I believe, in principle. But when I was sixteen, I saw the hypocrisy in all the things the priest had taught me. It's all very well to *say* the world values reason and compassion and justice, but if nothing in reality reflects those words, they're meaningless."

"Since the Gods' War, the world has enjoyed the longest period of peace and prosperity in its history."

"My people were once as wealthy and powerful as the Amn, Lady Serymn. Now we're refugees without even a homeland to call our own, forced to rely on Arameri charity."

"There have been losses, true," Serymn conceded. "I believe those are outweighed by the gains."

I was suddenly angry, *furious*, with her. I had heard Serymn's arguments from my mother, my priest, friends of the family— people I loved and respected. I had learned to endure my anger without protest, because my feelings were upsetting to them. But in my heart? Truly? I had never understood how they could be so ... so ...

Blind.

"How many nations and races have the Arameri wiped out of existence?" I demanded. "How many heretics have been executed, how many families slaughtered? How many poor people have been beaten to death by Order-Keepers for the crime of not knowing our place?" Hot droplets of tea sloshed onto my fingers. "The Bright is *your* peace. *Your* prosperity. Not anyone else's."

"Ah." Serymn's soft voice cut through my anger. "Not just lost faith, but *broken* faith. The Bright has failed you, and you reject it in turn."

I hated her patronizing, sanctimonious, knowing tone. "You don't know anything about it!"

"I know how your father died."

I froze.

She continued, oblivious to my shock. "Ten years ago—on the very day, it seems, that the Gray Lady's power swept the world—your father was in the village market. Everyone felt *something* that day. You didn't need magical abilities to sense that something momentous had just occurred."

She paused as if waiting for me to speak. I held myself rigid, so she went on.

"But it was only your father, out of all the people in that market, who burst into tears and fell to the ground, singing for joy."

I sat there, trembling. Listening to this woman, this *Arameri*, dispassionately recite the details of my father's murder.

* * *

It wasn't the singing that did him in. No one but me could detect the magic in his voice. A scrivener might have sensed it, but my village was far too poor and provincial to merit a scrivener at its small White Hall. No, what killed my father was fear, plain and simple.

Fear, and faith.

*   *   *

"The people of your village were already anxious." Serymn spoke more softly now. I did not believe it was out of respect for my pain. I think she just realized greater volume was unnecessary. "After the morning's strange storms and tremors, it must have seemed as though the world was about to end. There were similar incidents that day, in towns and cities elsewhere in the world, but your father's case is perhaps the most tragic. There had been rumors about him before that day, I understand, but... that does not excuse what happened."

She sighed, and some of my fury faded as I heard genuine regret in her tone. It might have been an act, but if so, it was enough to break my paralysis.

I got up from my chair. I couldn't have sat any longer, not without screaming. I put the teacup down and moved away from Serymn, seeking somewhere in the room with fresher, less constricting air. A few feet away, I found a wall and felt my way to a window; the sunlight coming through it helped to ease my agitation. Serymn remained silent behind me, for which I was grateful.

*   *   *

Who threw the first stone? It is something I have always wondered. The priest would not say, when I asked him over and over again. No one in town could say; they did not remember. Things had happened so quickly.

My father was a strange man. The beauty and magic that I loved in him was an easily perceptible thing, though no one else ever seemed to see it. Yet they noticed *something* about him, whether they understood it or not. His power permeated the space around him, like warmth. Like Shiny's light and Madding's chimes. Perhaps we mortals actually have more than five senses. Perhaps along with taste and smell and the rest there is *detecting the special*. I see the specialness with my eyes, but others do it in some different way.

So on that long-ago day, when power changed the world and everyone from senile elders to infants felt it, they all discovered that special sense, and then they noticed my father and understood at last what he was.

But what I had always perceived as glory, they had seen as a threat.

* * *

After a time, Serymn came to stand behind me.

"You blame our faith for what happened to your father," she said.

"No," I whispered. "I blame the people who killed him."

"All right." She paused a moment, testing my mood. "But has it occurred to you that there may be a cause for the madness that swept your village? A higher power at work?"

I laughed once, without humor. "You want me to blame the gods."

"Not all of them."

"The Gray Lady? You want to kill her, too?"

"The Lady ascended to godhood in that hour, it's true. But remember what else happened then, Oree."

Just Oree this time, no "Lady." Like we were old friends, the street artist and the Arameri fullblood. I smiled, hating her with all my soul.

She said, "The Nightlord regained his freedom. This, too, affected the world."

My heart hurt too much for politeness. "Lady, I don't care."

She moved closer, beside me. "You should. Nahadoth's nature is more than just darkness. His power encompasses wildness, impulse, the abandonment of logic." She paused, perhaps waiting to see if her words had sunk in. "The madness of a mob."

Silence fell. In it, a chill laced around my spine.

I had not considered it before. Pointless to blame the gods when mortal hands had thrown the stones. But if those mortal hands had been influenced by some higher power...

Whatever Serymn read on my face must have pleased her. I heard that in her voice.

"These godlings," she said, "the ones you call your friends. Ask yourself how many mortals they've killed over the ages. Far more than the Arameri ever did, I'm quite certain; the Gods' War alone wiped out nearly every living thing in this realm." She stepped closer still. I could feel her body heat radiating against my side, almost a pressure. "They live forever. They have no need of food or rest. They have no true shape." She shrugged. "How can such creatures understand the value of a single mortal life?"

In my mind, I saw Madding, a shining blue-green thing like nothing of this earth. I saw him in his mortal shape, smiling as I touched him, soft-eyed, longing. I smelled his cool, airy scent, heard the sound of his chimes, felt the purr of his voice as he spoke my name.

I saw him sitting at a table in his house, as he had often done during our relationship, laughing with his fellow godlings as they drew their blood into vials for later sale.

It was a part of his life I'd never let myself consider deeply. Godsblood was not addictive. It caused no deaths or sickness;

no one ever took too much and poisoned himself. And the favors Madding did for people in the neighborhood—for those of us who were too unimportant to merit aid from the Order or the nobles, Madding and his crew were often our only recourse.

But the favors were never free. He wasn't cruel about it. He asked only what people could afford, and he gave fair warning. Anyone who incurred a debt to him knew there would be consequences if they failed to repay. He was a godling; it was his nature.

What did he do to them, the ones who reneged?

I saw Trickster Sieh's child eyes, as cold as a hunting cat's. I heard Lil's chittering, whirring teeth.

And from the deepest recesses of my heart rose the doubt that I had not allowed myself to contemplate since the day Madding had broken my heart.

Did he ever love me? Or was my love just another diversion for him?

"I hate you," I whispered to Serymn.

"For now," she replied, with terrible compassion. "You won't always."

Then she took my hand and led me back to my room, and left me there to sit in silent misery.

10

"Indoctrination"
(charcoal study)

THAT AFTERNOON, Hado put me on a work crew to help clean the large dining hall. This turned out to be a group of nine men and women, a few older than me but most younger, or so I judged by their voices. They watched me with open curiosity as Hado explained about my blindness—though he did not, I noticed, tell them that I had been forced into the cult. "She's quite self-sufficient, as I'm sure you'll find, but of course there will be some tasks she can't complete," was all he said, and by that I knew what was coming. "Because of that, we've assigned several of our older initiates to shadow the work crew in case she needs assistance. I hope all of you don't mind."

They assured him that they did not in tones of such slavish eagerness that I immediately loathed all of them. But when Hado left, I made my way to the work crew's designated leader, a young Ken woman named S'miya. "Let me handle the mopping," I said. "I feel like working hard today." So she handed me the bucket.

The handle of the mop was much like a walking stick in my hands. I felt more secure with it, in control of myself for the first time since I'd come to the House of the Risen Sun. This was an illusion, of course, but I clung to it, needed it. The dining hall was huge, but I put my back into the work and paid no heed to the sweat that dripped down my face and made my shapeless tunic stick to my body. When S'miya finally touched my arm and told me we were done, I was surprised and disappointed it had gone so quickly.

"You do Our Lord proud with such effort," S'miya said in an admiring tone.

I straightened to ease my aching back and thought of Shiny. "Somehow I doubt that," I said. This earned me a moment of puzzled silence, and more when I laughed.

With that done, one of the older initiates led me to the baths, where a good soak helped ease some of the soreness I would certainly feel the next day. Then I was led back to my room, where a hot meal waited on the table. They still locked the door, and there was only a fork to eat with, no knife. But as I ate, I reflected on how quickly one could grow used to this sort of captivity— the simplicity of honest labor, soothing hymns echoing throughout the halls, free food and shelter and clothing. I had always wondered why anyone would join an organization like the Order, and now I began to see. Compared to the complexities of the outside world, this was easier on the body and the heart.

Unfortunately, this meant that once I'd bathed and eaten, the silence closed in. But as I sat miserable in my chair at the window, my head leaning against the glass as if that would somehow ease the ache in my heart, Hado returned. He had another person in tow, a woman I had not met before.

"Go away," I said.

He stopped. The woman paused as well. He said, "We're in a mood, I see. What's the problem?"

I laughed, once and harshly. "Our gods hate us. Aside from that, everything's right as rain."

"Ah. A *philosophical* mood." He moved to sit somewhere across from me. The woman, whose perfume was quite unpleasantly strong, took up position near the door. "Do you hate the gods?"

"They're gods. It doesn't matter if we hate them."

"I disagree. Hate can be a powerful motivator. Our whole world is the way it is because of a single woman's hate."

More proselytizing, I realized. I didn't feel like talking to him, but it was better than sitting alone and brooding, so I replied. "The mortal woman who became the Gray Lady?"

"One of her ancestors, actually: the founder of the Arameri clan, the Itempan priestess Shahar. Do you know of her?"

I sighed. "Nimaro might be a backwater, Master Hado, but I *did* go to school."

"White Hall lessons skim the details, Lady Oree, which is a shame, because the details are so very delicious. Did you know she was Itempas's lover, for example?"

Delicious, indeed. My mind tried to conjure an image of Shiny—stony, coldhearted, indifferent Shiny, indulging in a passionate affair with a mortal. Or anyone, for that matter. Hells, I couldn't even imagine him having sex. "No, I didn't. I'm not sure *you* know that, either."

He laughed. "For now, let's simply assume it's true, hmm? She was his lover—the only mortal he ever saw fit to honor in that way. And she truly loved him, because when Itempas fought his sibling gods, she hated them, too. Much of what the Arameri did after the war—forcing the Bright on every race, persecuting those who'd once worshipped Nahadoth or Enefa—is the result of her hate." He paused. "One of the gods we've captured is your lover. Isn't that also true?"

I made a great effort and did not react or speak.

"Apparently, you and Lord Madding were quite an item. Word is your relationship ended, but it doesn't escape me that you ran to him when you were in need."

From across the room, the woman who'd come in with Hado made a faint sound of disgust. I'd almost forgotten she was there.

"How do you feel now that someone's attacked him?" Hado asked. His voice was gentle, compassionate. Seductive. "You said the gods hate us, and for the moment I think you hate them, too, at least a little. Yet somehow I find it hard to believe your feelings have changed so completely toward the one who shared your bed."

I looked away. I didn't want to think about it. I didn't want to *think* at all. Why had Hado and the woman come, anyhow? Didn't a Master of Initiates have other duties?

Hado leaned forward. "If you could, would you fight us to save your lover? Would you risk your life to set him free?"

Yes, I thought immediately. And just like that, the doubts I'd felt since my conversation with Serymn faded.

Someday, when Madding and I were free of this place, I would ask him about his treatment of mortals. I would ask about his role in the Gods' War. I would find out what he did to people who failed to repay. I had been remiss in not doing this before. But would it make a difference, in the end? Madding had lived thousands of years to my few. In that time, he had surely done things that would horrify me. Would knowing about those things make me love him any less?

"Whore," said the woman.

I stiffened. "Excuse me?"

Hado made a sound of annoyance. "Erad, Brightsister, you will be silent."

"Then hurry up," she snapped. "He wants the sample as soon as possible."

I was already tense, ready to throw some harsh words—or the chair under me—at Erad. This caught my attention. "What sample?"

Hado let out a long sigh, plainly considering a few choice words of his own. "The Nypri's request," he said finally. "He has asked for some of your blood."

"Some of my *what*?"

"He's a scrivener, Lady Oree, and you have magical abilities no one has ever seen. I imagine he wants to study you in depth."

I clenched my fists, furious. "And if I don't want to give a sample?"

"Lady Oree, you know full well the answer to that question." There was no patience left in Hado now. I considered resisting, anyway, to see whether he and Erad were prepared to use physical force. That was stupid, though, because there were two of them and one of me, and there could easily be more of them if they just opened the door and called for help.

"Fine," I said, and sat down.

After a moment—and probably a last warning look from Hado—Erad came over and took my left hand, turning it over. "Hold the bowl," she said to Hado, and a moment later I gasped as something stabbed me in the wrist.

"Demons!" I cried, trying to jerk away. But Erad's grip was firm, as if she'd been expecting my reaction.

Hado gripped my other shoulder. "This won't take long," he said, "but if you struggle, it will take longer." I stopped fighting only because of that.

"What in the gods' names are you doing?" I demanded, yelping as Erad did something else, and it felt like my wrist was stabbed again. I could hear liquid—my blood—splattering into some sort of container. She had jabbed something into me, opening the wound further to keep the blood flowing. It hurt like the infinite hells.

"Lord Dateh requested about two hundred drams," muttered Erad. A moment passed, and then she sighed in satisfaction. "That should be enough."

Hado let go of me and moved away, and Erad took the painful thing out of my arm. She bandaged my wrist with only marginally more gentleness. I snatched my arm away from her as soon as her grip lessened. She uttered a contemptuous snort but let me go.

"We'll have someone bring you dinner shortly," Hado said as they both went to the door. "Be sure to eat; it will prevent weakness. Rest well tonight, Lady Oree." Then they closed the door behind them.

I sat where they'd left me, cradling my aching arm. The bleeding hadn't quite stopped; a stray droplet had seeped through the bandage and begun to thread its way down my forearm. I followed the sensation of its passage, my thoughts meandering in a similar way. When the droplet fell off my arm to the floor, I imagined its splatter. Its warmth, cooling. Its smell.

Its color.

There was a way out of the House of the Risen Sun, I understood now. It would be dangerous. Possibly deadly. But was it any safer for me to stay and find out whatever they planned to do with me?

I lay down, my arm tucked against my chest. I was tired—too tired to make the attempt right then. It would take too much of my strength. In the morning, though, the Lights would be busy with their rituals and chores. There would be time before they came for me.

My thoughts as dark as blood, I slept.

11

"Possession"
(watercolor)

SO, THERE WAS A GIRL.

What I've guessed, and what the history books imply, is that she was unlucky enough to have been sired by a cruel man. He beat both wife and daughter and abused them in other ways. Bright Itempas is called, among other things, the god of justice. Perhaps that was why He responded when she came into His temple, her heart full of unchildlike rage.

"I want him to die," she said (or so I imagine). "Please, Great Lord, make him die."

You know the truth now about Itempas. He is a god of warmth and light, which we think of as pleasant, gentle things. I once thought of Him that way, too. But warmth uncooled burns; light undimmed can hurt even my blind eyes. I should have realized. We should all have realized. He was never what we wanted Him to be.

So when the girl begged the Bright Lord to murder her father,

He said, "Kill him yourself." And He gifted her with a knife perfectly suited to her small, weak child's hands.

She took the knife home and used it that very night. The next day, she came back to the Bright Lord, her hands and soul stained red, happy for the first time in her short life. "I will love you forever," she declared. And He, for a rare once, found Himself impressed by mortal will.

Or so I imagine.

The child was mad, of course. Later events proved this. But it makes sense to me that this madness, not mere religious devotion, would appeal most to the Bright Lord. Her love was unconditional, her purpose undiluted by such paltry considerations as conscience or doubt. It seems like Him, I think, to value that kind of purity of purpose—even though, like warmth and light, too much love is never a good thing.

* * *

I woke an hour before dawn and immediately went to the door to listen for my captors. I could hear people moving about in the corridors beyond my door, and sometimes I caught snatches of the Lights' wordless, soothing song. More morning rituals. If they followed the pattern of previous mornings, I had an hour, maybe more, before they came.

Quickly I set to work, pushing aside the room's table as quietly as I could. Then I rolled aside the small rug to bare the wooden floor, which I inspected carefully. It was smoothly sanded, lightly finished. Dusty. It felt nothing like a canvas.

Neither had the bricks at the south promenade, though, the day I'd killed the Order-Keepers.

My heart pounded as I went through the room, collecting

the items I'd marked or hidden as potentially useful. A piece of cheese and a nami-pepper from a previous meal. Chunks of melted fakefern wax from the candles. A bar of soap. I had nothing that felt or smelled like the color black, though, which was frustrating. I had a feeling I would need black.

I knelt on the floor and picked up the cheese, and took a deep breath.

Kitr and Paitya had called my drawing a doorway. If I drew a place I knew and opened that doorway again, would I be able to travel there? Or would I end up like the Order-Keepers, dead in two places at once?

I shook my head, angry at my own doubts.

Carefully, clumsily, I sketched Art Row. The cheese was more useful as texture than color, because it felt rough, like the cobbles I'd walked across for the past ten years. I yearned for black to outline the cobbles but forced myself to do without. The candlewax ran out first—too soft—but between it and the soap I managed to suggest a table, and beyond that another. The pepper ran out next, its juice stinging my fingers as I ground it to a nub trying to depict the Tree's greenscent in the air. Finally, though I used my own saliva and blood to stretch it and properly color the cobbles, the cheese crumbled to bits in my fingers. (To get my blood, I'd had to scratch off the scab from the previous night's bloodletting. Inconveniently, I was not menstruating.)

When it was done, I sat back to gaze at my work, grimacing at the ache in my back and shoulders and knees. It was a crude, small drawing, only two handspans across since there hadn't been enough "paint" to do more. More impressionistic than I liked, though I had created such drawings before and seen the magic in them nevertheless. What mattered was what the depiction evoked in the mind and heart, not how it looked. And this one, however crude, had captured Art Row so well that I felt homesick just looking at it.

But how to make it real? And then, how to step through?

I put my fingers on the edge of the drawing, awkwardly. "Open?" No, that wasn't right. At the south promenade I had been too terrified for words. I closed my eyes and said it with my thoughts. *Open!*

Nothing. I hadn't really thought that would work.

Once, I had asked Madding how it felt for him, using magic. I'd had a bit of his blood in me at the time, making me restless and dreamy; that time, the only magic that had manifested in me was the sound of distant, atonal music. (I hadn't forgotten the melody, but I'd never once hummed it aloud. All my instincts warned against doing that.) I'd been disappointed, wishing for something more grandiose, and that had gotten me wondering what it felt like to *be* magic, not just taste it in dribs and drops.

He'd shrugged, sounding bemused. "Like walking down the street feels for you. What do you think?"

"Walking down the street," I had informed him archly, "is nothing like flying into stars, or crossing a thousand miles in one step, or turning into a big blue rock whenever you get mad."

"Of course it's the same," he'd said. "When you decide to walk down a street, you flex the muscles in your legs. Right? You feel out the way with your stick. You listen, make sure there's no one in the way. And then you will yourself to move, and your body moves. You believe it will happen, so it happens. That's how magic is for us."

Will the door open, and it will open. Believe, and it will be. Nibbling my bottom lip, I touched the drawing again.

This time, I tried imagining Art Row as I would one of my landscapes, cobbling together the memories of a thousand mornings. It would be busy now, the area thick with local merchants and laborers and farmers and smiths beginning their daily business. In some of the buildings just beyond my drawing, courtesans and restaurants would be opening their books for evening appointments. The pilgrims who'd prayed with the dawn would be giving way to minstrels singing for coins. I hummed a Yuuf tune that had been a favorite of mine. Sweating stonemasons, distracted accountants; I heard their hurrying feet and tense breath and felt their purposeful energy.

I was not aware of the change at first.

The Tree's scent had been thick around me since I'd been brought to the House of the Risen Sun. Slowly, subtly, it changed—becoming the fainter, more distant scent I was used to. Then that scent mingled with the smells of the Promenade, horseshit and sewage and herbs and perfumes. I heard murmuring voices and dismissed them...but they were not coming from within the House.

I did not notice the change at all, really, until the drawing opened up beneath my hands and I nearly fell into it.

Startled, I yelped and stumbled back. Then I stared. Blinked. Leaned close and stared more.

The cloth on the nearest Row table: *it moved*. I could not see people—perhaps because I hadn't drawn any figures—but I could hear the gabble of a crowd in the distance, moving feet, rattling wheels. A breeze blew, tossing a few fallen Tree leaves across the cobbles of the Promenade, and my hair lifted off my neck, just a little.

"Intriguing," said the Nypri, behind me.

Yelping in shock, I tried to simultaneously jump to my feet and scoot away from the voice. Instead I tripped over the rolled-up rug and went sprawling. While I struggled upright, grabbing for the bed to get my bearings, I realized too late that I had heard him enter, and had dismissed it. He had been standing in the room, watching me, for quite some time.

He came over, taking my hand and helping me to my feet. I snatched my hand away as soon as I could. Beyond him, I realized in dismay, the drawing had not only stopped being real, but also it had faded from view entirely, its magic gone.

"It takes great concentration to wield magic in a controlled fashion," he said. "Impressive given that you've had no training. And you did it with nothing but food and candlewax. Truly amazing. Of course, it means we'll have to watch you eat from now on, and search your quarters regularly for anything bearing pigment."

Damn! I clenched my fists before I thought to stop myself. "Why are you here?" I asked. It came out far more belligerent than it should have, but I couldn't help it. I was too angry over my lost chance.

"I came, ironically enough, to ask you to demonstrate your magical abilities for me. I'm still a scrivener, even if I've left the Order. Unique manifestations of inherited magic were my particular field of study." He sat down in one of the room's chairs, oblivious to my seething fury. "I should note, however, that if you meant to escape through that portal, your efforts would've ultimately been futile. The House of the Risen Sun is surrounded by a barrier that prevents magic from entering or leaving. A variation on my Empty, actually." He tapped the wooden floor with his foot. "If you had tried passing through it via that portal... Well, I'm not certain what would've happened. But you, or your remains, would not have gotten far."

Broken bowel, voices screaming... I felt ill, and defeated. "It wasn't big enough to pass through, anyway," I muttered, slumping onto the bed.

"True. With practice, however—and more paint—no doubt you *could* pass through these portals."

That got my attention. "What?"

"Your magic isn't that different from my own," he said, and abruptly I recalled the holes he'd used to capture me and Madding and the others. "Both are variants on the scrivening technique that permits instantaneous transport through matter and distance via a gate. Which is itself merely an approximation of the gods' ability to traverse space and time at will. It seems that your gift expresses itself extraversively, however, while mine is introversive."

I groaned. "Pretend I haven't spent my life studying musty old scrolls full of made-up words."

"Ah. My apologies. Let me try an analogy. Imagine that you hold a lump of gold in your hands. Gold is quite soft in its pure form; you can mold it with your fingers if you exert enough pressure. Then it can become many things: coins, a bracelet, a cup to hold water. Yet gold isn't useful for every purpose. A sword made of gold would bend easily and be too heavy to wield. For that, a different metal—say, iron—is better."

A rustle of cloth was my warning before Dateh took my hand. His fingers were dry, thick-skinned, callused at the tips. He turned over my hand, exposing my own calluses from carving wood and clipping linvin saplings, and also the stains from my makeshift paints. I did not pull away, though I wanted to. I did not like the feel of his hand.

"The magic in you is like gold," he said. "You've learned to shape it in one way, but there are others. I imagine you'll discover them with time and experimentation. The magic in me is more like iron: it can be shaped and used in similar ways, but its fundamental properties and uses are very different. And I, unlike you, have learned many ways to shape it. Now do you understand?"

I did. Dateh's holes, or portals, or whatever he called them, were like my doorways. He created them at will, perhaps using his own method to invoke them as I used painting. But while his magic opened a dark, cold space devoid of—*everything*—my magic opened the way to existing spaces...or created new spaces out of nothingness.

While I mulled this, I found myself rubbing my eyes with my free hand. They ached, though not as badly as on the previous occasions I'd used my magic. I supposed I hadn't overdone it this time.

"And your eyes," Dateh said. I stopped rubbing them, annoyed. He missed nothing. "That's even more unique. You saw Serymn's blood sigil. Can you see other magic?"

I considered lying, but in spite of myself, I was intrigued. "Yes," I said. "Any magic."

He seemed to consider this. "Can you see me?"

"No. You don't have any godwords, or you're masking them."

"What?"

I gestured vaguely with my hands, which gave me an excuse

to pull away from him. "With most scriveners, I see godwords written on their skin, glowing. I can't see the skin, but I can see the words, wrapped around their arms and so on."

"Fascinating. Most scriveners do that, you know, when they've mastered a new sigil or word-script. It's tradition. They write the sigils on their skin to symbolize their comprehension. The ink washes off, but I suppose there's a magical residue."

"You don't see it?"

"No, Lady Oree. Your eyes are quite unique; I have nothing that compares. Although—"

All at once, Dateh became visible to me. I was too distracted by his looks at first to realize the significance of what I saw. I couldn't help it, because he was *not Amn*. Or at least not completely, not with hair so straight and limp that it cupped his skull as if painted on. He wore it short, probably because the priests' fashion of long hair worn in a queue would look ridiculous on him. His skin was paler than Madding's, but there were other things about him that hinted at a less than pure Amn heritage. He was shorter than me, and his eyes were as dark as polished Darrwood. Those eyes would've been more at home among my own people or one of the High North races.

How in all the gods' names had an Arameri—proudest members of the Amn race and notorious for their scorn of anyone not pure Amn—contrived to marry a *non-Amn* rebel scrivener?

But as my shock at this realization faded, a more important one finally struck me: I could see him.

Him, that was, and not the markings of his scrivener power. In fact, I saw no godwords on him at all. He was simply visible, all over, like a godling.

But the Lights hated godlings...

"What the hells are you?" I whispered.

"So you *can* see me," he said. "I'd wondered. I suppose it works only when I use magic, though."

"When you...?"

He pointed above us, off toward a corner of the room. I followed his finger, confused, but saw nothing.

Wait. I blinked, squinted, as if that would help. There was something else etched against the dark of my vision. Something small, no bigger than a ten-meri coin, or Serymn's blood sigil. It hovered, glimmering with an impossible black radiance that shimmered faintly; that was the only way I'd been able to sift it from the darkness that I usually saw. It looked just like—

I swallowed. It *was*. A tiny, almost-unnoticeable version of the same holes that had attacked us at Madding's house.

"I can enlarge it at will," he said when I finally spotted it. "I often use portals at this size for surveillance."

I understood then why he'd compared me to gold and himself to iron: my magic was prettier, but his made a better weapon.

"You haven't answered my question," I said.

"What am I?" He looked amused. "I'm the same as you."

"No," I said. "You're a scrivener. I might have a knack for magic, but lots of people have that—"

"You have far more than a 'knack' for magic, Lady Oree. This?" He gestured toward the floor, where my drawing was. "Is something that only a trained, first-rank scrivener of many years' experience could attempt. And that scrivener would need hours of drawing time and half a dozen fail-safe scripts on hand in case the activation went wrong—neither of which you seem to need." He smiled thinly. "Neither do I, I should note. I am considered something of a prodigy among scriveners because of it. I imagine you would be, too, if you had been found and trained early."

My hands clenched into fists on my knees. *"What are you?"*

"I am a demon," he said. "And so are you."

I fell silent, more in confusion than in shock. That would come later.

"Demons aren't real," I said at last. "The gods killed them all aeons ago. There's nothing left but stories to frighten children."

Dateh patted my hand where it sat on my knee. At first I thought it was a clumsy attempt on his part to comfort me; the gesture felt awkward and forced. Then I realized he didn't like touching me, either.

"The Order of Itempas punishes unauthorized magic use," Dateh said. "Have you never wondered why?"

Actually, I had not. I'd thought it was just another way for the Order to control who had power and who didn't. But I said what the priests had taught me: "It's a matter of public safety. Most people *can* use magic, but only scriveners *should*, because they have the training to keep it safe. Write even one line of a sigil wrong and the ground could open up, lightning could strike, anything might happen."

"Yes, though that isn't the only reason. The edict against wild magic actually predates the scrivening art that tamed it." He was watching me. He was like Shiny, like Serymn; I could feel his gaze. So many strong-willed people around me, all of them dangerous. "The Gods' War was not the *first* war among the gods, after all. Long before the Three fought among themselves, they fought their own children—the half-breed ones they'd borne with mortal men and women."

All of a sudden, inexplicably, I thought of my father. I heard his voice in my ears, saw the gentle wavelets of his song as they rode the air.

Serymn's voice: *there had been rumors about him.*

"The demons lost that war," Dateh said. He spoke softly, for which I was grateful, because all at once I felt unsteady. Chilled, as if the room had grown colder. "It was foolish for them to fight, really, given the gods' power. Some of the demons no doubt realized this, and hid instead."

I closed my eyes and inwardly mourned my father all over again.

"Those demons survived," I said. My voice shook. "That's what you're saying. Not many of them. But enough." My father. His father, too, he'd told me once. And his grandmother, and an uncle, and more. Generations of us in the Maroland, the world's heart. Hidden among the Bright Lord's most devout people.

"Yes," said Dateh. "They survived. And some of them, perhaps to camouflage themselves, hid among mortals with more distant, thinner gods' blood in their veins—mortals who had to struggle to use magic, borrowing the gods' language to facilitate even simple tasks. The gods' legacy is what turned the key in humankind, unlocking the door to magic, but in most mortals that door is barely ajar.

"Yet there are some few among us who are born with more. In those mortals, the door is *wide open*. We need no sigils, no years of study. Magic is ingrained in our very flesh." He touched my face just under one eye, and I flinched. "Call us throwbacks, if you will. Like our murdered ancestors, we are the best of mortalkind—and everything our gods fear."

He dropped his hand onto mine again, and it was not awkward this time. It was possessive.

"You're never going to let me go, are you?" I said it softly.

He paused for a moment.

"No, Lady Oree," he said, and I heard him smile. "We aren't."

12

"Destruction"
(charcoal and blood, sketch)

I HAVE A REQUEST," I said to the Nypri when he rose to leave. "My friends, Madding and the others. I need to know what you plan to do with them."

"That isn't something you *need* to know, Lady Oree." Dateh's tone was gently chiding.

I set my jaw. "You seem to want me to join you willingly."

He fell silent for a moment, contemplating. That was gratifying, because my statement had been a gamble. I had no idea why he wanted me, beyond the fact that we were both demons. Perhaps he thought I could eventually develop magic as powerful as his, or perhaps demons had some symbolic value to the New Lights. Whatever the reason, I knew leverage when I saw it.

At last he said, "My wife believes you can be rehabilitated, made to see reason." He glanced at my drawing on the floor. "I, however, am beginning to wonder whether you're too dangerous to be worth the effort."

I nibbled my bottom lip. "I won't try that again."

"We are both Itempans here, Lady Oree. You'll try it if you think it will work. And if there is insufficient disincentive." He folded his arms, thoughtful. "Hmm. I've been trying to figure out what to do with him. . . ."

"What?"

"Your Maroneh friend."

"My—" I started. "You mean Shiny." So he hadn't escaped. Damnation.

"Yes, whatever his name is." For once, Dateh sounded annoyed. "I thought he was a godling, too, given his intriguing ability to return from death. But I've had him in the Empty for days now, and he's shown no sign of resistance, magical or otherwise. He just keeps dying."

The small hairs along my skin prickled. I opened my mouth to say, *That's our god you're torturing, you bastard*, but then I stopped. What would Dateh do, if he knew he had the Bright Lord of Order as his prisoner? Would he even believe it? Or would he question Shiny—and be shocked to learn, as I had been, that Shiny *loved* the Nightlord and would disapprove of any action that threatened him? What would these madmen do then?

"Maybe he's . . . like us," I said instead. "A d-demon." It was hard to say the words.

"No. I did test him. There are distinct properties that can be observed in the blood. . . . Aside from his peculiar ability, he's mortal in every way that I can determine." He sighed and did not see my start as I realized that was why they'd taken my blood. "The Order has discovered any number of minor magical variants over the centuries. I suppose he's just another of those." Dateh paused, long enough for the silence to unnerve me further. "This man lived with you in the city, I'm told. I can't kill him, but I think you've guessed the ways in which I can make his brief periods of life unpleasant. *You* are valuable to me; *he* is not. Do we understand each other?"

I swallowed. "Yes, Lord Dateh. I understand you perfectly."

"Excellent. I'll have him placed with you later today, then. I should warn you, though; after this much time in the Empty, he may require . . . assistance." I clenched my fists on my knees while he knocked on the door to be let out.

But as he did so, something changed.

It was just a momentary flicker, so fast that I thought I imagined it. For that instant, Dateh's body looked wholly different. Wrong. I saw his nearer arm, curiously doubled as he rested it on the door-sill. Two arms, not one. Two hands gripping the smooth wood.

I blinked in surprise and suddenly the image was gone. Then the door opened, and so was Dateh.

I slept. I didn't mean to, but I was exhausted after my effort to use magic. When I opened my still-twinging eyes, the light of sunset was thin and fading on my skin. Someone had been in the room during that time, which meant I'd slept hard; I was usually quick to wake at any untoward noise. My visitors had been busy. I found the furniture put back in place and a tray of food on the table. The candles were gone when I checked, replaced by a single small lantern of a design that I found odd—until I realized it held nothing more than a slow-burning moistened wick. No reservoir of oil that I could use for painting. Other items in the room had been removed or replaced, too, ostensibly because they could have been used for their pigment. The food was a bowl of some sort of porridge, as bland and textureless as they could've made it and kept it palatable. And the air smelled of floor cleanser. I felt a moment's grief for my drawing, poor as it had been.

I ate and then went to the window, wondering if I would ever escape from this place. I guessed that I had been imprisoned for five days, maybe six. Soon it would be Gebre, the spring equinox. All over the world, White Halls would deck themselves in festive ribbons and *encanda*, lanterns given a special fuel to make their flame burn white instead of red or gold. The Halls would throw open their doors to all comers, celebrating the approach of summer's long days—and even now, with so many doubting their faith, those Halls would be full. Yet at the same time, in every city, there would be ceremonies dedicated to the Nightlord, too, and to the Lady. That was something new and still strange to me.

An hour passed before the door of my cell opened again. Three men entered, carrying something heavy—two somethings, I realized, as they grunted and jostled the table and chairs out of the way. The first object they put down squeaked faintly, and I realized it was another cot, like the one I slept on.

The second object they put down was Shiny, dumped on the cot. He groaned once and then lay still.

"A present from the Nypri," said one of the men, and another laughed. They left, and I hurried to Shiny's side.

His flesh was as cold as a corpse's. I had never felt him that cold; he never stayed dead long enough to completely lose body temperature. Yet when I fumbled for his pulse, it was racing. His breath came in harsh, quick pants. They had cleaned him up; he was wearing the sleeveless white smock and pants of a new initiate. But what had they bathed him in, ice water?

"Shiny?" All thoughts of his real name fled my mind as I wrestled him onto his back, then tugged a blanket over him. I touched his face and he jerked away, making a quick animal sound. "It's Oree. Oree."

"Oree." His voice was hoarse, as mine had been, perhaps for the same reason. But he settled after that, no longer moving away from my touch.

He was mortal, Dateh had said, but I knew the truth. Beneath the mortal veneer, he was the god of light, and he had spent five days trapped in a lightless hell. Hurrying across the room, I found the lantern, which thankfully I had not yet blown out. Would such a tiny light help him? I brought it closer, putting it on the shelf above Shiny's bed. His eyes were shut tight, and all his muscles quivered like wires ready to snap. He was only a little warmer.

Seeing no better option, I slipped under the covers with him and tried to warm him with my body. This was not easy, as the cot was narrow and Shiny took up all but a few inches of it. Finally I had to climb on top of him, resting my head on his chest. I wasn't fond of the overly intimate position, but there was nothing else to be done.

I was completely caught by surprise when Shiny suddenly wrapped himself around me and turned us over, holding me solidly in place with an arm around the waist, a hand cupping my head against his shoulder, and his leg thrown over mine. I was not quite pinned but I couldn't move much, either. Not that I tried; I was too stunned for that, wondering what had prompted this sudden gesture of affection. If that it was.

He seemed reassured by the fact that I didn't fight him. The quivering tension gradually drained out of his body, his breath against my ear slowing to something more normal. After a while, we both grew warm, and despite spending the whole day asleep, I could not quite help it; I slept again.

When I awoke, I guessed that it was late. Near midnight, give or take a few hours. I was still sleepy but had a growing need to urinate, which was a problem because I was still neatly tucked into the complicated tangle of Shiny's body. His long, slow breaths told me he was asleep, and deeply, which he probably needed after his ordeal.

Working carefully and slowly, I extricated myself from his grip and then eased my way to a sitting position, from which I managed to clamber over him to reach the floor at last. By this point, the need had grown urgent, so I stood to hurry.

A hand caught my wrist, and I yelped.

"Where are you going?" Shiny rasped.

Taking a deep breath to slow my heart, I said, "The bathroom," and waited for him to let me go.

He didn't move. I shifted from one foot to the other uncomfortably. Finally I said, "If you don't let go, the floor is going to be very wet in a minute."

"I'm trying," he said, very softly. I had no idea what that meant. Then I realized his hand on my wrist was loosening and tightening and loosening again, as if he could not quite will it to open.

Confused, I reached out to touch his face. His brow was furrowed. He drew in another deep breath through gritted teeth, then jerkily, deliberately, released my wrist.

I puzzled over this for a moment, but nature warned me not to dawdle. I felt his eyes on me for the whole hurried walk across the room.

It was better when I came out; the room held less tension. When I went over to him, I reached for his face and found his bowed shoulders, head hanging between them, heaving like he'd just run a long and exhausting race.

I sat down beside him. "Want to tell me what that was about?"

"No."

I sighed. "I think I deserve an explanation, if only so I can plan my bathroom breaks accordingly."

Predictably, he said nothing.

Whatever lingering reverence I'd felt for him vanished. I was tired. For months I had endured his moods and his silence, his temper, his insults. Because of him, I had lost my life in Shadow. In my churlish moments, I could even blame him for my captivity. Dateh had found me because I'd killed the Order-Keepers, which wouldn't have happened if Shiny hadn't made them angry.

"Fine," I said, getting up to return to my own cot.

But when I stepped forward, his hand caught my wrist again, tighter this time. "You will stay," he said.

I tried to yank my arm free. "Let go of me!"

"Stay," he snapped. "I command you to stay."

I twisted my arm, breaking his hold, and stepped back quickly, finding the table and maneuvering so that it was between me and him. "You *can't* command me," I said, trembling with fury. "You're not a god anymore, remember? You're just a pathetic mortal as helpless as the rest of us."

"You dare—" Shiny rose to his feet.

"Of course I dare!" I gripped the table edge, hard enough to make my fingertips sting. "What's wrong with you? You think just because you say something, I'll obey? Will you kill me if I don't? You think that makes you *right*? My gods, no wonder the Nightlord hates you, if that's how you think!"

Silence fell. I had run out of rage. I waited for his, ready to throw it back at him, but he said nothing. And after a long, pent moment, I heard him sit down again.

"*Please* stay," he said at last.

"What?" But I had heard him.

For a moment, I almost walked away, anyway. I was that tired of him. But he said nothing more, and in the silence, my anger faded enough that I realized what that quiet plea must have cost. It was not the way of the Bright to *ask* for what one wanted.

So I went to him. But when he touched my hand, I pulled back. "A trade," I said. "You've taken enough from me. Give *something* back."

He let out a long sigh and touched my hand again. I was surprised to find it trembling.

"Later, Oree," he said, barely louder than a whisper. Completely confused, I reached up to touch his not-Maroneh hair with my free hand; his head was still bowed. "Later, I will tell you...everything. Not now. Please, just stay."

I didn't make a decision, not in any conscious way. I was still angry. But this time, when he tugged my hand, I let him draw me forward. I sat beside him again, and when he lay down, I let him pull me down as well, positioning me on my side and spooning himself behind me. He kept his arms loose so that I could get up if I needed to. He put his face into my hair, and I chose not to pull away.

I did not sleep for the rest of that night. I'm not certain he did, either.

*   *   *

"There may be a way for us to get free of this place," Shiny said the next day.

It was noon. One of the Lights' initiates had just left, after bringing us lunch and staying to see that we ate it all. He took away the leftovers and searched out my hiding places, too, to make sure there was no stored food under the mattress or rug. No chitchat this time, and no efforts to convert either of us. No one took me away for chores or lessons. I felt oddly neglected.

"How?" I asked, then guessed. "Your magic. It comes when you protect me."

"Yes."

I licked my lips. "But I'm in danger now—have been since the Lights took me." There wasn't the slightest glimmer of magic in him.

"It may be a matter of degree. Or perhaps a physical threat is required."

I sighed, wanting to hope. "That's more 'may be' and 'perhaps' than I like to hear. I don't suppose anyone thought to give you instructions on how...you...work now?"

"No."

"What do you propose, then? I pick a fight with Serymn, and when she fights back, you blow up the House and kill us all?"

There was a moment's pause. I think my levity annoyed him.

"In essence, yes. Though there would be little logic in me killing *you*, so I'll moderate the amount of force I use."

"I appreciate your consideration, Shiny, really I do."

So the rest of the day passed with aching slowness, as I waited and tried not to hope. Shiny, for all his promises to explain the previous day's bizarre behavior, said nothing more about it. I gathered he was still recovering from his ordeal in the Empty; he'd slept through dawn, which he'd never done before, though he'd glowed as usual. That, plus my company, seemed to restore him. He had been his old taciturn self since he'd woken.

Still, I felt his eyes on me more often than usual that day, and once he touched me. It was when I'd gotten up to pace, fruitlessly hoping to vent restless energy. I brushed past Shiny, and he reached out to touch my arm in passing. I would have dismissed it as a mistake or my imagination if not for the previous evening. It was as if he needed contact now and again, for some reason that made no sense to me. Though when had anything about Shiny made sense?

I didn't ask questions, preoccupied as I was with my own concerns—like Dateh's revelation that I was a demon. I did not feel much like a monster. That didn't make me eager to discuss it with Shiny, who had slaughtered my ancestors and banned his children from ever again creating more beings like me.

So I was content to let him keep his secrets for the time being.

Toward evening, I was almost relieved when there came a brisk knock at the door, followed by the arrival of another initiate. As I rose to follow the girl, Shiny simply stood and came to my side. I heard her splutter for a moment, caught off guard, but finally she sighed and took us both.

Thus we arrived in the private dining hall, where Serymn waited with Dateh. No one else this time, beyond the servants who were already busy setting out the meal and a few guards. If Serymn was bothered by Shiny's presence, she said nothing to that effect.

"Welcome, Lady Oree," she said as we sat down. I turned my face toward the faint glimmer of her Arameri blood sigil in an effort to be polite, though I was beginning to hate being called *Lady Oree*. I knew what they meant by it now. The demons of old had been the Three's offspring, too, and perhaps as deserving of respect as the godlings—and *not human*. Something I was not ready to think, about myself.

"Good afternoon, Lady Serymn," I said. "And Lord Dateh." I could not see him, but his presence was as palpable against my skin as cool moonlight.

"Lady Oree," Dateh said. Then, so subtly that I almost didn't catch it, his tone changed as he addressed Shiny. "And a good afternoon to your companion. Are you perhaps willing to introduce yourself today?"

Shiny said nothing, and Dateh let out a sigh of barely contained exasperation. I had to fight the urge to laugh, because as amusing as it was to hear Shiny drive someone else mad for a change, I was surprised at how quickly Dateh's temper broke. For whatever reason, Dateh seemed to have taken an instant dislike to him.

"He doesn't talk to me, either," I said, keeping my tone light. "Not much, anyway."

"Hmm," said Dateh. I waited for him to ask more questions about Shiny, but he fell silent, too, radiating hostility.

"Interesting," said Serymn, which annoyed *me* now because it was exactly what I'd been thinking. "In any case, Lady Oree, I trust your day went well?"

"I was bored, actually," I said. "I'd've preferred to be on another of those work crews. Then I could've at least gotten out of my room."

"I can imagine!" said Serymn. "You seem the type of woman to prefer a more spontaneous, energetic approach to life."

"Well...yes."

She nodded, the sigil bobbing in the dark. "You may find this difficult to accept, Lady Oree, but your trials have been a necessary step in cementing you to our cause. As you found today, having no other options makes even menial labor desirable. Sever one attachment and others become more viable. It's a harsh method, but one that has been used by both the Order and the Arameri family over the centuries, to great effect."

I refrained from saying what I really thought of that effect, and covered my anger by taking a sip from my wineglass. "I thought you people were opposed to the Order's methods."

"Oh, no—only their recent change in doctrine. In most other ways, the Order's methods have been proven by time, so we adopt them gladly. We are still devoted to the ways of the Bright Father, after all."

I should have known what that would set off.

"In what way," Shiny asked suddenly, startling me in mid-swallow, "does attacking Itempas's children serve Him?"

Silence fell around the table. Mine was astonishment; so was Serymn's. Dateh's...That I could not read. But he put down his fork.

"It is our feeling," he said, his words ever so slightly clipped, "that they do not belong in the mortal realm and that they defy the Father's will by coming here. We know, after all, that they vanished from this plane after the Gods' War, when Itempas took exclusive control of the heavens. Now that His control appears to have, hmm, slipped, the godlings—like rebellious children—take advantage. Since we have the ability to correct the matter..." I heard the fabric of his robes shift; a shrug. "We do as He would expect of His followers."

"Hold His children hostage," said Shiny, and only a fool would not have heard the kindling fury in his voice. "And... kill them?"

Serymn laughed, though it sounded affected. "You assume that *we*—"

"Why not?" Dateh, too, was coldly angry. I heard some of the servants shift uneasily in the background. "During the Gods' War, their kind used this world as a battleground. Whole cities died at the godlings' hands. They cared nothing for those mortal lives lost."

At this I grew angry myself. "What is this, then?" I asked. "Revenge? That's why you're keeping Madding and the others—"

"They are nothing," Dateh snapped. "Fodder. Bait. We kill them to attract higher prey."

"Oh, yes." I couldn't help laughing. "I forgot. You actually think you can kill the Nightlord!"

I heard, but did not think about, Shiny's swift intake of breath.

"I do, indeed," Dateh said coolly. He snapped his fingers, summoning one of the servants. There was a quick murmured exchange and then the servant left. "And I shall prove it to you, Lady Oree."

"Dateh," said Serymn. She sounded...concerned? Annoyed? I could not tell. She was Arameri; perhaps Dateh's temper was spoiling some elaborate plan.

He ignored her. "You forget, Lady Oree, there is ample precedent for what we've done. Or perhaps you don't know how the

Gods' War actually began? I assumed that you, having been a god's lover..."

I became acutely aware of Shiny. He sat very still; I could hardly even hear him breathe. It was ridiculous that I felt sorry for him in that instant. He had murdered his sister, enslaved his brother, bullied his children for two thousand years. He had so little concern for life in general, including mine and his own, that more deaths should have been meaningless to him.

And yet...

I had touched his hand, that day at Role's memorial. I had heard the waver in his steady, stolid voice when he'd spoken of the Nightlord. Whatever problems he had, however much of a bastard he was, Shiny was still capable of love. Madding had been wrong about that.

And how would any man feel, on learning that his daughter had been murdered in imitation of his own sins?

"I've...heard," I said uneasily. Shiny kept silent.

"Then you understand," said Dateh. "Bright Itempas desired, and killed to obtain that desire. Why should we not do the same?"

"Bright Itempas also embodies order," I said, hoping to change the subject. "If everyone in the world killed to get what they wanted, there would be anarchy."

"Untrue," Dateh said. "What would happen is what *has* happened. Those with power—the Arameri, and to a lesser degree the nobility and priests of the Order—kill with impunity. No others may do so without their permission. *The right to kill* has become the most coveted privilege of power in this world, as in the heavens. We worship Him not because He is the best of our gods, but because He is, or was, the greatest killer among them."

228

The dining room door opened then. I heard another murmur. The servant returning. Something flickered, and then abruptly a silvery, shifting gleam appeared in my vision. Startled, I peered at it, trying to figure out what it was. Something small, only an inch or so in length. Oddly shaped. Pointy, like the tip of a knife, but far too small to be used that way.

"Ah, so you *can* see it," Dateh said. He sounded pleased again. "This, Lady Oree, is an arrowhead—a very special one. Do you recognize it?"

I frowned. "I'm not exactly into archery, Lord Dateh."

He laughed, already in a better mood. "What I meant was, do you recognize the power in it? You should. This arrowhead—the substance that comprises it—was made from your blood."

I stared at the thing, which shone like godsblood. Not quite as bright. And stranger: a moving, inconstant swirl of magic, rather than the steady gleam I was used to.

My blood should have been nothing special; I was just a mortal. "Why would you make something from my blood?"

"Our blood has grown thin over the ages," said Dateh. He set the thing down on the table in front of him. "It was said that Itempas needed only a few drops to kill Enefa. These days, the quantity needed to be effective is... impractical. We therefore distill it, concentrating its power, then shape the resulting product into a more usable form."

Before I could speak, there was a sharp thump as wood hit the floor, and the dining table shook hard.

"*Demon,*" Shiny said. He was standing, his hands planted on the table. It shook with the force of his rage. "You *dare* to threaten—"

"Guards!" Serymn, angry and alarmed. "Sit down, sir, or—"

Whatever she might have said was lost. There was a crash of servingware and furniture as Shiny lunged forward, his weight making the table jolt hard against my ribs. More startled than hurt, I scrambled backward, my hand flailing for the stick that should've been beside me. Of course there was nothing, so I tripped on the dining hall's thick rug and went sprawling, practically into the fireplace. I heard shouts, a scream from Serymn, a violent scuffle of flesh and cloth. Men converged from several directions, though not on me.

I pushed myself upright to get away from the close heat of the fire, my hands scrabbling for purchase on the smooth sculpted stone of the hearth—and as I did so, my hands slipped in something warm and gritty. Ash.

Behind me, it sounded as though another Gods' War had broken out. Shiny cried out as someone hit him. An instant later, that person went flying. There were choking sounds, grunts of effort, more dishes shattering. But there was no magic, I realized in alarm. I could see none of them—nothing except the tiny pale glimmer of the arrowhead where it had fallen to the floor, and the swift-moving bob of Serymn's blood sigil as she ran to the door to shout for help. Shiny fought for his own rage, not to protect me, and that meant he was just a man. They would overcome him soon, inevitably.

The ash. I felt around, closer to the fire, ready to snatch my hand back if I encountered something hot. My fingers fumbled over a hard, irregular lump, quite warm but not painfully so. Bits of it crumbled away as I touched it. A chunk of old wood that had been burned to charcoal, probably over several days.

The color black.

Behind me, Dateh had managed to get free of Shiny, though he was wheezing and hoarse. Serymn had him; I heard her murmuring, worried, to see if he was all right. Beyond them, a flurry of blows and shouts as more men ran in.

Inspiration struck like a kick to the gut. Scrambling back with the charcoal in my hand, I shoved aside the rug and began to scrape the charcoal against the floor, grinding it in circles. Around and around—

Someone called for rope. Serymn shouted not to bother with rope, just kill him damn it—

—and around and around and—

"Lady Oree?" Dateh, his voice rough and puzzled.

—and around and around, feverishly, sweat from my forehead dripping down to smear the blackness, blood from my scraped knuckles, too, forming a circle as deep and dark as a hole into nowhere, cold and silent and terrible and *Empty*. And somewhere in that emptiness, blue-green and bright, warm and gentle and irreverent—

"Dearest gods, stop her! *Stop her!*"

I knew the texture of his soul. I knew the sound of him, like chimes. I knew that he owed Dateh and the New Lights a debt of pain and blood, and I wanted that debt repaid with all my heart.

Beneath my fingers and my eyes, the hole appeared, its edges ragged where bits of the charcoal had broken off with the force of my grinding. I shouted into it, "*Madding!*"

And he came.

What burst from the hole was light, a scintillating blue-green mass of it that roiled like a thundercloud. After an instant, it shivered and became the shape I knew better—a man formed of living, impossibly moving aquamarine. For a moment, he hovered where the cloud had been, turning slowly, perhaps disoriented by the Empty's deprivations. But I felt rage wash the room the instant he spied Dateh and Serymn and the others, and I heard his chimes rise to a harsh, brassy jangle of dire intent.

Dateh was shouting over the guards' panicked cries, demanding something. I saw a faint flicker from his direction, almost drowned out by Madding's blaze. Madding uttered a wordless, inhuman roar that shook the whole House, and shot forward—

—then jerked back, tumbling to the floor as something struck him. I waited for him to rise, angrier. Mortals could annoy gods but never stop them. To my surprise, however, Madding gasped, the light of his facets dimming abruptly. He did not get up.

Faintly, through shock, I heard Shiny cry out, in something that sounded much like anguish.

I should not have been afraid. Yet fear soured my mouth as I scrambled to my feet, stepping onto my own drawing in my haste to reach him. It was just inert charcoal now. I tripped over the rug again, righted myself, fell over a chair that lay across the floor, and finally crawled. I reached Madding, who lay on his side, and pulled him onto his back.

There was no light in his belly. The rest of him shone as usual, though dimmer than I'd ever seen, but that part of him I could not see at all. He clutched at it, and I followed his hands to find the smooth, hard substance of his body broken by something long and thin, made of wood, that jutted up. A crossbow bolt. I grasped its shaft in both hands and yanked it free. Madding cried out, arching—and the blotch of nothingness at his middle spread farther.

I could see the arrow's tip. Dateh's arrowhead—the one made from my blood. There wasn't much left; I touched it and found that it had the consistency of soft chalk, crumbling with just the pressure of my fingers.

All at once, Madding guttered like a candle flame, his jewel facets becoming dull mortal flesh and tangled hair. *But I still couldn't see part of him.* I felt for his belly and found blood and a deep puncture. It wasn't healing.

My blood. In him. Working through his body like poison, snuffing out his magic as it went along.

No. Not just his magic.

I threw aside the arrow and touched his face, my fingers shaking. "Mad? I...I don't know, this doesn't make sense, it's my blood, but..."

Madding drew in a harsh breath and coughed. Blood— godsblood, which should've shone with its own light—covered his lips, but it was dark, obscuring the parts of him that I could see. Those were fading from view, too. The arrow was killing him.

No. He was a god. They did not die.

Except Role had, and Enefa had, and—

Madding choked, swallowed, focused on me. It made no sense that he laughed, but he did. "Always knew you were special, Oree," he said. "A demon! A legend. Gods. Always knew... something." He shook his head. I could barely see for his dimness and my tears. "And here I thought I'd have to watch *you* die."

"No. I...I won't. This isn't. No." I shook my head, babbling. Madding caught my hand, his own slick and hot with blood.

"Don't let him use you, Oree." He lifted his head to make sure I heard him. I could barely see his face, though I could feel it, hot and fevered. "They never understood...too quick to judge. You aren't just a weapon." He shuddered, his head falling back, his eyes drifting shut. "I would have loved you...until..."

He vanished. I could feel him beneath my hands still, but he was not there.

"Don't hide from me," I said. My voice was soft and did not carry, but he should have heard me. Should have obeyed.

Hands seized me, dragged me to my feet. I dangled limply between them, trying to will it: *I want to see you.*

"You forced my hand, Lady Oree." Dateh. He came over, visible for once; he had used magic during the struggle. He was rubbing his throat, his face bruised and bloody. Someone had torn part of his robes. He looked thoroughly furious.

I hated that I could see him and not Madding.

"A doorway into my Empty." He laughed once, without humor, then grimaced, as this hurt his bruised throat. "Amazing. Did you plan this, you and your nameless companion? I should have known better than to trust a woman who would give her body to one of *them*." He spat downward, perhaps at Madding's corpse.

not Madding there's nothing there that isn't him

Then he turned and snarled at one of the guards to come over. "Bring your sword," he added.

I prayed then. I had no idea if Shiny could hear me, or if he cared. I didn't care. *Bright Father, please let this man kill me.*

"Must you?" asked Serymn, her voice edged with distaste. "She might still be turned to our cause."

"It must be done within moments of death. I don't intend to let this mess go to waste." He reached over to take something from the guard. I waited, feeling nothing as Dateh turned a look on me that was as cold as the wind in the Tree's highest branches.

"When Bright Itempas killed Enefa," he said, "He also tore her body open and took from it a piece of flesh that contained all her power. Had He not done so, the universe would've ended. Killing the Nightlord runs the same risk, so I've spent years researching where the seat of a god's soul lies when they incarnate themselves in flesh."

He lifted the sword then, two-handed, so fast that for an instant I saw six arms instead of two, and three sets of teeth bared in effort.

There was the hollow *whoosh* of cloven air. I felt a stirring of wind against my face. But the impact, when it came, was not in my body, though I heard the wet *chuff* as it struck flesh.

I frowned, horror struggling up through the numbness in my mind. Madding.

Dateh tossed the sword aside, gestured at another man to help. They bent. The smell of godsblood rose around me, thick and cloying, familiar, as flat and wrong here as it had been in the alley where I'd found Role. I heard ... gods. Sounds I would expect in one of the infinite hells. Meat tearing. Bone and gristle cracking apart.

Then Dateh rose. His hand had gone dark, holding something; his robes were splattered and intermittent, too. He gazed at the thing in his hand with a look that I could not interpret, not without the touch of fingers, but I guessed. Revulsion, some, and resignation. But also eagerness. Lust worthy of a god.

When he lifted Madding's heart to his lips and bit down—

I remember nothing more.

13

"Exploitation"
(wax sculpture)

IT ALL COMES DOWN to blood. Yours, mine. All of it.

No one knows how it was discovered that godsblood is an intoxicant for mortals. The godlings knew it already when they came; it had been common knowledge before the Interdiction. I suppose someone, somewhere, simply decided to try it one day. Likewise, gods have drunk mortal blood. Only a few of them, thankfully, seem to like the taste.

But some god, somewhere, eventually decided to try a demon's blood. And then the great paradox was revealed: that immortality and mortality do *not* mix.

How the heavens must have shaken at that first death! Until then, godlings had feared only each other and the wrath of the Three, while the Three feared no one. Suddenly it must have seemed to the gods that there was danger everywhere. Every poisonous drop, in every mortal vein, of every half-breed child.

There was only one way—one terrible way—that the gods' fears could be assuaged.

Yet the murdered demons had their vengeance. After the slaughter, the harmony that had once been unshakable between gods and godlings, immortals and mortals, was shattered. Those humans who'd lost demon friends and loved ones turned against humans who had aided the gods; tribes and nations fell apart under the strain. The godlings regarded their parents with new fear, aware now of what could happen should *they* ever become a threat.

And the Three? How much did it hurt them, horrify them, when the deed was done and the battle haze faded and they found themselves surrounded by the corpses of their sons and daughters?

Here's what I believe.

The Gods' War took place thousands of years after the demon holocaust. But for beings who live forever, would not the memory still be fresh? How much did the former event contribute to the latter? Would the war have even happened if Nahadoth and Itempas and Enefa had not already tainted their love for one another with sorrow and distrust?

I wonder. We all should wonder.

* * *

I stopped caring. The Lights, my captivity, Madding, Shiny. None of it mattered. Time passed.

They brought me back to my room and tied me to the bed, leaving one arm free. As an added measure, they went through the room and removed everything I might use to harm myself: the candles, the sheets, other things. There were voices, touches. Pain when something was done to my arm again. More of my blood-poison, drip, drip, dripping into a bowl. Long periods of silence. Somewhere amid this I felt the urge to urinate, and did so. The attendant who arrived next cursed like a Wesha beggar when he smelled it. He left, and presently women came. I was diapered.

I lay where they put me, in the darkness that is the world without magic.

Time passed. Sometimes I slept, sometimes I didn't. They took more of my blood. Sometimes I recognized the voices that spoke around me.

Hado, for example: "Shouldn't we at least allow her to recover from the shock first?"

Serymn: "Bonebenders and herbalists have been consulted. This won't do her any lasting harm."

Hado: "How convenient. Now the Nypri need no longer weaken himself to achieve our goals."

Serymn: "See that she eats, Hado, and keep your opinions to yourself."

I was fed. Hands put food into my mouth. I chewed and swallowed out of habit. I grew thirsty, so I drank when water was held to my mouth. Much of it spilled down my shirt. The shirt dried. Time passed.

Now and again, women returned to bathe me with sponges. Erad returned, and after some consultation with Hado, she put something into my arm that remained there, a constant niggling pain. When they came to take my blood the next time, it went faster, because all they had to do was uncap a thin metal tube.

If I could have mustered the will to speak, I would have said, *Don't cap it. Let it all run out.* But I didn't, and they didn't.

Time passed.

Then they brought Shiny back.

* * *

I heard men huffing and grunting with effort. Hado was with them. "Gods, he's heavy. We should've waited until he was alive again."

Something knocked over one of the chairs with a loud wooden clatter. "Together," said someone, and with a final collective grunt, they heaved something onto the other cot in the room.

Hado again, close by, sounding winded and annoyed. "Well, Lady Oree, it looks like you'll have company again soon."

"Much good it'll do her," said one of the other men. They laughed. Hado shushed him.

I stopped listening to them. Eventually they left. There was more silence for a time. Then, for the first time in a long while, light glimmered at the edge of my vision.

I did not turn to look at it. From the same direction, there was a sudden gasp of breath, then others, steadying after a moment. The cot creaked. Went still. Creaked again, louder, as its occupant sat up. There was more silence for a long while. I was grateful for it.

Eventually I heard someone rise and come toward me.

"You killed him."

Another familiar voice. When I heard it, something in me changed, for the first time in forever. I remembered something. The voice had spoken softly, tonelessly, but what I remembered was a shout filled with more emotion than I'd ever heard a human voice bear. Denial. Fury. Grief.

Ah, yes. He had screamed for his son that day.

What day?

It didn't matter.

Weight bore down the side of the cot as Shiny sat beside me. "I know this emptiness," he said. "When I understood what I had done..."

The room had grown cool with the sunset. I thought of blankets, though I stopped short of wishing for one.

A hand touched my face. It was warm and smelled of skin, old blood, and distant sunlight.

"I fought, when he came for me," he said. "It is my nature. But I would have let him win. I *wanted* him to win. When he failed, I was angry. I...hurt him." The hand trembled, once. "Yet it was my own weakness that I truly despised."

It didn't matter.

The hand shifted, covering my mouth. I was breathing through my nose, anyway; it was no hardship.

"I'm going to kill you, Oree," he said.

I should have felt fear, but there was nothing.

"No demon can be permitted to live. But beyond that..." His thumb stroked my cheek once. It was oddly soothing. "To kill what you love...I know this pain. You have been clever. Brave. Worthy, for a mortal."

Deep in the murk of my heart, something stirred.

His hand slid up, covering my nose. "I would not have you suffer."

I did not care about his words, but breathing mattered. I turned my head to one side, or tried to. His hand tightened steadily, almost gently, holding my face still.

I tried to open my mouth. Had to think of the word. "Shiny." But it was muffled by his hand, unintelligible.

I lifted my left arm, the one that was free. It hurt. The area around the metal thing was terribly sore, and hot, too, with the beginnings of infection. There was a moment of resistance, and then the metal thing tore loose, sending a flash of white pain through me. Startled out of apathy, I bucked upward, reflexively catching Shiny's wrist with my hand. Blood, hot and slick, coated the inner bend of my elbow and ran down my arm.

I froze for an instant as awareness flooded through me, the instant the apathy lifted. *Madding is dead.*

Madding was dead, and I was alive.

Madding was dead and now Shiny, his father, who had cried out in anguish while my blood-arrow worked its evil, was trying to kill me.

First had come awareness. On its heels came *rage*.

I tried again to shake my head, this time scrabbling at Shiny's wrist with my fingers. It was like grabbing cordwood; his hand didn't budge. Instinctively, I sank my nails into his flesh, having some irrational thought of piercing the tendons to weaken his grip. He shifted his hand slightly—I had an instant to suck a breath—and then pushed my hand away with his free hand, easily brushing off my efforts to regain a grip.

A drop of blood landed in my eye, and red filled my thoughts. The color of pain and blood. The color of fury. The color of Madding's desecrated heart.

I put my hand against Shiny's chest. *I paint a picture, you son of a demon!*

Shiny jerked once. His hand slipped aside; I quickly caught my breath. I braced myself for him to try again, but he did not move.

Suddenly I realized I could see my hand.

For a moment, I was not certain that it *was* my hand. I had never seen my hand before, after all. It looked too small to be mine, long and slender, more wrinkly than I'd expected. There was charcoal under some of the nails. Along the back of the thumb was a raised scar, old and perhaps an inch long. I remembered getting it last year when an awl I'd been using slipped.

I turned my hand to look at the palm and found it completely coated in blood.

There was a thud as Shiny fell to the floor beside me.

I lay where I was for a moment, grimly satisfied. Then I began working at the straps that held me down. Quickly I realized the buckles were meant to be opened with two hands. My other hand was solidly strapped down with a leather cuff, padded on the inside to prevent sores. For a moment, this stymied me until it occurred to me to use the blood on my free hand. I rubbed it on the other wrist, then began working it from side to side, pulling and twisting. I had such small, slender hands. It took time, but eventually the blood and sweat on my wrist made the leather slick, and I slipped that hand free. Then I could open the rest of the buckles and sit up.

When I did, though, I fell back again. My head spun, thick queasiness rolling in its wake. I slumped against the wall, panting and trying to blink away the stars across my vision, and wondering what in the gods' names the Lights had done to me. Only gradually did I realize: all the blood they had taken. Four times. In how many days? Time had passed, but not enough, clearly. I was in no shape to walk or even move much.

That was bad, because I would have to escape the House of the Risen Sun as soon as possible. I had no choice now.

While I lay sprawled across the bed, fighting for consciousness, light glimmered again on the floor. I heard Shiny draw breath, then slowly get to his feet. I felt his angry gaze, heavy as a lead weight.

"Don't touch me," I snapped before he could get any more ideas. "Don't you dare touch me!"

He said nothing. And did not move, looming over me in palpable threat.

I laughed at him. I felt no real amusement, just bitterness. Laughter let me vent it as well as anything else.

"Bastard," I said. I tried to sit up and face him but could not. Staying conscious and talking was the best I could do. My head had lolled to one side like a drunkard's. I kept talking, anyway. "The great lord of light, so merciful and kind. Touch me again and I'll put the next hole through your head. Then I'll bleed on you." I tried to lift my arm, but succeeded only in jerking it a bit. "See if I have enough left in me to kill one of the Three."

It was a bluff. I didn't have the strength to do any of it. Still, he stayed where he was. I could almost feel the fury in him, beating against me like insect wings.

"You cannot be permitted to live," he said. None of that fury was in his voice. He was so good at self-control. "You threaten the entire universe."

I swore at him in every language I could think of. That wasn't much: Senmite; a few epithets in old Maro, which were all I knew of the language; and a bit of gutter Kenti that Ru had taught me. When I finished, I was slurring again, on the brink of passing out. With an effort of will I fought it off.

"To the hells with the universe," I finished. "You didn't give a damn about the universe when you started the Gods' War. You don't give a damn about *anything*, including yourself." I managed to make a vague gesture with one hand. "You want to kill me? Earn it. Help me get free of this place. *Then* my life is yours."

He went very still. Yes, I'd thought that would get his attention.

"A bargain. You understand that, don't you? An *orderly*, fair thing, so you should respect it. You help me, I help you."

"Help you escape."

"Yes, damn you!" My voice echoed from the walls. There were guards outside, I remembered belatedly. I lowered my voice and went on. "Help me get away from this place and *stop these people*."

"If I kill you, they will have no more of your blood."

Such sweet words my Shiny spoke. I laughed again and felt his consternation.

"They'll still have Dateh," I said when the laughter had run out. I was tiring again. Sleepy. Not yet, though. If I didn't make this bargain with Shiny first, I would never wake up.

"With just Dateh's blood, they killed Role. With his power, they've captured others. Four times, Shiny! Four times they've taken my blood. How many more of your children have they poisoned with it?"

I heard the pause of his breath. That one had struck home, oh, yes. I had found his weakness at last, the chink in his apathy. Diminished and reviled and cold-blooded as he was, he still loved his family. So I readied my next lunge, knowing this one would cut even deeper.

"Maybe they'll even use my blood to kill Nahadoth."

"Impossible," Shiny said. But I knew him. That was fear in his voice. "Nahadoth could crush this world before Dateh blinks."

"Not if he's distracted." My eyes drifted shut while I said it. I could not open them, no matter how hard I tried. "They're killing the godlings to lure him here, to the mortal realm. Dateh kills them. *Eats* them." Madding's blood, running dark rivers down Dateh's chin as he bit into the heart like an apple. I gagged and fought the image back. "Takes their magic. I don't know how. How he." I swallowed, focused. *"The Nightlord.* I don't know how Dateh plans to do it. An arrow in the back, maybe. Who the hells knows if it'll work, but . . . do you want him to try? If there's even a chance he could . . . succeed . . ."

Too much. Too much. I needed rest and for no one to try and kill me for a while. Would Shiny let me have that?

One way to find out, I decided, and passed out.

*   *   *

I surfaced a little, bobbing beneath the threshold of consciousness.

Daytime warmth. More voices.

". . . infection," said one. Male. Nice old gravelly voice like Vuroy's, oh how I missed him. More murmured words, soothing. Something about "seizure," "blood loss," and "apothecary."

". . . necessary. There are signs . . ." Serymn. She had come to see me before, I remembered. Wasn't that sweet? She cared. ". . . must move quickly."

The gravelly voice rose and bobbed and dipped enough for me to hear one word, emphasized. ". . . *die.*"

A long sigh from Serymn. "We'll pause for a day or two, then."

More murmurs. Confusing. I was tired. I slept again.

N. K. Jemisin

* * *

Night again. The room felt cooler. I opened my eyes and heard a harsh, ragged panting from the cot nearby. Shiny. His breath bubbled and wheezed strangely. I listened to it for a while, but then his breathing slowed. Caught once, resumed. Ceased again. Stayed silent.

The room smelled of fresh blood again. Had they taken more from me? But I felt better, not worse.

I fell asleep again before Shiny could resurrect and tell me what the Lights had done to him.

* * *

Later. Still night, but deeper into it.

I opened my eyes as brightness flared against them. I glanced over to see Shiny. He lay on the cot, curled on his side, still shimmering from his return to life.

I tried moving and found that I had more energy. My arm was still very sore, and thickly bandaged now, but I could move it. The straps were back in place and cinched tight across my chest and hips and legs, but the other wrist's cuff had been left loose. I easily slipped my hand free.

Shiny's doing? Then he had agreed to my bargain.

I unbuckled myself and sat up slowly, cautiously. There was an instant of dizziness and nausea, but it passed before I could fall on my face. I sat where I was on the edge of the bed, taking deep breaths, becoming reacquainted with my body. Feet. Shaky legs. Diaper around my hips, thankfully clean. Slouched back. Sore neck. I lifted my head and it did not spin. With great care, I got to my feet.

The three steps from my cot to Shiny's exhausted me. I sat

down on the floor beside the cot, leaning my head on his legs. He didn't stir, but his breath tickled my fingers when I examined his face. His brow was furrowed, even in sleep. There were new lines on his face, around his sunken eyes. Not dead, but something had taken its toll on him. He usually woke as soon as he came back to life. Very strange.

As I took my hand away, it brushed against the cloth of his smock. Cooled wetness startled me. I touched, explored, and realized there was a wide patch of half-dried blood all down the lower half of his torso. Pulling up his shirt, I explored his belly. No wound now, but there had been a terrible one before.

He stirred while I was touching him, his glow fading rapidly. I saw him open his eyes and frown at me. Then he sighed and sat up beside me. We sat together, quiet, for a while.

"I have an idea," I said. "To escape. Tell me if you think it will work." I told him, and he listened.

"No," he said.

I smiled. "No, it won't work? Or no, you'd rather kill me on purpose than by accident?"

He stood up abruptly and walked away from me. I could see only a hazy outline of him as he went to the windows and stood there. His hands were clenched into fists, his shoulders high and tense.

"No," he said. "I doubt it will work. But even if it does…" A shudder passed through him, and then I understood.

My anger roiled again, though I laughed. "Oh, I *see*. I'd forgotten that day in the park. When you started this whole mess by attacking Previt Rimarn." I clenched my fists on my thighs, ignoring the twinge from the injured arm. "I remember the look on your face as you did it. That whole time I was in danger, scared out of my mind for you, but *you* were enjoying the chance to wield a bit of your old power."

He did not reply, but I was certain. I had seen his smile that day.

"It must be so hard for you, Shiny. Getting to be your old self again for so brief a time. Then it diminishes until there's nothing left of you but…*this*." I gestured toward his fading back, letting my disgust show. I didn't care what he thought of me anymore. I certainly didn't think much of him. "Bad enough you get a taste of it every morning, isn't it? Maybe it would be easier if you didn't have that little reminder of all you used to be."

He held rigid for a moment, his sullenness racheting toward anger in the usual pattern. Always predictable, he was. So satisfying.

And then, all at once, his shoulders slumped. "Yes," he said.

I blinked, thrown. That made me angrier. So I said, "You're a coward. You're afraid that it *will* work, but afterward it'll be like the last time—you'll be weaker than ever, unable even to defend yourself. Useless."

Again that inexplicable yielding. "Yes," he whispered.

I ground my teeth in thwarted rage. It gave me momentary strength to rise and glare at his back. I did not want his capitulation. I wanted…I did not know. But not this.

"Look at me!" I snarled.

He turned. "Madding," he said softly.

"What about him?"

He said nothing. I made a fist, welcoming the flash of pain as my nails cut my palm. "*What*, damn you?"

Infuriating silence.

If I'd had the strength, I would've thrown something. As it was, I had only words, so I made them count. "Let's talk about Madding, then, why don't we? Madding, your son, who died on the floor, killed by mortals who then *ripped out his heart and ate it*. Madding, who still loved you in spite of everything—"

"Be silent," he snapped.

"Or what, Bright Lord? Will you try to kill me again?" I laughed so hard that it winded me, and I had to gasp out the next words. "Do you think...I *care*...if I die anymore?" At that I had to stop. I sat down heavily, trying not to cry and hoping for the dizziness to pass. Thankfully, but slowly, it did.

"Useless," Shiny said. It was so soft, nearly a whisper, that I barely heard it over my own panting. "Yes. I tried to summon the power. I fought *for him*, and not myself. But the magic would not come."

I frowned, the back of my anger breaking. I felt nothing in its wake. We sat for a long while as the silence stretched on, and the last of his glow faded to nothingness.

Finally I sighed and lay back on Shiny's cot, my eyes closed. "Madding wasn't mortal," I said. "That's why your power didn't work for him."

"Yes," he said. He had control of himself again, his tone emotionless, his diction clipped. "I understand that now. Your plan is still a foolish risk."

"Maybe so," I breathed, drifting toward sleep. "But it's not like you can stop me, so you might as well help."

He came to the bed and stood over me for so long that I did fall asleep. He could've killed me then. Smother me, hit me, strangle me with his bare hands; he had a whole menu of options.

Instead he picked me up. The movement woke me, though only halfway. I floated in his arms, dreamlike. It felt like it took much longer for him to carry me to my cot than it should have. He was very warm.

He laid me down and strapped me back in, leaving the wrist cuff loose so that I could free myself.

"Tomorrow," he said.

I roused at the sound of his voice. "No. They might start taking my blood again. We should go now."

"You need to be stronger." Unspoken, the fact that I would be unable to count on his strength. "And my power won't come at night. Not even to protect you."

"Oh," I said, feeling stupid. "Right."

"Afternoon would be best. The sun will be unobstructed by the Tree then; that may provide some small advantage. I'll do what I can to convince them not to take more of your blood before that."

I reached up to touch his face, then trailed my hand down to his shirt and the stiff spot there. "You died again tonight."

"I have died many times in recent days. Dateh is most fascinated by my ability to resurrect."

I frowned. "What..." But, no, I could imagine all too easily what Dateh had done to him. Searching my hazy memories of the days since Madding's death, I realized this was not the first time Shiny had returned to the room dead, dying, or covered in gore. No wonder there had been no reaction from our captors when I'd blown a hole in him myself.

There were so many things I wanted to think about. So many questions unanswered. How *had* I killed Shiny? I had had no paint that time, not even charcoal. Were Paitya and the others still alive? (Madding, my Madding. No, not him, I could not think about him.) If my plan succeeded, I would try to get to Nemmer, the goddess of stealth. She would help us.

I would see Madding's killers stopped if it was the last thing I did.

"Wake me in the afternoon, then," I said, and closed my eyes.

14

"Flight"
(encaustic, charcoal, metal rubbing)

THERE WERE COMPLICATIONS.

I woke only gradually, which was fortunate, or I might have stirred and given myself away. Before I could do that, someone spoke, and I realized Shiny and I were not alone in the room.

"Let go of me."

My blood chilled. *Hado.* There was tension in the air, something that vibrated along my skin like an itch, but I did not understand it. Anger? No.

"*Let go*, or I call the guards. They're right outside the door."

A quick sound of motion, flesh and cloth.

"Who are you?" That was Shiny, though I hardly recognized his voice. It trembled, wavering from need to confusion.

"Not who you think."

"But—"

"*I am myself.*" Hado said this with such savagery that I nearly forgot myself and flinched. "Just another mortal, to you."

"Yes...yes." Shiny sounded more himself now, the emotion cooling from his voice. "I see that now."

Hado drew in a deep breath, as shaky as Shiny's voice had been, and some of the tension faded. Cloth stirred again and Hado came over to me, shadowing my face. "Has she shown any sign of recovery today? Spoken, maybe?"

"No, and no." Stiffer than usual, even for Shiny. The White Halls taught that the Bright Lord could not lie. I was relieved to hear that he could, though it plainly did not suit him.

"Everything is different now. They'll begin taking blood again tonight. Hopefully she's strong enough."

"That will likely kill her."

"Look outside, man. Two weeks have passed since Role died. Two weeks until the Nightlord's deadline—as he has so dramatically decided to remind us." He uttered a soft, humorless laugh. I wondered what he meant. "Dateh has been a man possessed since he saw it. There's no hope of my dissuading him this time."

Hado's hand stroked my face suddenly, brushing my hair back. I was surprised at such a tender gesture from him. He hadn't struck me as the type for tenderness, even to this small degree.

"In fact," he continued with a sigh, "if her mind doesn't return—or hells, even if it does—I fear he'll take *all* her remaining blood, and her heart, too."

Goose bumps prickled my skin. I prayed that Hado would not notice.

He touched the buckle across my midriff, silent now with his own thoughts—and showing no inclination to leave. I began to worry. The sunlight felt strange on my skin. *Thin*, sort of. Did that mean it was late afternoon? If Hado didn't leave soon, the sun would set and Shiny would become powerless. We needed his magic for this to work.

"You are not quite yourself," Shiny said suddenly. "Something of him lingers." Hado stiffened perceptibly beside me.

"Not the part that gives a damn about you," he snapped, and got up, stalking toward the door. "Speak of this again and I'll kill you myself."

With that he was gone, closing the door rather harder than necessary. And then Shiny was there, yanking at my midriff strap so roughly that I yelped.

"This place has been chaos all day," he said. "The guards are on edge; they keep checking the room. Every hour some interruption—servants bringing food, checking your arm, then that one." Hado, I gathered.

I pushed his hands away and fumbled with the midriff strap myself, gesturing for him to work on the leg straps, which he began to do. "What's happened to get them all upset?"

"When the sun rose this morning, it was black."

I froze, stunned. Shiny kept working.

"A warning?" I asked. The words of the quiet goddess came to me, from that day in South Root. *You know his temper better than I do.* Not Itempas, as I had assumed then. With more of his children dead or missing, it was the Nightlord whose temper would be at the breaking point. Would he even wait the full month he had promised?

"Yes. Though it seems Yeine has managed to contain his fury to some degree. The rest of the world can see the sun clearly. Only this city cannot."

So Serymn had been right in her prediction. I could still feel sunlight on my skin, just weak. There must have been some light remaining, or Shiny wouldn't have bothered trying to free me. Perhaps it was like an eclipse. I had heard those described as the sun going black. But an eclipse that lasted all day and moved with the sun across the sky? No wonder the Lights were a-tizzy. The whole city would be in a panic.

"How much time until sunset?" I asked.

"Very little."

Gods. "Do you think you'll be able to break that window? The glass is so thick." My hands would not work as quickly as I wanted; I was still weak. But better than I had been.

"The cot legs are made of metal. I've loosened one of them, which should serve well as a club." He spoke as if that answered my question, which I supposed was an answer in itself.

We got the straps undone and I sat up. There was no dizziness this time, though I swayed when I stood. Shiny turned away from me, and I heard him positioning the table in front of the door. This was to delay the guards, who would enter as soon as they heard Shiny break the window. Every second would matter once we began.

There was a quick grunt from him, and a metallic groan as he worked the loose leg off his cot. As quietly as he could, he moved the broken cot in front of the door, too. Then we went to the window. I could still feel sunlight on my skin, but it was weak, cooling. Soon it would be gone.

"I don't know how long it will take for the magic to come," he said. *Or whether it will come at all,* he did not say, but I knew he thought it. I was thinking it myself.

"So I'll fall for a while," I said. "It's a long way down."

"Fear alone has killed mortals in moments of danger."

The anger I'd felt since Madding's death had never gone away, just quieted. It rose in me again as I smiled. "Then I won't be afraid."

He hesitated a moment more but finally lifted the cot leg.

The first blow spiderwebbed the window. It was also so loud, echoing in the partially emptied room, that almost immediately I heard men's voices through the door, raised in alarm. Someone fiddled with the lock, rattling keys.

Shiny drew back and heaved the cot leg forward again, grunting with effort as he did so. I felt the wind of the leg's passing; a truly mighty blow. It finished the window, knocking out several large pieces. A startlingly cold wind blew into the room, plastering my smock to my skin and making me shiver.

The guards had gotten the door partially open but were impeded by the table and cot. They were shouting at us, shouting for aid, trying to jostle the furniture out of the way. Shiny tossed aside the cot leg and kicked out as much of the glass as he could. Then he took my hands and guided them forward. I felt the cloth of his smock, removed to cover the jagged edges along the bottom sill.

"Try to push out, away from the Tree, as you jump," he said. As if he told women how to leap to their deaths all the time.

I nodded and leaned out over the drop, trying to figure out how best to push off. As I did so, a breeze wafted up from below, lifting a few stray strands of my hair. For an instant, my resolve faltered. I am only human, after all—or mortal, if not human.

Deliberately, I summoned the image of Madding as he had

gazed at me in that last moment. He had known he was dying, known that I was the cause—but there had been no hatred or disgust in his expression. He'd still loved me.

My fear faded. I moved back, away from the window.

Shiny said over the guards' shouts, urgently, "Oree, you must—"

"Shut up," I whispered, and took a running dive through the opening, spreading my arms as I flew into the open air.

Roaring wind became the only sound I could hear. My clothes flapped around me, stinging my skin. My hair, which someone had tied back into a puff in an effort to control it, broke the tie and clouded loose behind me. Above me. I was falling, but it did not feel like falling. I floated, buoyed on an ocean of air. There was no sense of danger, no stress, no fear. I relaxed into it, wishing it would last.

A hand swatted at my leg, jarring me out of bliss. I turned onto my back, lazy, graceful. Was that Shiny? I could not see him. My plan had failed, then, and we would both die when we struck the ground. He would come back to life. I would not.

I reached up, offering my hands to him. He caught them this time, fumbling once, then drawing me close and wrapping his arms around me. I relaxed against his warm solidity, lulled by the rushing wind. Good. I would not die alone.

Because my ear was against his chest, I felt him stiffen and heard his harsh gasp. His heart thudded hard once, against my cheek. Then—

Light.

By the Three, so bright! All around me. I shut my eyes and still saw Shiny's form blazing before me, thinning the darkness of my vision. I could *feel* it against my skin, like the pressure of sunbeams. We streaked toward the earth like things I had imagined but would never see with my own eyes. Like a comet. Like a falling star.

Our descent slowed. The wind's roar grew softer, gentler. Something had reversed gravity's pull. Were we flying now? Floating. How far had we fallen, how much farther to go? How long before the sun was gone, and—

Shiny cried out. His light vanished, snuffed all at once, and with it went the force that had kept us afloat. We fell again, helpless now, with nothing left to stop us.

I felt no fear.

But Shiny was doing something. Twisting, panting with effort or perhaps the aftermath of his magic. I felt us turn in the air—

And then we hit the ground.

15

"A Prayer to Dubious Gods"
(watercolor)

SOMEONE WAS SCREAMING. High, thin, incessant. Irritating. I was trying to sleep, damn it. I turned over, hoping to orient my ears away from the sound.

The instant I moved my head, nausea struck with stunning speed and force. I had enough time to open my mouth and drag in a loud, wheezing breath before the heaves came. I vomited a thin stream of bile, but nothing more. I must not have eaten for some time.

My stomach seemed determined to dry heave nevertheless, regardless of my lungs' need for air. I fought the urge, my eyes watering and head pounding and ears ringing, until at last I managed to draw in a quick half breath. That helped. The heaving slowed; I breathed more. At last the clenching in my gut ceased—though only for the moment. I could still feel the muscles there trembling, ready to resume their onslaught.

Finally able to think, I lifted my head, trying to figure out where I was and what had happened. The ringing in my ears—which I had mistaken for screaming—was loud and incessant, maddening. The last thing I recalled was...I frowned, though this made the pain worse. Falling. Yes. I had leapt from a window of the House of the Risen Sun, determined to escape or die trying. Shiny had caught me, and—

I caught my breath. *Shiny.*

Beneath me.

I scrambled off him, or tried to. The instant I moved my right arm, I screamed, which touched off another spate of stomach heaves. I fought through the pain and the retching, dragging myself off him with my left arm, which was still sore from infection and whatever the Lights had inserted to draw my blood. Still, the pain in that arm was nothing compared to the agony in my right, and the clenching of my belly, and the shooting pains in my ribs, and the roiling grinding hell of my head. For a few moments I could do nothing but lie where I was, whimpering and helpless with misery.

At last the pain faded enough for me to function. When I finally struggled to a half-upright position, I tried again to assess my surroundings. My right arm would not work at all. I reached out with my left. "Shiny?"

He was there. Alive, breathing. I brushed his eyes, which were open. They blinked, the lashes tickling my fingertips. I wondered if he had decided to stop speaking to me again.

That was when I realized my knees and the hip I sat on were soaking wet. Confused, I felt the ground. Brick cobbles, greasy and thick with dirt. Cold dampness that grew warmer, closer to Shiny's body. As warm as—

Dearest gods.

He was alive. His magic had saved us—not completely, but enough to soften our fall. Enough that when he had turned us in the air, orienting so that he would hit the ground first, we had both survived. But if I was this injured...

My fingers found the back of his head, and I gasped, jerking my hand back. Gods, gods, gods.

Where the hells were we? How long had we been lying here? Did I dare call for help? I looked around, listened. The air felt cool and misty with deep night. Fat drops of water touched my skin now and again with the intermittent gentleness that was rain in Shadow. I could hear it, a light drizzle all around us, but in the immediate vicinity, I heard nothing, no one. I could smell a great deal, though—garbage and fermented urine and rusting metal. Another alley? No, the space around us felt more open. Wherever we were, it was isolated; if anyone had seen us land, sheer curiosity should've brought them to find us.

Shiny had begun to gasp irregularly. I put my hand on his bare chest—he had removed his shirt in the House—and almost drew it back, repelled by the unnatural *flatness* of his torso. Yet his heart still beat steadily, in contrast to the bubbling, jerky breaths that he was struggling to draw in. At this rate, his natural death might take an agonizingly long time.

I had to kill him.

Panic gripped me, though that might have been queasiness, too. I knew it was foolish. It wasn't as though he would stay dead, and when he returned to life, he would be whole. It was, as Lil had concluded, the easiest way to "heal" him. It wouldn't even be the first time I'd done it.

But it was one thing to kill in the heat of anger. Doing it in cold-blooded calculation was a whole other matter.

I wasn't even certain I *could* kill him. My right arm was useless, dislocated or broken, though thankfully it seemed to be going numb. Everything else hurt. I might've survived the fall better than him, but that didn't make me whole. At the very least, I would need two working arms to break his neck.

All at once it hit me: I was lost in some part of Shadow, helpless, with a companion as good as dead. It was only a matter of time before the Lights came looking. They knew Shiny, at least, would come back to life. I was sick, injured, weak. Terrified. And, damn it all, blind.

"Why the hells is everything so *hard* with you?" I demanded of Shiny, blinking away tears of frustration. "Hurry up and die!"

Something rattled nearby.

I gasped, my heart leaping in my chest. Frustration forgotten, I pushed myself to my knees and listened hard. It had come from my right, somewhere above me, a quick metal sound. Water falling on exposed pipe, maybe. Or someone searching for us, reacting to the sound of my voice.

On my hands and knees, I quickly felt around me. A few feet to my left I found wood, old and splintery. A barrel, its binding rings rusty, one side staved in. Above it another, and then something that felt like a wide, flat piece of roof-shingle planking, leaning against the barrels. Jammed against it, a rotted-out crate.

I was in a junkyard. The only junkyard anywhere near the Tree was Shustocks, in Wesha, where all the area's smiths and carters dumped their useless materials and carriageworks.

The roof planking formed a kind of lean-to against the barrels, with a narrow space underneath. As carefully as I could, I pushed the planking farther back, praying there was nothing balanced against it that would fall and give us away—or crush us. Nothing happened, so I felt around more, finally crawling under the planking to inspect the space.

Just enough room.

I backed out and got to my feet, and nearly fell again as another retching spasm took me. The pain in my head was truly awful, worse than it had ever been. I must've hit my head in the fall—not enough to break it, but certainly enough to rattle things around inside.

Another sound from the same direction, something thumping against wood. Then silence.

Panting my way through the pain, I stumbled back to Shiny's body. Hooking my good hand into his pants, I leaned back with my hips and pushed with my legs and whimpered through my teeth as I dragged him back, inch by inch. It took everything I had to get him into the little hiding space, and he did not fit well. His feet stuck out. I crawled in beside him, panting, and listened, hoping the rain would wash away Shiny's blood quickly.

Shiny groaned suddenly and I jumped, glaring at him in consternation. The dragging must have injured him even further. No choice now; if I didn't kill him, he would give us away.

Swallowing hard, I did as he had done to me in the House of the Risen Sun. I pressed my hand over his mouth, pinching his nose shut with my fingers.

For five breaths—I counted my own—it seemed to work. His chest rose, fell. Stilled. And then he bucked upward, fighting me. I tried to hold on, but he was too strong, even damaged as he was, jostling me loose. As soon as I let go, he sucked in air again, louder than before. *Demons, he's going to get us both killed!*

Demons. I flexed my hand, remembering.

There was plenty of blood to use as paint, at least. I reached under his neck and got a generous handful. My hand shook as I put it on his chest, gingerly. Before, I had imagined that I was painting, and then I had *believed* the painting real. Slowly I moved my hand, smoothing the blood in a wide circle on his skin. I would make another hole, like the one I had used to kill Shiny before, like the one that had pierced Dateh's Empty. Not a circle drawn with blood-paint. A hole.

His chest rose and fell beneath my hand, belying this. I scowled and lifted my hand so that I couldn't feel him breathe.

A hole. Through flesh and bone, like a grave dug in soft earth, edges neatly cut by an unseen shovel blade. Perfectly circular.

A hole.

My hand appeared. I saw it hovering in the darkness, fingers splayed, trembling with effort.

A *hole*.

Compared to the sickening throb already in my head, what arced through my eyes was almost pleasant. Either I was getting used to it or I was already in so much pain that it didn't matter. But I noticed when Shiny stopped breathing.

My heart pounding, I lowered my hand to where his chest should have been. I felt nothing at first; then my hand drifted a little to the side. Meat and bone, cut neatly as if with a knife. I snatched my hand back, my gorge rising again all on its own.

"How peculiar!" cried a bright voice, right behind me.

I nearly screamed. Would have done it if my chest hadn't hurt. I did whirl and jump and scramble back, jarring my arm something fierce.

The creature that crouched at Shiny's feet was not human. It had a human structure, more or less, but it was impossibly squat, nearly as wide as it was tall—and it wasn't very tall. Maybe the size of a child, if that child had broad, yokelike shoulders and long arms rippling with muscle. The creature's face was not that of a child, either, though it was cheeky, with huge round eyes. It had a receding hairline, and its gaze was both ancient and half feral.

But I could see it, and that meant it was a godling—the ugliest one I had yet seen.

"H-hello," I said when my heart had stopped jumping around. "I'm sorry. You startled me."

It—he—smiled at me, a quick flash of teeth. Those were not human, either; he had no canines. Just perfectly flat squares, straight across on top and bottom.

"Didn't mean to," he said. "Didn't think you'd see me. Most don't." He leaned close, squinting at my face. "Huh. So you're that girl. The one with the eyes."

I nodded, accepting that bizarre designation. Godlings gossiped like fishermen; enough of them had encountered me that word must've spread. "And you are?"

"Dump."

"Pardon?"

"*Dump.* That's a neat trick you did." He jerked his chin toward Shiny. "Always wanted to pop a hole or two in him myself! What're you doing with him?"

"It's a long story." I sighed, suddenly weary. If only I dared rest. Maybe..."Um. Lord D-Dump." I felt very foolish saying that. "I'm in a lot of trouble here. Please, will you help me?"

Dump cocked his head, like a puzzled dog. Despite this, the look in his eyes was quite shrewd. "You? Depends. Him? No way."

I nodded slowly. Mortals constantly asked godlings for favors; a lot of godlings were prickly about it. And this one didn't like Shiny. I would have to tread carefully, or he might leave before I could explain about his missing siblings. "First, can you tell if anyone else is around? I heard something before."

"That was me. Coming to see what had dropped into my place. Lots of people get tossed out and end up here, but never from so high up." He gave me a wry look. "Thought you'd be messier."

"Your place?" A junkyard was not my idea of a home, but godlings had no need of the material comforts we mortals liked. "Oh. Sorry."

Dump shrugged. "Not like you could help it. Won't be mine much longer, anyway." He gestured upward, and I remembered the blackened sun. The Nightlord's warning.

"You're going to leave?" I asked.

"Got no choice, do I? Not stupid enough to stick around when Naha's this pissed. Just glad he hasn't cursed us, too." He sighed, looking unhappy. "All the mortals, though...They're marked—everybody who was in the city at the time Role and the others died. Even if they leave, they still see the black sun. I tried to send some of my kids down south to one of the coast towns, and they just came back. Said they wanted to be with me when..." He shook his head. "Kill 'em all, guilty and innocent alike. He and Itempas never were all that damn different."

I lowered my head and sighed, weary in more than body. Had it even done any good, escaping the Lights? Would it make any difference if I found a way to expose them? Would the Nightlord destroy the city anyway, for sheer spite?

Dump shifted from foot to foot, abruptly looking uncomfortable. "Can't help you, though."

"What?"

"Someone wants you. Him, too. Can't help either of you."

All at once I understood. "You're the Lord of Discards," I said. I could not help smiling. I'd grown up on tales of him, though I'd never known his true name. They'd been favorites of my childhood. He was another trickster figure, humorous, appearing prominently in stories of runaway children and lost treasures. Once something was thrown away, unwanted, or forgotten, it belonged to him.

He grinned back at me with those unnervingly flat teeth. "Yeah." Then his smile faded. "But you ain't thrown away. Someone wants you *bad*." He took a step back as if my very presence pained him, grimacing in distaste. "You're gonna have to go. I'll send you somewhere, if you can't walk—"

"I know about the missing godlings," I blurted. "I know who's been killing them."

Dump stiffened all at once, his massive fists clenching. "Who?"

"A cult of crazy mortals. Up there." I pointed back toward the Tree. "There's one of them, a scrivener who..." I hesitated, suddenly aware of the danger of naming Dateh a demon. If the gods knew there were still demons in the world...

No. I no longer cared what happened to me. Let them kill me, as long as they dealt with Madding's killers, too.

But before I could say the words, Dump suddenly caught his breath and whirled away from me, his image flaring brighter as he summoned his magic. There was a scream in the distance, and then I heard small feet come pelting around a pile of rubbish, scrabbling once as they trotted along what sounded like a loose board.

"Dump!" a young girl cried. "People in the yard! Rexy told 'em to get the hells out and they hit him! He's bleedin'!"

Abruptly I was jostled as Dump shoved the girl into the little alcove with me and Shiny. "Stay there," he commanded. "I'll go take care of 'em."

I squirmed around the girl. There wasn't much room for her, but she was small. I pushed at her; she was all lanky bones and ragged clothes. "Lord Dump, be careful! The scrivener I told you about, his magic—"

Dump made a sound of annoyance and vanished.

"Damn it!" I pounded my good fist into Shiny's unresponsive leg. If Dateh was among the Lights who had come looking for me, or if they had another arrowhead made from demons' blood...

"Hey," said the girl, annoyed. "Shove the dead guy, not me."

Dead, dead, uselessly dead. I couldn't say he hadn't warned me, though; this was why he'd wanted me stronger before we attempted the escape. So that I could leave him behind? For a moment, the possibility turned in my thoughts. If the Lights didn't find him, Shiny would return to life and make his own way in the city, however he'd done it before meeting me. If they did find him... Well, perhaps he would slow them down enough for me to escape.

Even as I thought it, though, I knew I couldn't do it. As much as I wanted to hate Shiny for his self-absorption and his temper and his miserable personality, he had loved Madding, too. For that alone, he deserved some loyalty.

In the meantime, I needed help. I couldn't count on Dump returning. I had no way to reach mortal aid. If I could summon another godling to help, or better still . . .

My first thought was so repellent that I actually had trouble considering it. I forced myself to do so, anyhow, because Shiny had said it himself: there was one god who would want to deal with his children's killers. Yet I also knew from my people's history that Lord Nahadoth would not stop there. He might decide to wipe out the Lights by wiping out the entire city of Shadow, or perhaps the whole world. He was already angry, and we were nothing to him—worse than nothing. His betrayers and tormentors. It would probably please him to see us all die.

The Gray Lady, then. She had been mortal and still showed some concern for mortalkind. Yet how could I reach her? I wasn't a pilgrim, though I had exploited them for years. To pray to a god—to get a god's attention—one had to thoroughly understand that god's nature. I didn't even know the Lady's real name. The same went for nearly all of the godlings I could think of, including Lady Nemmer. I didn't know enough about any of them.

Then an idea came to me. I swallowed, my hands suddenly clammy. There was one godling whose nature was simple enough, terrible enough, that any mortal could summon her. Though the Maelstrom knew I didn't want to.

"Move," I said to the girl. Muttering, she slipped out, and I crawled one-handed out into the open. The girl started to crawl back in, but I caught her bony leg. "Wait. Is there anything around here like a stick? Something at least this long." I started to lift both arms, then gasped as the muscles of my bad arm cramped agonizingly. I finally approximated the gesture with my good arm. If I had to flee, I would need some means of finding my way.

The girl said nothing, probably glaring at me for a second or two; then she slipped out. I waited, tense, hearing the sounds of battle in the distance—adult shouts, children's screams, debris crashing and splintering. Disturbingly close. That the fight had lasted this long with a godling involved meant there were either a lot of Lights, or Dateh had already gotten him.

The girl came back, pressing something into my hand. I felt it and smiled: a broomstick. Broken off and jagged at one end, but otherwise perfect.

Now came the hard part. I knelt and bowed my head, taking a deep breath to settle my thoughts. Then I reached inside myself, trying to find one feeling amid the morass. One singular, driving need. One *hunger*.

"Lil," I whispered. "Lady Lil, please hear me."

Silence. I fixed my thoughts upon her, framed her in my mind: not her appearance, but the feel of her presence, that looming sense of so many things held in precarious containment. The scent of her, spoiling meat and bad breath. The sound of her whirring, unstoppable teeth. What did it feel like to *want* as she did, constantly? How did it feel to crave something so powerfully that you could taste it?

Perhaps a little like the way I felt, knowing Madding was lost to me forever.

I clenched my hand around the broomstick as my heart

flooded with emotion. I planted the jagged end of it in the dirt and fought the urge to weep, to scream. I wanted him back. I wanted his killers dead. I could not have the former—but the latter was within my grasp, if I could only find someone to help me. Justice was so close I could taste it.

"Come to me, Lil!" I cried, no longer caring if any Lights roving the junkyard heard me. "Come, darkness damn you! I have a feast even you should like the taste of!"

And she appeared, crouching in front of me with her gold hair tangled around her shoulders, her madness-flecked eyes sharp and wary.

"Where?" Lil asked. "What feast?"

I smiled fiercely, flashing my own sharp teeth. "In my soul, Lil. Can you taste it?"

She regarded me for a long moment, her expression shifting from dubious to gradual amazement. "Yes," she said at last. "Oh, yes. Lovely." Her eyes fluttered shut, and she lifted her head, opening her mouth slightly to taste the air. "Such longing in you, for so many things. Delicious." She opened her eyes and frowned in puzzlement. "You were not so tasty before. What has happened?"

"Many things, Lady Lil. Terrible things, which is why I called you. Will you help me?"

She smiled. "No one has prayed to me for centuries. Will you do it again, mortal girl?"

She was like a bauble-beetle, scuttling after any shiny thing. "Will you help me, if I do?"

"Hey," said the girl behind me. "Who's that?"

Lil's gaze settled on her, suddenly avid. "I'll help you," she said to me, "if you give me something."

My lip curled, but I fought back disgust. "I'll give you anything that is mine to give, Lady. But that child is Lord Dump's."

Lil sighed. "Never liked him. No one wants his junk, but he doesn't share." Sulky, she flicked a fingertip at something I couldn't see on the ground.

I reached out and gripped her hand, making her focus on me again. "I've learned who's been killing your siblings, Lady Lil. They're hunting me now, and they may catch me soon."

She stared at my hand on hers in surprise, then at me. "I don't care about any of that," she said.

Damnation! Why did I have to be plagued by *crazy* godlings? Were the sane ones avoiding me? "There are others who do," I said. "Nemmer—"

"Oh, I like her." Lil brightened. "She gives me any bodies her people want to get rid of."

I forgot what I'd meant to say for a moment, then shook it off. "If you tell her this," I said, gambling, "I'm sure she'll give you more bodies." There would be many dead New Lights by the time this business was done, I hoped.

"Maybe," she said, suddenly calculating, "but what will *you* give me to go to her?"

Startled, I tried to think. I had no food on hand, nothing else of value. But I could not escape the feeling that Lil knew what she wanted of me; she just wanted me to say it first.

Humility, then. I had prayed to her, made her *my* goddess in a way. It was her right to demand an offering. I put my good hand on the ground and bowed my head. "Tell me what you want of me."

"Your arm," she said, too quickly. "It's useless now, worse than useless. It may never heal right. Let me have it."

Ah, of course. I looked at the arm dangling at my side. There was a swollen, hot-to-the-touch knot in the upper arm that probably meant a bad break, though fortunately it hadn't come through the skin. I had heard of people dying from such things, their blood poisoned by bits of bone, or infection and fever setting in.

It wasn't the arm I preferred to use; I was left-handed. And I had already decided that I would not need it for much longer.

I took a deep breath. "I can't be incapacitated," I said softly. "I need to ... to still be able to run."

"I can do it so quickly that you'll feel no pain," Lil said, leaning forward in her eagerness. I smelled it again, that fetid whiff of breath from her real mouth, not the false one she was using to coax me. Carrion. But she preferred fresh meat. "Burn the end so it won't bleed. You'll hardly miss it."

I opened my mouth to say yes.

"No," snapped Shiny, startling us both. Leaning on one arm, I nearly fell as I tried to whirl around. I could see him; the magic of his resurrection was still bright.

Dump's girl yelped and scuttled away from us. "You was dead! What the demonshit is this?"

"Her flesh is hers to bargain with!" Lil said, her fists clenching in thwarted anger. "You have no right to forbid me!"

"I think even you would find her flesh disagreeable, Lil." I heard wood rattle and dust grit as he climbed out of the alcove. "Or do you mean to kill another of my children, Oree?"

I flinched. My demon blood. I had forgotten. But before I could explain to Lil, another voice spoke that chilled every drop of poison in my veins.

"There you are. I knew your companion would be alive, Lady Oree, but I'm surprised—and pleased—to see you in the same condition."

Above and behind Lil: one of the tiny, marble-sized portals that Dateh used for spying. I had not noticed it, not with Lil in front of me as a distraction. Too late I realized the sounds of battle in the distance had faded into silence.

Lil turned and stood, cocking her head from one side to the other, birdlike. I scrambled to my feet, leaning heavily on the broomstick for balance against my deadweight arm. To the girl, wherever she was, I hissed, "Run!"

"Now, Lady Oree." Dateh's voice was chiding, reasonable, despite the strangeness of it issuing from the tiny hole. "We both know there's no point in your resisting. I see that you're injured. Must I risk hurting you further by taking you into my Empty? Or will you come quietly?"

From my left, a startled cry. The girl. She had run—and been caught by the people converging on us from that direction. Many sets of feet, ten or twelve. There were others moving around the other end of the junkyard row. The New Lights had come.

"There's no need for you to take that child," I said, trying to keep my voice from shaking. So close! We had almost done it. "Can't you let her go?"

"She's a witness, unfortunately. Don't worry; we take care of children. She won't be mistreated, so long as she joins us."

"Dump!" shouted the girl, who was apparently struggling against her captors. "Dump, help!"

Dump did not appear. My heart sank.

"You're the one!" Lil said, suddenly brightening. "I tasted your ambition weeks ago and warned Oree Shoth to beware of you. I knew if I stayed near her, I might meet you." She beamed like a proud mother. "I am Lil."

"Lil." I gripped the broomstick. "He has powerful magic. He's already killed several godlings, and"—I fought back a shudder of revulsion, which might've been enough to touch off my nausea again—"and eaten them. I don't want to see you join them."

Lil looked at me, startled. "What?"

Shiny's hand gripped my good shoulder; I felt him move in front of me.

"I don't want *you* anymore," Dateh said, cold now. To Shiny. "You're useless, whatever you are. But I have no qualms about going through you to get to her, so step aside."

Lil was still staring at me. "What do you mean, *eaten* them?"

My eyes welled with tears of grief and frustration. "He cuts out their hearts and eats them. He's been doing that to all the missing ones. Gods know how many by now."

"*Lady Oree,*" Dateh said, his voice tight with anger. All at once, the hole doubled in size, tearing the air as it grew. It drifted toward us, a warning. There was no suction—yet.

"You didn't say they were being eaten. You should have said that in the first place," Lil said, looking annoyed. Then she turned on Dateh's hole, and her expression darkened. "It is bad, very bad, for a mortal to eat one of us."

I felt the suction the instant it began. It was gentler than that night in front of Madding's, but still enough to stagger me. In front of me, Shiny grunted and set his feet, his power rising, but it dragged him forward, anyway—

Lil shoved both of us roughly aside, stepping in front of the hole.

The suction increased sharply, to full force. Shiny and I had both fallen to the ground; I was sprawled and half sensible, as the fall had jarred both my head and my broken arm. Through a haze, I saw Lil, her legs braced, her gown whipping about her scrawny form, her long yellow hair tangling in the wind. The hole was huge now, nearly as big as her body, yet somehow it had not claimed her.

She lifted her head. I was behind her, but I knew the instant her mouth lengthened, without seeing it.

"Greedy mortal boy." Lil's voice was everywhere, echoing, shrill with delight. "Do you really think that will work on *me*?"

She spread her arms wide, blazing with golden power. I heard the buzz and whir of her teeth, so loud that it made my bones rattle and my spine vibrate, so powerful that even the earth shivered beneath me. The whir rose to a scream as she lunged at the portal—and *tried to eat it*. Sparks of pure magic shot past us, each one burning where it landed. A concussion of force flattened me even more and shattered the piles of junk around us. I heard wood splintering, debris tumbling, the Lights screaming, and Lil laughing like the insane monster she was.

And then Shiny had my good arm, hauling me up. We ran, him half dragging me because my legs would not work and I kept trying to vomit. Finally he scooped me into his arms and ran, as behind us the junkyard erupted in earthquakes and chaos and flames.

16

"From the Depths to the Heights"
(watercolor)

I GRAYED OUT FOR A TIME. The jostling, the running, and the blurring cacophony of sounds proved too much for my already-abused senses. I was vaguely aware of pain and confusion, my sense of balance completely thrown; it felt as though I tumbled through the air, unconnected to anything, uncontrolled. A blurry voice seemed to whisper into my ear: *Why are you alive when Madding is dead? Why are you alive at all, death-filled vessel that you are? You are an affront to all that is holy. You should just lie down and die.*

It might have been Shiny speaking, or my own guilt.

* * *

After what felt like a very long time, I regained enough wit to think.

I sat up, slowly and with great effort. My arm, the good one, did not obey my will at first. I told it to push me up, and instead it flailed about, scrabbling at the surface beneath me. Hard, but not stone. I sank my nails into it a little. Wood. Cheap, thin. I patted it, listening, and realized it was all around me. When I finally regained control of myself, I managed a slow, shaky exploration of my environment, and finally understood. A box. I was in some kind of large wooden crate, open at one end. Something heavy and scratchy and smelly lay upon me. A horse blanket? Shiny must have stolen it for me. It still reeked of its former owner's sweat, but it was warmer than the chilly pre-dawn air around me, so I drew it closer.

Footsteps nearby. I cringed until I recognized their peculiar weight and cadence. Shiny. He climbed into the crate with me and sat down nearby. "Here," he said, and metal touched my lips. Confused, I opened my mouth, and nearly choked as water flooded in. I managed not to splutter too much of it away, fortunately, because I was desperately thirsty. As Shiny turned up the flask for me again, I greedily drank until there was nothing left. I was still thirsty but felt better.

"Where are we?" I asked. I kept my voice soft. It was quiet, wherever we were. I heard the *bap-plink* of morning dew—such a welcome sound after days without it in the House of the Risen Sun. There were people about, but they moved quietly, too, as if trying not to disturb the dew.

"Ancestors' Village," he said, and I blinked in surprise. He had carried me across the city from the Shustocks junkyard, from Wesha into Easha. The Village was just north of South Root, near the tunnel under the rootwall. It was where the city's homeless population had made a camp of sorts, or so I'd been told. I'd never visited it. Many of the Villagers were sick in body or mind, too harmless to be quarantined, but too ugly or strange or pitiful to be acceptable in the orderly society of the Bright. Many were lame, mute, deaf... blind. In my earliest days in Shadow, I'd been terrified of joining them.

I didn't ask, but Shiny must have seen the confusion on my face. "I lived here sometimes," he said. "Before you."

It was no more than I'd already guessed, but I could not help pity: he had gone from ruling the gods to living in a box among lepers and madlings. I knew his crimes, but even so...

Belatedly I noticed more footsteps approaching. These were lighter than Shiny's, several sets—three people? One of them had a bad limp, dragging the second foot like deadweight.

"We have missed you," said a voice, elderly, raspy, of indeterminate gender, though I guessed male. "It's good to see you well. Hello, miss."

"Um, hello," I said. The first words had not been directed at me.

Satisfied, the maybe-man turned his attention back to Shiny. "For her." I heard something set down on the crate's wooden floor; I smelled bread. "See if she can get that down."

"Thank you," said Shiny, surprising me by speaking.

"Demra's gone looking for old Sume," said another voice, younger and thinner-sounding. "She's a bonebender—not a very good one, but sometimes she'll work for free." The voice sighed. "Wish Role was still around."

"That won't be necessary," said Shiny, because of course he intended to kill me. Even I could tell that these people didn't have many favors to call in; best they not spend such a precious one on me. Then Shiny surprised me further. "Something for her pain would be good, however."

A woman came forward. "Yes, we brought this." Something

else was set down, glass. I thought I heard the slosh of liquid. "It isn't good, but it should help."

"Thank you," Shiny said again, softer. "You are all very kind."

"So are you," said the thin voice, and then the woman murmured something about letting me sleep, and all three of them went away. I lay there in their wake, not quite boggling. I was too tired for real astonishment.

"There's food," Shiny said, and I felt something dry and hard brush my lips. The bread, which he'd torn into chunks so I wouldn't have to waste strength gnawing. It was coarse, flavorless stuff, and even the small piece he'd torn made my jaws ache. The Order of Itempas took care of all citizens; no one starved in the Bright. That did not mean they ate *well*.

As I held a piece in my mouth, hoping saliva would make it more palatable, I considered what I had heard. It had had the air of long habit—or ritual, perhaps. When I'd swallowed, I said, "They seem to like you here."

"Yes."

"Do they know who you are? What you are?"

"I have never told them."

Yet they knew, I was certain. There had been too much reverence in the way they'd approached and presented their small offerings. They had not asked about the black sun, either, as a heathen might have done. They simply accepted that the Bright Lord would protect them if He could—and that it was pointless to ask if He could not.

I had to clear my dry throat to speak. "Did you protect them while you were here?"

"Yes."

"And...you spoke to them?"

"Not at first."

With time, though, same as me. For a moment, an irrational competitiveness struck me. It had taken three months for Shiny to deem me worthy of conversation. How long had he taken with these struggling souls? But I sighed, dismissing the fancy and refusing when Shiny tried to offer me another piece of bread. I had no appetite.

"I've never thought of you as kind," I said. "Not even when I was a child, learning about you in White Hall. The priests tried to make you sound gentle and caring, like an old grandfather who's a little on the strict side. I never believed it. You sounded... well-intentioned. But never kind."

I heard the glass thing move, heard a stopper come free with a faint *plonk*. Shiny's hand came under the back of my head, lifting me gently; I felt the rim of a small flask nudge my lips. When I opened my mouth, acid fire poured in—or so it tasted. I gasped and spluttered, choking, but most of the stuff went down my throat before my body could protest too much. "Gods, no," I said when the bottle touched my lips again, and Shiny took it away.

As I lay there trying to regain the full use of my tongue, Shiny said, "Good intentions are pointless without the will to implement them."

"Mmm." The burn was fading now, which I regretted, because for a moment I had forgotten the pain of my arm and head. "The problem is, you always seem to implement your intentions by stomping all over other people's. That's pretty pointless, too, isn't it? Does as much harm as good."

"There is such a thing as greater good."

I was too tired for sophistry. There had been no greater good in the Gods' War, just death and pain. "Fine. Whatever you say."

I drifted awhile. The drink went to my head quickly, not so much dulling the pain as making me care less about it. I was contemplating sleeping again when Shiny spoke. "Something is happening to me," he said, very softly.

"Hmm?"

"It isn't my nature to be kind. You were correct in that. And I have never before been tolerant of change."

I yawned, which made my headache grow in a distant, warm sort of way. "Change happens," I said through the yawn. "We all have to accept it."

"No," he replied. "We don't. *I* never have. That is what I am, Oree—the steady light that keeps the roiling darkness at bay. The unmoving stone around which the river must flow. You may not like it. You don't like *me*. But without my influence, this realm would be cacophony, anarchy. A hell beyond mortal imagination."

Surprised into wakefulness, I blurted the first thing that came to mind. "Does it bother you that I don't like you?"

I heard him shrug. "You have a contrary nature. I suspect you are of Enefa's lineage."

I almost laughed at the sour note in his voice, though that would've hurt my head. I sobered, though, as I realized something. "You and Enefa weren't always enemies."

"We were never enemies. I loved her, too." And I could hear that, suddenly, in the soft interstices of his tone.

"Then"—I frowned—"why?"

He did not answer for a long while.

"It was a kind of madness," he said at last, "though I did not think so at the time. My actions seemed perfectly rational, until...after."

I shifted a little, uncomfortable, both from my arm and the conversation topic. "That's pretty normal," I said. "People snap sometimes. But afterward—"

"Afterward I had no recourse. Enefa was dead and could not—I thought—be restored. Nahadoth hated me and would shatter all the realms for vengeance. I dared not free him. So I committed myself to the path I had chosen." He paused for a moment. "I...regret...what I did. It was wrong. Very wrong. But regret is meaningless."

He fell silent. I knew I should have let it go then, with the echoes of his pain still reverberating in the air around me. He was ancient, unfathomable; there was so much about him I would never understand. But I reached out with my good hand and found his knee.

"Regret is never meaningless," I said. "It's not *enough*, not on its own; you have to change, too. But it's a start."

Shiny let out a long sigh of almost unbearable weariness. "Change is not my nature, Oree. Regret is all I have."

More silence then, for a long while.

"I'd like some more of that stuff," I said at length. The throb of my arm was becoming more present; the liquor had worn off. "But I think I'd better eat something beforehand."

So Shiny resumed feeding me, giving me more water, too, from among the offerings the Villagers had made. I had the presence of mind to keep a little in my mouth and use that to soften the horrid bread. "In the morning there will be soup," he said. "I'll have the others bring some to us. It would be best if neither you nor I are seen for a while."

"Right," I said, sighing. "So what do we do now? Live here among the beggars until the New Lights find us again? Hope I don't die of infection before Mad's killers are brought to justice?" I rubbed my face with my good hand. Shiny had given me more of the fiery liquor, and already it was making me feel warm and feather-light. "Gods, I hope Lil is all right."

"They are both children of Nahadoth. In the end, it will be a matter of strength."

I shook my head. "Dateh's not..." Then I understood. "Oh. That explains a lot." I felt Shiny throw me a look. Well, too late to take it back.

"She is my daughter, too," he said, at length. "He will not defeat her easily."

For a moment I puzzled over this, wondering how on earth the Lord of Night and the Bright Father had managed to have a child together. Or was he speaking figuratively, counting all godlings as his children regardless of their specific parentage? Then I dismissed it. They were gods; I didn't need to understand.

We fell silent for a while, listening to the dew fall. Shiny ate the rest of the bread, then sat back against a wall of the crate. I lay where I was and wondered how long it would be 'til dawn and whether there was any point in living long enough to see it.

"I know who we can go to for help," I said at length. "I don't dare call another godling; I won't be responsible for more of their deaths. But there are some mortals, I think, who are strong enough to take on the Lights. If you help me."

"What do you want me to do?"

"Take me back to Gateway Park. The Promenade." The last place I had been happy. "Where they found Role. Do you remember it?"

"Yes. There are often New Lights in that area."

Yes. This time of year, with the Tree about to bloom, all the heretic groups would have people at the Promenade, hoping to convert some of the Lady's pilgrims to their own faiths. Easier to start with people who had already turned their backs on Bright Itempas.

"Help me get there unseen," I said. "To the White Hall."

He said nothing. All at once, tears sprang to my eyes, inexplicable. Drunkenness. I fought them back.

"I have to see this through, Shiny. I have to make sure the New Lights are destroyed. They still have my blood—they can make more of those arrow things. Madding isn't like Enefa. He won't come back to life."

I could still see him in my head. *I always knew you were special*, he'd said, and my specialness had killed him. His death had to be the last.

Shiny got up, climbed out of the crate, and walked away.

I could not help it. I gave in to the tears, because there was nothing else I could do. I didn't have the strength to make it to the Promenade on my own, or elude the Lights for much longer. My only hope was the Order. But without Shiny—

I heard his heavy footfalls and caught my breath, pushing myself up and wiping the tears off my face.

Something heavy and loose landed in front of me. I touched it, puzzled it out. A cloak. It reeked of someone's unwashed filth and stale urine, but I caught my breath as I realized what he meant for us to do.

"Put that on," Shiny said. "Let's go."

* * *

The Promenade.

Dawn had not yet come, but the Promenade was far from still. People stood in knots on streets and corners, murmuring, some weeping, and for the first time I noticed the tension that filled the city, as it must have since the sun had turned black the day before. The city was never quiet at night, but by the sounds that I could hear on the wind, many of its denizens had not slept the night before. A good number must have risen to wait for the sunrise, perhaps in hopes of seeing a change in the sun's condition. There were none of the usual vendors about—and no one at Art Row, though it was still too early for that—but I could hear the pilgrims. Many more than usual seemed to have gathered, kneeling on the bricks and murmuring prayers to the Gray Lady in her dawn guise. Hoping she would save them.

Shiny and I made our way along quietly, keeping close to buildings rather than crossing the Promenade. That would've been faster—the White Hall was directly across from us—but also more conspicuous, even amid the milling crowd. Most Villagers knew better than to enter those parts of the city frequented by visitors; doing so was a good way to get rousted by Order-Keepers. They would be tense today, and a good many of them were young hotheads who would just as soon take Shiny and me into an empty storehouse to deal with themselves. We needed to reach the White Hall itself, where they were more likely to do the proper thing and take us in.

I had discarded my makeshift stick, as it was too much of a giveaway. I barely had the strength to hold it, anyhow; a fever had sapped what little energy I'd gained from resting in the Village, forcing us to stop frequently. I walked close behind Shiny, holding on to the back of his cloak so that I could feel it when he stepped over an obstacle or skirted around milling folk. This forced me to keep low and shuffle a bit, which added to the disguise, though I could feel that Shiny hadn't done the same, walking with his usual stiff-backed, upright pride. Hopefully no one would notice.

We had to pause at one point while a line of chained people came down the street with push brooms, sweeping the bricks clean for the day's business. Debtors, most likely, only a step away from life in the Ancestors' Village themselves. Working despite the tension in the city. Of course the Order of Itempas would not disrupt the city's daily functions, even under a god's death sentence.

Then they were gone, and Shiny started forward again—and abruptly paused. I bumped into his back, and he put back an arm to push me aside, into the doorway alcove of a building. Unfortunately, he touched the broken arm in the process; I managed not to scream, but just barely.

"What is it?" I whispered, when I'd regained enough self-control to speak. I was still panting. It helped me feel cooler, given the fever.

"More Order-Keepers, patrolling," he said tersely. The Promenade must have been crawling with them. "They did not see us. Be still."

I obeyed. We waited there long enough that Shiny's morning

glow began. Irrationally I worried that it would somehow draw the Lights, even though no one had ever seen the glow of his magic but me. Though perhaps it would work in our favor and draw some godling instead.

I jerked back, blinking and disoriented. Shiny held me up, bracing me against the door.

"What?" I asked. My thoughts were blurry.

"You collapsed."

I took a deep breath, shivering before I could help myself. "Just a little farther. I can make it."

"It might be best if—"

"No," I said, trying to sound firmer. "Just get me to the steps. I can crawl from there if I have to."

Shiny obviously had his doubts, but as usual he said nothing.

"You don't have to go in with me," I said as I recovered. "They'll just kill you."

Shiny sighed and took my hand, a silent rebuke. We resumed our careful movement around the circle.

That we reached the White Hall steps without trouble was so amazing that without thinking, I whispered a prayer of thanks to Itempas. Shiny turned to stare at me for a moment, then led me on up the steps.

My first knock on the big metal door got no response, but then I hadn't knocked hard. When I tried to lift my hand again and swayed on my feet, Shiny caught my hand and knocked himself. Three booming strikes, seeming to echo through the whole building. The door opened before the third blow's echoes had faded. "What the hells do you want?" asked an annoyed-sounding guard. He grew more annoyed as he assessed us. "Food distribution will be at noon, the way it is every day, *in the Village*," he snapped. "Get back there or I'll—"

"My name is Oree Shoth," I said. I tugged back the hood so he could see I was Maroneh. "I killed three Order-Keepers. You've been looking for me. For us." I gestured tiredly at Shiny. "We need to speak to Previt Rimarn Dih."

*   *   *

They separated us and put me in a small room with a chair, a table, and a cup of water. I drank the water, begged the silent guard for more, and when he brought no more, I put my head down on the table and slept. The guard had obviously been given no instructions about this, so he let me sleep for some time. Then I was roughly shaken awake.

"Oree Shoth," said a familiar voice. "This is unexpected. I'm told you *asked* to see me."

Rimarn. I had never been so glad to hear his cold voice.

"Yes," I said. My voice was hoarse, dry. I was hot all over and shaking a little. I probably looked like all the infinite hells combined. "There's a cult. Not heretics—Itempans. They're called the New Lights. One of their members is a scrivener. Dateh." I tried to remember Dateh's family name and could not. Had he ever told me? Unimportant. "They call him the Nypri. He's a demon, a real one, like in the stories. Demon blood is poison to gods. He's been capturing godlings and killing them. He's the one who killed Role and...and others." My strength ran out. I hadn't had much of it to begin with, which was why I'd spoken as quickly as I could. My head drooped, the table beckoning. Perhaps they would let me sleep some more.

"That's quite a tale," Rimarn said after an astonished moment.

"*Quite* a tale. You do seem…distressed, though that could simply be because your protector, the god Madding, has gone missing. We keep expecting his body to turn up, like the other two we found, but so far, nothing."

He'd said it to hurt me, to see my reaction, but nothing could hurt more than the fact of Madding's death. I sighed. "Ina, probably, and Oboro. I…heard they'd gone missing." Perhaps the discovery of their bodies had triggered the Nightlord's dramatic warning.

"You'll have to tell me how you heard that, since we'd witheld that information from the public." I heard Rimarn's fingers tap against the tabletop. "I imagine you've had a difficult few weeks. Been hiding out among the beggars, have you?"

"No. Yes. Just today, I mean." I dragged my head up, trying to orient on his face. People who could see took me more seriously when I seemed to look at them. I willed him to believe me. "Please. I don't care if you go after them yourself. You probably shouldn't; Dateh's powerful, and his wife is an Arameri. A *full-blood*. They've probably got an army up there. The godlings. Just tell the godlings. Nemmer."

"Nemmer?" At that, at last, he sounded surprised. Did he know Nemmer, or perhaps know *of* her? That would figure; the Order-Keepers had to be keeping track of the various gods of Shadow. I imagined they would keep an especially close eye on Nemmer given that her nature defied the pleasant, comfortable order of the Bright.

"Yes," I said. "Madding was…they were. Working together. Trying to find their siblings." I was so tired. "Please. Can I have some water?"

For a moment, I thought he would do nothing. Then to my surprise, Rimarn rose and went to the room's door. I heard him speak to someone outside. After a moment, he returned to the table, pressing the refilled cup into my hand. Someone else came in with him and stood along the room's far wall, but I had no idea who this was. Probably just another Order-Keeper.

I spilled half the water trying to lift it. After a moment, Rimarn took it from my hands and held it to my lips. I drank it all, licked the rim, and said, "Thank you."

"How were you injured, Oree?"

"We jumped out of the Tree."

"You..." He fell silent for a moment, then sighed. "Perhaps you should begin at the beginning."

I contemplated the monumental task of talking more and shook my head.

"Then why should I believe you?"

I wanted to laugh, because I had no answer for him. Did he want proof that I'd leapt from the Tree and survived? Proof that the Lights were up to no good? What would sway him, me dying on the spot?

"Proof isn't necessary, Previt Dih." This was a new voice, and it was enough to startle me awake, because I recognized it. Oh, dear gods, how well I recognized it.

"Faith should be enough," said Hado, the New Lights' Master of Initiates. He smiled. "Shouldn't it, Eru Shoth?"

"No." I would have leapt to my feet and fled if I could have. Instead I could only whimper and despair. "No, I was so close."

"You did better than you realize," he said, coming over and patting my shoulder. It was the shoulder of the bad arm, which was now swollen and hot. "Oh, you're not well at all. Previt, why hasn't a bonebender been summoned for this woman?"

"I was just about to, Lord Hado," said Rimarn. I could hear anger in his tone, underlying the careful respect in his speech. *What...?*

Hado humphed a little, pressing the back of his hand to my forehead. "Is the other one prepared? I'm not keen on wrestling him into submission."

"If you like, my men can bring him to you later." I could actually hear Rimarn's frosty smile. "We would make certain he is sufficiently subdued."

"Thank you, but no. I have orders, and no time." A hand took my good arm and pulled me up. "Can you walk, Lady Oree?"

"Where..." I couldn't catch my breath. Fear ate at my thoughts, but I was more confused by the conversation. Was Rimarn turning me over to the Lights? Since when had the Order of Itempas been subservient to some cult? Nothing here made sense. "Where are you taking me?"

He ignored my question and pulled me along, and I had no choice but to shuffle at his side. He had to go slow, as it was the best pace I could do. Outside the little room, we were joined by two other men, one of whom grabbed my injured arm before I could evade him. I screamed, and Hado cursed.

"Look at her, you fool. Be more careful." With that, the man let me go, though his companion kept a grip on my good arm. Without that, I might not have remained standing.

"I will take her," said Shiny, and I blinked, realizing I had grayed out again. Then someone lifted me in strong arms, and I felt warm all over like I'd been sitting in a patch of sun, and though I should not have felt safe at all, I did. So I slept again.

*   *   *

Waking, this time, was very different.

It took a long time, for one thing. I was very conscious of this as my mind moved from the stillness of sleep to the alertness of waking, yet my body did not keep up. I lay there, aware of silence and warmth and comfort, able to recall what had happened to me in a distant, careless sort of way, but unable to move. This did not feel restrictive or alarming. Just strange. So I drifted, no longer tired, but helpless while my flesh insisted upon waking in its own good time.

Eventually, however, I did succeed in drawing a deeper breath. This startled me because it did not hurt. The ache that had been deepening in one side where I thought the ribs were cracked was gone. So surprising was this that I drew another breath, moved my leg a little, and finally opened my eyes.

I could see.

Light surrounded me on all sides. The walls, the ceiling. I turned my head: the floor, too. All of it shone, some strange, hard material like polished stone or marble, but it glowed bright and white with its own inner magic.

I turned my head. (More surprise there: this did not hurt, either.) An enormous window, floor to very high ceiling, dominated one wall. I could not see beyond it, but the glass shimmered faintly. The furniture around the room—a dresser, two huge chairs, and an altar for worship in the corner—did not glow. I could see them only as dark outlines, silhouetted by the white of the walls and floor. I supposed not everything could be magic here. The bed that I lay on was dark, a negative shape against the pale floor. And threading up and down through the walls at random were long patches of darker material that looked like nothing I had ever seen before. This material glowed, too, in a faint green that was somehow familiar. Magic of a different sort.

"You're awake," said Hado from one of the chairs. I started, because I had not noticed the silhouette of legs against the floor.

He rose and came over, and as he did, I noticed something else strange. Though the other nonmagical objects in the room were dark to my vision, Hado was darker. It was a subtle thing, noticeable only when he moved past something that should have been equally shadowed.

Then he bent over me, reaching for my forehead, and I remembered that he was one of the people who had killed Madding. I slapped his hand away.

He paused, then chuckled. "And I see you're feeling stronger. Well, then. If you'll get up and get dressed, Lady, you have an appointment with someone very important. If you're polite—and lucky—he may even answer your questions."

I sat up, frowning, and only belatedly realized my arm was encumbered. I examined it and found that the upper arm had been set and splinted with two long metal rods, which had then been bound tightly in place with bandages. It still hurt, I found when I tried to bend it; this triggered a deep, spreading ache through the muscles. But it was infinitely better than it had been.

"How long have I been here?" I asked, dreading the answer. I was clean. Even the blood that had been crusted under my nails was gone. Someone had bound my hair back in a single neat braid. There was no bandaging on my ribs or head; those injuries were completely healed.

That took days. Weeks.

"You were brought here yesterday," Hado said. He set clothing on my lap. I touched it and knew at once that it was not the usual New Light smock. The material under my fingers was something much finer and softer. "Most of your injuries were easily treated, but your arm will require a few more days. Don't disturb the script."

"Script?" But now I saw it as I lifted the sleeve of the nightgown I wore. Wrapped into the bindings was a small square of paper, on which had been drawn three interlinked sigils. The characters glowed against my silhouette, working whatever magic they did just by existing.

Bonebenders might use the odd sigil, generally the most commonly known or simple to draw, but never whole scripts. Anything this complex and intricate was scriveners' work—the kind that cost a fortune.

"What is this, Hado?" I turned my head to follow him as he went over to a window. Now that I knew to look for that distinctive darkness, he was easy to see. "This isn't the House of the Risen Sun. What's going on? And you—what the hells are you?"

"I believe the common term is *spy*, Lady Oree."

That hadn't been what I'd meant, but it distracted me. "Spy? *You?*"

He uttered a soft, humorless laugh. "The secret to being an effective spy, Lady Oree, is to *believe* in your role and never step out of character." He shrugged. "You may not like me for it, but I did what I could to keep you and your friends alive."

My hands tightened on the sheets as I thought of Madding. "You didn't do a very good job of it."

"I did an excellent job of it, all things considered, but blame me for your lover's death if it makes you feel better." His tone said he didn't care whether I did or not. "When you have time to think about it a little, you'll realize Dateh would have killed him, anyhow."

None of this made sense. I pushed back the covers and tried to get up. I was still weak; no amount of magical healing could fix that. But I was stronger than I had been, a clear sign of improvement. It took me two tries to stand, but when I did, I did not sway. As quickly as I could, I changed out of the nightgown and into the clothes he'd given me. A blouse and an elegantly long skirt, much more my usual style than the shapeless Light clothing. They fit perfectly, even the shoes. There was also a sling for my arm, which eased the lingering pain greatly once I worked out how to put it on.

"Ready?" he asked, then took my arm before I had a chance to answer. "Come, then."

We left the room and walked through long, curving corridors, and I could see all of it. The graceful walls, the arched ceiling, the mirror-smooth floor. As we mounted a set of shallow, wide stairs, I slowed, figuring out by trial and error how to gauge height using just my eyes and not a walking stick. Once I mastered the technique, I found that I didn't need Hado's hand on my arm to guide me. Eventually I shook him off entirely, reveling in the novelty of making my way unassisted. All my life I had heard arcane terms like *depth perception* and *panorama*, yet never fully understood. Now I felt like a seeing person—or how I had always imagined they must feel. I could see *everything*, except for the man-shaped shadow that was Hado at my side and the occasional shadows of other people passing by, most of them moving briskly and not speaking. I stared at them shamelessly, even when the shadows turned their heads to stare back.

Then a woman passed close to us. I got a good look at her forehead and stopped in my tracks.

An Arameri blood sigil.

Not the same as Serymn's—this had a different shape, its meaning a mystery to me. The servants of the Arameri were rumored to be Arameri themselves, just more distantly related. All marked, though, in some esoteric way that only other family members might understand.

Hado paused as well. "What is it?"

Compelled by a growing suspicion, I turned away from him and went to one of the walls, touching the green patch there. It was rough under my fingers, scratchy and hard. I leaned close, sniffed. The scent was faint but unmistakably familiar: the sweet living wood of the World Tree.

I was in Sky. The Arameri's magical palace. This was *Sky*.

Hado came up behind me, but this time he said nothing. Just let me absorb the truth. And at last, I did understand. The Arameri had been watching the New Lights, perhaps because of Serymn's involvement, or perhaps realizing that they were the most likely of the heretic groups to pose a threat to the Order of Itempas. I'd wondered about Hado's odd way of talking—like a nobleman. Like a man who'd spent his whole life surrounded by power. Was he Arameri himself? He had no mark, but maybe it was removable.

Hado had infiltrated the group on the Arameri's behalf. He must have warned them that the Lights were more dangerous than they seemed. But then—

I turned to Hado. "Serymn," I said. "Is she a spy, too?"

"No," said Hado. "She's a traitor. If you can call anyone in this family that." He shrugged. "Remaking society is something of a tradition with Arameri. When they succeed, they get to rule. When they fail, they get death. As Serymn will learn soon."

"And Dateh? What is he? Her unwitting pawn?"

"*Dead*, I hope. Arameri troops began attacking the House of the Risen Sun last night."

I gasped. He smiled.

"Your escape gave me the opportunity I'd been waiting for, Lady. Though my role as Master of Initiates allowed me access to the Lights' inner circle, I could not communicate beyond the House of the Risen Sun easily without rousing suspicion. Once Serymn turned out nearly the entire complement of Lights to search for you, I was able to get word to certain friends, who made sure the information reached the right ears." He paused. "The Lights were right about one thing: the gods have ample cause to be angry with mortalkind, and the deaths of their kin have done little to endear us to them. The Arameri understand this and so have taken steps to control the situation."

My hand on the Tree's bark began to tremble. I had never realized the Tree grew *through* the palace, integrated with its very substance. At the roots, its bark was rougher, with crevices deeper than the length of my hand. This bark, high on the

Tree's trunk, was fine-lined, almost smooth. I stroked it absently, seeking comfort.

"Lord Arameri," I said. T'vril Arameri, head of the family that ruled the world. "Is that who you're taking me to see?"

"Yes."

I had walked among gods, wielded the magic they'd given my ancestors. I had held them in my arms, watched their blood coat my hands, feared them and been feared by them in turn. What was one mortal man to all that?

"All right, then." I turned back to Hado, who offered me his arm. I walked past him without taking it, which caused him to shake his head and sigh. Then he caught up with me, and together we continued through the shining white corridors.

17

"A Golden Chain"
(engraving on metal plate)

T'VRIL ARAMERI WAS A VERY BUSY MAN. As we walked the long hallway toward the imposing set of doors that led to his audience chamber, they opened several times to admit or release brisk-walking servants and courtiers. Most of these carried scrolls or whole stacks thereof; a few wore long sharp shapes that I assumed were swords or spears; still more were very well dressed, their foreheads bearing the marks of Arameri. No one lingered in the corridor to chat, though some spoke while on the move. I heard Senmite flavored with exotic accents: Narshes, Min, Veln, Mencheyev, others I did not recognize.

A busy man, who valued useful people. Something to keep in mind if I hoped to enlist his aid.

At the doors, we paused while Hado announced us to the two women who stood there. High Northers, I guessed by the fact that both were shorter than average and by their telltale straight hair, which hung long enough that I could see its sway.

They did not appear to be guards at first glance—no weapons that I could see, though they could have had something small or close to their bodies—but something in the set of their shoulders let me know that was exactly what they were. They were *not* Arameri, or even Amn. Were they here, then, to guard the lord from his own family? Or was their presence emblematic of something else?

One of the women went inside to announce us. A moment later, a knot of other people emerged and filed past us. They stared at me with open curiosity. They looked at Hado, too, I noticed, especially the two fullbloods who emerged together and immediately fell to whispering at each other. I glanced at Hado, who seemed not even to see them. I wished I dared touch his face, because there was a pleased air about him that I wasn't sure how to interpret.

The guard emerged from the chamber and, without a word, held the door open for us. I followed Hado inside.

The audience chamber was open and airy. Two enormous windows, each many paces in width and twice Shiny's height, dominated the walls on either side of the door. As we walked, the sounds of our footsteps echoed from high overhead. I was too nervous to look up. The room's sole piece of furniture, a great blocklike chair, sat at the farthest point from the door, atop a tiered dais. And though I could not see the chair's occupant, I could hear him, writing something on a piece of paper. The scratching of his pen sounded very loud in the room's vast silence.

I could see his blood sigil, too, a stranger mark than anything I'd seen yet: a half-moon, downturned, bracketed on either side by glimmering chevrons.

We waited, silent, while he finished whatever he was doing. When the lord set his pen down, Hado abruptly dropped to one knee, his head bowed low. Quickly I followed suit.

After a moment, Lord T'vril said, "You'll both be pleased to know, I think, that the House of the Risen Sun is no more. Its threat has been removed."

I blinked in surprise. The Lord Arameri's voice was soft, low-pitched and almost musical—though the words he spoke were anything but. I wanted very much to ask what *removed* meant, but I suspected that would be a very foolish thing to do.

"What of Serymn?" asked Hado. "If I may ask."

"She's being brought here. Her husband has not yet been captured, but the scriveners tell me it's only a matter of time. We aren't the only ones seeking him, after all."

I wondered at first, then realized—of course he would have informed the city's godlings. I cleared my throat, unsure of how to pose a question without offending this most powerful of men.

"You may speak, Eru Shoth."

I faltered a moment, realizing this had been another clue I'd missed—Hado's gesture of using Maroneh honorifics. It was the sort of thing one did in dealing with folk of foreign lands, to be diplomatic. An Arameri habit.

I took a deep breath. "What about the godlings being held captive by the New Lights, ah, Lord Arameri? Have they been rescued?"

"Several bodies have been found, both in the city where the Lights dumped them and at the House. The local godlings are dealing with the remains."

Bodies. I forgot myself and stared at the man in gape-mouthed shock. More than the four I knew of? Dateh had been busy. "Which ones?" In my mind, I heard the answer to this question, too: Paitya. Kitr. Dump. Lil.

Madding.

"I haven't been given names as yet. Though I've been informed that the one who called himself Madding was among them. I believe he was important to you; I'm very sorry." He sounded sincere, if distant.

I lowered my eyes and muttered something.

T'vril Arameri then crossed his legs and steepled his fingers, or so I guessed from his movements. "But this leaves me with a dilemma, Eru Shoth: what to do with you. On the one hand, you've done a great service to the world by helping to expose the New Lights' activities. On the other, you are a weapon—and it is foolish in the extreme to leave a weapon lying about where anyone can pick it up and use it."

I lowered my head again, dropping lower than I had before, until my forehead pressed against the cold, glowing floor. I had heard this was the way to show penitence before nobles, and penitent was exactly how I felt. *Bodies.* How many of those dead, desecrated godlings had been poisoned by my blood, rather than Dateh's?

"Then again," said the Lord Arameri, "my family has long known the value of dangerous weapons."

Against the floor, my forehead wrinkled in confusion. *What?*

"The gods know now that demons still exist," said Hado, through my shock. He sounded carefully neutral. "This isn't something you'll be able to hide."

"And we will give them a demon," said the Lord Arameri.

"The very one responsible for murdering their kin. That should satisfy them—leaving you, Eru Shoth, for us."

I pushed myself up slowly, trembling. "I ... don't understand." But I did, gods help me. I did.

The Lord Arameri rose, an outline against the pale glow of the room. As he walked down the steps of the dais, I saw that he was a slender man, very tall in the way of Amn, wearing a long, heavy mantle. Both it and his loose-curled hair, the latter tied at the tip, trailed along the steps behind him as he came to me.

"If there's one lesson the past has taught us, it is that we mortals exist at the bottom of a short and pitiless hierarchy," he said, still in that warm, almost-kind voice. "Above us are the godlings, and above those, the gods—and they *do not like us*, Eru Shoth."

"With reason," drawled Hado.

The Lord Arameri glanced at him, and to my surprise seemed to take no offense from this. "With reason. Nevertheless, we would be fools not to seek some means of protecting ourselves." He gestured away, I think toward the windows and the blackened sun beyond. "The art of scrivening was born from such an effort, initiated long ago by my forebears, though it has proven too limited to do humanity much good against gods. *You*, however, have been far more effective."

"You want to use me as the Lights did," I said, my voice shaking. "You want me to kill gods for you."

"Only if they force us to," the Arameri said. Then, to my greater shock, he knelt in front of me.

"It will not be slavery," he said, and his voice was gentle. Kind. "That time of our history is done. We will pay you as we do any of the scriveners or soldiers who fight for us. Provide you housing, protection. All we ask is that you give some of your blood to us—and that you allow our scriveners to place a mark upon your body. I will not lie to you about this mark's purpose, Eru Shoth: it is a leash. Through it we will know whenever your blood has been shed in sufficient quantity to be a danger. We will know your location in the event of another kidnapping, or if you attempt to flee. And with this mark, we will be able to kill you if necessary—quickly, painlessly, and thoroughly, from any distance. Your body will turn to ash so that no one else will be able to use its...unique properties." He sighed, his voice full of compassion. "It will not be slavery, but neither will you be wholly free. The choice is yours."

I was so tired. So very tired of all of this. "Choice?" I asked. My voice sounded dull to my own ears. "Life on a leash or death? That's your choice?"

"I'm being generous even to offer, Eru Shoth." He reached up then, put a hand on my shoulder. I thought he meant to be reassuring. "I could easily force you to do as I please."

Like the New Lights did, I considered saying, but there was no need for that. He knew precisely what a hellish bargain he'd offered me. The Arameri got what they wanted either way; if I chose death, they would take what blood they could from my body and store it against future need. And if I lived...I almost laughed as it occurred to me. They would want me to have children, wouldn't they? Perhaps the Shoths would become a shadow of the Arameri: privileged, protected, our specialness permanently marked upon our bodies. Never again to live a normal life.

I opened my mouth to tell him no, that I would not accept the life he offered. Then I remembered: I had already promised my life to another.

That would be better, I decided. At least with Shiny I would die on my own terms.

"I'd...like some time to think about it," I heard myself say, as from a distance.

"Of course," said the Lord Arameri. He rose, letting go of me. "You may remain as our guest for another day. By tomorrow evening, I'll expect your answer."

One day was more than enough. "Thank you," I said. It echoed in my ears. My heart was numb.

He turned away, a clear dismissal. Hado rose, gesturing me up, too, and as we had entered, we left in silence.

*   *   *

"I want to see Shiny," I said, once we were back in my room. Another cell, though prettier than the last. I did not think Sky's windows would break so easily. That was all right, though. I wouldn't need to try.

Hado, who had gone to stand at the window, nodded. "I'll see if I can find him."

"What, you aren't keeping him locked up someplace?"

"No. He has the run of Sky if he wants it, by the Lord Arameri's own decree. That has been so since he was first made mortal here ten years ago."

I was sitting at the room's table. A meal had been laid out, but it sat untouched before me. "He became mortal...here?"

"Oh, yes. All of it happened here—the Gray Lady's birth, the Nightlord's release, and Itempas's defeat, all in a single morning."

My father's death, my mind added.

"Then the Lady and the Nightlord left him here." He shrugged. "Afterward, T'vril extended every courtesy to him. I think some of the Arameri hoped he would take over the family and lead it on to some new glory. Instead he did nothing, said nothing. Just sat in a room for six months. Died of thirst once or twice, I heard, before he realized he no longer had a choice about eating and drinking." Hado sighed. "Then one day he simply got up and walked out, without warning or farewell. T'vril ordered a search, but no one could find him."

Because he had gone to the Ancestors' Village, I realized. Of course the Arameri would never have thought to look for their god there.

"How do you know all this?" I frowned. "You don't have an Arameri mark."

"Not yet." Hado turned to me, and I thought that he smiled. "Soon, though. That was the bargain I struck with T'vril: if I proved myself, I could be adopted into the family as a fullblood. I think bringing down a threat to the gods should qualify."

"Adopted..." I'd had no idea such a thing was even possible. "But...well...You don't seem to like these people very much."

He did chuckle this time, and again I had an odd sense about him, of someone wise beyond his years. Of something dark and strange.

"Once upon a time," he said, "there was a god imprisoned here. He was a terrible, beautiful, angry god, and by night when he roamed these white halls, everyone feared him. But by day, the god slept. And the body, the living mortal flesh that was his ball and chain, got to have a life of its own."

I inhaled, understanding, just not believing. He was speaking of the Nightlord, of course—but the body that lived by day was...?

Near the window, Hado folded his arms. I saw this easily, despite the window's darkness, because he was darker still.

"It wasn't much of a life, mind you," he said. "All the people who feared the god did *not* fear the man. They quickly learned they could do things to the man that the god would not tolerate. So the man lived his life in increments, born with every dawn, dying with every sunset. Hating every moment of it. For two. Thousand. Years."

He glanced back at me. I gaped at him.

"Until suddenly, one day, the man became free." Hado spread his arms. "He spent the first night of his existence gazing at the stars and weeping. But the next morning, he realized something. Though he could finally die, as he had dreamt of doing for centuries, he did not want to. He had been given a life at last, a whole life all his own. Dreams of his own. It would have been... wrong... to waste that."

I licked my lips and swallowed. "I..." I stopped. I had been about to say *I understand*, but that wasn't true. No mortal, and probably no god, could comprehend Hado's life. *Children of Nahadoth*, Shiny had called Lil and Dateh. Here was another of the Nightlord's children, stranger than all the rest.

"I can see that," I said. "But"—I gestured around at the walls of Sky—"*is* this life? Wouldn't something more normal—"

"I've spent my whole life serving power. And I've suffered for it—more than you can possibly imagine. Now I'm free. Should I go build a house in the country and grow vegetables? Find a lover I can endure, raise a litter of brats? Become a commoner like you, penniless and helpless?" I forgot myself and scowled. He chuckled. "Power is what I know. I would make a good family head, don't you think? Once I'm a fullblood."

He sounded sincere; that was the truly frightening thing.

"I think Lord Arameri would be a fool to let you anywhere near him," I said slowly.

Hado shook his head in amusement. "I'll go find Lord Itempas for you."

How jarring, to hear Shiny called that. I nodded absently as Hado headed for the door. Then, when he was at the door, a thought occurred to me. "What would you do?" I asked. "If you were me. What would you choose? Life in chains or death?"

"I would be grateful to have that much of a choice."

"That's not an answer."

"Of course it is. But if you must know, I would choose life. So long as it *was* a choice, I would live."

I frowned, mulling this over. Hado hesitated a moment, then spoke again. "You've spent time among the gods, Eru Shoth. Haven't you noticed? They live forever, but many of them are even more lonely and miserable than we are. Why do you think they bother with us? *We teach them life's value.* So I would live, if only to spite them." He let out a single mirthless laugh, then sighed and offered me a sardonic bow. "Good afternoon."

"Good afternoon," I said. After he was gone, I sat thinking for a long time.

*   *   *

I ate something, more out of habit than necessity, and then eventually I took a nap. When I woke up, Shiny was there.

I heard him breathing as I sat up, bleary and stiff. Still weary from my ordeals, I'd fallen asleep at the table beside the remains of my meal, cradling my head on my good arm. I bumped the sling-bound arm against the table as I lifted my head, but this elicited only a mild twinge. The sigil had nearly finished its work.

"Hello," I said. "Thank you for letting me sleep." He said nothing, but that didn't bother me. "What happened to you?"

He shrugged. He was sitting across from me, near enough that I could hear his movements. "I was questioned at the White Hall; then we came here."

Obviously. I did not say it, because one took what one could get with him. "Where did you go after they brought you here?" Silently I made a wager with myself that he would say *nowhere*.

"Nowhere that matters."

I could not help smiling. It felt good, because it had been a long time since I'd felt the urge to genuinely smile. It reminded me of days long past, a life long gone, when my only worries had been putting food on the table and keeping Shiny from bleeding on my carpets. I almost loved him for reminding me of that time.

"Does anything matter to you?" I asked, still smiling. "Anything at all?"

"No," he said. His voice was flat, emotionless. Cold. I was beginning to understand just how wrong that was for him, a being who had once embodied warmth and light.

"Liar," I said.

He fell silent. I picked up the paring knife they'd given me for my meal, liking the slightly rough texture of its wooden hilt. I would have expected something finer to be used in Sky—porcelain, maybe, or silver. Nothing so common and utilitarian as wood. Maybe it was expensive wood.

"You care about your children," I said. "You feared Dateh would harm your old love, the Nightlord, so it seems you still care about him. You could probably even get to like this new Lady, if you gave her half a chance. If she's willing to take a chance on you."

More silence.

"I think you care about a great many things, more than you want to. I think life still holds some potential for you."

"What do you want from me, Oree?" Shiny asked. He sounded...not cold, not anymore. Just tired. I heard Hado's words again: *they're even more miserable than we are.* With Shiny, I could believe it.

At his question, I shook my head and laughed a little. "I don't know. I keep hoping you'll tell me. You're the god, after all. If I prayed to you for guidance, and you decided to answer, what would you tell me?"

"I wouldn't answer."

"Because you don't care? Or because you wouldn't know what to say?"

More silence.

I put the knife down and got up, walking around the table. When I found him, I touched his face, his hair, the lines of his neck. He sat passive, waiting, though I felt the tension in him. Did it bother him, the idea of killing me? I dismissed the thought as vain on my part.

"Tell me what happened," I said. "What made you like this? I want to understand, Shiny. See, Madding loved you. He—" My throat tightened unexpectedly. I had to look away and take a deep breath before continuing. "He hadn't given up on you. I think he wanted to help you. He just didn't know how to begin." Silence before me. I stroked his cheek. "You don't *have* to tell me. I won't break my promise; you helped me escape, and now you can remove one more demon from the world. But I deserve that much, don't I? Just a little bit of the truth?"

He said nothing. Beneath my fingers, his face was marble-still. He was looking straight ahead, through me, beyond me. I waited, but he did not speak.

I let out a sigh, then reached for an empty soup bowl. It wasn't very big, but there was a glass, too, which had held the best wine I'd ever tasted. I was slightly tipsy because of it, though mostly I had slept that off. I set the bowl and glass in front of me and carefully shrugged my right arm out of the sling. I could use it now, though there was still an ache in the muscles of my upper arm. They had healed, but the memory of pain was still fresh.

"Wait until I'm unconscious before you do it," I said. I couldn't tell if he was paying any attention to me. "Then pour the blood down the toilet. Don't leave any for them to use, if you can."

That same stubborn silence. It didn't even make me angry anymore; I was so inured to it.

I sighed and raised the knife to make the first cut to my wrist.

Then the glass broke against the floor, and a hand gripped my wrist tight, and suddenly we were across the room, against the wall, me pinned by the wire-taut weight of Shiny's body.

He pressed against me, breathing hard. I tried to pull my wrist from his hand, and he made a tight sound of negation, shaking my arm until I stilled. So I waited. I had managed to graze my wrist, but nothing more. A drop of my blood welled around his gripping hand and fell to the floor.

He bent. Slow, slow, like a tall old tree in the wind, fighting it every inch of the way. Only when he had bent to his fullest did he stop, his face pressed against the side of mine, his breath hot and harsh in my ear. It must have been an uncomfortable posture for him. But he stopped there, torturing himself, trapping me, and only in this manner was he able, at last, to speak. It was a whisper the whole time.

*   *   *

"They did not love me anymore. He was born first, I came next. I was never alone because of him. Then she came and I did not mind, I did not mind, as long as she understood that he was mine, too. It was not the sharing, do you see? It was good having her with us, and then the children, so many of them, all perfect and strange. I was happy then, *happy*, she was with us and we loved her, he and I, but I was first in his heart. I knew that. She respected it. It was never the sharing that troubled me.

"But they changed, changed, they always changed. I knew the possibility, but after so long, I did not believe. He had been alone for eternities before me. I did not understand. Even when we were enemies, he thought of me. How could I know? In all the time of my existence, it had never occurred, not once! Even apart from them, I knew their presence, felt their awareness of me. But then... but then..."

*   *   *

At this point, he pulled me against him. His free hand, the one that wasn't holding my wrist, fisted in the cloth at the small of my back. It wasn't a hug; that much I was sure of. It didn't feel like a gesture of comfort. It was closer to the way he'd held me after his release from the Empty. Or the way I sometimes gripped my walking stick when I was adrift in some place I didn't know, with no one to help me if I stumbled. Yes, very much like that.

*   *   *

"I didn't think it possible. Was it a betrayal? Had I offended them somehow? I didn't think they could forget me so completely.

"But they did.

"They forgot me.

"They were together, he and she, yet I could not feel them. They thought only of each other. I was not part of it.

"They left me alone."

*   *   *

I have always understood bodies better than voices or faces or words. So when Shiny whispered to me of horror, of a single moment of solitude after an eternity of companionship, it was not his words that conveyed the devastation this had wreaked on his soul. He was pressed against me as intimately as a lover. There was no need for words.

*   *   *

"I fled to the mortal realm. Better human company than nothing. I went to a village, to a mortal girl. Better any love than none. She offered herself and I took her, I needed her, I have never felt such need. After, I stayed. Mortal love was safer. There was a child, and I did not kill him. I knew he was demon, forbidden, I had written the law myself, but I needed him, too. He was...I had forgotten how beautiful they could be. The mortal girl whispered to me, in the night when I was weak. My siblings were wrong, wicked, hateful to have forgotten me. They would betray me again if I went back to them. Only she could love me truly; I needed only her. I needed to believe it, do you understand? I needed something certain. I lived in dread of her death. Then *they* came for me, found me. They apologized—apologized! Like it was nothing."

*　　*　　*

He laughed once, here. It was half a sob.

*　　*　　*

"And they brought me home. But I knew: I could no longer trust them. I had learned what it meant to be alone. It is the opposite of all that I am, that emptiness, that...*nothing*. I fought ten thousand battles before time began, burned my soul to shape this universe, and never before have I experienced such agony.

"The mortal girl warned me. She said they would do it again. That they would forget they loved me. That they would turn to each other and I would be alone—*left* alone—forever.

"They would not.

"They would *not*.

"Then the mortal girl killed our son."

*　　*　　*

He fell silent here for just a moment, his body utterly still.

*　　*　　*

"'Take it,' she told me, and offered me the blood. And I thought...I thought...I thought...*when there were only two of us, I was never alone*."

*   *   *

A final silence, fortelling the story's end.

Slowly, he let me go. All the tension and strength ran out of him, like water. He slid down my body to his knees, his cheek pressed to my belly. He had stopped trembling.

I have spent time studying the nature of light. It is part curiosity and part meditation; someday I hope to understand why I see the way I do. Scriveners have studied light, too, and in the books that Madding read to me, they claimed that the brightest light—true light—is the combination of all other kinds of light. Red, blue, yellow, more; put it all together and the result is shining white.

This means, in a way, that true light is dependent on the presence of other lights. Take the others away and darkness results. Yet the reverse is not true: take away darkness and there is only more darkness. Darkness can exist by itself. Light cannot.

And thus a single moment of solitude had destroyed Bright Itempas. He might have recovered from that in time; even a river stone wears into new shapes. But in the moment of his greatest weakness, he had been manipulated, his already-damaged soul struck an unrecoverable blow by the mortal woman he'd trusted to love him. That had driven him so mad that he had murdered his sister to keep from ever experiencing the pain of betrayal again.

"I'm sorry," he said. It was very soft, and not meant for me. But the next words were. "You don't know how much I've thought of taking your blood for myself."

I folded my arm around his shoulders and bent down to kiss his forehead. "I do know, actually." Because I did.

So I straightened, took his hand, and pulled him up. He came without resistance, letting me lead him to the bed, where I pulled him to lie down. When we'd settled, I snuggled into the crook of his arm, resting my head on his chest as I'd so often done with Madding. They felt and smelled very different—sea salt to dry spice, cool to hot, gentle to fierce—but their heartbeats were the same. Steady, slow, reassuring. Could a son inherit such a thing from a father? Apparently so.

I could always die tomorrow, I supposed.

18

"The Gods' Vengeance"
(watercolor)

I THINK MADDING ALWAYS SUSPECTED THE TRUTH.

Throughout my childhood, I had a strange memory of being someplace warm and wet and enclosed. I felt safe, yet I was lonely. I could hear voices, yet no one spoke to me. Hands would touch me now and again, and I would touch back, but that was all.

Many years later, I told this story to Madding, and he looked at me oddly. When I asked him what was wrong, he didn't answer at first. I pressed him, and finally he said, "It sounds like you were in the womb."

I remember laughing. "That's crazy," I said. "I was thinking. Listening. *Aware*."

He shrugged. "So was I, before I was born. I guess that happens sometimes with mortals, too."

But it isn't supposed to, he did not say.

* * *

"What do you intend to do?" Shiny asked me the next morning.

He stood at the window across the room, glowing softly with the dawn. I sat up blearily, stifling a yawn.

"I don't know," I said.

I wasn't ready to die. That was easier to admit than I'd thought. I had killed Madding; to live with that knowledge would be—had been—almost unbearable. But killing myself, or letting Shiny or the Arameri do it, felt worse somehow. In the wake of Madding's death, it felt like throwing away a gift.

"If I live, the Arameri will use me for the gods know what. I won't have more deaths on my conscience." I sighed, rubbing my face with my hands. "You were right to want to kill us. You should've gotten us all, though. That was the only mistake the Three made."

"No," said Shiny. "We were wrong. Something had to be done about the demons—that I will not deny—but we should have sought a different solution. They were our children."

I opened my mouth. Closed it. Stared, though he was now little more than a pale relief against the dimmer sheen of the window. I wasn't really sure what to say. So I changed the subject. "What do *you* plan to do?"

He stood as he had on so many mornings at my house, facing the rising sun with back straight and head high and arms folded. Now, however, he let out a soft sigh and turned to me, leaning against the window with an almost palpable weariness. "I have no idea. Nothing in me is whole or right, Oree. I am the coward you named me, and the fool you did not. Weak." He lifted his hand as if he'd never seen it before and made a fist. It didn't look weak to me, but I imagined how a god might see it. Bones that could be broken. Skin that would not instantly heal if torn. Tendons and veins as fine as gossamer.

And underneath this fragile flesh, a mind like a broken tea-cup, badly mended.

"It's solitude, then?" I asked. "That's your true antithesis, not darkness. You didn't realize?"

"No. Not until that day." He lowered his hand. "But I should have realized. Loneliness is a darkness of the soul."

I got up and went over to him, stumbling once over the rugs. Finding his arm, I reached up to touch his face. He allowed this, even turning his cheek against my hand. I think he was feeling alone in that very moment.

"I'm glad they put me here in this mortal form," he said. "I can do no harm when I go mad. When I was trapped in that realm of darkness, I thought I would. Having you there after-ward . . . Without that, I would have broken again."

I frowned, thinking of the way he'd clung to me that day, barely able to let go even for a moment. No human being could bear solitude forever—I would've gone mad in the Empty, too—but Shiny's need was not a human thing.

I thought of something my mother had said to me, many times during my childhood. "It's all right to need help," I said. "You're mortal now. Mortals can't do everything alone."

"I wasn't mortal then," he said, and I could tell he was think-ing of the day he'd killed Enefa.

"Maybe it's the same for gods." I was still tired, so I turned to lean against the window beside him. "We're made in your image, right? Maybe your siblings didn't send you here so you'd do no harm as a mortal, but rather so that you could learn to deal with this as mortals do." I sighed and closed my eyes, tired of Sky's constant glow. "Hells, I don't know. Maybe you just need friends."

He fell silent, but I thought I felt him look at me.

Before I could say anything more, there was a knock at the door. Shiny went to answer it.

"My lord." A voice that I did not recognize, with the professional briskness of a servant. "I bear a message. The Lord Arameri requests your presence."

"Why?" Shiny asked—something I would never have done myself. The messenger was taken aback, too, though he paused for only a beat before answering.

"Lady Serymn has been captured."

*   *   *

As before, the Lord Arameri had dismissed his court. I suppose making bargains with demons and disciplining wayward full-bloods were not matters for public consumption.

Serymn stood between four guards—Arameri as well as High Norther—though they were not actually touching her. I could not tell if she looked any worse for the wear, but her silhouette stood as straight and proud as any other time I'd met her. Her hands had been bound in front of her, which seemed to be the only concession made to her status as a prisoner. She, the guards, Shiny, and I were the only people in the room.

She and the Lord Arameri regarded each other in stillness and silence, like elegant marble statues of Defiance and Mercilessness.

After a moment of this perusal, she looked away from him—even blind, I could tell this was dismissive—and faced me. "Lady Oree. Does it please you to stand beside those who let your father die?"

Once, those words would have bothered me, but now I knew better. "You misunderstood, Lady Serymn. My father didn't die because of the Nightlord, or the Lady, or the godlings, or anyone who supports them. He died because he was different—something ordinary mortals hate and fear." I sighed. "With reason, I'll admit. But give credit where credit is due."

She shook her head and sighed. "You trust these false gods too much."

"No," I said, growing angry. Not just angry but furious, *incandescent* with rage. If I'd had a walking stick, there would have been trouble. "I trust the gods to be what they are, and I trust mortals to be mortals. *Mortals*, Lady Serymn, stoned my father to death. *Mortals* trussed me up like livestock and milked me of blood until I nearly died. Mortals killed my love." I was very proud of myself; my throat did not close and my voice did not waver. The anger buoyed me that far. "Hells, if the gods *do* decide to wipe us out, is it such a bad thing? Maybe we've earned a little annihilation." At that, I couldn't help looking at Lord T'vril, too.

He ignored me, sounding bored when he spoke. "Serymn, stop toying with the girl. This rhetoric might have swayed your poor, lost spiritual devotees, but everyone here sees through you." He gestured at her, a graceful hand wave encompassing all that she was. "What you may not understand, Eru Shoth, is that this whole affair is a family squabble gotten out of hand."

I must have looked confused. "Family squabble?"

"I am a mere halfblood, you see—the first who has ever ruled this family. And though I was appointed to this position by the Gray Lady herself, there are those of my relatives, particularly the fullbloods, who still question my qualifications. Foolishly, I counted Serymn among the less dangerous of those. I even believed she might be useful, since her organization seemed to give direction to those members of the Itempan faith who have been disillusioned lately." I could not see him glance at Shiny, but I guessed that he did. "I did not believe they could do true harm. For this, you have my apologies."

I stiffened in surprise. I knew nothing of nobles or Arameri, but I knew this: they did not apologize. Ever. Even after the destruction of the Maroland, they had offered the Nimaro peninsula to my people as a "humanitarian gesture"—not an apology.

Serymn shook her head. "Dekarta appointed you his heir only under duress, T'vril. Ordinarily you'd do well enough, half-blood or not. But in these dark times, we need a family head strong in the old values, someone who will not waver from devotion to Our Lord. You lack the pride of our heritage."

I felt the Lord Arameri smile, because it was a brittle, dangerous thing, and the whole room felt less safe for it.

"Have you anything else to say?" he asked. "Anything worthy of my time?"

"No," she replied. "Nothing worthy of *you*."

"Very well," said the Lord Arameri. He snapped his fingers, and a servant appeared from a curtain behind T'vril's seat. He crouched beside T'vril's chair, holding something; there was the faint clink of metal. T'vril did not take it, and I could not see what it was. I did, however, see Serymn's flinch.

"This man," said the Lord Arameri. He gestured toward Shiny. "You left Sky before the last succession. Do you know him?"

Serymn glanced at Shiny, then away. "We were never able to determine *what* he was," she said, "but he is the Lady Oree's companion and perhaps lover. He had no value to us, except as a hostage against her good behavior."

"Look again, Cousin."

She looked, radiating disdain. "Is there something I should be seeing?"

I reached for Shiny's hand. He had not moved—did not seem to care at all.

The Lord Arameri rose and descended the steps. At the foot of the steps, he abruptly turned toward us in a swirl of cloak and hair and dropped to one knee, with a grace I would never have expected of a man so powerful. From this, he said in a ringing tone, "Behold Our Lord, Serymn. Hail Itempas, Master of Day, Lord of Light and Order."

Serymn stared at him. Then she looked at Shiny. There had been no sarcasm in T'vril's tone, no hint of anything other than reverence. Yet I could guess what she saw when she looked at Shiny: the soul-deep weariness in his eyes, the sorrow beneath his apathy. He wore borrowed clothing, as I did, and said nothing at T'vril's bow.

"He's Maroneh," Serymn said, after a long perusal.

T'vril got to his feet, flicking his long tail of hair back with practiced ease. "That is a bit of a surprise, isn't it? Though it would not be the first lie our family has told until it forgot the truth." He turned and went to her, stopping right in front of her. She did not step back from his nearness, though I would have. There was something about the Lord Arameri in that moment that made me very afraid.

"You knew he had been overthrown, Serymn," he said. "You've seen many gods take mortal form. Why did it never occur to you that your own god might be among them? Hado tells me that your New Lights were not kind to him."

"No," Serymn said. Her strong, rich voice wavered with uncertainty for the first time since I'd met her. "That's impossible. I would have…Dateh…We would have *known*."

T'vril glanced back at the servant, who hurried forward with the metal object. He took it and said, "I suppose your pure Arameri blood doesn't entitle you to speak for our god after all. Just as well, then. Hold her mouth open."

I didn't realize the last part was a command until the guards suddenly took hold of Serymn. There was a struggle, a jumble of silhouettes. When they stilled, I realized the guards had taken hold of Serymn's head.

T'vril lifted the metal object so that I could see it at last, outlined by the glow of the far wall. Scissors? No, too large and oddly shaped for that.

Tongs.

"Oh, gods," I whispered, understanding too late. I turned away, but there was no avoiding the horrible sounds: Serymn's gagging cry, T'vril's grunt of effort, the wet tear of flesh. It took only a moment. T'vril handed the tongs back to the servant with a sigh of disgust; the servant took them away. Serymn made a single, raw sound, not so much a scream as a wordless protest, and then she sagged between the guards, moaning.

"Hold her head forward, please," T'vril cautioned. I heard him as if from a distance, through fog. "We don't want her to choke."

"W-wait," I said. Gods, I could not think. That sound would echo in my nightmares.

"Yes, Eru Shoth?" Other than sounding a bit winded, the Lord Arameri's tone was the same as always: polite, soft-spoken, warm. I wondered if I would throw up.

"Dateh," I said, "and the missing godlings. She...she could have told us...." Now Serymn would say nothing, ever again.

"If she knew, she would never tell," he said. He mounted the steps and sat down again. The servant, having disposed of the tongs behind the curtain, hurried back out and handed him a cloth for his hands, which he used to wipe each finger. "But most likely, she and Dateh agreed to separate in order to protect each other. Serymn is a fullblood, after all; she would have known to expect harsh questioning in the event of capture."

Harsh questioning. Noble language for what I'd just witnessed.

"And unfortunately, the matter is out of my hands," he continued. I caught a hint of a gesture. The main doors opened and another servant entered, carrying something that caught my eye at once because it glowed as brightly as the rest of this so-magical palace. And unlike the walls and floor, the object that the servant carried was a bright, cheerful rose color. A small rubber ball, like something a child might play with.

T'vril took this ball from the servant and continued. "Not only has my cousin forgotten that Bright Itempas no longer rules the gods, but she has also forgotten that we Arameri now answer to several masters rather than one. The world changes; we must change with it or die. Perhaps, after hearing of Serymn's fate, more of my fullblood cousins will remember this."

He turned his hand and let the pink ball fall. It bounced against the floor beside his chair and he caught it, then bounced it twice more.

A boy appeared before him. I recognized him at once and gasped. Sieh, the child-godling who had once tried to kick Shiny to death. The Trickster, who had once been an Arameri slave.

"What?" he asked, sounding annoyed. He glanced toward my gasp once, then looked away with no change in his expression. I prayed to no god in particular that he had not recognized me—though with Shiny standing beside me, that was a thin hope.

T'vril inclined his head respectfully. "Here is one of the killers of your siblings, Lord Sieh," he said, gesturing at Serymn.

Sieh raised his eyebrows, turning to her. "I remember her. Dekarta's third-removed niece or something, left years ago." A wry, unchildlike smile crossed his face. "Really, T'vril, the tongue?"

T'vril handed the pink ball back to the servant, who bowed and took it away. "There are those in the family who believe I am...too gentle." He shrugged, glancing at the guards. "An example was necessary."

"So I see." Sieh trotted down the steps until he stood before Serymn, though I saw him fastidiously step around the blood that darkened the floor. "Having her will help, but I don't think Naha will restore the sun until you have the demon. Do you?"

"No," said T'vril. "We're still looking for him."

Serymn made a sound then, and the little hairs on my skin prickled. I could feel her attention, could see her straining toward me as she made the sound again. There was no way to make out words, or even be certain she had tried to speak, but somehow I knew: she was trying to tell Sieh about me. She was trying to say, *There is a demon.*

But T'vril had seen to it she would never tell my secret, not even to the gods.

Sieh sighed at Serymn's struggles to speak. "I don't care what you have to say," he said. Serymn went still, watching him in fresh apprehension. "Neither will my father. If I were you, I'd save my strength to pray he's not in a creative mood."

He waved a hand, lazy, careless, and perhaps only I saw the flood of black, flamelike raw power that lashed out from that hand, coiling for a moment like a snake before it lunged forward and swallowed Serymn whole. Then it vanished, and Serymn went with it.

And then Sieh turned to us.

"So you're still with him," he said to me.

I was very aware of my hand, holding Shiny's. "Yes," I replied. I lifted my chin. "I know who he is now."

"Do you really?" Sieh's eyes flicked to Shiny, stayed there. "Somehow I doubt that, mortal girl. Not even his children know him anymore."

"I said I know him *now*," I said, annoyed. I had never liked being patronized, regardless of who was doing it—and I had been through enough in recent weeks to no longer fear a godling's temper. "I don't know what he was like before. That person is gone, anyway; he died the day he killed the Lady. *This* is just what's left." I jerked my head toward Shiny. His hand had gone slack, I think with shock. "It's not much, I'll grant you. Sometimes I want to kick him senseless myself. But the more I get to know him, the more I realize he's not as much of a lost cause as all of you seem to think."

Sieh stared at me for a moment, though he recovered quickly. "You don't know anything about it." He clenched his fists. I half expected him to stamp his feet. "He killed my mother. *All* of us died that day, and he's the one who killed us! Should we forget that?"

"No," I said. I could not help it; I pitied him. I knew how it felt to lose a parent in a way that defied all sense. "Of course you can't forget. But"—I lifted Shiny's hand—"*look* at him. Does it look like he spent the centuries gloating?"

Sieh's lip curled. "So he regrets what he did. Now, *after* we've freed ourselves, and *after* he's been sentenced to humanity for his crimes. So very remorseful."

"How do you know he didn't regret it before?"

"Because he didn't set us free!" Sieh thumped a hand against his chest. "He left us here, let humans do as they pleased with us! He tried to *force* us to love him again!"

"Maybe he couldn't think of another way," I said.

"*What?*"

"Maybe that was the only thing that made sense, mad as it was, after the mad thing he'd already done. Maybe he wanted time to fix things, even though it was impossible. Even though he was making things worse." My anger had already faded. I remembered Shiny the night before, on his knees before me, empty of hope. "Maybe he thought it was better to keep you prisoner and be hated than lose you entirely."

I knew it was a pointless argument. Some acts were beyond forgiveness; murder, unjust imprisonment, and torture were probably among them.

And yet.

Sieh closed his mouth. He looked at Shiny. His jaw tightened, eyes narrowing. "Well? Does this mortal speak for you, Father?"

Shiny said nothing. His whole body radiated tension, but none of that found its way into words. I wasn't surprised. I loosened my hand from his to make it easier for him to let me go when he walked away.

His hand snapped closed on mine, suddenly, tightly. I couldn't have pulled away if I'd wanted to.

While I blinked and wondered at this, Sieh sighed in disgust. "I don't understand you," he said to me. "You don't seem stupid. He's a waste of your energy. Are you the sort of woman who tortures herself to feel better or who takes only lovers who beat her?"

"Madding was my lover," I said quietly.

At that, Sieh actually looked chagrined. "I forgot. Sorry."

"So am I." I sighed and rubbed my eyes, which were aching again. Too much magic in Sky; I wasn't used to being able to see like this. I missed the familiar magic-flecked darkness of Shadow.

"It's just that...all of you will live forever." Then I remembered and amended myself, smiling bleakly. "Barring murder, I mean. You'll have forever with one another." *As Madding and I could never have had, even if he hadn't been killed.* Oh, I was tired; it was harder to keep the sorrow at bay. "I just don't see the point of spending all that time full of hate. That's all."

Sieh gazed at me, thoughtful. His pupils changed again, becoming catlike and sharp, but this time there was no sense of threat accompanying the transformation. Perhaps, like me, he needed strange eyes to see what others couldn't. He turned those eyes on Shiny then, for a long, silent perusal. Whatever he saw didn't make his anger fade, but he didn't attack again, either. I counted that as a victory.

"Sieh," Shiny said suddenly. His hand tightened more on mine, on the threshold of pain. I set my teeth and bore it, afraid to interrupt. I felt him draw in a breath.

"Never apologize to me," Sieh said. He spoke very softly, perhaps sensing the same thing that I did. His face had gone cold, devoid of anything but a skein of anger. "What you did can never be absolved by mere words. To even attempt it is an insult—not just to me, but to my mother's memory."

Shiny went stiff. Then his hand twitched on mine, and he seemed to draw strength from the contact, because he spoke at last.

"If not words," he said, "will deeds serve?"

Sieh smiled. I was almost sure his teeth were sharp now. "What deeds can make up for your crimes, my bright father?"

Shiny looked away, his hand loosening on my own at last. "None. I know."

Sieh drew in a deep breath and let it out heavily. He shook his head, glanced at me, shook his head again, and then turned away.

"I'll tell Mother you're doing well," Sieh said to T'vril, who had sat silent throughout this conversation, probably holding his breath. "She'll be glad to hear it."

T'vril inclined his head, not quite a bow. "And is she well, herself?"

"Very well, indeed. Godhood suits her. It's the rest of us who are a mess these days." I thought I saw him hesitate for a moment, almost turning back to us. But he only nodded to T'vril. "Until the next time, Lord Arameri." He vanished.

T'vril let out a long sigh in his wake. I felt that this spoke for all of us.

"Well," he said. "With that business out of the way, we are left with only one matter. Have you considered my proposal, Eru Shoth?"

331

I had latched on to one hope. If I lived and let the Arameri use me, I might someday find a way free. Somehow. It was a thin hope, a pathetic one, but it was all I had.

"Will you settle things with the Order of Itempas for me?" I asked, trying for dignity. Now it was I who clung to Shiny for support. It was easier, somehow, to give up my soul with him there beside me.

T'vril inclined his head. "Already done."

"And"—I hesitated—"can I have your word that this mark, the one I must wear, will do nothing *but* what you said?"

He lifted an eyebrow. "You have little room to bargain here, Eru Shoth."

I flinched, because it was true, but I clenched my free hand, anyhow. I hated being threatened. "I could tell the godlings what I am. They'll kill me, but at least they won't use me the way you mean to."

The Lord Arameri sat back in his chair, crossing his legs. "You don't know that, Eru Shoth. Perhaps the godling you tell will have her own enemies to get rid of. Would you really risk exchanging a mortal master for an immortal one?"

That was a possibility that had never occurred to me. I froze, horrified by it.

"You will not be her master," Shiny said.

I jumped. T'vril drew in a deep breath, let it out. "My lord. I'm afraid you weren't privy to our earlier conversation. Eru Shoth is aware of the danger if she remains free." *And you are in no position to negotiate on her behalf*, his tone said. He did not have to say it aloud. It was painfully obvious.

"A danger that remains if *you* lay claim to her," Shiny

snapped. I could hardly believe my ears. Was he actually trying to fight for me?

Shiny let go of my hand and stepped forward, not quite in front of me. "You cannot keep her existence a secret," he said. "You can't kill enough people to safely make her your weapon. It would be better if you had never brought her here—then at least you could deny knowledge of her existence."

I frowned in confusion. But T'vril uncrossed his legs.

"Do you intend to tell the other gods about her?" he asked quietly.

And then I understood. Shiny was not powerless. He could not be killed, not permanently. He could be imprisoned, but not forever, because he was supposed to be wandering the world, learning the lessons of mortality. At some point, inevitably, one of the other gods would come looking for him, if only to gloat over his punishment. And then T'vril's plan to make me the Arameri's latest weapon would come apart.

"I will say nothing," Shiny said softly, "if you let her go."

I caught my breath.

T'vril was silent for a moment. "No. My greatest concern hasn't changed: she's too dangerous to leave unprotected. It would be safer to kill her." Which would erase Shiny's leverage, besides ending my life.

It was a game of *nikkim*: feint against feint, each trying to outplay the other. Except I had never paid attention to such games, because I could not see them, so I had no idea what happened if there was a draw. I definitely didn't like being the prize.

"She *was* safe until the Order began to harass her," Shiny

333

said. "Anonymity has protected her bloodline for centuries, even from the gods. Give that to her again, and all will be as it was." Shiny paused. "You still have the demon blood you took from the House of the Risen Sun before you destroyed it."

"He took—" I blurted, then caught myself. But my hands clenched. Of course they would never have let such a valuable resource go to waste. My blood, Dateh's blood, the arrowheads— perhaps they had even learned Dateh's refining method. The Arameri had their weapon, with or without me. Damn them.

Shiny was right, though. If the Lord Arameri had that, then he didn't need me.

T'vril rose from his chair. He descended the steps and walked past the guards, moving to stand at one of the long windows. I saw him pause there, gazing out at the world that he owned— and at the black sun, warning sign of the gods who threatened it. He clasped his hands behind his back.

"Make her anonymous, you say," he said, and sighed. At that sigh, my heart made an uneasy leap of hope. "Very well. I'm willing to consider it. But how? Shall I kill anyone in the city who knows her? As you say, that would require more deaths than is practical."

I shuddered. Vuroy and the others from Art Row. My landlord. The old woman across the street who gossiped to the neighbors about the blind girl and her godling boyfriend. Rimarn, the priests of the White Hall, a dozen nameless servants and guards, including the ones standing here listening to all this.

"No," I blurted. "I'll leave Shadow. I was going to do it anyway. I'll go somewhere no one knows me, never talk to anyone, just don't—"

"Kill her," Shiny said.

I flinched and stared at his profile. He glanced at me. "If she is dead, her secrets no longer matter. No one will look for her. No one can use her."

I understood then, though the idea made me shiver. T'vril turned to look at us over his shoulder. "A false death? Interesting." He thought for a moment. "It would have to be thorough. She could never speak to her friends again, or even her mother. She could no longer be Oree Shoth at all. I can arrange for her to be sent elsewhere, with resources and a concocted past. Perhaps even hold a magnificent funeral for the brave woman who gave her life to expose a plot against the gods." He glanced at me. "But if my spies hear any rumor, any *hint* of your survival, then the game ends, Eru Shoth. I will do whatever is necessary to prevent you from falling into the wrong hands again. Is that understood?"

I stared at him, and at Shiny, and then at myself. At the body that I could see, as a shadowy outline against the constant glow of Sky's light. Breasts, gently rolling. Hands, fascinatingly complex as I lifted them, turned them, flexed the fingers. The tips of my feet. A spiraling curl of hair at the edge of my vision. I had never seen myself so completely before.

To die, even in this false way, would be terrible. My friends would mourn me, and I would mourn even more the life I'd already lost. My poor mother: first my father and now this. But it was the magic, the strangeness of Shadow, all the beautiful and frightening things that I had learned and experienced and *seen*, that would hurt most to leave behind.

I had once wanted to die. This would be worse. But if I did it, I would be free.

I must have stayed silent too long. Shiny turned to me, his heavy gaze more compassionate than I had ever imagined it could be. He understood; of course he did. It was a hard thing, sometimes, to live.

"I understand," I said to the Lord Arameri.

He nodded. "Then it shall be done. Remain here another day. That should be sufficient time for me to make the arrangements." He turned back to the window, another wordless dismissal.

I stood there unmoving, hardly daring to believe it. I was free. *Free*, like old times.

Shiny turned to leave, then turned back to me, radiating irritation at my failure to follow. Like old times.

Except that he had fought for me. And won.

I trotted after him and took his arm, and if it bothered him that I pressed my face against his shoulder as we walked back to my room, he did not complain.

19

"The Demons' War"
(charcoal and chalk on black paper)

It SHOULD HAVE ENDED THERE. That would have been best, wouldn't it? A fallen god, a "dead" demon, two broken souls limping back toward life. That would have been the end that this tale deserved, I think. Quiet. Ordinary.

But that wouldn't have been good for you, would it? Too lacking in closure. Not dramatic enough. I will tell myself, then, that what happened next was a fortunate thing, though even now it feels anything but.

*   *   *

I slept deeply that night, despite my fear of what was to come, despite my worry about Paitya and the others, despite my cynical suspicion that the Lord Arameri would find some other way to keep me under his graceful, kindly thumb. My arm had healed completely, so I stripped off the bandages and the sling and the sigil-script, took a long, deep bath to celebrate the absence of pain, and curled up against Shiny's warmth. He shifted on the bed to make room for me, and I felt him watching me as I fell asleep.

Sometime after midnight, I woke with a start, blinking in disorientation as I rolled over. The room was quiet and still; Sky's magical walls were too thick to let me hear movement in the halls beyond, or even the sound of the wind that must surely be fierce outside, up so high. In that, I preferred the House of the Risen Sun, where at least there had been small sounds of life all around me—people walking through the corridors, chanting and songs, the occasional creaking and groaning of the Tree as it swayed. I would not miss the House, or its people, but being there had not been wholly unpleasant.

Here there was only the quiet, bright-glowing stillness. Shiny was asleep beside me, his breathing deep and slow. I tried to remember if I'd had a nightmare but could recall nothing. Pushing myself up, I looked around the room because I could. There would be things I'd miss about Sky, too. I saw nothing, but my nerves still jumped and my skin still tingled, as if something had touched me.

Then I heard a sound behind me like tearing air.

I whirled, my thoughts frozen, and it was behind me: a hole the height of my body, like a great, open mouth. Stupid, stupid. I had known he was still out there but thought myself safe in the stronghold of the Arameri. Stupid, stupid, stupid.

I was halfway across the bed, dragged by the hole's power, before I could open my mouth to cry out. Convulsively, my hands locked on the sheets, but I knew it was futile. In my mind's eye, I saw the sheets simply pull free of the bed, fluttering uselessly as I disappeared into whatever hell Dateh had built to hold me.

There was a jerk, so hard that friction heat burned my knuckles. The sheets had caught on something. A hand wrapped around my wrist. *Shiny.*

I shot backward into the terrible metal roar, and he came with me. I felt his presence even as I screamed and flailed, even as the feel of his hand on my wrist faded into cold numbness. We tumbled through trembling darkness, falling sideways into—

Sensation and solidity. I struck the ground—ground?—first, hard enough to jar the breath from my body. I *felt* the breath. Shiny landed nearby, uttering a grunt of pain, but at once he rolled to his feet, pulling me up, too. I caught my breath and looked around wildly, though I could see only darkness.

Then my eyes caught on something: a faint, blurry form, curled and fetal, hovering amid the dark. Dateh? But it did not move, and then I saw the shimmer of something between me and the form. Like glass. I turned again, trying to comprehend, and saw another murky form, hovering in the dark beyond the glass. This one I recognized by her brown skin: Kitr. She did not move. I reached for her, but when my hands encountered the glassy dark, they stopped. It was solid, enclosing us entirely above and around, a bubble of normality carved out of the Empty's hellish substance.

I turned again, and there was Dateh.

He was closer to us than the blurry forms, on the other side of the wide room that the bubble formed. I wasn't sure he knew we were there (though his will had brought us here), because his back was to us, and he crouched amid sprawled bodies. I could not see the bodies, except where their dimness occluded my view of Dateh, but I could taste blood in the air, thick and sickly and fresh. I heard the sounds I had hoped never to hear again: tearing flesh. Chewing teeth.

I stiffened and felt Shiny's hand tighten on my wrist. So he, too, could see Dateh, which meant there was light in this empty world. And it meant Shiny could see which of his children lay around us, sprawled and desecrated, the magic of their lives long gone.

Tears of helpless rage pricked my eyes. Not again. *Not again.* "Gods damn you, Dateh," I whispered.

Dateh paused in whatever he was doing. He turned to us, still in a crouch, moving in an odd, scuttling manner. His mouth, robes, and hands were stained dark, and his left hand was closed around a dripping lump. He blinked at us like a man coming out of a fugue. I could not see the demarcation between pupil and iris in his eyes; they looked like a single dark pit, too large, carved into the white.

He seemed to recall himself slowly. "Where is Serymn?" he asked.

"Dead," I snapped.

He frowned at this, as if confused. Slowly he rose to his feet. He drew a breath to speak again, then paused as he noticed the heart in his hand. Frowning, he tossed it aside and stepped closer to us. "Where is my wife?" he asked again.

I scowled, but behind my bravado, I was terrified. I could feel power sluicing off him like water, pressing against my skin, making it crawl. It shimmered around him, making the whole chamber flicker unsteadily. He had been missing since the Arameri raid on the House of the Risen Sun. Had he spent all that time hiding here, killing and eating godlings, making himself stronger? And madder?

"Serymn is *dead*, you monster," I said. "Didn't you hear me? The gods took her to their realm for punishment, and she deserved it. They'll find you, too, soon."

Dateh stopped. His frown deepened, and he shook his head. "She isn't dead. I would know."

I shuddered. So the Nightlord had been in a creative mood after all. "Then she will be. Unless you mean to challenge the Three now?"

"I have always meant to challenge them, Lady Oree." Dateh shook his head again, then smiled with bloody teeth. It was the first hint of his old self I had seen, but it chilled me nevertheless. He had eaten the godlings in hope of stealing their power, and it seemed he had managed to do so. But something else had gone very, very wrong. That was plain in his smile and in the emptiness of his eyes.

It is bad, very bad, for a mortal to eat one of us, Lil had said.

He turned, surveying his handiwork. The bodies seemed to please him, because he laughed, the sound echoing within the space of his bubble. "We demons are the gods' children, too, are we not? Yet they have hunted us nearly to extinction. *How is that right?*" I jumped at the last, because he shouted it. But when he spoke again, he laughed. "I say that if they fear us so, we should give them something to fear: their despised, persecuted children, coming to take their place."

"Don't be absurd," said Shiny. He still gripped my wrist; through this I felt the tension in his body. He was afraid—but along with the fear, he was *angry*. "No mortal can wield a god's power. Even if you could defeat the Three, the very universe would unravel under your feet."

"I can create a new one!" Dateh cried, delighted, demented. "You hid yourself within my Emptiness, didn't you, Oree Shoth? Untrained, in terror, with nothing but instinct, you carved out a safer realm for yourself." To my horror, he held his hand out as if he actually expected me to take it. "It is why Serymn hoped to win you to our cause. I can create only this one realm, but you've already built dozens. You can help me build a world where mortals need never live in fear of their gods. Where you and I will *be* gods, in our own right, as we should be."

I stumbled back from his outstretched hand and stopped as I felt the solid curve of Dateh's barrier behind me. Nowhere to run.

"Your gift has existed before among our kind," said Dateh. He gave up reaching for me but watched me around Shiny's shoulder with a hunger that was almost sexual. "It was rare, though—even when there were hundreds of us. Only Enefa's children possessed it. I need that magic, Lady Oree."

"What in the Maelstrom are you talking about?" I demanded. I frantically groped along the hard surface behind me, half hoping to find a doorknob. "You've already made me kill for you. What, you expect me to eat godling flesh and go mad with you, too?"

He blinked, startled. "Oh...no. No. You were a godling's lover. *I* never believed you could be trusted. But your magic need not be lost. I can consume *your* heart and then wield your power myself."

I froze, my blood turning to ice. Shiny, however, stepped forward, in front of me.

"Oree," he said softly. "Use your magic to leave this place."

I started out of horror and fumbled for him, finding his shoulder. To my confusion, he was not tense at all, unafraid. "I . . . I don't—"

He ignored my babbling. "You've broken his power before. Open a door back to Sky. I will make certain he doesn't follow."

I could see him, I realized. He had begun to glow, god-power rising as he committed himself to protecting me.

Dateh bared his teeth and spread his arms. "Get out of my way," he snarled.

I blinked, squinted, flinched. *He* had begun to glow as well, but with a jarring, sickening clash of colors, more than I could name. It made my stomach churn to look at him. The colors were bright, though, so bright. He was more powerful than I had ever dreamt.

I did not understand why until I blinked and my eyes made that strange, involuntary adjustment that hurt so much—and suddenly I *saw* Dateh, through whatever veil he'd cast around himself with his scrivening skills.

And I screamed. Because what stood there, enormous and heaving, rocking on twenty legs and flailing with as many arms—*and oh gods, oh gods, his FACE*—was too hideous for me to take without some outlet for my horror.

Shiny rounded on me. "Do as I say! Now!"

And then he charged forward, blazing, to meet Dateh's challenge.

"No," I whispered, shaking my head. I could not take my eyes from the great gabbling thing Dateh had become. I wanted to deny what I had seen in Dateh's face: Paitya's gentle smile, Dump's square teeth, *Madding's eyes*. And many others. There was almost nothing left of Dateh himself—nothing but will and hate. How many godlings had he consumed? Enough to overwhelm his humanity and grant him unimaginable power.

No one could fight such a creature and hope to survive. Not even Shiny. Dateh would kill him and then come eat my heart. I would be trapped within him, my very soul enslaved, forever.

"No!" I ran for the wall of the bubble, slapping its cold shimmering surface with my hands. I could not think through my terror. My breath came in gasps. I wanted nothing more than to escape.

My hands suddenly became visible. And between my hands, something new flickered into view.

I stopped, startled out of panic. The new thing rotated before me, flickering faintly, a bauble of silvery light. As I stared at it, I realized there was a face in its surface. I blinked, and the face blinked, too. It was *me*. The image—a mirror reflection, I realized, something else I had heard of but never seen—was distorted by the bubble's shape, but I could make out the curve of cheekbones, lips open in a sob, white teeth.

But most clearly, I could see my eyes.

They were not what I expected. Where my irises should have been, dull disks of twisted gray, I saw instead brilliance: tiny winking, wavering lights. My malformed corneas had withdrawn, opening like a flower, to reveal something even stranger inside.

What—?

There was a cry behind me and the sound of a blow. As I turned, something streaked across my vision like a comet. But this comet screamed as it fell, trailing fire like blood. Shiny.

Dateh uttered a rattling hiss, raising two of his stolen arms. Light, sickly mottled, dripped from his hands like oil and splattered the floor of the Empty realm. Where it fell, I heard hissing.

The small bubble winked out of existence between my hands.

Escape and strange magic forgotten, I ran to where Shiny lay, not so shiny now, and not moving. He was alive, I found as I pulled him onto his back; breathing, at least, though raggedly. But crossing his chest from shoulder to hip was a streak of darkness, an obscene obliteration of his light. I touched it, my hand trembling, but there was no wound. No magic, either.

Then I understood: whatever it was that made demon blood negate the magic of a god's life-essence, Dateh had found a way to channel it—or perhaps this was simply the culmination of what he had become. Not just a demon but a god whose very nature was mortality. He was turning Shiny back into an ordinary man, piece by piece. And once that was done, he would tear Shiny apart.

"Lady Oree," breathed the thing that had been Dateh. I could no longer think of it as a man. Its voice overlapped upon itself: I heard him echo in female registers, other males, older, younger. It wheezed as it lumbered toward me. Perhaps it had developed multiple lungs, or whatever godlings shaped within their bodies to simulate breath.

It said, "We are the last of our kind, you and I. I was wrong, wrong, wrong to threaten you." It paused, shook its massive head as if to clear it. "But I need your power. Join me, use it for me, and I'll do you no harm." It took a step closer, six feet shuffling at once.

I did not, dared not, trust the Dateh creature. Even if I agreed to its plan, its sanity was as distorted as the rest of its form; it might still kill me on a whim. It would kill Shiny regardless, I was certain—permanently, irreversibly. What would happen to the universe if one of the Three died? Would this god-eating madman even care?

Unthinking, I clutched at Shiny, a bulwark against fear. He stirred under my hands, semiconscious, no protection at all. Even his light had begun to fade. But he was not dead. Perhaps if I stalled for time, he could recover.

"J-join you?" I asked.

Dateh's form shivered, then resolved again into the ordinary, mortal shape that I had known in the House of the Risen Sun. It was an illusion. I could *feel* the warped reality still present, even if it had found a way to fool my eyes. Dateh was like Lil, safe on the surface, horror underneath.

"Yes," it said, and this time it spoke in a single voice. It gestured behind itself, toward the corpses I knew were there. "I could train you. Make you st-st-strong." The Dateh-creature paused then, eyes unfocusing for a moment, and there was that curious blurring again, the outward mask cracking for an instant. The effort needed to hold that mask in place was a taut, palpable thing. No wonder the Dateh-creature hesitated to devour me; one more heart, one more stolen soul, might be too much to contain.

Shiny groaned, and the creature's face hardened. "But you

must do something for me." Its voice had changed. I choked back a sob. It spoke with Madding's voice, gentle and persuasive. Its hands flexed from fists to claws and back. "That creature in your lap. I thought he had no true magic, but now I see I underestimated him."

My vision blurred with tears as I shook my head, and I reached across Shiny's body as if I could somehow protect him. "No," I blurted. "I won't let you kill him, too. No."

"I want *you* to kill him, Oree. Kill him, and take his heart."

I froze, staring at Dateh, my mouth falling open.

It smiled again, its teeth flickering from Dateh's to Dump's back to Dateh's. "You love too many of these gods," it said. "I need proof of your commitment. So kill him, Oree. Kill him and take that shining power for your own. When you've done it, you'll understand how much more you were meant to be."

"I can't." I was trembling all over. I barely heard myself. "I can't."

The Dateh-creature smiled, and this time its teeth were sharp, like a dog's. "You can. Your blood will work, if you use enough of it." He gestured, and a knife appeared on Shiny's chest. It was black, shimmering like solid mist—a piece of the Empty given form. "I will have your power one way or another, Lady Oree. Eat him and join me, or I eat you. Choose."

*   *   *

You may think me a coward.

You'll remember that I fled when Shiny told me to, instead of staying to fight at his side. You will remember that throughout this final horror, I was useless, helpless, too terrified to be any good to anyone, including myself. It may be that by telling you this, I have earned your contempt.

I won't try to change your mind. I'm not proud of myself or the things I did in that hell. I can't explain it, anyhow—no words can capture the terror that I felt in those moments, faced with the starkest, ugliest choice that any creature on this earth must face: kill, or die. Eat, or be eaten.

I will say this, though: I think I made the choice that any woman would when confronted by the monster that murdered her beloved.

*   *   *

I set the knife aside. Didn't need it. Shiny's chest heaved like a bellows. Whatever Dateh had done had hurt him badly, despite the magic that still wavered around him. Unnecessarily, I smoothed the cloth across his chest, then rested my hands there, one on either side of his heart.

My tears fell onto my hands in a patter of threes: one two *three*, one two *three*, one two *three*. Like the weeper-bird's cry. *Oree, oree, oree.*

*   *   *

I chose to live.

*   *   *

The paint was the door, my father had taught me, and belief was the key that unlocked it. Beneath my hands, Shiny's heart beat steady, strong.

"I paint a picture," I whispered.

*   *   *

I chose to fight.

*   *   *

Dateh let out a rattling sigh of pleasure as the shimmering bubble formed again between my hands, hovering just above Shiny's heart. I knew what it was at last—the visible manifestation of my will. My power, inherited from my god ancestors and distilled through generations of humanity, given shape and energy and *potential*. That was all magic was, really, in the end. Possibility. With it I could create anything, provided I believed. A painted world. A memory of home. A bloody hole.

I willed it into Shiny's body. It passed through his flesh harmlessly, settling amid the steady, strong pulses of his heart.

I looked up at Dateh. Something changed in me then; I don't know what. All at once, Dateh hissed in alarm and stepped back, staring at my eyes as if they had turned to stars.

Perhaps they had.

* * *

I chose to believe.

* * *

"*Itempas*," I said.

Lightning blazed out of nothingness.

The concussion of it stunned both Dateh and me. I was flung backward, slamming against Dateh's barrier with enough force to knock the breath from my body. I fell to the ground, dazed but laughing, because this was so familiar to me and because I was no longer afraid. I *believed*, after all. I knew it was over, even if Dateh had yet to learn that lesson.

A new sun blazed in the middle of Dateh's Empty, too bright to look upon directly. The heat of it was terrible even from where I lay, enough to tighten my skin and take my breath away. Around this sun glimmered an aura of pure white light—but it did not merely glow in every direction, this aura. Lines and curves seared my sight before I looked away, forming rings within rings, lines connecting, circles overlapping, godwords forming and marching and fading out of thin air. The sheer complexity of the design would have stunned me in itself, but each of the rings turned in dizzying, graceful gyroscopic patterns around a human form.

I stole a series of sweeping glances through the brilliance and made out a corona of glowing hair, a warrior's garments done in shades of pale, and a slender, white-metaled straightsword held in one perfect black hand. I could not see his face—too bright— but it was impossible not to see his eyes. They opened as I watched, piercing the unrelenting white with colors I had only heard of in poetry: fire opal. Sunset's cloak. Velvet and desire.

I could not help remembering a day, so long ago, when I'd found a man in a muckbin. They had been the same eyes then, but so much more beautiful now, incandescent, assured, that there was no sense in comparing.

"Itempas," I said again, reverent.

Those eyes turned to me, and it did not bother me that I saw no recognition in them. He saw me and knew me for one of His children, but no more than that. An entity so far beyond humanity had no need of human ties. It was enough for me that He saw, and His gaze was warm.

Before Him huddled the Dateh-creature, thrown by the same blast of power that had flattened me. As I watched, it clambered unsteadily to its many feet, the mask of its humanity shattered.

"What the hells are you?" the Dateh-creature demanded.

"A shaper," said the Lord of Light. He raised his sword of white steel. I saw hundreds of godwords in filigree patterns along the blade's length. "I am all knowledge and purpose defined. I strengthen what exists and cull that which should not."

His voice made the darkness of the Empty tremble. I laughed again, filled with inexpressable joy. Pain suddenly blossomed in my eyes, grinding, terrible. I clung to my joy and fought back against it, unwilling to look away. My god stood before me. No Maroneh had seen Him since the earliest days of the world. I would not let a simple thing like physical weakness interfere.

The Dateh-creature shouted with its many voices and let loose a wave of magic so tainted that the air turned brown and foul. Itempas batted this aside with all the effort of an after-thought. I heard a clear ringing note in the wake of His movement.

"Enough," He said, His eyes turning dark and red like a cold day's sunset. "Release my children."

The creature stiffened all over. Its eyes—Madding's eyes—grew wide. Something stirred at its midriff, then bulged obscenely in its throat. It fought this with an effort of sheer will, setting its teeth and straining. I felt it struggling to hold all the power it had swallowed into itself. This was futile, however, and a moment later it threw back its head and screamed, streams of viscous color fountaining from its throat.

Each color evaporated in the blaze of Itempas's white heat, becoming thin, shimmering mist. The mists flew to Him, swirl-ing and entwining until they formed a new ring of His multilay-ered aura, this one turning in front of Him.

He lifted a hand and the mists contracted to encircle it. Even through my agony I felt their delight.

"I'm sorry," He said, His beautiful eyes full of pain. (So familiar, that.) "I have been a poor father, but I will do better. I will become the father you deserve." The ring coalesced further, becoming a swirling sphere that hovered over His palm. "Go and be free."

He blew on the gathered souls, and they scattered into nothingness. Did I imagine that one of them, a green-blue helix, lingered a moment longer? Perhaps. Even so, it vanished, too.

Then Dateh stood alone, half slumped and knees buckling, just a man again.

"I didn't know," he whispered, gazing at the shining figure in wonder, in fear. He fell to his knees, his hands shaking as if palsied. "I didn't know it was *you*. Forgive me!" Tears ran down his face, some caused by fear, but some, I understood, were tears of awe. I knew, because the same tears ran slow and thick down my own face.

Bright Itempas smiled. I could not see His face through the glory of His light, or my hot tears, but I felt that smile along every inch of my skin. It was a warm smile—loving, benevolent. Kindly. Everything I had always believed Him to be.

The white blade flashed. That was the only way I knew that it moved; otherwise I would have thought it had simply appeared, conjured from one place to another, through the center of Dateh's chest. Dateh did not cry out, though his eyes widened. He looked down and saw his lifeblood begin threading the Bright Lord's narrow blade in pulses: one-one, two-two, three-three. The sword was so fine, the strike so precise even through bone, that his pierced heart just kept beating.

I waited for the Bright Lord to withdraw the sword and let

Dateh die. But He reached out then, with the hand that did not hold the sword. The smile was still on His face, warm and gentle and utterly merciless. There was no contradiction in this as He took hold of Dateh's face.

I had to look away then. The pain in my eyes had grown too great. I saw only red now, and it was not anger. I *heard* it, though, when Dateh began to scream. I *felt* reverberations in the air as bones cracked and ground together, as Dateh flailed and struggled and finally just twitched. I smelled fire, smoke, and the greasy acridity of burned flesh.

I tasted satisfaction then. It was not sweet, or filling, but it would do.

Then the Empty was gone, shattering around us, but I was barely aware of it. There was only the red, red pain. I thought I saw Sky's glowing floor beneath me, and I tried to push myself up, but the pain was too great. I fell, curling in on myself, too sick to retch.

Warm hands lifted me, so familiar. They touched my face, brushing away the strange thick tears that issued from my eyes. I worried, irrationally, about staining His perfect white garments with blood.

"You have given me back myself, Oree," said that shining, knowing voice. I wept harder and loved it helplessly. "To be whole again, after all these centuries…I had forgotten the feeling. But you must stop now. I would not add your death to my crimes."

It hurt so much. I had believed, and belief had become magic, but I was only mortal. The magic had limits. Yet how could I stop myself from believing? How did one find a god, and love Him, and let Him go?

The voice changed, becoming softer. Human. Familiar. "Please, Oree."

My heart called him Shiny even though my mind insisted on something else. That was enough to stop me doing whatever I was doing, and I felt the change in my eyes. Suddenly I could no longer see the glowing floor, or anything else, but the pain in my head immediately diminished from a shriek to a chronic moan. My whole body went limp with relief.

"Rest now." The disordered bed beneath me. Sheets came up to my chin. I began to shiver violently—shock. A big hand stroked the soft mass of my hair. I whimpered because this made my head hurt worse. "Shhh. I will care for you."

I did not plan what I said then. I was in too much pain, half delirious. But I asked through chattering teeth, "Are you my friend now?"

"Yes," he replied. "As you are mine."

I could not help smiling all the way into dreams.

20

"Life"
(oil study)

MORE THAN A YEAR it took me to heal.

The first two weeks of that I spent in Sky, comatose. The Lord Arameri, summoned to my room to find a barely alive demon, an exhausted fallen god, several dead and nearly dead godlings, and a human-shaped pile of ash, reacted remarkably well. He sent for Sieh again and apparently spun a magnificent tale of Dateh attacking Sky only to be repelled and ultimately destroyed by Shiny, the latter acting to defend mortal lives. Which was more or less true, as the Lord Arameri had learned long ago that it was difficult to lie to gods. (Not for nothing was he ruler of the world.)

I slept right through the restoration of the sun. I'm told the whole city celebrated for days. Wish I could have been there.

Later, when I regained consciousness and the scriveners at last pronounced me well enough to travel, I was quietly relocated to the city of Strafe, in a small barony called Ripa on the northeastern coast of the Senm continent. There I became

Desola Mokh, a tragically blind young Maroneh woman who had been fortunate enough to come into money after the death of her only remaining relative. Strafe was a midsized city, really a large small town, best known for cheap fishskin leather and mediocre wine. I had a modest town house near the ocean, with—I am told—a lovely view of both the placid town center and the churning Repentance Sea. I liked the sea, at least; the smell reminded me of good days in Nimaro.

With me traveled Enmitan Zobindi, a taciturn Maro man who was neither my husband nor a relative. (This was the talk of the town for weeks.) He earned the not-unfriendly nickname of Shadow, as in Desola's Shadow, because he was most often seen running errands around town for me. The town ladies, who eventually overcame their nervousness about approaching us, dropped polite hints during their weekly visits that I should just go ahead and marry the man, since he was doing the work of a husband, anyhow. I merely smiled, and eventually they got over it.

If they had asked, I might have felt contrary enough to tell them: Shiny wasn't doing *all* the work of a husband. At night we shared a bed, as we had done since the House of the Risen Sun. It was convenient, since the town house was drafty; I saved a lot of money on firewood. It was comforting, too, since more often than not, I awoke crying or screaming in the night. Shiny held me, and often caressed me, and occasionally kissed me. That was all I needed to regain my emotional equilibrium, so it was all I asked of him, and all he offered. He could not be Madding for me. I could not be Nahadoth or Enefa. Still, each of us managed to fulfill the other's basic needs.

He talked more, I should note. In fact, he told me many

things about his former life, some of which I've now told you. Some of what he told me I'll never tell.

And—oh, yes. I had become blind, fully and truly.

My ability to see magic never returned after the battle with Dateh. My paintings were just paint now, nothing special. I still enjoyed creating them, but I could not see them. When I went for walks in the evening, I went slower, because there was no Tree glimmer or godling leavings to see by. Even if I'd still been able to perceive such things, there would have been nothing to see. Strafe was not Shadow. It was a very unmagical town.

It took me a long while to get used to this.

But I was human, and Shiny was more or less the same, so it was inevitable that things would change.

* * *

I had been in the garden planting, since it was finally full spring-time. I had some winter onions cradled in my skirt, and my hands and clothes were stained with soil and grass. I'd put a kerchief on my head to hold back my hair and was thinking about anything but Shadow and old times. This was a good thing. A new thing.

So I was less than pleased to walk into my toolshed and find a godling waiting for me.

"Don't you look good," said Nemmer. I recognized her voice, but it still startled me. I dropped the onions. They thumped to the floor and rolled around for what sounded like an obscene amount of time.

Not bothering to pick them up, I stared in her direction. She may have thought I was astonished. I wasn't. It was just that I remembered the last time I'd seen her, at Madding's house. With Madding. It took me a moment to master my feelings.

Finally I said, "I thought godlings weren't allowed to leave Shadow."

"I'm the goddess of stealth, Oree Shoth. I do a lot of things that I'm not supposed to." She paused in surprise. "You can't see me, can you?"

"No," I said, and left it at that.

So did she, thankfully. "Wasn't easy to find you. The Arameri did a good job of covering your tracks. I honestly thought you were dead for a while. Lovely funeral, by the way."

"Thank you," I said. I hadn't attended. "Why are you here?"

She whistled at my tone. "You certainly aren't happy to see me. What's wrong?" I heard her push aside some of the tools and pots on my workbench and sit down. "Afraid I'll out you as the last living demon?"

I had lived without fear for more than a year, so it was slow to awaken in me. I only sighed and knelt to begin collecting the spilled onions. "I suppose it was inevitable you would find out *why* the Arameri 'killed' me."

"Mmm, yes. Nummy secrets." I heard her kick her feet idly, like a little girl nibbling a cookie. "I promised Mad, after all, that I'd find out who was killing our siblings."

At that, I sat back on my heels. I still felt no fear. "I had nothing to do with Role. That was Dateh. The rest, though . . ." I had no idea, so I shrugged. "It could have been either of us. They started taking my blood not long after they kidnapped me. The only one I'm sure was my fault was Madding."

"I wouldn't say it was your *fault*—" Nemmer began.

"I would."

An uncomfortable silence fell.

"Are you going to kill me now?" I asked.

There was another pause that told me she'd been considering it. "No."

"Do you want my blood for yourself, then?"

"Gods, no! What do you take me for?"

"An assassin."

I felt her stare at me, her consternation churning the air of the small room. "I don't want your blood," she said finally. "In fact, I'm planning to do all I can to make sure anyone *else* who figures out your secret dies before they can act on it. The Arameri were right about anonymity being your surest protection. I intend to make sure even *they* don't remember your existence for long."

"Lord T'vril—"

"Knows his place. I'm sure he could be persuaded to remove certain records from the family archive in exchange for my silence about his carefully hidden stash of demons' blood. Which isn't hidden as well as he thinks it is."

"I see." My head was beginning to hurt. Not from magic, just pure irritation. There were aspects of life in Shadow that I did not miss. "Why did you come, then?"

She kicked her feet again. "I thought you'd want to know. Kitr runs Madding's organization now, with Istan."

I didn't know the latter name, but I was relieved—more than I'd ever expected to be—to hear that Kitr was alive. I licked my lips. "What about... the others?"

"Lil is fine. The demon couldn't take her." With the clarity of intuition, I realized Dateh had become "the demon" for Nemmer. I was something else. "She almost killed him, in fact;

he fled from their battle. She's taken over the Shustocks junkyard—Dump's old place?—and Ancestors' Village." At my look of alarm, she added, "She doesn't eat anyone who doesn't want to be eaten. In fact, she's rather protective of the children; their hunger for love seems to fascinate her. And for some reason, she's gained a taste for being worshipped lately."

I couldn't help laughing at that. "What about—"

"None of the others survived," she said. My laughter died.

After a moment of silence, Nemmer added, "Your friends from Art Row are all fine, though."

That was very good, but it hurt me most of all to think about that part of my old life, so I said, "Did you have a chance to check on my mother?"

"No, sorry. Getting out of the city is difficult enough. I could make only one trip."

I nodded slowly and resumed picking up onions. "Thank you for doing it. Really."

Nemmer hopped down and helped me. "You seem to have a good life here, at least. How is, ah…" I smelled her discomfort, like a toe of garlic amid the onions.

"He's better," I said. "Do you want to talk to him? He went to the market. Should be back soon."

"Went to the market." Nemmer weakly let out a little laugh. "Will wonders never cease."

We got the onions into a basket. I sat back, mopping my now-sweaty brow with a dirty hand. She sat there beside me on her knees, thinking a daughter's thoughts. "I think he'd be happy if you stayed," I said softly. "Or came back at some point in the future. I think he misses all of you."

"I'm not sure I miss him," she said, though her tone said something entirely different. Abruptly she got to her feet, brushing off her knees unnecessarily. "I'll think about it."

I rose as well. "All right." I considered whether to invite her to stay for dinner, then decided against it. Despite what it might have meant to Shiny, I didn't really want her to stay. She didn't really want to, either. An awkward silence descended between us.

"I'm glad you're well, Oree Shoth," she said finally.

I extended my hand to her, not worrying about the dirt. She was a god. If dirt bothered her, she could will it away. "It was good seeing you, Lady Nemmer."

She laughed, easing the awkwardness. "I told you not to call me 'Lady.' You mortals all make me feel so *old*, I swear." But she took my hand and squeezed it before vanishing.

I puttered about in the shed awhile, then went into the house and upstairs to bathe. After that, I put my hair back in a braid, donned a thick, warm robe, and curled up in my favorite chair, thinking.

Evening fell. I heard Shiny come in downstairs, wipe his feet, and begin putting away the supplies he'd bought. Eventually he came upstairs and stopped, standing in the doorway, looking at me. Then he came over to the bed and sat down, waiting for me to tell him what was wrong. He talked more these days, but only when the mood took him, and that was rare. For the most part, he was just a very quiet man. I liked that about him, especially now. His silent presence soothed my loneliness in a way that talking would only have irritated.

So I got up and went over to the bed. I found his face with my hands, traced its stern lines. He shaved his head bald every morning. That kept people from realizing it was completely white, which was too striking for the low profile we were trying to keep. He was handsome enough without it, but I missed pushing my fingers into his hair. I ran my fingers across his smooth scalp instead, wistful.

Shiny regarded me for a moment, thoughtful. Then he reached up and untied the sash of my robe, tugging it open. I froze, startled, as he gazed at me—nothing more than that. But as he had somehow done long ago, on a rooftop in another life, just that look made me incredibly aware of my body, and his nearness, and all the potential that lay therein. When he took hold of my hips, there was absolutely no doubt as to what he intended. Then he pulled me closer.

I pulled back instead, too stunned to react otherwise. If my skin hadn't still tingled where he'd touched me, I would have thought I'd imagined the whole thing. But that, and the roaring-awake of certain parts of me that had been mostly asleep for a long while, told me it was very real.

Shiny lowered his hands when I stepped back. He didn't seem upset, or concerned. He just waited.

I laughed weakly, suddenly nervous. "I thought you weren't interested."

He said nothing, of course, because it was obvious that had changed.

I fidgeted, pushing up my sleeves (they fell back down immediately), tucking back a stray curl of hair, shifting from foot to foot. I didn't close the open robe, though.

"I don't know—" I began.

"I have decided to live," he said quietly.

That, too, was obvious from the way he'd changed in the past year. I felt his gaze as he spoke, heavier than usual along my skin. He had been my friend, and now offered more. Was *willing to try* more. But I knew: he was not the sort of man who loved easily, or casually. If I wanted him, I would have all of him, and he wanted all of me. All or nothing; that was as fundamental to his nature as light itself.

I tried to joke. "It took you a year to decide that?"

"Ten, yes," Shiny replied. "This last year was for *you* to decide."

I blinked in surprise, but then I realized he was right. *Such a strange thing*, I thought, and smiled.

Then I stepped forward again, found his face, and kissed him.

It was much better than that long-ago night on Madding's roof, probably because he wasn't trying to hurt me this time. The same incredible gentleness without malice—nice. He tasted of apples, which he must've eaten on his way back from town, and radishes, which were not so pleasant. I didn't mind. I felt his eyes on me the whole time. *He would be the type*, I thought, but then I hadn't closed mine, either.

It did feel strange, though, and until he'd taken hold of my waist again, pulling me where he wanted so he could do all the things his gaze had implied, I didn't realize what it was that had me confused. Then he did something that made me gasp, and I realized Shiny's kiss had been just a kiss. Just one mouth on another, with no impression of colors or music or soaring on unseen winds. It had been so long since I'd kissed a mortal that I'd forgotten we couldn't do that.

That was all right, though. There were other things we could do just fine.

*   *   *

I slept well into the small hours, until a dream made me start awake. I kicked Shiny in the shin inadvertently, but he did not react. I touched his face and realized he was awake, untroubled by my thrashing.

"Did you sleep at all?" I yawned.

"No."

I couldn't remember the dream, but the feeling of unease it had given me lingered. I pushed myself up from his chest and rubbed my face, bleary and painfully aware of the unlovely taste of my mouth. Outside I could hear a few determined birds beginning their morning song, though the chill in the air told me it wasn't yet dawn. Otherwise it was quiet—that eerie, not-quite-comforting quiet one finds in small towns before dawn. Not even the fishermen were up. In Shadow, I thought with fleeting sadness, the birds would not have been so alone.

"Everything all right?" I asked. "I can make some tea."

"No." He reached up then to touch my face, as I so often did with him. Since his eyes worked just fine, I wondered if I dared take it as a gesture of affection. Maybe the room was just dark. He was always a hard man to read, and now I had to learn a whole new set of interpretations for the things he did.

"I want you," he said.

Or he could just tell me. I couldn't help laughing, though I nuzzled his hand to let him know his advance wasn't unwelcome. "We're going to have to work on your bedroom talk, I think."

He sat up, shifting me easily to his lap, and pulled me into a kiss before I could warn him about my breath. His was no better. But it was my turn to be surprised, because as he deepened the kiss and smoothed his hands down my arms, gently pulling them behind me, I felt something. A flicker. A trickle of heat— real heat. Not passion, but *fire*.

I gasped, my eyes widening as he pulled back.

"I want to be inside you," he said, his voice low, implacable. One of his hands pinned my wrists behind my back; the other massaged elsewhere, just right. I think I made a sound. I'm not sure. "I want to watch the dawnlight break across your skin. I want you to scream as the sun rises. I don't care what name you call."

That has to be the most unromantic thing I've ever heard, I thought giddily. He touched me more then, kissing, tasting, caressing. He had learned much about me in our previous session, which this time he used to ruthless effect. When his teeth grazed my throat, I cried out and arched backward, not quite voluntarily. The way he was holding my wrists meant that I bent how he wanted me to bend. He wasn't hurting me—I could feel the care he took to avoid that—but I couldn't break his grip. I trembled, my eyelids fluttering shut, fear and arousal making me light-headed as I finally understood.

Sunrise was coming. I had made love to a godling, but this was different. I could no longer see the glow rise in Shiny's body, but I had tasted the first stirrings of magic in his kiss. He was not quite my Shiny, not anymore, and he would be nothing like my cool, carefree Madding. He would be a thing of heat and intensity and absolute power.

Could I lie down with something like that and get up whole?

"I want to be myself for you, Oree," he whispered against my skin. "Just once." Not a plea—never that. An explanation.

I closed my eyes and made myself relax. I couldn't bring myself to speak, but I didn't have to. My trust was enough.

So he lifted us, turning to put me under him on the bed, this time pinioning my arms above my head. I lay passive, knowing that he needed this. The control. He had so little power these days; what he could claim was precious to him. For some moments, he simply looked at me. His gaze was like feathers on my skin, a torment. When he actually touched me, it had the weight of command. I arched and shuddered and opened myself to him. I could not help it. As he pressed against me, into me, I felt the impossible heat of his body rise. He moved slowly at first, concentrating, whispering something. Godwords, like a prayer, almost at the threshold of my ability to hear them. The magic would not work for him, would it?

but he is different now, this is different—

and then I felt the words on my skin. I don't know how I knew they were words. I shouldn't have. Usually only my fingers were that sensitive, but now my thighs made out the arcs and curves and jagged turns of gods' language, each character perfectly clear in my mind. It was more than words; there were strange tilted lines, too, and numbers, and other symbols whose purpose I could not decipher. Too complex. He had created language at the beginning of time, and it had always been his most subtle instrument. The words slid along my skin, wending down my legs, circling my breasts—gods. There are no mortal words for how it felt, but I writhed, how I writhed. He watched me, heard me whimper, and was pleased. I felt that, too.

"Oree," he said. Only that. I heard whispers behind it, a dozen voices—all his—overlapping. The word took on a dozen different layers of meaning, encompassing lust, fear, dominance, tenderness, reverence.

Then he kissed me again, fiercely this time, and I would have cried out if I could have because it *burned*, like lightning arcing down my throat and setting all my nerves afire. It made me writhe anew, which he generously permitted. It made me cry, but the tears dried almost at once.

My sweat became steam. I felt the heat of the encroaching sun soak in and then gather within me, rising close to the skin, boiling. It would either find an outlet or it would burn me up; it did not care. *I* did not care. I was shouting wordlessly, straining against him, begging for just that little bit extra, just that final touch, just a taste of the god within the man, because he was both, and I loved them both, and I needed both with all my soul.

Then came the day, and with it the light, and all my awareness dissolved amid the rush and roar and incomprehensible glory of ten thousand white-hot suns.

21

"Still Life"
(oil on canvas)

THIS PART IS HARD FOR ME, harder than all the rest. But I will tell it, because you need to know.

*   *   *

When I awoke, it was early evening. I'd slept all day, but as I sat up, kicking my way free of the entangling sheets, I gave serious thought to lying back down. I could have slept a week more, so tired was I. Still, I was hungry, thirsty, and in sore need of a toilet, so I got up.

Shiny, asleep beside me, didn't stir, even when I tripped over my discarded robe and cursed loudly. I supposed the magic had worn him out even more than it had me.

In the bathroom, I took stock, having reached the conclusion that I was alive and had not been burned to a crisp. I felt fine, in fact, other than the tiredness and a bit of soreness here and there. More than fine. It struck me as I stood there rubbing my face: I was happy again, perhaps for the first time since I'd left Shadow. Truly, completely, happy.

So when the first tickle of cold air brushed my ankles, I barely noticed. Not until I left the bathroom, and walked into a space of coldness so sharp and alien that it made me stop short, did I realize Shiny and I were not alone.

There was only silence, at first. Only a growing feeling of presence and *immensity*. It filled the bedroom, oppressive, making the walls creak faintly. Whatever had come to visit us, it was not human.

And it did not like me. Not one whit.

I stood very still, listening. I heard nothing—and then something inhaled, very near the back of my neck.

"You still smell of him."

Every nerve in my body screamed. I stayed silent only because fear had robbed me of breath. I knew who this was. I had not heard his approach, didn't dare speak his name, but *I knew who he was*.

The voice behind me—soft, deep, malevolent—chuckled. "Prettier than I expected. Sieh was right; you were a lucky find for him." A hand stroked my hair, which was a mess, the braid half undone. The finger that snaked out to graze the back of my neck was ice cold. I could not help jumping. "But so delicate. So soft a hand to hold his leash."

I was not surprised, not at all, when those long fingers suddenly gripped my hair, pulling my head back. I barely registered the pain. The voice, which now spoke into my ear, was of far greater concern.

"Does he love you yet?"

I could not process the words. "Wh-what?"

"Does he." The voice moved closer. "Love you." I should have felt his body by now, leaning against my shoulder, but there was only a feeling of stillness and cool, like midnight air. "*Yet.*"

The last word was so close to my ear that I felt the caress of his breath. I expected to feel his lips in the next instant. When I did, I would start screaming. I knew this as surely as I knew he would kill me when I did it.

Before I could doom myself, however, another voice spoke from across the room.

"That's not a fair question. How could she know?" This one was a woman, a cultured contralto, and I recognized her voice. I'd heard it a year before, in an alley, with the scents of piss and burned flesh and fear heavy in the air. The goddess Sieh had called Mother. I knew, now, who she really was.

"It's the only question that matters," said the man. He released my hair, and I stumbled forward to a trembling halt, wanting to run and knowing there was no point.

Shiny was not awake. I could hear him in the bed, still breathing slow and even. Something was very wrong with that.

I swallowed. "Do you prefer Y-Yeine, Lady? Or, ah—"

"Yeine will do." She paused, a hint of amusement in her voice. "Aren't you going to ask my companion's name?"

"I think I know it already," I whispered.

I felt her smile. "Still, we should at least observe the formalities. You are Oree Shoth, of course. Oree, this is Nahadoth."

I made myself nod, jerkily. "Very nice to meet you both."

"Much better," said the woman. "Don't you think?"

I didn't realize this wasn't directed at me until the man—*not a man, not a man at all*—replied. And I jumped again, because suddenly his voice was farther away, over near the bed. "I don't care."

"Oh, be nice." The woman sighed. "I appreciate your asking, Oree. I suppose someday my own name will be better known, but until then, I find it irritating when others treat me and my predecessor as interchangeable."

I could guess her location now: over by the windows, in the big chair where I sometimes sat to listen to the town. I imagined her sitting daintily, one leg crossed over the other, her expression wry. Her feet would still be bare, I felt certain.

I tried not to imagine the other one at all.

"Come with me," said the woman, rising. She came closer, and I felt a cool hand take my own. Though I had gotten a taste of her power on that long-ago day in the alley, I felt nothing of her right then, even this close. It was all the Nightlord's cold that filled the room.

"Wh-wha—" I turned to go with her out of sheer unthinking self-preservation. But as she tugged my hand, my feet stopped moving. She stopped as well, turning to me. I tried to speak and could not muster words. Instead I turned, not wanting to but *needing* to. I faced the Nightlord, who stood near the bed, looming over Shiny.

There was a hint of kindness in the Lady's voice. "We will do him no harm. Not even Naha."

Naha, I thought dizzily. *The Nightlord has a pet name.* I licked my lips. "I don't…he's." I swallowed again. "Usually a light sleeper."

She nodded. I couldn't see her, but I knew it. I didn't need to see her to know anything she did.

"The sun has just set, though it still lights the sky," she said, taking my hand again. "This is my time. He'll wake when I let him—though I don't intend to let him until we're gone. It's better that way."

She led me downstairs. In the kitchen, she sat with me at the table, taking the other chair. Here, away from Nahadoth, I could feel something of her, but it was restrained somehow, nothing like that moment in the alley. She had an air of stillness and balance.

I debated whether I should offer her tea.

"Why is it better that Shiny stay asleep?" I asked at last.

She laughed softly. "I like that name, Shiny. I like *you*, Oree Shoth, which is why I wanted to talk to you alone." I started as her fingers, gentle—and strangely, callused—tilted my face down so she could see me more clearly. I remembered she was much shorter than me. "Naha was right. You really are lovely. Your eyes accentuate it, I think."

I said nothing, worried that she hadn't answered my question.

After a moment, she let me go. "Do you know why I prohibit the godlings from leaving Shadow?"

I blinked in confusion. "Um...no."

"I think you do know—better than any other, perhaps. Look what happens when even one mortal gets too closely involved with our kind. Destruction, murder...Shall I let the whole world suffer the same?"

I frowned, opened my mouth, hesitated, then finally decided to say what was on my mind.

"I think," I said slowly, "that it doesn't matter whether you restrict the godlings or not."

"Oh?"

I wondered if she was genuinely interested, or whether this was some sort of test.

"Well... I wasn't born in Shadow. I went there because I had heard about the magic. Because..." *I would be able to see there*, I had intended to say, but that wasn't true. In Shadow I had seen wonders on a daily basis, but in practical terms, I hadn't been much better off than I was in Strafe; I'd still needed a stick to get around. I hadn't cared about being able to see, anyway. I had come because of the Tree and the godlings, and the rumors of still greater strangeness. I had yearned to find a place where my father could have felt at home. And I had not been the only one. All my friends, most of whom were not demons or godlings or magic-touched in any way, had come to Shadow for the same reason: because it had been a place like no other. Because...

"Because the magic called to me," I said at last. "That will happen wherever magic is. It's part of us now, and some of us will always be drawn to it. So unless you take it away completely, which even the Interdiction never managed to do"—I spread my hands—"bad things will happen. And good."

"Good?" The Lady sounded thoughtful.

"Well... yes." I swallowed again. "I regret some of what's happened to me. But not all of it."

"I see," she said.

Another silence fell, almost companionable.

"Why is it better that Shiny stay asleep?" I asked, very softly this time.

"Because we've come to kill you."

My innards turned to water. Yet strangely, I found it easier to talk now. It was as if my anxiety had passed some threshold, beyond which it became pointless.

"You know what I am," I guessed.

"Yes," she replied. "You bent the chains we placed on Itempas and released his true power, even if only for a moment. That got our attention. We've been watching you ever since. But"—she shrugged—"I was a mortal for longer than I've been a god. The possibility of death is nothing new or especially frightening to me. So I don't care that you're a demon."

I frowned. "Then what...?"

But I remembered the Nightlord's question. *Does he love you yet?*

"Shiny," I whispered.

"He was sent here to suffer, Oree. To grow, to heal, to hopefully rejoin us someday. But make no mistake—this was also a punishment." She sighed, and for an instant I heard the sound of distant rain. "It's unfortunate that he met you so soon. In a thousand years, perhaps, I could have persuaded Nahadoth to let this go. Not now."

I stared at her with my sightless eyes, stunned by the monstrosity of what she was saying. They had made Shiny nearly human, the better to experience the pain and hardship of mortal life. They had bound him to protect mortals, live among them, understand them. Like them, even. But he could not love them.

Love *me*, I realized, and ached with both the sweetness of the knowledge and the bitterness that followed.

"That isn't fair," I said. I wasn't angry. I wasn't that stupid. Still, if they were going to kill me, anyway, I was damn well going to speak my mind. "Mortals love. You can't make him one of us and keep him from doing that. It's a contradiction."

"Remember why he was sent here. He loved Enefa—and murdered her. He loved Nahadoth and his own children, yet tormented them for centuries." She shook her head. "His love is dangerous."

"It wasn't—" *His fault*, I almost said, but that was wrong. Many mortals went mad; not all of them attacked their loved ones. Shiny had accepted responsibility for what he'd done, and I had no right to deny that.

So I tried again. "Have you considered that having mortal lovers may be what he needs? Maybe—" And again I cut myself off, because I had almost said, *Maybe I can heal him for you.* That was too presumptuous, no matter how kind the Lady seemed.

"It may be what he needs," said the Lady, evenly. "It isn't what *Nahadoth* needs."

I flinched and fell silent then, lost. It was as Serymn had guessed: the Lady knew what another Gods' War would cost humanity, and she had done what she could to prevent it. That meant balancing the needs of one damaged brother against the other—and for the time being, at least, she had decided that the Nightlord's rage deserved more satisfaction than Shiny's sorrow. I didn't blame her, really. I had felt that rage upstairs, that hunger for vengeance, so strong that it ground against my senses like a pestle. What amazed me was that she actually thought there was some hope of reconciling the three of them. Maybe she was as crazy as Shiny.

Or maybe she was just willing to do whatever it took to fill the chasm between them. What was a little demon blood, a little cruelty, compared to another war? What were a few ruined mortal lives, so long as the majority survived? And if all went well, then in a thousand years or ten thousand, the Nightlord's wrath might be appeased. That was how gods thought, wasn't it?

At least Shiny will have forgotten me by then.

"Fine," I said, unable to keep the bitterness out of my voice. "Get it over with. Or do you mean to kill me slowly? Give Shiny's knife an extra turn?"

"He'll suffer enough knowing *why* you died; *how* makes little difference." She paused. "Unless."

I frowned. Her tone had changed. "What?"

She reached across the table and cupped my cheek, her thumb brushing my lips. I nearly flinched but managed to master the reflex in time. That seemed to please her; I felt her smile.

"Such a lovely girl," she said again, and sighed with what might have been regret. "I might be able to persuade Nahadoth to let you live, provided Itempas still suffers."

"What do you mean?"

"If, perhaps, you were to leave him..." She trailed off, letting her fingers trail away from my face. I stiffened, sick with understanding.

When I finally managed to speak, I was shaking inside. I was angry at last, though; that steadied my voice. "I see. It's not enough for you to hurt him; you want *me* to hurt him, too."

"Pain is pain," said the Nightlord, and all the small hairs on my skin prickled, because I had not heard him come into the room. He was somewhere behind the Lady, and already the room was turning cold. "Sorrow is sorrow. I don't care where it comes from, as long as it is all he feels."

Despite my fear, his careless, empty tone infuriated me. My free hand tightened into a fist. "So I'm to choose between letting you kill me and stabbing him in the back myself?" I snapped. "Fine, then—kill me. At least he'll know *I* didn't abandon him."

Yeine's hand brushed mine, which I suspected was meant to be a warning. The Nightlord went silent, but I felt his rigid fury. I didn't care. It made me feel better to hurt him. He had taken my people's happiness and now he wanted mine.

"He still loves you, you know," I blurted. "More than me. More than anything, really."

He hissed at me. It was not a human sound. In it I heard snakes and ice, and dust settling into a deep, shadowed crevice. Then he started forward—

Yeine stood, turning to face him. Nahadoth stopped. For a span of time that I could not measure—perhaps a breath, perhaps an hour—they stared at one another, motionless, silent. I knew that gods could speak without words, but I was not certain that was happening here. This felt more like a battle.

Then the feeling faded and Yeine sighed, stepping closer to him. "Softly," she said, her voice more compassionate than I could have imagined. "Slowly. You're free now. Be what you choose to be, not what they made you."

He let out a long, slow sigh, and I felt the cold pressure of him fade just a little. When he spoke, however, his voice was just as hard as before. "I am of my choosing. But that is *angry*, Yeine. They burn in me, the memories... They hurt. The things he did to me."

The room reverberated with betrayals unspoken, horrors and

loss. In that silence, my anger crumbled. I had never been able to truly hate anyone who'd suffered, no matter what evils they'd done in the aftermath.

"He has not earned such happiness, Yeine," the Nightlord said. "Not yet."

The Lady sighed. "I know."

I heard him touch her, perhaps a kiss, perhaps just taking her hand. It reminded me at once of Shiny and the way he often touched me, wordlessly, needing the reassurance of my nearness. Had he done that with Nahadoth, once upon a time? Perhaps Nahadoth—underneath the anger—missed those days, too. He had the Lady to comfort him, however. Shiny would soon have no one.

Silently, the Nightlord vanished. Yeine stayed where she was for a moment, then turned back to me.

"That was foolish of you," she said. I realized she was angry, too, with me.

I nodded, weary. "I know. Sorry."

To my surprise, that actually seemed to mollify her. She returned to the table, though she didn't sit. "Not wholly your fault. He's still...fragile, in some ways. The scars of the War, and his imprisonment, run deep. Some of them are still raw."

And I remembered, with some guilt, that this was Shiny's fault.

"I've made my decision," I said, very softly.

She saw what was in my heart—or perhaps it was just obvious. "If what you said was true," she said, "if you do care about him, then ask yourself what's best for him."

I did. And in that moment I imagined Shiny, what he might

become, long after I died and had turned to dust. A wanderer, a warrior, a guardian. A man of soft words and swift decisions and little in the way of kindness—yet he would have some, I understood. Some warmth. Some ability to touch, and be touched by, others. I could leave him that much, if I did it right.

But if I died, if his love killed me, there would be nothing in him. He would distance himself from mortalkind, knowing the consequences of caring too deeply for us. He would snuff that small ember of warmth in himself, fearful of the pain it brought. He would live among humanity yet be wholly alone. And he would never, ever heal.

I said nothing.

"You have one day," Yeine said, and vanished.

I sat at the table for a long while.

Whatever the Lady had done to still time, it faded once she was gone. Through the kitchen windows, I felt night fall, the air turning cool and dry. I could hear people walking outside, cicadas in the distant fields, and a carriage rattling along a cobbled street. There was the scent of flowers on the wind...though not the flowers of the World Tree.

In time, I heard movement upstairs. Shiny. The pipes rattled as he ran a bath. Strafe was not Shadow, but it had better plumbing, and I shamelessly wasted wood and coal to give us hot water whenever we wanted it. After a time, I heard him let the water out, moving around some more; then he came downstairs. As before, he stopped in the doorway of the room, reading something in my stillness. Then he came over to the table and sat down—where the Lady had sat, though that meant nothing. I didn't have many chairs.

I had to hold very still as I spoke. Otherwise, I would break, and it would all be for nothing.

"You have to leave," I said.

Silence from Shiny.

"I can't be with you. It never works between gods and mortals; you were right about that. Even to try is foolish."

As I spoke, I realized with a shock that I believed some of what I was saying. I had always known, in part of my heart, that Shiny could not stay with me forever. I would grow old, die, while he stayed young. Or would he grow old, too, die of old age, and then be reborn young and handsome again? Not good for me, either way. I wouldn't be able to help resenting him, feeling guilty for burdening him. I would cause him unimaginable pain as he watched me fail, and in the end we would be separated forever, anyway.

But I had wanted to try. Gods, how I'd wanted to try.

Shiny sat there, gazing at me. No recriminations, no attempts to change my mind. That was not his way. I had known from the moment I began this that it wouldn't take much. Not in words, anyhow.

Then he got up, came around the table, and crouched in front of me. I turned, moving slowly and oh so carefully to face him. Control. That was his way, wasn't it? I tried for it and held myself still. I fought the urge to touch his face and learn how badly he now thought of me.

"Did they threaten you?" he asked.

I froze.

He waited, then when I did not answer, sighed. He got to his feet.

"That isn't why," I blurted. Suddenly it was powerfully important that he know I was not acting out of fear for my own life. "I didn't . . . I would rather have let them——"

"No." He touched my cheek then, once and briefly. It hurt. Like breaking my arm all over again. Worse. That was all it took to shatter my careful control. I began to tremble, so much that I could barely get the words out.

"We can fight them," I blurted. "The Lady, she doesn't really want to do this. We can run or——"

"No, Oree," he said again. "We can't."

At this, I fell silent. It was not the inability to think this time, just the utter certainty of his words. They left me with nothing to say.

He rose. "You should live, too, Oree," he said.

Then he went to the door. His boots were there, neatly placed beside mine. He pulled them on, his movements neither swift nor slow. Efficient. He put on the lambskin coat I'd bought for him at the beginning of the winter, because he kept forgetting he could get sick, and I hadn't felt like nursing him through pneumonia.

I inhaled to say something. Let the breath out. Sat there, trembling.

He walked out of the house.

I had known he would go like that, too, with nothing but the clothes on his back. He wasn't human enough to care about possessions or money. I heard his heavy tread move down the steps, then down the dusty street. They faded into the distance, lost in the sounds of night.

I went upstairs. The bathroom was spotless as usual. I took

off my robe and had a long soak, as hot as I could bear the water. I steamed even after I dried off.

It did not hit me until I picked up a sponge to clean the tub. Now that Shiny was gone, I would have to do that myself from now on.

I finished the tub, then sat down in it and wept for the rest of the night.

*   *   *

So now you know it all.

You needed to know it, and I needed to tell it. I've spent the past six months trying not to think about all that's happened, which wasn't the wisest thing to do. It was easier, though. Better to go to bed and simply sleep, rather than lie there all night feeling lonely. Better to concentrate on the *tap-tap* of my stick as I walk, rather than think of how, once, I could have navigated by the faint outline of some godling's footprints. I've lost so much.

But I've gained some things, too. Like you, my little surprise.

On some level I knew it was a risk. Gods don't breed as easily as us, but they made him more mortal than any god has ever been. I don't know what it means that they left him this ability when they took so much else. I suppose they just forgot.

Then again, I can't help remembering that evening, at my kitchen table, when the Lady Yeine touched me. She is the Mistress of Dawn, the goddess of life; surely she sensed you, or at least your imminence, while we sat there. That makes me wonder: did she notice you and let you live? Or did she . . . ?

She's a strange one, the Lady.

Even more strangely, she listened to me.

I've now heard the news from too many merchants and gossips to discount: there are gods everywhere. Singing in rain forests, dancing atop mountains, staking out beaches and flirting with the clam-boys. Most large cities have a resident godling these days, or two or three. Strafe is trying to attract one right now; the town elders say it's good for business. I hope they succeed.

Soon the world will be a far more magical place. Just right, I think, for you.

And—

No.

No, I know better than to think it.

No.

And yet.

I lie here in my lonely bed, watching for the sunrise. I feel it coming—the light warms its way along the blankets and my skin. The days are getting shorter with the coming of winter. I'm guessing you'll be born around the solstice.

Are you still listening? Can you hear me in there?

I think you can. I think you were made that second time, when Shiny became his true self for me, just a little. Just enough. I think he knew it, too, like the Lady knew it, and maybe even the Nightlord. This isn't the sort of thing he would do by accident. He'd seen that I missed my old life. This was his way of helping me focus on the new one. And also...his way of making up for past mistakes.

Gods. Men. Damn him; he should've asked me. I could die giving birth to you, after all. Probably not, but it's the principle of the thing.

Well.

I hope you're listening, because sometimes gods—and

demons—do that. I think that you're awake, aware, and that you understand everything I've said.

Because I think I saw you, yesterday morning when I woke up. I think my eyes worked again, just for a moment, and you were the light I saw.

I think that if I wait 'til dawn and watch closely, I'll see you again this morning.

And I think that if I wait long enough and listen carefully, one day I'll hear footsteps on the road outside. Maybe a knock at the door. He'll have learned basic courtesy by then from someone. We can hope for that, can't we? Either way, he'll come inside. He'll wipe his feet, at least. He'll hang his coat.

And then you and I, together, will welcome him home.

APPENDIX

1

A Glossary of Terms

Amn: Most populous and powerful of the Senmite races.

Arameri: Ruling family of the Amn; advisors to the Nobles' Consortium and the Order of Itempas.

Art Row: Artists' market at the Promenade, in East Shadow.

Blood sigil: The mark of a recognized Arameri family member.

Bonebender: A healer, often self-taught, with knowledge of herbalism, midwifery, bonesetting, and basic surgical techniques. Some bonebenders illegally utilize simple healing sigils.

Bright, the: The time of Itempas's solitary rule, after the Gods' War. General term for goodness, order, law, righteousness.

Darkwalkers: Worshippers of the Lord of Shadows.

Dateh Lorillalia: A scrivener, formerly of the Order of Itempas. Husband of Serymn Arameri.

Dekarta Arameri: Most recent former head of the Arameri family.

Demon: Children of forbidden unions between gods/godlings and mortals. Mortal, though they may possess innate magic that is equivalent, or greater, to that of godlings in strength.

Dump: A godling who dwells in West Shadow, overseeing the Shustocks junkyard. The Lord of Discards.

Easha: Local term for East Shadow.

Enefa: One of the Three. Former Goddess of Earth, creator of godlings and mortals, Mistress of Twilight and Dawn (deceased).

Eo: A godling who dwells in Shadow. The Merciful.

Gateway Park: A park built around Sky and the World Tree's base, in East Shadow.

God: Immortal children of the Maelstrom. The Three.

Godling: Immortal children of the Three. Sometimes also referred to as gods.

Godsblood: A popular and expensive narcotic. Confers heightened awareness and temporary magical abilities on consumers.

God spots: Local/colloquial name for locations in Shadow that have been temporarily or permanently made magical by godlings.

Gods' Realm: All places beyond the universe.

Gods' War: An apocalyptic conflict in which Bright Itempas claimed rulership of the heavens after defeating his two siblings.

Hado: A member of the New Lights. Master of Initiates.

Heavens, Hells: Abodes for souls beyond the mortal realm.

Heretic: A worshipper of any god but Itempas.

A Glossary of Terms

High North: Northernmost continent. A backwater.

House of the Risen Sun: A mansion. One of several attached to the World Tree's trunk.

Hundred Thousand Kingdoms, the: Collective term for the world since its unification under Arameri rule.

Ina: A godling who dwells in Shadow.

Interdiction, the: The period during which no godlings appeared in the mortal realm, per order of Bright Itempas.

Islands, the: Vast archipelago east of High North and Senm.

Itempan: General term for a worshipper of Itempas. Also used to refer to members of the Order of Itempas.

Itempas: One of the Three. The Bright Lord; master of heavens and earth; the Skyfather.

Kitr: A godling who dwells in Shadow. The Blade.

Lil: A godling who dwells in Shadow. The Hunger.

Madding: A godling who dwells in Shadow. The Lord of Debts.

Maelstrom: The creator of the Three. Unknowable.

Magic: The innate ability of gods and godlings to alter the material and immaterial world. Mortals may approximate this ability through the use of the gods' language.

Maroland, the: Smallest continent, which once existed to the east of the islands; site of the first Arameri palace. Destroyed by Nahadoth.

Mortal realm: The universe, created by the Three.

Nahadoth: One of the Three. The Nightlord. Also called the Lord of Shadows.

Nemmer: A godling who dwells in Shadow. The Lady of Secrets.

Nimaro Reservation: A protectorate of the Arameri, established after the Maroland's destruction to provide a home for survivors. Located at the southeast edge of the Senm continent.

Nobles' Consortium: Ruling political body of the Hundred Thousand Kingdoms.

Oboro: A godling who dwells in Shadow.

Order of Itempas: The priesthood dedicated to Bright Itempas. In addition to spiritual guidance, also responsible for law and order, education, public health and welfare, and the eradication of heresy. Also known as the Itempan Order.

Order-Keepers: Acolytes (priests in training) of the Order of Itempas, responsible for maintenance of public order.

Order of New Light: An unauthorized priesthood dedicated to Bright Itempas, comprised mainly of former members of the Order of Itempas. Colloquially known as the "New Lights."

Paitya: A godling who dwells in Shadow. The Terror.

Pilgrim: Worshippers of the Gray Lady who journey to Shadow to pray at the World Tree. Generally High Northers.

Previt: One of the higher rankings for priests of the Order of Itempas.

Promenade, the: Northernmost edge of Gateway Park in East Shadow. A site popular with pilgrims, due to its view of the World Tree. Also the site of Art Row and the city's largest White Hall.

Role: A godling who dwells in Shadow. The Lady of Compassion.

Salon: Headquarters for the Nobles' Consortium.

Script: A series of sigils, used by scriveners to produce complex or sequential magical effects.

Scrivener: A scholar of the gods' written language.

Senm: Southernmost and largest continent of the world.

Senmite: The Amn language, used as a common tongue for all the Hundred Thousand Kingdoms.

Serymn Arameri: An Arameri fullblood, husband of Dateh Lorillalia. Owner of the House of the Risen Sun.

Shadow: Local/colloquial name for the largest city on the Senm continent (official name is Sky).

Shahar Arameri: High priestess of Itempas at the time of the Gods' War. Her descendants are the Arameri family.

Shustocks: A neighborhood in Wesha.

Sieh: A godling, also called the Trickster. Eldest of all the godlings.

Sigil: An ideograph of the gods' language, used by scriveners to imitate the magic of the gods.

Sky: Official name of the largest city on the Senm continent. Also, the palace of the Arameri family.

Strafe: A city along the northwestern coast of the Senm continent.

Teman Protectorate, the: A Senmite kingdom.

Time of the Three: Before the Gods' War.

T'vril Arameri: Current head of the Arameri family.

Velly: A cold-water fish, normally smoked and salted. A Maroneh delicacy.

Wesha: Local term for West Shadow.

White Hall: The Order of Itempas's houses of worship, education, and justice.

World Tree, the: A leafy evergreen tree estimated to be 125,000 feet in height, created by the Gray Lady. Sacred to worshippers of the Lady.

Yeine: One of the Three. The current Goddess of Earth, Mistress of Twilight and Dawn. Also called the Gray Lady.

Historical Record;
First Scriveners' notes, volume 96;
from the collection of T'vril Arameri.

(Interview conducted and originally transcribed by First Scrivener Y'li Denai/Arameri, at Sky, year 1512 of the Bright, may He shine upon us forever. Recorded in fixed messaging sphere. Secondary transcription completed by Librarian Sheta Arameri, year 2250 of the Bright. WARNING: contains heretical references, marked "HR." Used with permission of the Litaria.)

FIRST SCRIVENER Y'LI ARAMERI: Are you comfortable?

NEMUE SARFITH ENULAI[1]: Should I be?

YA: Of course. You are a guest of the Arameri, Enulai Sarfith.

---

1. Interviewer's note: "Enulai" (HR) is apparently a hereditary title among the Maro.

NS: Exactly! (laughs) I suppose I should enjoy it while I can. I doubt you'll have many more Maro guests here in the future.

YA: I see you've decided not to use the new word. Maroneh[2]—

NS: Three words, actually, in the old tongue. *Maro n neh.* Nobody says it right. Too much of a mouthful. I was Maro all my life; I'll be Maro 'til I die. Not long, now.

YA: For the record, would you be willing to state your age?

NS: The Father has blessed me with two hundred and two years.

YA: (laughs) I was told you liked to claim that age.

NS: You believe I'm lying?

YA: Well... madam—I mean, Enulai...

NS: Call me what you like. But remember that enulai always speak the truth, boy. Lying is dangerous. And I wouldn't bother lying about something so trivial as my age. So write it down!

YA: Yes, madam. I have done so.

NS: You Amn never listen. In the days following the War,[3] we warned you to respect the Dark Father (HR). He is not our enemy—we told you—even if he is Bright Itempas's. Before the War, he loved us better than Enefa (HR) herself. The things you must have done to him, to fill his heart with such rage.

YA: Madam, please. We do not speak... that name you mentioned, the—

2. Reference: The Survivors' Provisional Council of Nimaro Territory issued an official pronouncement on behalf of their royal family (deceased), indicating that their people were henceforth to be known as "Maroneh," not "Maro."

3. Interviewers' note: The Gods' War.

NS: What? Enefa? (shouts) Enefa, Enefa, Enefa!

YA: (sighs)

NS: Roll your eyes at me one more time.

YA: My apologies for disrespecting you, madam. It is only…
The absolute dominance of Itempas is the fundamental
principle of the Bright.

NS: I love the White Lord as much as you do. It was my people He chose as the model for His mortal appearance
(HR), and we were the first to receive His blessing of
knowledge (HR). Mathematics and astronomy and writing and—all of that, all of it, we did it before any of you
Senmites, or those ignorant bastards up in the north, or
that bunch of pirates on the islands. Yet for all He gave us,
we have always remembered that He is one of *Three*. Without His siblings, He is nothing (HR).

YA: Madam!

NS: Report me to your family head if you like. What will he
do, kill me? Destroy my people? I have nothing left to lose,
boy. That's the only reason I came.

YA: Because the Maro royal family is gone.[4]

NS: No, fool, because *the Maro* are gone. Oh, if we get to
making babies, there might be enough of us to limp along
for a while longer, but we'll never be what we were. You
Amn will never let us get that strong again.

YA: Er, yes, madam. But specifically, it was the duty of the
enulai to serve the royal family, was it not? As, ah, let's see,
bodyguards and storytellers—

4. Interviewers' note: See *Post-Cataclysm Maro: Census.*

NS: Historians.

YA: Well, yes, but much of that history . . . I have a list here . . . legends and myths . . .

NS: It was all true.

YA: Madam, really.

NS: Why did you bother to invite me here?

YA: Because I am a historian as well.

NS: Then *listen*. That's the most important thing any historian can do. Hear clearly with just your ears, not with ten thousand Amn lies garbling everything—

YA: But, madam, an example, one of the enulai stories recorded . . . the tale of the Fish Goddess.

NS: Yes. Yiho, of the Shoth clan, though they're all dead now, too, I suppose.

YA: The tale speaks of her sitting by a river for three days during a famine and causing schools of ocean fish to swim up the river—from salt water to fresh water—and fling themselves into nets.

NS: Yes, yes. And ever since then, those breeds of fish have continued to swim up the river to spawn, every year. She changed them forever.

YA: But that's . . . Is the tale from before the War? Was this Yiho a godling?

NS: No, of course not. She dies an old woman at the end of the tale, doesn't she?

YA: Well, then—

NS: Though the gods had many children.

YA: (pause) My gods. (sound of a blow) Ah!

NS: That's for blaspheming.

YA: I don't believe this. (sighs) You're right, my apologies. I forgot myself. I was only... You're suggesting that the woman described in the tale was... was a half-breed, a child of the gods—

NS: All of us are children of the gods. But Yiho was special.

YA: (silence)

NS: (laughs) What's that I see in your pale eyes, boy? Have you suddenly started listening? Figures.

YA: Remembering, actually. Many of the Maro stories in my records prominently feature enulai themselves.

NS: Yes, go on...

YA: Every member of the royal family had an enulai. The enulai would educate them, advise them, protect them from danger.

NS: (laughs) Get to the point, boy. I'm not getting any younger.

YA: Protect them, often using strange abilities that the Litaria has designated unlikely or impossible—

NS: Because you scriveners don't make your own magic. You borrow it, secondhand, using the gods' language. But if you spoke the magic yourselves—if that didn't kill you—or, better still, if you could simply *will* a thing into being, you could do all that the gods do. And more.

YA: Enulai Sarfith, I wish you had not told me this.

NS: (laughs)

YA: You know what I must do.

NS: (more laughter) Ah, boy. What does it matter? I am the last descendant of Enulai—daughter of Enefa, last-born of the mortal gods who chose to spend their brief days among humankind. All the Maro's kings and queens are dead. All my children and grandchildren are dead. All of us who carried the Gray Mother's blood—we're as dead as she is. Why should I bother hiding anymore?

YA: (speaks to a servant, sending for guards)

NS: (while he speaks, softly) All gone, demonkind. All gone. No need to search for more. None left.[5]

YA: I'm sorry. (garbled)

NS: Don't be. (garbled) destroyed the last of demonkind. No need to search for more now.

YA: No need to search for more.

NS: There are no demons left in the world, anywhere.

YA: None left. (garbled, until the guards come) Farewell, Enulai. I'm sorry it had to turn out this way.

NS: (laughing) I'm not. Good-bye, boy.

[Interview ends][6]

---

5. Librarian's note: Original transcript ends here. The message sphere recording is partially inaudible from this point on. There appears to be no damage to the sphere's controlling script; however, consultation with scriveners suggests magical interference. I have transcribed the remainder of the interview as best I could.

6. Librarian's note: This transcript and sphere were misfiled by First Scrivener Y'li Arameri in the Library of Sky and thus lost for some 600 years. Recovered when an exhaustive search of the Library vaults was conducted per order of Lord T'vril Arameri.

Acknowledgments

Since I thanked everybody and everybody's sister in the acknowledgments of *The Hundred Thousand Kingdoms*, here I'll offer some literary/artistic acknowledgments. Fitting, since *The Broken Kingdoms* is a more, hmm, *aesthetic* book than its predecessor.

For the vocabulary of encaustic painting, sculpture, and watercolor used herein, I again thank my father, artist Noah Jemisin, who taught me more of his craft than I ever realized, given that I can't draw a straight line. (No, Dad, fingerpainting when I was five doesn't count.)

For the city of Shadow, I owe an obvious debt to urban fantasy—both the Miéville kind and the "disaffected hot chick with a weapon" kind (to quote a detractor of the latter, though I'm a fan of both). But a lot of it I owe to a lifetime spent in cities: Shadow's Art Row is the Union Square farmers' market in New York, maybe with a bit of New Orleans's Jackson Square thrown in.

Acknowledgments

For several of the godlings, particularly Lil, Madding, and Dump, I thank my subconscious, because I had a dream about them (and several godlings you'll meet in the third book of the Inheritance Trilogy). Lil tried to eat me. Typical.

Oh—and for a taste of how people in a major city might cope with a giant tree looming overhead, I acknowledge my past as an anime fangirl. In this case, the debt is owed to a lovely little shoujo OAV and TV series called *Mahou Tsukai Tai*, which I highly recommend. The problems caused by the giant tree were handled in a much more lighthearted manner there, but the beauty of the initial image lingers in my mind.

extras

orbitbooks.net

about the author

N. K. Jemisin is the first author in the genre's history to win three consecutive Best Novel Hugo Awards, for her Broken Earth trilogy. She is a MacArthur 2020 Genius Grant Fellow. Her work has won the Nebula and Locus Awards, and the first book in her current Great Cities trilogy, *The City We Became*, is a *New York Times* bestseller. Among other critical work, she was formerly the speculative book reviewer at the *New York Times*. In her spare time she's a gamer and gardener, responsible for saving the world from Ozymandias, her dangerously intelligent ginger cat, and his destructive sidekick Magpie. Essays and fiction excerpts are available at nkjemisin.com.

Find out more about N. K. Jemisin and other Orbit authors by registering for the free monthly newsletter at orbitbooks.net

if you enjoyed

THE BROKEN KINGDOMS

look out for

THE KINGDOM
OF GODS

Book Three of the Inheritance Trilogy

by

N. K. Jemisin

For two thousand years the Arameri family has ruled the world by enslaving the very gods that created mortalkind. Now the gods are free, and the Arameri's ruthless grip is slipping. Yet they are all that stands between peace and world-spanning, unending war.

Shahar, last scion of the family, must choose her loyalties. She yearns to trust Sieh, the godling she loves. Yet her duty as Arameri heir is to uphold the family's interests, even if that means using and destroying everyone she cares for.

As long-suppressed rage and terrible new magics consume the world, the Maelstrom - which even gods fear - is summoned forth. Shahar and Sieh: mortal and god, lovers and enemies. Can they stand together against the chaos that threatens the kingdom of gods?

SHE LOOKS so much like Enefa, *I think, the first time I see her.*

Not this moment, as she stands trembling in the lift alcove, her heartbeat so loud that it drums against my ears. This is not really the first time I've seen her. I have checked in on our investment now and again over the years, sneaking out of the palace on moonless nights. (Nahadoth is the one our masters fear most during those hours, not me.) I first met her when she was an infant. I crept in through the nursery window and perched on the railing of her crib to watch her. She watched me back, unusually quiet and solemn even then. Where other infants were fascinated by the world around them, she was constantly preoccupied by the second soul nestled against her own. I waited for her to go mad, and felt pity, but nothing more.

I next visited when she was two, toddling after her mother with great determination. Not mad yet. Again when she was five; I watched her sit at her father's knee, listening raptly to his tales of the gods. Still not mad. When she was nine, I watched her mourn her father. By that point, it had become clear that she was not, and would never go, insane. Yet there was no doubt that Enefa's soul affected her. Aside from her looks, there was the way she killed. I watched her climb out from beneath the corpse of her first man, panting and covered in filth, with a bloody stone knife in her hand. Though she was only thirteen years old, I felt no horror from her— which I should have, her heart's fluctuations amplified by her double souls. There was only satisfaction in her face, and a very familiar coldness at her core. The warriors' council women, who had expected to see her suffer, looked at each other in unease. Beyond the circle of older women, in the shadows, her watching mother smiled.

I fell in love with her then, just a little.

So now I drag her through my dead spaces, which I have never shown to another mortal, and it is to the corporeal core of my soul that I take her. (I would take her to my realm, show her my true soul, if I could.) I love her wonder as she walks among my little toy worlds. She tells me they are beautiful. I will cry when she dies for us.

Then Naha finds her. Pathetic, isn't it? We two gods, the oldest and most powerful beings in the mortal realm, both besotted by a sweaty, angry little mortal girl. It is more than her looks. More than her ferocity, her instant maternal devotion, the speed with which she lunges to strike. She is more than Enefa, for Enefa never loved me so much, nor was Enefa so passionate in life and death. The old soul has been improved, somehow, by the new.

She chooses Nahadoth. I do not mind so much. She loves me, too, in her way. I am grateful.

And when it all ends and the miracle has occurred and she is a goddess (again), I weep. I am happy. But still so very alone.

1

Trickster, trickster
Stole the sun for a prank
Will you really ride it?
Where will you hide it?
Down by the riverbank!

*   *   *

There will be no tricks in this tale. I tell you this so that you can relax. You'll listen more closely if you aren't flinching every other instant, waiting for the pratfall. You will not reach the end and suddenly learn I have been talking to my other soul or making a lullaby of my life for someone's unborn brat. I find such things disingenuous, so I will simply tell the tale as I lived it.

But wait, that's not a real beginning. Time is an irritation, but it provides structure. Should I tell this in the mortal fashion? All right, then, linear. Slooooow. You require context.

Beginnings. They are not always what they seem. Nature is cycles, patterns, repetition—but of what we believe, of the beginning I understand, there was once only Maelstrom, the unknowable. Over a span of uncountable aeons, as none of us were here yet to count, It churned forth endless substances and concepts and creatures. Some of those must have been glorious, because even today the Maelstrom spins forth new life with regular randomness, and many of those creations are indeed beautiful and wondrous. But most of them last only an eyeblink or two before the Maelstrom rips them apart again, or they die of instant old age, or they collapse in on themselves and become tiny Maelstroms in turn. These are absorbed back into the greater cacophony.

But one day the Maelstrom made something that did not die. Indeed, this thing was remarkably like Itself — wild, churning, eternal, ever changing. Yet this new thing was ordered enough to think, and feel, and dedicate itself to its own survival. In token of which, the first thing it did was get the hells away from the Maelstrom.

But this new creature faced a terrible dilemma, because away from the Maelstrom there was nothing. No people, no places, no spaces, no darkness, no dimension, no EXISTENCE.

A bit much for even a god to endure. So this being — whom we shall call *Nahadoth* because that is a pretty name, and whom we shall label male for the sake of convenience if not completeness — promptly set out to create an existence, which he did by going mad and tearing himself apart.

This was remarkably effective. And thus Nahadoth found himself accompanied by a formless immensity of separate substance. Purpose and structure began to cohere around it simply as a side effect of the mass's presence, but only so much of that could occur spontaneously. Much like the Maelstrom, it churned and howled and thundered; unlike the Maelstrom, it was not in any way *alive*.

It was, however, the earliest form of the universe and the gods' realm that envelops it. This was a wonder—but Nahadoth likely did not notice, because he was a gibbering lunatic. So let us return to the Maelstrom.

I like to believe that It is aware. Eventually It must have noticed Its child's loneliness and distress. So presently, It spat out another entity that was aware and that also managed to escape the havoc of its birth. This new one—who has always and only been male—named himself Bright Itempas, because he was an arrogant, self-absorbed son of a demon even then. And because Itempas is also a gigantic screaming twit, he attacked Nahadoth, who...well. Naha very likely did not make a good conversation partner at the time. Not that they talked at all, in those days before speech.

So they fought, and fought, and fought times a few million jillion nillion, until suddenly one or the other of them got tired of the whole thing and proposed a truce. Both of them claim to have done this, so I cannot tell which one is joking. And then, because they had to do *something* if they weren't fighting and because they were the only living beings in the universe after all, they became lovers. Somewhere between all this—the fighting or the lovemaking, not so very different for those two—they had a powerful effect on the shapeless mass of substance that Nahadoth had given birth to. It gained more function, more structure. And all was well for another Really Long Time.

Then along came the Third, a she-creature named Enefa, who should have settled things because usually three of anything is better, more stable, than two. For a while this was the case. In fact, EXISTENCE became the universe, and the beings soon became a family, because it was Enefa's nature to give meaning to anything she touched. I was the first of their many, many children.

So there we were: a universe, a father and a mother and a Naha, and a few hundred children. And our grandparent, I suppose—the Maelstrom, if one can count It as such given that It would destroy us all if we did not take care. And the mortals, when Enefa finally created them. I suppose those were like pets—part of the family and yet not really—to be indulged and disciplined and loved and kept safe in the finest of cages, on the gentlest of leashes. We only killed them when we had to.

Things went wrong for a while, but at the time that this all began, there had been some improvement. My mother was dead, but she got better. My father and I had been imprisoned, but we'd won our way free. My other father was still a murdering, betraying bastard, though, and nothing would ever change that, no matter how much penance he served—which meant that the Three could never be whole again, no matter that all three of them lived and were for the most part sane. This left a grating, aching void in our family, which was only tolerable because we had already endured far worse.

That is when my mother decided to take things into her own hands.

* * *

I followed Yeine one day, when she went to the mortal realm and shaped herself into flesh and appeared in the musty inn room that Itempas had rented. They spoke there, exchanging inanities and warnings while I lurked incorporeal in a pocket of silence, spying. Yeine might have noticed me; my tricks rarely worked on her. If so, she did not care that I watched. I wish I knew what that meant.

Because there came the dreaded moment in which she looked at him, really *looked* at him, and said, "You've changed."

And he said, "Not enough."

And she said, "What do you fear?" To which he said nothing, of course, because it is not his nature to admit such things.

So she said, "You're stronger now. She must have been good for you."

The room filled with his anger, though his expression did not change. "Yes. She was."

There was a moment of tension between them, in which I hoped. Yeine is the best of us, full of good, solid mortal common sense and her own generous measure of pride. Surely she would not succumb! But then the moment passed and she sighed and looked ashamed and said, "It was...wrong of us. To take her from you."

That was all it took, that acknowledgment. In the eternity of silence that followed, he forgave her. I knew it as a mortal creature knows the sun has risen. And then he forgave himself— for what, I cannot be sure and dare not guess. Yet that, too, was a palpable change. He suddenly stood a little taller, grew calmer, let down the guard of arrogance he'd kept up since she arrived. She saw the walls fall—and behind them, the him that used to be. The Itempas who'd once won over her resentful predecessor, tamed wild Nahadoth, disciplined a fractious litter of child-gods, and crafted from whole cloth time and gravity and all the other amazing things that made life possible and so interesting. It isn't hard to love that version of him. I know.

So I do not blame her, not really. For betraying me.

But it hurt so much to watch as she went to him and touched his lips with her fingers. There was a look of dazzlement on her face as she beheld the brilliance of his true self. (She yielded so easily. When had she become so weak? Damn her. Damn her to her own misty hells.)

She frowned a little and said, "I don't know why I came here."

"One lover has never been enough for any of us," said Itempas, smiling a sad little smile, as if he knew how unworthy he was of her desire. Despite this, he took her shoulders and pulled her close and their lips touched and their essences blended and I hated them, I hated them, I despised them both, how dare he take her from me, how dare she love him when I had not forgiven him, how dare they both leave Naha alone when he'd suffered so much, how could they? I hated them and I loved them and gods how I wanted to be with them, why couldn't I just be one of them, it wasn't fair—

—no. No. Whining was pointless. It didn't even make me feel better. Because the Three could never be Four, and even when the Three were reduced to two, a godling could never replace a god, and any heartbreak that I felt in that moment was purely my own damned fault for wanting what I could not have.

When I could bear their happiness no more, I fled. To a place that matched the Maelstrom in my heart. To the only place within the mortal realm I have ever called home. To my own personal hell...called Sky.

I was sitting corporeal at the top of the Nowhere Stair, sulking, when the children found me. Total chance, that. Mortals think we plan everything.

They were a matched set. Six years old—I am good at gauging ages in mortals—bright-eyed, quick-minded, like children who have had good food and space to run and pleasures to stimulate the soul. The boy was dark-haired and -eyed and -skinned, tall for his age, solemn. The girl was blonde and green-eyed and pale, intent. Pretty, both of them. Richly dressed. And little tyrants, as Arameri tended to be at that age.

"You will assist us," said the girl in a haughty tone.

Inadvertently I glanced at their foreheads, my belly clenched for the jerk of the chains, the painful slap of the magic they'd once used to control us. Then I remembered the chains were gone, though the habit of straining against them apparently remained. Galling. The marks on their heads were circular, denoting fullbloods, but the circles themselves were mere outlines, not filled in. Just a few looping, overlapping rings of command, aimed not at us but at reality in general. Protection, tracking, all the usual spells of safety. Nothing to force obedience, theirs or anyone else's.

I stared at the girl, torn between amazement and amusement. She had no idea who—or what—I was, that much was clear. The boy, who looked less certain, looked from her to me and said nothing.

"Arameri brats on the loose," I drawled. My smile seemed to reassure the boy, infuriate the girl. "Someone's going to get in trouble for letting you two run into me down here."

At this they both looked apprehensive, and I realized the problem: they were lost. We were in the underpalace, those levels beneath Sky's bulk that sat in perpetual shadow and had once been the demesne of the palace's lowblood servants—though clearly that was no longer the case. A thick layer of dust coated the floors and decorative moldings all around us, and aside from the two in front of me, there was no scent of mortals anywhere nearby. How long had they been wandering down here alone? They looked tired and frazzled and depleted by despair.

Which they covered with belligerence. "You will instruct us in how we might reach the overpalace," said the girl, "or guide us there." She thought a moment, then lifted her chin and added, "Do this now, or it will not go well with you!"

I couldn't help it: I laughed. It was just too perfect, her fumbling attempt at hauteur, their extremely poor luck in meeting me, all of it. Once upon a time, little girls like her had made my life a hell, ordering me about and giggling when I contorted myself to obey. I had lived in terror of Arameri tantrums. Now I was free to see this one as she truly was: just a frightened creature parroting the mannerisms of her parents, with no more notion of how to *ask* for what she wanted than how to fly.

And sure enough, when I laughed, she scowled and put her hands on her hips and poked out her bottom lip in a way that I have always adored—in children. (In adults it is infuriating, and I kill them for it.) Her brother, who had seemed sweeter-natured, was beginning to glower, too. Delightful. I have always been partial to brats.

"You have to do what we say!" said the girl, stamping her foot. "You will help us!"

I wiped away a tear and sat back against the stair wall, exhaling as the laughter finally passed. "You will find your own damn way home," I said, still grinning, "and count yourselves lucky that you're too cute to kill."

That shut them up, and they stared at me with more curiosity than fear. Then the boy, who I had already begun to suspect was the smarter if not the stronger of the two, narrowed his eyes at me.

"You don't have a mark," he said, pointing at my forehead. The girl started in surprise.

"Why, no, I don't," I said. "Imagine that."

"You aren't...Arameri, then?" His face screwed up, as if he had found himself speaking gibberish. *You curtain apple jump, then?*

"No, I'm not."

"Are you a new servant?" asked the girl, seduced out of anger by her own curiosity. "Just come to Sky from outside?"

I put my arms behind my head, stretching my feet out in front of me. "I'm not a servant at all, actually."

"You're dressed like one," said the boy, pointing.

I looked at myself in surprise and realized I had manifested the same clothing I'd usually worn during my imprisonment: loose pants (good for running), shoes with a hole in one toe, and a plain loose shirt, all white. Ah, yes—in Sky, servants wore white every day. Highbloods wore it only for special occasions, preferring brighter colors otherwise. The two in front of me had both been dressed in deep emerald green, which matched the girl's eyes and complemented the boy's nicely.

"Oh," I said, annoyed that I'd inadvertently fallen prey to old habit. "Well, I'm not a servant. Take my word for it."

"You aren't with the Teman delegation," said the boy, speaking slowly while his eyes belied his racing thoughts. "Datennay was the only child with them, and they left three days ago, anyway. And they dressed like Temans. Metal bits and twisty hair."

"I'm not Teman, either." I grinned again, waiting to see how they handled that one.

"You *look* Teman," said the girl, clearly not believing me. She pointed at my head. "Your hair barely has any curl, and your eyes are sharp and flat at the corners, and your skin is browner than Deka's."

I glanced at the boy, who looked uncomfortable at this comparison. I could see why. Though he bore a fullblood's circle on his brow, it was painfully obvious that someone had brought non-Amn delicacies to the banquet of his recent heritage. If I hadn't known it was impossible, I would have guessed he was some variety of High Norther. He had Amn features, with their long-stretched facial lines, but his hair was blacker than Nahadoth's void and as straight as windblown grass, and he was indeed a rich all-over brown that had nothing to do with a suntan. I had seen infants like him drowned or head-staved or tossed off the Pier, or marked as lowbloods and given over to servants to raise. Never had one been given a fullblood mark.

The girl had no hint of the foreign about her — no, wait. It was there, just subtle. A fullness to her lips, the angle of her cheekbones, and her hair was a more brassy than sunlit gold. To Amn eyes, these would just be interesting idiosyncracies, a touch of the exotic without all the unpleasant political baggage. If not for her brother's existence, no one would have ever guessed that she was not pure-blooded, either.

I glanced at the boy again and saw the warning-sign wariness in his eyes. Yes, of course. They would have already begun to make his life hell.

While I pondered this, the children fell to whispering, debating whether I looked more of this or that or some other mortal race. I could hear every word of it, but out of politeness I pretended not to. Finally the boy stage-whispered, "I don't think he's Teman at *all*," in a tone that let me know he suspected what I really was.

With eerie unity they faced me again.

"It doesn't matter if you're a servant or not, or Teman or not," said the girl. "*We're* fullbloods, and that means you have to do what we say."

"No, it doesn't," I said.

"Yes, it does!"

I yawned and closed my eyes. "Make me."

They fell silent again, and I felt their consternation. I could have pitied them, but I was having too much fun. Finally, I felt a stir of air and warmth nearby, and I opened my eyes to find that the boy had sat down beside me.

"Why won't you help us?" he asked, his voice soft with honest concern, and I nearly flinched beneath the onslaught of his big dark eyes. "We've been down here all day, and we ate our sandwiches already, and we don't know the way back."

Damnation. I'm partial to cuteness, too. "All right," I said, relenting. "Where are you trying to go?"

The boy brightened. "To the World Tree's heart!" Then his excitement flagged. "Or at least, that was where we *were* trying to go. Now we just want to go back to our rooms."

"A sad end to a grand adventure," I said, "but you wouldn't have found what you were looking for anyhow. The World Tree was created by Yeine, the Mother of Life; its heart is her heart. Even if you found the chunk of wood that exists at the Tree's core, it would mean nothing."

"Oh," said the boy, slumping more. "We don't know how to find her."

"I do," I said, and then it was my turn to sag, as I remembered what had driven me to Sky. Were they still together, she and Itempas? He was mortal, with merely mortal endurance, but she could renew his strength again and again for as long as she liked. How I hated her. (Not really. Yes, really. Not really.)

"I do," I said again, "but that wouldn't help you. She's busy with other matters these days. Not much time for me or any of her children."

"Oh, is she your mother?" The boy looked surprised. "That sounds like our mother. She never has time for us. Is your mother the family head, too?"

"Yes, in a way. Though she's also new to the family, which makes for a certain awkwardness." I sighed again, and the sound echoed within the Nowhere Stair, which descended into shadows at our feet. Back when I and the other Enefadeh had built this version of Sky, we had created this spiral staircase that led to nothing, twenty feet down to dead-end against a wall. It had been a long day spent listening to bickering architects. We'd gotten bored.

"It's a bit like having a stepmother," I said. "Do you know what that is?"

The boy looked thoughtful. The girl sat down beside him.

"Like Lady Meull, of Agru," she said to the boy. "Remember our genealogy lessons? She's married to the duke now, but the duke's children came from his first wife. His first wife is the mother. Lady Meull is the stepmother." She looked at me for confirmation. "Like that, right?"

"Yes, yes, like that," I said, though I neither knew nor cared who Lady Meull was. "Yeine is our queen, sort of, as well as our mother."

"And you don't like her?" Too much knowing in both the children's eyes as they asked that question. The usual Arameri pattern, then, parents raising children who would grow up to plot their painful deaths. The signs were all there.

"No," I said softly. "I love her." Because I did, even when I hated her. "More than light and darkness and life. She is the mother of my soul."

"So, then..." The girl was frowning. "Why are you sad?"

"Because love is not enough." I fell silent for an instant, stunned as realization moved through me. Yes, here was truth, which they had helped me find. Mortal children are very wise, though it takes a careful listener or a god to understand this. "My mother loves me, and at least one of my fathers loves me, and I love them, but that just isn't *enough*, not anymore. I need something more." I groaned and drew up my knees, pressing my forehead against them. Comforting flesh and bone, as familiar as a security blanket. "But what? What? I don't understand why everything feels so wrong. Something is changing in me."

I must have seemed mad to them, and perhaps I was. All children are a little mad. I felt them look at each other. "Um," said the girl. "You said *one* of your fathers?"

I sighed. "Yes. I have two. One of them has always been there when I needed him. I have cried for him and killed for him." Where was he now, while his siblings turned to each other? He was not like Itempas—he accepted change—but that did not make him immune to pain. Was he unhappy? If I went to him, would he confide in me? Need me?

It troubled me that I wondered this.

"The other father..." I drew a deep breath and raised my head, propping my folded arms on my knees instead. "Well, he and I never had the best relationship. Too different, you see. He's the firm disciplinarian type, and I am a brat." I glanced at them and smiled. "Rather like you two, actually."

They grinned back, accepting the title with honor. "We don't have any fathers," said the girl.

I raised my eyebrows in surprise. "*Someone* had to make you." Mortals had not yet mastered the art of making little mortals by themselves.

"Nobody important," said the boy, waving a hand dismissively. I guessed he had seen a similar gesture from his mother. "Mother needed heirs and didn't want to marry, so she chose someone she deemed suitable and had us."

"Huh." Not entirely surprising; the Arameri had never lacked for pragmatism. "Well, you can have mine, the second one. I don't want him."

The girl giggled. "He's your father! He can't be ours."

She probably prayed to the Father of All every night. "Of course he can be. Though I don't know if you'd like him any more than I do. He's a bit of a bastard. We had a falling-out some time ago, and he disowned me, even though he was in the wrong. Good riddance."

The girl frowned. "But don't you miss him?"

I opened my mouth to say *of course I don't* and then realized that I did. "Demonshit," I muttered.

They gasped and giggled appropriately at this gutter talk. "Maybe you should go see him," said the boy.

"I don't think so."

His small face screwed up into an affronted frown. "That's silly. Of course you should. He probably misses you."

I frowned, too taken aback by this idea to reject it out of hand. "What?"

"Well, isn't that what fathers do?" He had no idea what fathers did. "Love you, even if you don't love them? Miss you when you go away?"

I sat there silent, more troubled than I should have been. Seeing this, the boy reached out, hesitating, and touched my hand. I looked down at him in surprise.

"Maybe you should be happy," he said. "When things are bad, change is good, right? Change means things will get better."

I stared at him, this Arameri child who did not at all look Arameri and would probably die before his majority because of it, and I felt the knot of frustration within me ease.

"An Arameri optimist," I said. "Where did you come from?"

To my surprise, both of them bristled. I realized at once that I had struck a nerve, and then realized which nerve when the girl lifted her chin. "He comes from right here in Sky, just like me."

The boy lowered his eyes, and I heard the whisper of taunts

around him, some in childish lilt and some deepened by adult malice: *where did you come from did a barbarian leave you here by mistake maybe a demon dropped you off on its way to the hells because gods know you don't belong here.*

I saw how the words had scored his soul. He had made me feel better; he deserved something in recompense for that. I touched his shoulder and sent my blessing into him, making the words just words and making him stronger against them and putting a few choice retorts at the tip of his tongue for the next time. He blinked in surprise and smiled shyly. I smiled back.

The girl relaxed once it became clear that I meant her brother no harm. I willed a blessing to her, too, though she hardly needed it.

"I'm Shahar," she said, and then she sighed and unleashed her last and greatest weapon: politeness. "Will you *please* tell us how to get home?"

Ugh, what a name! The poor girl. But I had to admit, it suited her. "Fine, fine. Here." I looked into her eyes and made her know the palace's layout as well as I had learned it over the generations that I had lived within its walls. (Not the dead spaces, though. Those were mine.)

The girl flinched, her eyes narrowing suddenly at mine. I had probably slipped into my cat shape a little. Mortals tended to notice the eyes, though that was never the only thing that changed about me. I put them back to nice round mortal pupils, and she relaxed. Then gasped as she realized she knew the way home.

"That's a nice trick," she said. "But what the scriveners do is prettier."

A scrivener would have broken your head open if they'd tried what I just did, I almost retorted, but didn't because she was mortal and mortals have always liked flash over substance and because it didn't matter, anyway. Then the girl surprised me further, drawing herself up and bowing from the waist. "I thank you, sir," she said. And while I stared at her, marveling at the novelty of Arameri thanks, she adopted that haughty tone she'd tried to use before. It really didn't suit her; hopefully she would figure that out soon. "May I have the pleasure of knowing your name?"

"I am Sieh." No hint of recognition in either of them. I stifled a sigh.

She nodded and gestured to her brother. "This is Dekarta."

Just as bad. I shook my head and got to my feet. "Well, I've wasted enough time," I said, "and you two should be getting back." Outside the palace, I could feel the sun setting. For a moment I closed my eyes, waiting for the familiar, delicious vibration of my father's return to the world, but of course there was nothing. I felt fleeting disappointment.

The children jumped up in unison. "Do you come here to play often?" asked the boy, just a shade too eagerly.

"Such lonely little cubs," I said, and laughed. "Has no one taught you not to talk to strangers?"

Of course no one had. They looked at each other in that freakish speaking-without-words-or-magic thing that twins do, and the boy swallowed and said to me, "You should come back. If you do, we'll play with you."

"Will you, now?" It *had* been a long time since I'd played. Too long. I was forgetting who I was amid all this worrying. Better to leave the worry behind, stop caring about what mattered, and do what felt good. Like all children, I was easy to seduce.

"All right, then," I said. "Assuming, of course, that your mother doesn't forbid it"—which guaranteed that they would never tell her—"I'll come back to this place on the same day, at the same time, next year."

They looked horrified and exclaimed in unison, "Next *year*?"

"The time will pass before you know it," I said, stretching to my toes. "Like a breeze through a meadow on a light spring day."

It would be interesting to see them again, I told myself, because they were still young and would not become as foul as the rest of the Arameri for some while. And, because I had already grown to love them a little, I mourned, for the day they became true Arameri would most likely be the day I killed them. But until then, I would enjoy their innocence while it lasted.

I stepped between worlds and away.